*For everyone who has wondered
if you can ever belong anywhere
because of where you were born
or how you were raised...
this is for you.*

CHAPTER ONE

uzhou, Fukien Province, China, 1870

    It was midsummer in tea-trading season, yet Captain Grayson Hunter had not come to Fuzhou for tea. Tea was the treasure of traders with small aspirations—those who wished only to build fortunes through buying and selling. Grayson's smaller aspirations had combusted in battle five years ago. He had come here to pursue much grander ambitions.

He had walked halfway up the hill on the southern side of the Min River where the Westerners lived. From this height, he could see all the signs of the warring empires. His cousin's ship, brought carefully up the Min, was docked in the harbor below. From here, the *Lenity* seemed like a toy, barely distinguishable from the other Western steamships that clamored for space, fighting—politely, always politely!—for trade goods that would bring them their little fortunes.

Crowding the northern docks were Chinese river junks, low and flat, that had come from the tea plantations that were scattered through the hills and mountains farther inland.

Every single one of the people in the harbor believed that

1

they traded in goods—tea, silk, grain—and every single one of them was wrong.

Grayson intended to control what really mattered, and the next step was here in Fuzhou.

His journey had been directed here after a chance meeting in Hong Kong two weeks ago. He'd been talking to a missionary by the name of Leland Acheson. Grayson had been gathering the principal item that he traded in: information.

He hadn't mentioned the disruption in his plans. He hadn't mentioned the two separate men who had quit his employ, claiming his aim was impossible. Grayson wasn't a chatterbox to spill his secrets. But he had mentioned *other* people's plans, and when Acheson had heard what they were doing, he'd laughed.

"Ridiculous," he'd said. "That's the most simplistic, useless scheme I've ever heard. I've an acquaintance who came up with a superior implementation years ago."

It had not taken much—another glass of whiskey—for Acheson to provide more details. Now Grayson was here, looking for a man known as the Silver Fox.

"Brilliant," Acheson had said before adding with a shake of his head, "Criminally underutilized."

Grayson had never been one to mince words. "Would the Silver Fox be willing to be employed by a Black man?"

Acheson had looked at him again, and then at his whiskey. "I honestly cannot say. That exact topic has not come up. But I think that *broad-minded* is a fair description of my friend." He'd said that with a conspiratorial smile.

So here Grayson was, with no actual name—only a direction, a code name, a letter of introduction Acheson claimed would give him as good a shot as any at a fair hearing, and the intense, unbounded requirements of his ambition.

The path curved up and up, past homes decorated with the Union Jack or the Stars and Stripes, proclaiming fealty to countries that ruled from half the globe away. Grayson could see the other hills that made up Fuzhou—terraced gardens filled with trees and waving grain manned by the occasional worker who was visible only at this distance by a wide-brimmed hat. It wasn't quite the height of summer yet. The air was still moving, and it was warm but not yet stiflingly humid.

A narrow-leafed lychee tree, boughs bending with strings of red-skinned fruit, had been planted at a curve in the road. He pulled one off as he went by, rolling the rough shell between his fingers. A little longer and Grayson's plan would be moving forward once more.

He was eating the fruit when a woman came into view ahead of him. She was walking the same path as he, on the side of the cart ruts closer to the inner slope. She was dressed in Western garb—full skirts, bustle, long sleeves, bonnet and everything.

Grayson found himself grimacing involuntarily. At this time of year? Grayson was going to see an Englishman, so he'd brought a coat (currently slung over one arm) and a necktie (currently stuffed in one pocket). The buttons on his shirt were undone to his chest. Even with that degree of undress, he was uncomfortable walking uphill. The wool of his trousers was a little too warm, the linen of his shirt a little too close.

Luckily, Grayson didn't care what foolishness Western women wore in China. He had one objective: Hire the Silver Fox. Pay him what he demanded so he could work his magic. Grayson's telegraphic company would then gain an advantage over everyone else. It would become the swiftest, least expensive mode of communication in the entire world. Profit wildly; own everything; make up for all that had been lost.

He nonetheless could not begin to fathom the mindset that demanded women wear petticoats and corsets and whatever else it was that got shoved underneath their clothing in this climate. Grayson shook his head. It would be hotter still by noontime, but none of this was his problem.

By noon, hopefully, he'd have met the Silver Fox, ascertained what the man wanted, made and negotiated offers, and already shaken hands on an agreement to work together. He could be done with Fuzhou by the next high tide.

Even though the sun was high overhead, this walk felt like he was coming through the dawn—a transitional space between sleeping and waking—like that moment lying in bed when it was not yet time to get up but the mind started running through all the things that needed to be done, slotting them into their proper place.

Envisioning every step of the plan that had been made so many years ago always brought a sense of melancholy. But it also solidified his ambition. Each stride brought him closer to a future that had once been just pencil sketches on paper.

He was coming up behind the woman. He was taller than her and unencumbered by skirts; it was hardly a surprise to pass her. A moment's hesitation hit him—what language to greet her in?

Western women were often surprisingly touchy about being addressed in any Chinese dialect. French? English? Either would probably serve, but at this point, he was growing close to the direction he had been given. The Westerners here all knew each other anyway. She might know the Silver Fox, and if he could address her in whatever her native tongue was…

He was ten paces behind her when she turned and glanced over her shoulder at him. Or, he supposed, it was intended to be a glance. But when she looked in his direction, her eyes widened.

Leland Acheson had told him that the Silver Fox would be able to work fairly with a Black man; there was no such guarantee with this woman.

Don't, he thought. *Don't scream.*

"Good day," he said clearly in his American-accented English. He touched the wide brim of his hat, lifting it enough so she could get a clear view of his face.

She tripped over her skirts, hands flailing, attempting to catch her balance.

She was still a few yards ahead of him—a little too far ahead to attempt anything gallant like catching her, even if he had thought it wise to touch her. Her hands stretched in front of her, bracing as she hit the ground. He heard a loud snapping sound, like the breaking of a branch.

She stayed on hands and knees for a few long seconds.

Lovely. Just lovely. For a moment he contemplated leaving her behind. But civility mattered to people like this.

False gallantry won out. "Ma'am?" Grayson tried. "Have you hurt yourself? Can I offer you some assistance?"

The woman pushed herself up to kneel. Her bonnet was askew, and her bustle looked oddly misshapen. The blue fabric of her gown had somehow split right over her buttocks—and how a fall that didn't land on her behind managed that, Grayson had no idea. He caught a hint of white underthings—and God, he knew better than to even look like he was getting an illicit eyeful.

He turned to face the river so that he could only see her in the periphery of his vision.

She wiped her hands and drew a deep breath. "Ga—" She cut off whatever word she had been intending to say. "Oh drat," she said instead.

She was English then, by the sound of her speech.

"Well." She dusted off the front of her gown, then slowly stood. "That's two ideas that have gone completely wrong, and it's not yet ten in the morning. *Please* don't tell my mother."

Grayson frowned at the harbor. "Do I *look* like the sort of person who would tell your mother?"

"*Everyone* looks like the sort of person who would tell my mother. If you haven't met her, you wouldn't understand." There was a hint of wry humor in her voice.

From the corner of his vision, he could see her turning to look over her shoulder, as if assessing the damage to her behind. "H—" Again, she cut herself off. He heard the rustle of fabric and saw her lift her skirts.

He hastily turned to face entirely away. "How are you?" he asked the river below him.

"I will never recover." She sounded mournful. More fabric rustled; something clacked. "How am I going to explain *this?* And Mrs. Flappert is supposed to arrive today. It's going to be nonstop criticism. 'I told you so, Amelia. You should be satisfied with what you have, Amelia. Why are you still talking, Amelia?'" Her voice dropped lower on those last sentences, as if she were imitating someone else. "I am doing ill, sir. Very ill."

Grayson had no idea what any of that meant. "I was asking if you had been physically injured."

"Oh." A pause. "*Physically.* Well. *That's* no problem. Are you any good at explaining things? I need a good explanation."

"Is there a reason 'I tripped, and it was an accident' will not work?"

"'I tripped' won't explain *this!*"

He turned back. It was the first time he had looked at her straight on, and his mind came to a standstill, sticking on three things that seemed utterly irrelevant.

Thing number one: Her eyelashes. They were long and black, framing large, dark eyes that were looking at him. Thing number two: Her nose. It was wide and small. Thing number three: Her skin. She was browner than the average Englishwoman even beneath that bonnet, possibly because she *was* not the average Englishwoman. She wasn't any kind of Englishwoman at all.

Her hair was dark and glossy, what he could see of it. Her

6

cheekbones were soft and tilted, the planes of her face smooth. She had a silver locket about her neck. She *sounded* English. She *dressed* like she was English. But if he'd encountered her in a Chinese robe, he would have thought her a native.

She was also inexplicably brandishing what looked like a rounded, broken cage of bamboo that contained a tiny bamboo version of the sort of wheel he might have expected to find on a paddle steamer.

"You're right." He blinked at her. "'I tripped' won't explain that. What is that?"

"My bustle." She sounded as if a tragedy had occurred. "Maybe? I had this *idea*, you see, because my real bustle is made of horsehair and it's so dreadfully hot."

"Hot." He couldn't take his eyes off her now that he'd looked. That little locket nestled right above her cleavage, drawing his eyes away from her bamboo...bustle? There was something engraved on the silver jewelry. Maybe a dog? He couldn't tell, and he was hesitant to draw nearer.

"I thought I would make a bamboo cage instead of a big horsehair lump."

He had no idea how he had come to be talking about a woman's bustle. "That sounds reasonable."

"And since it was a cage, I thought, well, what if I put a little paddle inside? That way when I walk, it will spin, and I'll get a little air to cool me off. It would be like a fan."

"Ingenious."

"No, not really." She sighed. "I was just testing it. It doesn't work; the paddle only spins if it has airflow, but with skirts over the top, it just sits in place, unmoving. I would have to propel it to make it spin." Her eyes lit. "I could make a little wheel that ran on the ground! And then attach it so that—" Her fists clenched; she brought her hands up by her side. He could see her thoughts dart excitedly across her face. She bit her lip and looked up as if tracking something in the sky.

Then her shoulders slumped. "Because, oh yes," she said bitterly, "my mother would *definitely* not ask why I was making a rattling noise like wheels over cobblestones when I walked."

"I see," Grayson said.

He didn't see at all. He didn't know who her mother was, to have such distinctly English strictures when this woman looked to be so clearly Chinese. He didn't know her age, but she seemed well into her twenties—too old to be clinging to her mother's opinions on such frivolous matters. And he didn't know why this delightful woman who immediately thought of ways to make paddles turn inside bustles had to *hide* the fact she was putting paddles inside bustles.

Her brow furrowed. "It would also make sitting down rather difficult. Which was admittedly a problem with this prototype as well. But the bamboo cracked when I tripped, and this bit jabbed through my skirt and tore the fabric. I don't know how I'm going to explain it. She'll be upset."

He shouldn't ask. He shouldn't entertain any curiosity at all about her. Grayson looked over at the harbor, reminding himself why he was here. And yet he asked anyway. "Why would she be upset?"

"I'm always trying to make things easier on myself," she admitted. "It's a personal failing. You know what they say about when the devil comes courting."

"I don't, actually."

"'When the devil comes courting,'" she quoted, dropping into that same imitated voice once again, "'he offers you what you want.' Primrose path, et cetera and so forth. And look—my skirt has split, so she was right." She sighed. "Again. Maybe if I sneak in quietly and sew it carefully, she just won't notice."

Grayson took his coat from around his arm and handed it to her. "If you tie it about your waist, it should shield you from any prying eyes for the time being."

"Thank you." She looked up at him, then smiled. "You're very kind."

He wasn't. Kindness was an instrument, one that often got him what he wanted. She—he suspected—was just very naïve.

Still, he had a ridiculous thought. He had no idea how this woman had come to be on the south side of the river, living among the Westerners, and he frankly didn't care. But the thought came unbidden—he could offer to take her away. She was pretty and clever and obviously unappreciated. *Come with me,* he imagined saying. *You don't need them. Come with me on my ship and make all the little paddles you want.*

But he didn't know her, and his ambition forcibly intruded. She was connected with the English people in this area. The mother that she spoke of—the one that Grayson was already writing off in his mind—might very well know the Silver Fox. And she probably didn't deserve to be seduced away from the home she knew, however unappreciative it might have been, by a man who wouldn't be interested in her for much longer than a handful of months.

He was going to be very, very polite to her. He was going to find the Silver Fox. And then he was going to leave this delightful woman precisely the same way he found her. He wasn't going to touch her. He was just going to imagine it.

He touched his pocket in reminder—the letter of introduction was still there, all sealed up, with no notation on the front but two words—Silver Fox, in English—and two Chinese characters. He recognized the first, and was fairly certain that inscription said the same thing in a different language.

"I'm Captain Grayson Hunter." He held out his hand.

"Oh!" She glanced at his hand and then colored. "My manners! Where have they been? Mrs. Amelia Smith."

Mrs. Ah. She was married. The seduction plan might not have worked in any event.

"It's very good to meet you, Mrs. Smith. I'm heading up to

9

the Acheson household on some business. Maybe you can assist me in finding the person I'm looking for."

"The Acheson household." Her cheeks colored with a hint of pink. "Are you—you're not, you're not Mr. Flappert by any chance? No, of course not. You just told me your name." Her eyes narrowed. "I'm sorry. I've already forgotten it."

"Captain Grayson Hunter."

"Captain Hunter. If I can assist you, I will, but as you may already have surmised, I have no memory for names. Who are you looking for?"

"If you don't know him, perhaps your mother or your husband will." There. He'd said it. *Her husband.*

"Oh. I'm not— That is, I'm a widow. Now who is it that you were looking for?"

She hardly looked old enough to be a widow. Grayson ignored the pulse of interest that went through him. It didn't matter; none of his transient feelings mattered. *Silver Fox*, he reminded himself. *Telegraphic empire. Ambition.* Those were the things he cared about. "Yes. Well. As to that—the who of it—this is going to sound odd. I don't have a name for the person I'm looking for."

"You don't have a name." She frowned.

"I heard of him from a Mr. Leland Acheson—"

Her eyes widened, and she made a startled noise.

"You know him then."

"Leland! But that's my brother!" Her eyes lit. "You've come from Hong Kong? Did he give you a letter for me? Is that part of your business?"

Her brother. He'd *met* Acheson. The man had been white as white could be—orange hair, sideburns, and everything. "I— No. I'm sorry."

He watched her face fall. Damn it. He didn't care if he disappointed her. He didn't care about her. He really didn't. It was just that her face was so expressive that he couldn't help but feel her emotions tugging at him.

"He sent me here because I was looking for someone who invented a telegraphic method for transmitting Chinese characters. The person involved is extremely clever, not doing much—criminally underutilized, he said—and might agree to work with me."

Her eyes rounded.

"If Leland is your brother, you might know who I'm looking for," Grayson said. "A man who goes by—" He stopped himself before the words came out of his mouth.

His eyes fell to the silver locket around her neck. The silver figurine of an animal was worked on that round locket, and it rose and fell against her breast. Not a dog. Of *course* it wasn't a dog. That was a fox in brambles worked in silver, lifting with every one of her breaths.

Extremely clever. Criminally underutilized. Of *course.*

What a buffoon he had been. No *wonder* Acheson had been so cagey about the matter, refusing to give him a name. Come to think of it, had he ever referred to the Silver Fox as *he?*

Grayson looked down into Mrs. Smith's eyes and thought about his plan. Hire the Silver Fox. Build an empire. Swim in profits.

So the Silver Fox was a woman. Did it matter? Yes, in the sense that Grayson had met her and wanted her.

But in the grander scheme of things? It mattered not one whit that he wanted her because now that he knew what she could be, he would never allow himself to have her. Not that way. Plans changed.

The calculation didn't take long. If he walked up to her mother—whoever that woman was, with her ridiculous aphorisms about *devils* and *courting* and her constant scolding of her daughter—he would be tossed out on his ear. He would need a moment to figure out how to proceed, but proceed he would. If

Mrs. Amelia Smith, criminally underutilized, was the one who had developed a telegraphic method for transmitting Chinese characters, then Grayson would hire her, give her all the money she demanded, and leave her very thoroughly alone.

He had a moment of regret in the Fuzhou sun—a single moment, which he immediately put behind him.

"Mrs. Amelia Smith," he said with a nod of his head. "I believe I was incorrect. I *do* have correspondence for you from your brother." He reached into his pocket and pulled out the letter of introduction Acheson had given him, holding it so that the Chinese characters faced toward her. "I believe this is yours."

CHAPTER TWO

Silver Fox.

The Chinese characters seemed embedded in the grain of the paper, fixed there as a reminder of what Amelia had once had.

It had been years since Amelia had seen Leland, years since she'd received more from him than his diligent weekly letters or the occasional telegram. *He indulges you,* her mother had used to say before he'd left Fuzhou for good. Amelia had never felt indulged in her brother's company; just an easiness of heart. Leland was the one person in the world with whom she felt safe.

She took the letter in both hands, wanting to clutch it to her chest. Instead, she dropped it into a pocket. "Thank you." She smiled at him. "How incredibly kind of you to bring it all this way."

He gave her a nod.

"You're going up the hill?" she asked.

"Are you?"

It wasn't an answer, she noticed. An odd point to be evasive on. "My home isn't far. I can accompany you there at least."

He nodded, and they resumed their walk. He seemed like the sort who would converse easily. He'd been so friendly just a moment earlier. Now he cast a sidelong glance at her. Probably contemplating the difficult paradox of a native Chinese woman speaking English with the Queen's accent while garbed in a heavy gown. A *British* gown, albeit somewhat punctured.

But he didn't seem sure how to restart their discussion once more. Despite her many flaws, Amelia knew what politeness required. It was up to her to move the talk along.

"Thank you, Captain...," she started.

Drat it all. She had forgotten his name already. Captain Something. Captain Some Name Unremarkable. Had it been Captain Turner? Captain Jones? She couldn't very well call him Captain Handsome, not even in her mind, because if she started doing that, knowing her, she would inevitably blurt it out by mistake.

Luckily, he took her confused dithering for a complete sentence, as if she were addressing him by title rather than name.

"Don't thank me," he said dryly. "I'm not here for your convenience."

"What are you here for then?" Her mind raced ahead of her. "Oh of course! You had said that you were looking for someone on business. I don't know how much assistance I can provide, but—"

As she spoke, they came around another turn in the road climbing the hill. This brought into view Amelia's childhood home—the place where she had grown up, the place where she had returned after her husband had so abruptly perished. She'd come back here in a cloud of confusion, technically in mourning but actually plagued with what felt like guilty relief.

This was the place where she belonged most out of anywhere in the world. Home? Home.

The house stood before them, a row of mulberry trees

flanking each side. All but the last fruits had been picked over by birds, and now a pair of magpies tussled in the broad green leaves over the final remains. The Union Jack lay limp on the flagpole by the road, occasionally kicking up a desultory end when a tiny breeze swept past. The two stories of the house were crammed into the side of the hill.

But the thing that made Amelia's heart race was the cart pulled up to one side. A piebald mare was tied to a trough in the back; the driver, an unfamiliar man, sat in the shade. He nodded to the two of them.

A cart and an unfamiliar driver. It meant only one thing.

Mrs. Flappert had arrived.

A sick sensation rose in Amelia's belly. Her palms prickled; cold fear ran down her spine. Expectation, she told herself. Hope. And if that emotion maybe felt something a little more like dread, surely that was because of her ruined gown and the failed experiment she should not have been conducting.

Certainly it was not because she felt any consternation at Mrs. Flappert's arrival. How could she when she had never met the woman?

She looked behind her at the captain. He was here, he had said, looking for someone. He had smiled, and his smiles had seemed genuine, and Amelia had talked to him and shown him her invention, which did not sound so bad when she said it that way, but, oh God. She had, in essence, shown him her under-things, and Mrs. Flappert was *here.*

There was nothing to be done. She turned to him. "I must beg a favor of you."

"Don't say that." He sounded amused. "I'm a trader. If you beg a favor of me, I'll expect one in return."

"I don't care about that," she said with a wave of her hands. "I'll *give* one in return. I will owe you dreadfully. It's like this." How to set forth a logical explanation of Mrs. Flappert? Or her son, Alden Flappert? Amelia thought about trying to convey

her situation to this man in front of her—he had been understanding thus far; surely, he would understand now?—and felt
a well of inexplicable shame rise in her. She finally settled on
this: "I am supposed to marry Mrs. Flappert's son."

He blinked once, then glanced at her hand, which had crept
to the pocket where she had placed the letter he'd given her.
"Ah. Are congratulations in order then?"

He didn't have to sound so doubtful. It was rather rude of
him. "Not yet." She shut her eyes. "His mother has yet to
approve of me." She pointed at the cart. "His mother is here.
Early."

That same slow, steady blink giving nothing of his thoughts
away. "He's fallen in love without parental permission, I
suppose?"

Oh. God. She could feel herself blushing. "Of course not.
I've never actually met him."

He blinked a third time. "Of *course* not? You've never *met*
him? Did you just say you were marrying?"

She could feel the heat rising under the collar of her blouse.
"You see my dilemma," she forged on, ignoring his all-too-
salient questions. "I can't meet Mrs. Flappert with my skirt
split and..." She gestured around them.

He did not blink at this. "And a man like me in tow?"

She winced. "*Any* man would be a problem. You know what
they say about women like me."

"And about men like me." He looked into her eyes. "Plus
there's this: I make you smile too much, and your skirt is split."

He said that without a hint of expression, but she felt her
face flame. He had hit precisely on half the problem. He made
her smile too much. He'd talked to her, and he hadn't pshawed
her invention. He'd talked *to* her instead of *about* her, and she
had hoped for one moment against all possible hope that *he*
was Mr. Flappert, come in his mother's place.

It was an obvious fiction—her mother would have

mentioned before now if Mr. Flappert were a Black man. She wouldn't have approved.

Still. She'd wanted to believe. *He* would likely have been more than just bearable. Amelia wouldn't have had to muster up all her courage to marry *him* on no acquaintance. If he was the one coming for her, she would have worried all these last nights for nothing.

Mr. Captain of Uncertain Name did not ask again why Amelia was set to marry a man she had never met. Instead, he looked her in the eye with an intensity that sent a shiver through her.

"Mrs. Amelia Smith," he said. "Also known as the Silver Fox."

Unfair that he could remember two of her appellations when she couldn't recall a single one of his. "If by *known as* you mean *teased by my brother with,* then yes."

"You seem like the sort of person who keeps her word once she gives it."

She found herself blushing. "Well. Yes. Don't most people?"

"You're too old to believe that." He had not looked away from her, and the fierceness of his gaze was unnerving. "You haven't actually committed to Flappert the Unmet, have you?"

She exhaled. "How could I when his mother hasn't yet approved of me?"

His brow furrowed. "Then I'm asking for that favor you granted. Don't. Not until you've had a chance to read that letter from your brother. Not until you've had a chance to talk with me. I have an offer to make you."

Amelia had heard of stupider things happening than a ship's captain proposing to a woman within fifteen minutes of their meeting. She had *contemplated* stupider things than accepting such a proposal. For instance, she was meeting a man's mother who intended to propose marriage on zero minutes of acquaintance. For a moment, she let herself believe this wild fiction. There was a heat in his eyes, a low intensity to his words.

"An offer of...?" Her heart slammed against her chest.

"Employment," he said, bringing her down to earth.

He must have seen the alarmed look in her eyes because he immediately added: "Respectable employment. In an office."

Respectable employment. Of course there was no other offer a man like him would make her.

But—employment? In an office? Really?

"I'm a woman," she informed him.

"Thank you for explaining." A hint of a smile touched his lips. "Women are also employed in offices. With some regularity. I'll be back in half an hour. Find an excuse to come out with me. I came here looking for someone whose name I did not know; pick someone you can take me to. Alone. I'll need no more than an hour of your time to explain."

"Employment." She spoke the word dubiously.

"Employment," he confidently echoed back at her. "As in I want your labor in exchange for money. That's the offer. We can quibble over the exact details in a little while." He smiled. His smile was so easy, so sunny, that she felt her spirits lift inexplicably.

"You must be an excellent trader." She bit her lip. "People will just give you anything you want, won't they?"

"Not really," the captain whose name she could not remember said. "But in this moment I do not care about people in general. I only care about you."

Thump, went Amelia's heart. *Thump. Thump. Thump.* She could feel the heat rising on her cheeks. *I only care about you.* God, she'd wished for so long for someone to say such a thing to her. She'd wanted and wanted, and the more she'd wanted, the more invisible she had seemed.

I only care about you.

He didn't mean it. He couldn't mean it. Not like that; he wanted to employ her.

She'd been offered employment before; somedays it felt as if she could scarcely meet a British man who looked her up and down *without* him offering a certain kind of employment. But since Captain Who Knows came bearing a letter from Leland, this employment was not for immoral purposes.

Which was a good thing. Amelia didn't *want* to be employed for immoral purposes. She'd never understood the appeal of the act once she'd finally done it. Perhaps one far corner of her mind whispered that immoral purposes with *this* man might prove useful as an additional point of experience. But one did not need to dwell on all one's stray thoughts.

"So you'll hear me out before you agree to anything?" he asked, bringing her back to the present.

Amelia shut her eyes. "Yes," she told him because she was foolish and undoubtedly as bad at negotiation as he was good at it. "Of course. But I really must be going."

He raised a hand. "Farewell for the moment."

She took hold of her ruined gown, clutching the split edges together before returning his jacket to him. Then she fled round the back of the house.

~

The back way was clear from entry to staircase. Amelia retreated to her room, her heart pounding, the sliced edges of her gown clutched in her hands and her mind full of the letter from her brother in her pocket.

There was no reason for her heart to beat so, stupid organ that it was. There was something about the captain—the way he looked at her, maybe, or the words he said or *something* undefinable in the air that followed him. She didn't know what it was, but look at her, fool that she was—he'd asked, and she'd promised. Why?

She closed the door to her room behind her as quietly as she could and shed her ruined gown.

How bad were matters? The bamboo had snapped and slit a hole right over her buttocks. Bad. Luckily, the bamboo shard had been sharp, so the slit was a single, clean line. A clever needle would fix it almost as good as new. *Her* needle was more competent than clever, but as long as the fabric wasn't examined closely, she might not be found out at all.

How bad were matters? Amelia shut her eyes and thought of the look in Captain Something's eyes, dark and compelling. That roil in her stomach started up again.

No, no. She took a breath. She'd promised not to agree to marry Mr. Flappert until after she and the captain had spoken. She hadn't made promises beyond the space of a conversation. Her duty was simple: Speak to Mrs. Flappert. Be as encouraging as possible. Ask for time to pray? Yes. Time to pray about the matter. Surely that could not be faulted.

She hadn't promised to speak *seriously* with the captain. She had only agreed to let him say words in her direction, and people did that to her all the time without asking for her permission.

She nodded to herself, having justified her enormous breach of protocol with such bare reasoning, and rewarded her own mental chicanery by opening her brother's letter.

My dear Amelia,

I know this letter will come as a surprise, as we have never spoken of this before. I have already apologized for not attending your antici-pated upcoming nuptials to Mr. Flappert; allow me to do so again, but more honestly.

I have not bowed out of your wedding simply because I am busy. I have made myself busy on purpose so as not to attend your wedding. You see, if I have to sit through another ceremony like the last one, watching you tie yourself to a man who doesn't know you, let alone value you, I will punch someone, and I do not believe in violence. I hope you understand the moral dilemma that has led to my absence.

Captain Hunter is going to offer you employment. I didn't tell him you were a woman—just about the code you came up with in Hyderabad. He's seen a few of your letters describing it. This is the spot where I am supposed to offer you reassurances, things like, "He is a good man" et cetera et cetera. I cannot offer those. Alas, I understand Captain Hunter too well. He is utterly ruthless in his dealings and has not one iota of mercy for those who oppose him. I know full well that setting him on you, telling him what you can do, is an utterly cruel thing to do to my dearest sister because Hunter tends to get what he wants.

But employment only lasts as long as both parties wish it. By contrast, marriage is forever. Consider this a wedding present then, or preferably a not-wedding present. On the eve of being shipped off to another man, I want you to have a choice. Whatever you choose, I will always care for you.

Hunter is not a good man, but he values what is valuable, and I've never known him to do anything to anyone without their full and willing consent. Watch out for that latter, and you will do well.

Your very worried brother,

Leland

She stared at her brother's big, loopy signature.

Postscript, he had written beneath this. *His name is Captain Grayson Hunter, in case you forget it.*

How well he knew her.

Yes, Leland had come up with some reason why he was unable to make the journey from Hong Kong for her possible wedding ceremony. Beyond the disappointment in not seeing her brother, she had accepted it. Of *course* he was too busy to see her. But—

A single rap on the door interrupted her musing.

"Amelia!" The word was a whispered hiss.

Amelia shot up straight and looked about. She was still in her shift; her split dress and the bamboo cage were in full view. She yanked them up. The bottom of the wardrobe was a mess —fallen garments mixed with some fossilized teeth from her megalodon stage that she'd tossed in last night when her mother told her she couldn't keep such things out for anyone to see.

She shoved the evidence of her morning crimes in her wardrobe, swiftly grabbed replacements, and eased the wardrobe doors shut so they wouldn't slam and cause suspicion.

"Mother?" Her heart was pounding.

"Mrs. Flappert is here. Where have you *been?*"

Amelia did not consider herself a liar, but she was a pointed teller of insufficient truths. "Out for a morning constitutional. The Flemings have those puppies. I wanted to see them."

The exhale that followed this could have blown a less sturdy door down. "Amelia. I have already said. Dogs are messy, noisy, horrible beasts. And Mrs. Flappert will expect you to leave with her in any event. You can't bring a dog on a ship."

"But *these* puppies are—" She cut herself off. They'd had the dog conversation multiple times. *Small! Yellow! Squirming! Cute!*

None of these things moved her mother.

She tried again. "I had not realized Mrs. Flappert was set to arrive so early."

An exasperated sigh. "Of *course* she was set to arrive early. The tide was in overnight."

"Was it?" Amelia wrestled her bustle—the one made of heavy horsehair, not the bamboo replacement—into place, securing it as best as she could. The river Min, which cut through Fuzhou, was only navigable by larger vessels when the tide was high; traffic and visitors had a natural ebb and flow. "I'm sorry. When the, um. That tall couple? When they arrived, the tide was in around midmorning."

The weighty bustle was not perfectly in place, but maybe nobody would notice? Amelia squeezed her eyes shut and shrugged into her gown. She had been a missionary's wife once and was expected to become a missionary's wife once more. Her clothing, despite its heavy layers, was simple to put on for a single woman on her own, buttoning up the front. Still, there were so many buttons.

"Amelia, the Lorrings arrived two weeks ago. You *know* how tides work."

"Oh?" She grimaced. "Was that two weeks ago? Already?"

"Amelia." A gentle thump alerted her to the fact that her mother had likely placed her forehead against the door. *"Amelia.* Honestly. You're twenty-three. You're a widow. You ought to have *some* sense by now."

He values what is valuable. That line from her brother's letter came back to Amelia.

Truth was she had always been just a little difficult. Despite expectations, despite everything she was told, somehow she kept setting her sights above her acknowledged value.

She constantly had to remind herself of the truth: She was a woman of Chinese descent. She'd be lucky to find a husband, *any* husband, let alone a decent, Christian man.

Hold on to your heart, some rebellious part of her whispered. But that came from the final vestiges of a false memory. She had to relinquish it.

Reality was here in this house where she had grown to adulthood. *This* was Amelia's truth: the constant certainty that someone held basic expectations for her behavior, and that she was failing to meet them.

Hold on to her heart? Ha. Amelia had never met anyone's expectations. She was always falling short. Her mother; her father; her first husband. She had no memory of the woman who had given birth to her, only shadows of feelings, thoughts that had long since lost their vitality from being probed so often. But whoever that mysterious woman was, whatever her name, whatever her language, Amelia must not have met her expectations either. She'd been given up.

Valuable. The word from Leland's letter seemed to drop deep inside her, smoking like coal fallen out of the fire. Amelia stopped in the process of buttoning, her fingertips over her heart, trying her best not to burst into flame.

"Amelia? *Hurry.*"

She jumped.

"I'm almost ready. Just three more buttons." She did one, then two, then winced and stopped. She looked up at the ceiling. Really? *Really?*

"Amelia?"

"I, um." She looked down at her gown, and now she could see her error. There it was, down past her navel. In her haste, she'd misaligned the buttons when she'd started. Now she had one extra button at the top of her cleavage and the only empty buttonhole was down by her toes. "I may be a bit longer? I did my buttons up wrong."

A long pause. She could imagine her mother counting to ten, trying not to lose her temper. Finally, she heard a deep sigh through the door. "Honestly, Amelia. I'll go tell Mrs. Flappert that you've returned from your walk, that you're changing your clothing and will be down shortly. Hurry *up,* Amelia. You know how important this is. Whatever will she think of you if you dawdle?"

CHAPTER THREE

The sun had climbed ten degrees higher in the sky by the time Grayson went up the path to the Achesons' home. It was a formal two-story affair of brownstone, built in the English style: straight walls rising to an angular roof. The large glass windows must have been imported from some distance. They proclaimed the wealth of those who lived here to all who passed by.

He knocked at the door, and while the servant who answered stiffened at the sight of him, the promise of a letter from Mr. Leland Acheson and the offer of news from out of the country eventually gave him reason to be allowed inside.

The parlor where he was led had windows thrown wide in the summer heat. A bit of a breeze circulated comfortably. The table was set with tea things—biscuits, little sandwiches—as if the ladies were pretending they lived in a fashionable London address.

Mrs. Smith was already present. She sat uncomfortably in a single straight-backed chair. Next to her were two women, both white, and presumably both English if the stiffness of their spines was any guide. The one closest to Mrs. Smith was dressed with an extravagance that spoke of particular effort. She wore a lavender muslin gown with little embroidered blossoms floating over layers of skirts, which were bright white lace at the cuffs with a hem that looked as if they might brush the ground. White lace trailing against the ground? That shouted *wealthy trader's wife, money to burn* louder than any words. This must be Mr. Acheson's mother then. Unlike Mr. Acheson, she was short and slim and dark-haired.

The other woman, in a serviceable dark gingham, with her modest neckline and excessively stuffed expression? Grayson had met her like too. She was a missionary. Most likely the dreaded Mrs. Flappert.

Both of them were staring at him as if he were some poisonous insect that had crawled out of the woodwork.

"Ladies." He bowed from the waist and used his best British accent. "Captain Grayson Hunter from Lord Traders Telegraphic Company."

They continued to look at him as if he were a talking centipede who had suddenly developed a fatal case of the manners.

"My mother was Lady Elizabeth Denmore," he explained. "She met my father in England where he was a speaker on the abolitionist circuit."

He did not mention that his parents had eloped without her family's support. He did not need to; that would be assumed by all present. But the affronted gazes fixed on him softened ever so slightly.

Sometimes Grayson felt as if he were a walking repository of accents and mannerisms. When pressed, he could do a reasonable approximation of a wealthy British accent. He'd spent time in England and his mother had been an English lady. Furthermore, he'd grown up with his elderly many-greats-not-actually-uncle Henry who had, before he'd run off to sail ships with his equally many-greats-but-actually-an-uncle John, been English gentry himself.

They had now slotted him in place. Not *British* in their minds, no matter who his mother had been. But British-adjacent. British enough to know the rules. British enough to converse with.

A conversation was all he needed. He didn't care about them and their small minds, not when Mrs. Amelia Smith was sitting next to them, soaking in every word he said with wide, interested eyes.

"I've come from Hong Kong," he explained, "with intent to trade in Fuzhou. An acquaintance of mine—Leland Acheson—asked me to carry a letter and his regards to you."

The trader's wife—Mrs. Acheson—melted at that. "Oh. *Leland.* My Leland."

Mrs. Flappert squinted at him as if she were not yet sure of her eyes. "How very good of Mr. Acheson to think of his family." Another pause. "He is a missionary like my Alden. Has he converted you to Christianity then?"

Mrs. Smith winced. She *tried* not to, but her emotion—that deep embarrassment, the way she looked down, keeping her expression rigidly unchanging—showed all too plainly.

Grayson tried not to have real emotions at all, let alone in public. His feelings now were a carefully managed affair. He kept the smile on his face. Friendly. Open. "My mother is the daughter of the Duke of Castleford. My uncle is a bishop in the Church of England. My father was active in the abolitionist community in Britain, which I am sure you are familiar with. I was baptized in London before I could walk. I was not in need of conversion."

A single blink was the only sign of discomfort. "Oh, but of course you are not. Who would say otherwise?"

It was so utterly brazen, her attempt to pretend that it had not just been *she* who said it. But Grayson was not trying to stir things up, which meant leaving this woman to her petty untruths.

"I won't bother you ladies much longer." He took the letter from his pocket and set it on the table. "I will say that when I saw Leland, he was well. He particularly pressed upon me that I was to assure his mother that he was eating well and looked in fine health."

"How lovely to hear," said Mrs. Acheson with a real smile. "I'm lucky to have such an attentive son."

It had not escaped Grayson's notice that none of the ladies here had introduced themselves to him, nor did they seem likely to do so. They had not thanked him for the delivery. Perhaps they had not noticed that it had taken time and effort on his part.

At one point in his life, he had harbored emotions about that sort of oversight. Now he refused to let such things bother him. He took all the frustration, all the rage, and siphoned it off into determination. They'd pay him back, all of them. They would pay it all back eventually.

Mrs. Smith leaned forward. "Well. *Was* he?"

Grayson blinked.

"*Was* he eating well? *Did* he look in fine health? You said that he asked you to assure us that this was the case; you didn't say it actually *was* the case."

Mrs. Acheson's smile froze. "Amelia," she half whispered. "Leland wouldn't ask someone to lie on his behalf. Think of what you are saying about your dear brother."

"Do you not remember the time he had cholera?" Mrs. Smith's back straightened. "He had—would you believe—a stash of undated, nonspecific letters which he ordered sent out for two straight months during the worst of his illness so we wouldn't worry about him. Lying is *exactly* the sort of thing he would do to assuage our fears."

"Amelia." Mrs. Acheson's smile wavered. She glanced at the

woman next to her as if trying to think of what to do. "Amelia, that is so like you." She smiled again at the woman, this time ingratiatingly. "She is the sort to care, you see. To want the best for those around her, and to see to their health."

Mrs. Flappert's nose wrinkled. "Perhaps a little vociferously."

Mrs. Acheson just beamed wider. "But you know how it is. In these less civilized places, with these less civilized people, a little vociferousness goes a long way. You *have* to tell them what to do, you know. I see that as an integral part of Amelia's utility—she knows how to communicate with natives wherever she goes."

Grayson glanced at Amelia once more. She didn't flinch at that, and he'd observed her enough that he suspected she would have if this kind of treatment were unfamiliar.

Did they always say such things in front of her? Talking about her as if she were nothing but a conduit, as if she could translate from civilized to uncivilized? It took some real inattention to detail, reality, and history to call either the Chinese or the varied nations that made up what Britain called India uncivilized, but then English propriety was that rare combination of inattention to everything that mattered coupled with a minute fascination with everything that didn't. After all, they were accusing China of being uncivilized while residing in the territory of one of the oldest civilizations in the world.

Criminally underutilized, Mr. Acheson had said of his sister, and Grayson was beginning to understand that this had been an understatement. He could not imagine what it would be like for a Chinese woman of her intelligence to be raised in such an atmosphere.

There was nothing to do but cut off the conversation before it did any further damage. He just nodded. "No need to worry, ma'am. I didn't have a chance to see him eat, but Mr. Acheson looked to be in good health when we spoke. I won't impose on you much longer; I only wish to ask for one small point. He mentioned earlier that a personal friend of his worked in the British records office here. He knows I have some small interest in an introduction. Might I prevail upon you to make it?"

Mr. Acheson had not mentioned any such thing, but he was the sort of personable, voluble fellow who made intimate friends everywhere he went with literally everyone. The records office was large; there would be *someone* who fit the bill.

Grayson let his eyes meet Mrs. Smith's. He did not do anything so obvious as raise an eyebrow; he just looked at her. *You promised,* he thought at her. *You promised to hear me out.*

If this was what her life was like here, he could have her for a song.

His request was met with a beat of silence, and in that moment Grayson realized his mistake. He shouldn't have asked for an introduction. He'd fallen too far into British manner-isms; introductions were things that were made between near equals, and no matter who Grayson was, no matter where his parents came from or what he had accomplished, people like these would never see him as an equal. He should have asked for a kind word or some such.

Then Mrs. Smith spoke. "You must mean Mr...." She trailed off. "At the customs house? The blond fellow? The one with the sideburns, who wears the hat?" She gestured with her hands, describing what seemed to be absurdly tall dimensions.

"Mr. Waterman," Mrs. Acheson said after a beat. "Amelia, you've met him a dozen times."

"Waterman," Amelia repeated, an expression somewhat like concentration crossing her face. "Of course. He lives by water and is a man. Waterman."

"She really is very bright," Mrs. Acheson said to Mrs. Flap-pert in something that was not quite an aside. "You mustn't think much of this. She occasionally fails to remember names, but—"

The other woman shrugged. "You don't need to sell me on whatever finer points you're imagining. I wasn't expecting much by way of intelligence. We both know what a missionary needs in a wife. A woman with a good constitution who can manage a household and meet his other needs so he needn't bother the natives. I only wanted to make sure she spoke English well enough. I've seen plenty; your daughter will do with enough training."

In that moment Grayson could see Mrs. Smith gathering up a response. Her eyes, dark brown, glittered. A rebellious spark rose visibly in the twitch of her nose. He inhaled, waiting to see what would happen.

Then all of that was repressed in the bite of her lip.

Grayson considered himself an excellent judge of character; he'd had far too much opportunity to judge it over the years. In this short space of time, he'd developed as clear a picture of Mrs. Smith as he could. He had no idea how Mrs. Smith had been taken into this household, but he could imagine precisely how it had been for her, with the talk of *conversion to Christianity* and *civilized people.* It had been hell, and she'd likely been taught that anything other than compliance would damn her even further.

And yet she'd talked to him so openly. Mrs. Smith kept her heart on her sleeve. It was almost as if she were begging for someone to *not* casually crush her into dust.

Criminally underutilized. Criminally undervalued. Not a surprise. When it came to valuing people other than themselves, colonialists were masters of a vast criminal conspiracy.

"Excellent," said Mrs. Acheson. "When will you leave?"

They had not asked her for a response, Grayson noticed.

"On high tide two days from now. That should be enough time for her to pack, yes?"

Mrs. Smith stood abruptly. "If it's no bother, I believe I will go with Captain…" She trailed off, glanced at him, and bit her lip once more, blushing. "The captain," she amended.

Her mother had not been lying. She *was* bad at remembering names. She didn't remember his. If he hadn't seen her stumble on another name, he might have been offended.

"I can introduce him to Mr. Water…something before he has to leave."

Mrs. Acheson glanced at Amelia, then at Grayson. Perhaps she was not as unobservant as Grayson had thought because she sighed. "It's Waterman. His name is Waterman. And take a servant, Amelia."

"Surely there's no need to worry about proprieties, when—"

"It's not about the proprieties, Amelia," she said. "It's about the circumstances. Take a servant."

~

On the walk down the hill with Mrs. Smith, pollen drifted on the air. The servant who had let him in— an Indian woman of about forty years or so— followed behind them at about ten or twelve paces. And Mrs. Smith looked at him, casting him glances that were laden with discomfort.

Finally, she let out a sigh. "I'm sorry."

"For what are you apologizing?"

She glanced at the house behind them. But for the landscape beyond—dark green mountains, higher and more angular than any peak in England—the vista behind would have fit in England with that square, heavy architecture.

Mrs. Smith compressed her lips and looked up at him. "All of it."

Grayson shrugged. "You have my condolences as well."

"It wasn't your home! They weren't polite to you."

"And it is yours. All things considered, it seems a far worse burden to permanently live there than to visit for a quarter of an hour. My sincerest regrets on your situation, Mrs. Smith."

"But—that is—" She looked up at him and her jaw squared. "That is my *mother* you are talking about."

"Yes, well." For a second, Grayson wondered—tell the truth? Or paper it over? Which would be better for his plans?

His attempts at calculation failed, and obstinacy won out over good sense. "As I said. My condolences. My sincere sympathies as well. I also have dreadful white relations who don't understand basic civility."

Her mouth gaped. "What are you talking about?"

"For me," Grayson continued, "it's my uncle on my mother's side. He spent years saying that the family would eventually recognize my mother's marriage instead of pretending she had perished. As soon as the time was right." He glanced over at her. "If you guessed that the time was never going to be right, you would be correct. I know the type."

"She is…" Mrs. Smith's eyes grew rounder. "She may have been…" She shook her head. "She may not always succeed, but she *tries.*"

"Ah, see. The problem with that argument is that I know what trying looks like. My mother is white. *She* tries. She does not always succeed—even now after decades of marriage to a Black man she met because they were both working to abolish slavery in the British empire, she sometimes fails to understand things that I have known since I was three. But she *does* try. Trying means that if someone calls even the least favorite of her children uncivilized in her own drawing room, she would demand that they apologize sincerely. If they are unwilling, she has them tossed out."

Mrs. Smith's eyes grew rounder. "But that would be uncivil! To say the least."

"Is it though? *Is* it uncivil to demand that your dearest loved ones be treated with basic respect?"

Mrs. Smith frowned. "But she loves me."

Grayson rolled his eyes. "Mrs. Smith, you do not strike me as the sort of person whom it would be difficult to like. It says absolutely nothing about anyone's character that they have chosen to do so."

She colored faintly.

"I can pretend with the best of them," he said. "I will bite my tongue when speaking won't do any good. But I have a great deal of experience. I know when a white trader will knife me in the back for ten cents in profit and then turn around and claim they did me a favor. They always tell on themselves before it happens. Does she use those words often in your company, by the way?"

"What words?"

"Lesser races. Uncivilized. Savage."

Mrs. Smith did not answer.

"So she does," Grayson said. "That *is* what you were apologizing to me for, yes?"

Out of the corner of his eye, he saw her give a quick nod.

"Enough of her. Let's talk about you and your plan here. You're supposed to be marrying a man who—what did Mrs. Flappert say again?—looks for a woman with a healthy constitution, a working grasp of English, and the ability to do all the boring chores. Sexual favors are an added incentive for him. Did I understand that correctly?"

Mrs. Smith bristled. "That's *not* what she said."

"It's close enough. Is that what you really want out of life? Some people do. I doubt I could convince you if you were one of them."

She glanced up at him, her brow furrowed in puzzlement. She did not answer immediately. Instead, she chewed her lip as if she had never contemplated the question.

Finally she spoke. "You said you were going to make me an offer of employment. What sort of employment?"

"I need someone to invent a telegraphic encoding for Chinese characters."

She was no good at hiding her thoughts. He saw it all: the flash of interest, the light that crossed her face, the way her mouth opened as she turned to him. That was her first reaction. Then she froze in that moment of excitement. The spark leached from her eyes. She shut her mouth, compressing her lips. Then she shook her head.

"No." She sounded regretful. "I don't know what Leland told you about me. You were obviously expecting someone else. You didn't even realize it was me at first. No." Her voice was very soft. "I couldn't do that."

"Couldn't?" Grayson asked. "Or don't wish to?"

She looked out over the hill. "It wouldn't be honest of me to take such an offer. Anyone who knows me would say the same thing. I'm flighty and forgetful. It takes me an age to remember anyone's name at all. I cannot keep details in my head. I make stupid, ridiculous mistakes. I could not even do my buttons up properly this morning because I was distracted thinking of other things. So inventing an actual code for use by real people?" She shook her head rapidly. "I could not."

"I see," he said. "Then let us just converse about a Chinese telegraphic code in general. Did you know there's a Frenchman who is working on his own version of Morse code for Chinese characters?"

"You see? That's the sort of person you should hire."

He had hired someone like that before. Two someones.

"I wonder what you would think of his premise," Grayson said, looking off into the distance. "This is all intelligence I've received, so I trust you'll keep it confidential."

She nodded.

"The basic idea is that he'll take the thousand most common

Chinese characters and assign them a value from one to one thousand. Let us say the character for 'life'—a very common one, I'm told—is assigned the value of one. To send that, one would send the numeral 'one' in Morse. For a less common character—"

"Stop," she interrupted him. "That can't be right. Are you telling me that he's encoding *Chinese characters* for telegraph by first creating a Western code for each character, without regard to construction or appearance or radicals, and then encoding them *a second* time in Morse code only using numbers?" Her brow wrinkled. "Unencoding would be, I suppose, a matter of looking up numbers in the chart. But if the characters are arranged in order from most commonly used, the encoding itself..." She was talking as much to herself as to him. "How would that even be done? I suppose you would have to make a dictionary of some sort based on stroke number, although I've always found that method to be ridiculous and time-consuming. There would have to be an index to the code, and if you're going to do that, why not make the *index* the code—" She cut herself off.

Grayson found himself smiling. "I see. You couldn't do it?"

Her eyes met his.

Grayson had spent the past years of his life planning out his telegraphic enterprise. That meant he had seen enough people get excited about the telegraph to know what true passion looked like. Her uncertainty had fled while she was talking. Her entire posture had opened up. Her eyes had lit from within. She had listed, in thirty seconds, precisely the issues with a Chinese telegraphic code that the hapless fellow he'd hired before her had mentioned when he quit—encoding, decoding, ease of transmission. She had come alive when she was talking.

Her eyes dropped from his.

"Mrs. Smith, you cannot possibly believe that you're flighty and forgetful."

"But I am."

He waved a hand. "It may be true about some things, but I'd wager it's never true for the things you care about. When I met you this morning, you were trying to invent a bamboo bustle replacement."

"*Trying* is too kind. *Failing* is more like it. It won't work. The material is too friable."

"Your brother showed me some of your letters. I've seen your idea for a Chinese telegraphic code. I listened to you talk. I just saw you light up like a second sun. You can't actually fool me into thinking you can't do this. You can only fool yourself."

She seemed taken aback by this. "Captain. Um. I have forgotten your name again."

"Hunter."

"Captain Hunter. You seem to have misapprehended my capabilities."

"Please enlighten me."

"I am not an expert in Chinese telegraphic code," she said. "It is simply that in my prior marriage, my late husband was stationed in Hyderabad."

She hardly looked old enough to have married and lost a husband.

"The telegraphic office was close by. I helped out a bit."

"A bit." He looked at her. "I thought we weren't engaging in these polite fictions. How much was a bit?"

"You know, decoding messages, sending them on." She looked away. "The man who was ostensibly in charge of the telegraph office, um, took leave a bit more than usual, so on occasion, when I had the time, I would fix the machinery, splice cable, that sort of thing. Nothing difficult."

"You learned to splice cable." He spoke evenly.

"Anyone could," she said dismissively. "It's not difficult so long as you've been taught properly."

"And you developed a Chinese telegraphic code while you were there."

"It is wildly incomplete. Do you know how many characters there are in the Chinese language? It's just that Leland and I used to speak Mandarin with one another, and since he was in Hong Kong and I was in Hyderabad, I had nobody to practice with. It took up much of my time because..." Her eyes slid away. "I'm the wrong person for this. I'm not a native speaker of any dialect of Chinese. I've scarcely fumbled into the writing of it."

That surprised him. "Are you not native?"

"Technically, I must have spoken some dialect before I was taken in." She looked away, off over the green foothills to the east. Her hand clenched at her side. "But my mother wanted me to learn English and forbade me from speaking any other tongue. I had forgotten most of what I knew by the time I was seven."

Her tone tried to communicate that was no real loss. Her eyes, fixed to the east, with just a hint of a wrinkle in her brow, said otherwise.

"Did she now," Grayson said, keeping his tone as mild as possible.

"She did." Mrs. Smith pasted a smile on her face and turned to him. "So you see how it is. I could not possibly accept employment under false pretenses."

"Well. You've convinced me. You're not an expert in Chinese telegraphic code."

She seemed to withdraw into herself. "Good. Then let's forget—"

"Mrs. Smith. There is no such thing as a Chinese tele-graphic code expert. The expertise does not exist, which is why I need someone to invent it. I need someone who will think clearly, react creatively, and work independently."

"That doesn't sound like me?" She made the sentence into a question.

He stopped in his tracks and turned to her. "It *absolutely* sounds like you. Your explanation of why you were inadequate included the information that you basically ran the telegraph office in Hyderabad for amusement because the man who was supposed to be in charge of it was a drunkard."

"I didn't say he was a drunkard!"

"No," he said, giving her a smile. "But we've already established I'm rather more to the point than you are. You've likely been told all your life that you should be humble and not think well of yourself, but I think you know the truth. You cannot possibly be unaware."

"Unaware?" She tilted her head. "Of what?"

"You are absolutely wasted here. It took me two minutes to realize that you are one of the brightest people I have ever met in my life. I want to hire you and set you loose on my problems, and you're here wasting all that power of imagination determining whether you can endure marriage to Mr. Flappert."

"Well. I see we are to be frank."

"By all means."

She turned to look at him. She had changed gowns from when he'd first seen her. She was now wearing something blue and sprigged and buttoned. His gaze caught momentarily on the slight swell of those buttons over her breasts before he looked into her eyes.

"This feels unlikely. Unrealistic. Impossible. You keep telling me I'm clever, and I'll admit it. I *am*. I'm clever enough to know I'm less than excited about the prospect of impending nuptials."

"Good."

"I'm clever enough to be suspicious. Someone I've only just met appears out of nowhere, offering me a chance to escape something I dread by being paid to do something I enjoy so much I have done it for amusement." Her nose wrinkled. "'When the devil comes courting...'"

He held up a hand. "Am I the devil here?"

"No. Of course not. *I* am. That's the point of the aphorism. You make mistakes when you want things too much. You have to stop and ask yourself if it's right, if it makes sense, or if you're only deluding yourself."

She had a point. She truly did.

"You don't trust me."

"I don't know you."

He glanced at her. "You probably shouldn't trust me. I intend to change the world. I've had a vision in mind for over a decade now: of messages that can be sent in an instant. Local control over the flow of information. I want telegrams to be sent not just by a few companies for the purpose of furthering trade, but by anyone. From peasants in Beijing to the Shehu of Borno. Think about how that will change the world."

Her eyes were wide and bright on his.

"I'm going to upend the world," he said, "so you probably shouldn't trust me. But I am telling you now that you can be a part of this."

He had her imagination working. He could see it in the faint flush that spread across her cheeks, as if she'd caught the scent of his ambition on the warm breeze between them.

"I have an office in Shanghai," he told her. "You'll receive an appropriate salary and I will turn you loose on the most difficult telegraphic encoding the world has encountered."

"But—"

"Don't answer yet." He smiled at her confidently. "I'm leaving with the tide in two days. You'll have that long to decide if you want to change the world." He let that thought stretch a long moment between them before he gave her the alternative. "Or if you'll let the world change you instead."

CHAPTER FOUR

Amelia felt dazed. This morning, she'd awoken feeling trapped by the certainty of Mrs. Flappert's arrival.

Then she'd met *him* on her wanderings. Captain... Captain... Oh bother his name anyway. He'd offered her employment. To work on telegraphic code. In Shanghai. To connect all parts of China, first, and then the world.

Honestly, she was half-convinced this was all a dream. She would wake at any moment to the news of Mrs. Flappert's imminent arrival.

Awakening after *this* to a world without escape would be crushing.

They had descended the hill now. Residences crowded in between mulberry trees gave way to stone stores and businesses. They passed the Flemings' mercantile, where Daisy's puppies were just old enough to leave their mother, then the bank, then the social club.

He didn't say anything now. There were people about; he'd cautioned her to confidentiality, and so perhaps he didn't want to expound on his plans for a telegraph. She brought them to a halt just outside the customs house. It was close enough to the water's edge that the nearest ships—low-keeled enough for river travel at high tide but large enough to survive a bit of an ocean voyage along the coasts—towered overhead. The five hills of Fuzhou rose beyond them.

Like all European architecture, the customs house was wide and blocky, squares upon squares upon squares softened only by stone garlands of laurel leaves above the windows.

Amelia turned to Captain Hunter.

"Did you really want the introduction," Amelia asked, "or was this all a pretext to speak with me?"

"No such thing as a pretext," he said. Perhaps he could see the hesitation she felt writ across her face because he leaned in and lowered his voice. "Don't worry. His name is Waterman. He lives by water and he is a man, remember?"

She looked away.

She'd voyaged once out of Hong Kong through deep waters. She'd thought of the depths of the ocean underneath her—of all the creatures that might be lurking unseen in those leagues of water—and felt her feet itch with the certainty that something was down there where it couldn't be seen.

That was how she felt right now. As if something waited in the deeps, and she didn't know what it was.

He gave her a little smile. "If you forget his name again, I'll remind you."

Her mother would scoff at that. *If I keep telling you, you'll never learn on your own. You can't expect people to make your life easy for you, Amelia. How is it that you can remember the most obscure Chinese characters, but you can't remember someone's name?*

They entered the building. A young man stood to bar their passage, but an elderly fellow near him shook his head.

"It's all right. She's with the Acheson family. You must have some message, Miss Amelia?"

"Of course. Thank you."

They were left on their own. Amelia took them to a back office with a view along the harbor.

That did bring something back to her. *Waterman,* she reminded herself. *His name is Waterman.*

She stopped in the doorway and waited for the man to look up. No; not *the man. Waterman.* That was his name. He set down his pen, and as he did, his eyes lifted. His gaze fell on her; he frowned, then nodded.

"Miss Amelia, isn't it?"

"It's Mrs. Smith now."

"Ah, is it? Time flies. It was a bit ago you were married; I remember now. You hardly seem old enough for that."

Amelia was well into adulthood—old enough not only to marry, but to have had a handful of children had things gone well in that first marriage. Another of the things that was subtly wrong with her: the relief she'd felt every month when their weekly exercise had once again failed to bear fruit.

"But never mind that. What can I do for you?"

"I've come on Leland's request to introduce a friend of his." She turned to the captain.

Oh God. Panic ensued. What was the captain's name again?

She turned back to the man at the desk because at least she remembered *his* name. She'd told it to herself three times just now. His name was something man? Something about what he did or where he was. Harborman?

Her head was full of answers, every one of them completely wrong.

The captain strode forward. "Captain Grayson Hunter," he said, "of Lord Traders, Incorporated, out of Maine. You must be Mr. Waterman."

Oh thank God.

"Lord Traders." Mr. Waterman's eyebrow rose. "Well, you lot are stirring things up a bit."

"Nothing brings me greater joy."

Hunter, Amelia reminded herself. His name was Hunter. The handsome captain's name was Hunter, and she would remember it because she was being hunted. He had pointed at her as if she were a pigeon on the wing and he was intending to take his shot. She was prey, and he was on the hunt. At least he was, if by *prey* one meant *a woman who knew Morse code.* And if by *hunting* one meant *offering employment.*

The conversation didn't need her input—it jumped immediately to tea and cinnamon, things she knew little about—and she sat and contemplated.

Decide if you want to change the world, or let the world change you. What immense hubris.

What fun, some small part of her mind whispered. She squashed that down.

He'd insulted Amelia's mother. He'd implied such terrible things about her. Amelia knew better. Her mother worked as a nurse in the missionary hospital when she was needed for no compensation but thanks, and little enough of that. Amelia knew her to be the sort who would make outright gifts to those in need—sailors left in port with no income, women down on their luck. Her kindness wasn't restricted to Europeans. She would bring gifts to the Chinese women she knew when they gave birth. She was a good woman. She wanted the best for Amelia.

The two men were still talking.

Amelia put a smile on her face and pretended to be interested in the conversation, which had switched to a discussion of the weather that year in the surrounding mountains and what that meant for this year's crop of tea.

Mrs. Acheson was a good woman, but Captain... What was his name? Employment. Morse code. Prey. Pigeon. Shoot? Rifle? Those didn't quite seem right, but then, that was the problem with trying to remember names. They never quite seemed right, even if they were.

Captain Name Not Rifle was not exactly correct, but he had not been entirely wrong in his estimations either.

Her mother wanted the best for Amelia, but what she came up with... Perhaps she lacked imagination.

Amelia had been married at seventeen to a man more than twice her age. She probably hadn't hated it? The marital bed had been boring rather than painful. He had taken her on his mission to India. The English wives around had had acquaintances enough that they didn't need to interact with Amelia beyond the pleasantries. She had hired Indian women to assist in the household, as had been typical, but she'd not wanted to impose more on their employment. Amelia would have been dreadfully lonely, but there had been a tame fox in Hyderabad that she'd enjoyed spending time with.

Between letters from Leland and her time in the telegraph office, she'd made do. Amelia had never fit in anywhere; not doing so in her marriage had felt depressingly ordinary.

Amelia had tried to be friendly, and she had some acquaintances. She would even say she had friends in Fuzhou. There was, after all, Daisy, the very nice yellow dog who had whelped the litter Amelia had cooed over just this morning. She was *definitely* friends with Daisy.

Mrs. Fleming, Daisy's owner, spoke to anyone and everyone who would stop to listen, so she counted as well. But neither Daisy nor Mrs. Fleming was particularly picky. Most other British women looked at Amelia as if she were an oddity.

The Chinese women treated her warily. She'd been introduced to the Chinese population early, brought out regularly as proof that the missionaries who took in children treated them with love and kindness. But the end result of having to be proof, not a person, was that there was nobody she could talk to, no one among their number whom she dared confide in. She'd tried to learn the local Fuzhou dialect once she'd been allowed to do so. She managed only a passable competence.

Captain Something and Mr. Whatever Man were still conversing. Amelia had no idea what they were talking about. She pasted an interested smile on her face and tried to mind their words.

She lasted half a sentence. Import duties? Bleah. There was only so much attention she could pay to *that*.

What she needed was a pocket watch, except instead of sounding the hour, it would poke her in the thigh every minute to remind her to notice whatever was happening around her. An excellent idea, but then she would have to invent a pocket watch that stopped her other pocket watch from poking her in the thigh because being continually prodded would drive her into madness.

Her mother would sigh if she could hear her thoughts.

Her mother wanted Amelia to marry again.

"But of course," Mr. Something-man was saying with a laugh. "We couldn't allow *that*."

Getting married again was the right thing to do. It was the moral thing to do. It was a failure in Amelia that she didn't want it.

But employment. What was the difference between being employed by a man and being married to one? She'd worked all the time during her last marriage. She would clearly be expected to do the same in the next one. She enjoyed keeping busy.

But what if she worked for a man and *didn't* have to lie there awkwardly, once a week, as he heaved himself over her? What if she worked for a man and he gave her money and she could decide what to have for dinner for *herself* instead of consulting his preferences?

That might be nice.

There was a woman in Fuzhou who made tea flowers. Unlike the square compressed bricks that were sent back to England to be broken apart and brewed, tea flowers were made by winding tea leaves and jasmine flowers cleverly together and tying them with silk threads. They were compressed into balls, then dried into what looked like boring, indiscriminate lumps.

When you dropped one into hot water, they unfurled, leaf by leaf, forming gorgeous flowers constructed of tea leaves.

Amelia felt as if she were a boring, indiscriminate lump held above hot water. She didn't know what would happen if she were dropped. Maybe she would unfold into a masterpiece.

It spoke to something inside her, that concept. The idea that underneath her awkward clumsiness there might be something beautiful. She *liked* that idea.

Unfortunately, most boring, indiscriminate lumps turned into still boring, looser, less discriminate lumps when made into tea. *When the devil comes courting, he offers you what you want.* She'd grown up with those words, a check on her flightiness, on her willingness to throw herself into whatever odd tidbit had piqued her interest that week.

And yet she had never been able to give up the hope that there *was* something inside her waiting to unfold. Amelia knew why.

In the depths of her heart, buried underneath years of neglect, she still held on to a lie. She *knew* it was a lie. It had been proven to be one again and again.

Hold on to your heart.

It seemed a strange echo of Leland's words: *what is valuable.*

"Well." Mr. Whatever stood, and Captain Something rose alongside him. The conversation was coming to an end; Amelia scrambled to her feet.

"A pleasure speaking with you," Captain Something said, holding out his hand. "I'll be in touch, Mr. Waterman."

"You as well. Surprising, really. But I see why Leland sent you my way. He always did collect interesting folk."

Captain Whatsit smiled gently at that—not quite reprovingly. "It's growing late." It was barely past noon. "I had best get Mrs. Smith home before the sun grows too hot."

"Of course, of course. My best to your mother, Mrs. Smith."

"My best to your wife." She did not add *Mr. Waterman* to the end of the speech because while Captain Question Mark had used the name, she was only *fairly* certain that was his name, not *extremely* certain. It would be extraordinarily awkward if she were wrong.

They left the building together. They walked back the way they had come, past the stand of mulberry trees with their slippery leaves, past the ginkgoes with their tiny green fruits.

He glanced at her once they'd started up the hill, away from those who might overhear.

"I understand now why your brother gave me a code name."

She tilted her head toward him.

"He knows about your coming nuptials, I take it?"

She nodded. "I write to him every week."

"Why 'Silver Fox,' by the way?"

Her hand crept to her locket. "It's a silly story."

"Indulge me."

"Leland was twelve when my mother took me in," Amelia said. "He was tasked with helping me learn English."

He just nodded at that.

"Those first few years, sometimes people would make fun of me for my way of speaking." She looked away. "And I forgot my Chinese name." She couldn't meet his eyes as she said this. "So he started calling me Silver Fox so that I would remember that I was quick. And clever. It's not really the sort of name one would give a girl in Chinese though."

She glanced up at him, realized he was looking at her, and felt herself flush and turn her gaze to the road.

"He must not think much of you marrying Mr. Pale."

Amelia grimaced. "I'm bad with names, but I'm not *that* bad. His name is Mr. Flappert. Mr. Alden Flappert."

"Ah. This *is* serious. You know his name." He was smiling at her—teasing her, she suspected—and she found her own smile creeping out in return.

"My first husband was an Alden. Alden Smith. When I found out this one was also named Alden, it seemed extremely convenient. I wouldn't have to learn a second name!"

"A match made in heaven. But consider this extremely important countervailing point—*my* name is *also* Alden."

Her eyes widened, and she turned to him. "It *is?*"

"I'm joking." His smile practically split his face. "It's funny because you actually believed me. You really *don't* know my name."

"Of course I know your name. You're Captain…" Pigeon. Shoot. Prey. "Hunter," she guessed.

"Look at that," he said, as if he were actually impressed. Which he assuredly wasn't. And even if he were, the feat was less impressive than it appeared, as she'd been half guessing. "What's my Christian name then?"

"G—Gabriel?"

"Close. It's Grayson."

She felt herself grimace.

"Soooo." His conversation had an idle quality to it, as if he were simply trying to be friendly. She doubted he had ever done anything idle in his life. "Your brother, who knows you well, who has encouraged you to think of yourself as clever and quick, doesn't want you to marry Mr. Flappert."

Hold on to your heart. Without Leland, Amelia would have given no credence to those falsely remembered words. She'd held on to her heart for so long, and to what purpose?

It had caused so much trouble.

"But what he wants is immaterial," the captain went on. "What do *you* want?"

"You make it sound so easy. The wanting, I mean."

"On the contrary. Wanting well is extraordinarily difficult."

She was aware that he was easy to talk to. Leland had told her that he was utterly ruthless. That he got what he wanted.

He didn't seem ruthless. He was being so, so nice.

"You are a ship's captain," she said to him. "When you're out in the middle of the ocean, do you ever worry about what lies beneath you?"

He took this wild change of subject with aplomb. "I lay submarine telegraphic cable. I worry about the ocean floor all the time."

"I'm speaking less geographically and more animalistically."

He wrinkled his nose. "You mean plankton and such?"

"I was thinking more along the lines of a megalodon."

He stopped and turned to her. "A megalodon."

"Yes," she couldn't stop herself from saying. "The massive sharks from the Jurassic period. The teeth that have been found can be as much as six inches in length, and they believe—"

She managed to bite back her words before her mega-lodonic enthusiasm overwhelmed the conversation. She could imagine her mother's reproach. *Nobody wants to know more megalodon facts, Amelia.*

But he was watching her with a bemused expression on his face. "Anyone who has been out to sea knows there are things in the world that can't easily be explained," he said slowly. "When we were laying the telegraphic line from Singapore to Hong Kong, somewhere in the middle of the South China Sea, something sheared the cable through."

She couldn't help herself. She gasped.

His eyes were twinkling as he faced her. "Whatever it was, it sliced the line as if were cheese instead of copper."

"What did you do?"

He shrugged. "Dredged the ocean floor until we found the fallen end of the cable." He met her eyes with a smile. "Hoped the megalodon beneath the waves took pity on us and didn't make matters worse for our vessel."

Amelia narrowed her eyes. "You're teasing."

"I am. A little. We were talking about your wants and somehow we ended up over here, discussing species of gargantuan extinct sharks. I trust you'll make the connection?"

She shook her head. "If there are megalodons beneath the waves, there's no point thinking about what's waiting in the deeps. They're too big, and they're full of massive, sharp teeth."

"As much as six inches long, you said." He was still smiling at her.

"You see my problem. There's nothing to be done with a creature of that size. All you can do is stay on the surface and hope for the best."

He let out a long sigh. "Very well, Mrs. Smith. Tell me about your surface worries."

"Aren't those obvious? I don't fit in much of anywhere. I'm not anyone's first choice for anything. I'm not their second choice. I'm perhaps the seventh, if they get around to choosing me at all."

The way he was looking at her changed.

She waved an annoyed hand at him. "For God's sake. Don't pity me. It is what it is. I've accepted it. But you see what I mean. There's enough for me to contend with in these shallow waters. I can't go hunting megalodons. Your entire proposition is preposterous."

Amelia's home was just around the bend now. He didn't answer, not as they grew closer. Not as the glinting glass of her household windows greeted her.

"Well," he said casually, turning to her. "Then that's a no from you?"

She nodded.

"What a pity."

Leland had said he was ruthless. Was he giving up so easily? Amelia felt strangely bereft.

"For curiosity's sake," he said as they came to a stop a few yards from the front door, "how large *are* megalodons?"

She'd been expecting a different question. A harder question. She felt herself brightening at this instead. "As much as fifty feet long," she informed him. "They've found megalodon vertebrae the size of dinner plates before. Jaws so large that I could walk through them."

His lips pressed together in ill-concealed amusement.

"You're laughing at me."

He didn't answer. Instead, he reached into a pocket and took out a card. "I'll be here two more days. In case you forget my name again and need to come looking. It's Captain Grayson Hunter. Don't ask what my ship is; that's complicated." He smiled. "I'm here on the *Lenity*. Come find me."

She blinked at him. "I thought you'd given up on employing me."

"Not in the slightest. I was just establishing basic facts."

"Basic facts? Basic facts about megalodons?"

"About you." He reached out and took her hand. Amelia's breath caught. He was standing close and he was very tall and very handsome. The rays of the early afternoon sun reflected off the rich brown of his skin in golds and oranges.

The want that threatened to envelop her was no megalodon, just a hint of wistfulness. If he had been Mr. Flappert after all...

They could have talked of telegraphs and he might have only laughed at her a little instead of bidding her to be quiet, please, for God's sake.

She let him draw her hand to him, unwilling to pull away when she didn't know what he intended to do.

He put the card in her palm.

"Mrs. Smith," he said. "Your analogy was spot on. You may, however, wish to reconsider your conclusion."

"What do you mean?"

"You should make friends with your megalodon." His fingers curled around hers, warm and substantial, closing her fingers around the solid edges of his card.

"But..."

"But nothing," he told her. "You *like* megalodons. Why are you avoiding this one?"

CHAPTER FIVE

Evening had come and with it, stronger winds sweeping in from the faraway mountains. They hissed and howled around Amelia's home, a constant chorus whispering through the evening meal.

You should make friends with your megalodon, she could still hear Captain Hunter saying. But Amelia's megalodon was nowhere to be found. Instead Mrs. Flappert had stayed for dinner. She talked of Amelia's departure with her the day after tomorrow as if the matter were already decided. She had not asked for Amelia's opinion; she did not seem to think it relevant.

You should make friends with your megalodon.

After Mrs. Flappert returned to her lodgings for the evening, Amelia absconded to her room and took out her trunk. She had used it for her first marriage, packing her things into it and unpacking them and then packing them again, and unpacking yet another time, moving from place to place alongside Alden the First.

It had felt like a relief to unpack it here—a relief and a wonder.

It was time to start packing again. Her future seemed hidden, like a river blanketed in mist. She didn't know where the current was bringing her or what her surroundings would look like when the fog lifted.

A rap sounded on her door. "Amelia?"

She crossed and opened the door. "Mother."

Mrs. Acheson glanced at her trunk, at the open wardrobe. "May I come in?"

"Of course. It's your home."

"It's your chamber." But her mother smiled and entered. "You're packing, I see."

"Of course," Amelia said even though there was no *of course* about it.

Her mother sat on the edge of the bed. "I hardly know how to bring this up, but I notice that you did not actually agree to marry Mr. Flappert."

Amelia picked up a pile of her shifts, shook them out, and refolded them. "I didn't. I haven't met him. At least I met Mr. Smith before we were engaged."

"His mother is a good woman."

Maybe it was the memory of the afternoon with Captain Hunter that made her speak more freely. "Mrs. Flappert finds it surprising that I can speak English despite having been raised in an English household from the age of six years old."

There was a long silence. Her mother drove a knuckle into her forehead as if staving off a headache.

"It doesn't make her *not* a good woman," Amelia said. "But it does make her company very uncomfortable. She looks at me as if at any moment I might have an unaccountable outbreak of savagery."

"Well, you'll have to teach her that you won't. Kindness will win her over. I'm sure of it."

Amelia wasn't sure where the courage to speak her mind came from. "She's fifty-five. If she were capable of learning such a lesson, shouldn't she have figured it out by now?" Amelia took a day gown out of the wardrobe and folded it with a little more vigor than necessary.

Her mother exhaled. "You're not happy with the prospect."

It wasn't that she was *unhappy*. She merely felt compressed. Ever since she had read Leland's letter, ever since she'd seen the words *what is valuable*, she had felt as if megalodons were teeming beneath the surface.

"In truth," her mother said, "neither am I. I wouldn't have said anything if you were delighted, but…" She sighed. "The family money. It's not as good as what Mr. Smith had, and even he didn't leave you anything. It wasn't expected of him, so he left his funds to his cousin. He treated you more like a servant than a wife, but a servant should at least expect something for their service."

Maybe now was the time to mention that she had been made an offer of employment.

Amelia let the gown she was holding drop into the trunk and peered back into the mess of her wardrobe. "Leland said much the same thing to me."

"Did you get a letter from him?"

"Captain…" She grimaced. The name was in Leland's letter and on his card, and it had once again slipped from her mind. "The captain brought it." She glanced at her mother. "I encountered him on my morning constitutional before he arrived at our house. We spoke."

You should make friends with your megalodon. But she didn't need more things to want. That was exactly the problem. She was hardly short on regular wants.

She wanted a place to call her own. She wanted the winds to die down; the sound of their howling would keep her awake tonight. She wanted her mother to be proud of her, to feel she had done the right thing on that long-ago road when she'd agreed to take charge of Amelia.

Her mother looked at her, a hint of wariness in her tone. "What think you of Captain Hunter?"

Amelia didn't know how to answer. Instead, she frowned at the fossilized teeth in her wardrobe and, after a little thought, added them to her trunk. "In his letter, Leland says that he's utterly ruthless, that he's possessed of an incisive mind, but that…" How had Leland put it? "That he's never done anything to anyone without their full and enthusiastic participation."

Her mother bit her lip. "That's extremely alarming."

"Is it? It sounded reassuring to me."

Her mother was looking off into the distance, her lips pursed. When she spoke, her tone was dry. "You're only saying that because you've never met a man who was able to obtain your full and enthusiastic participation."

Amelia frowned. "You say that as if it's a bad thing."

Her mother pursed her lips. "Amelia, you're…" The woman turned to look at her, but didn't finish her sentence.

Amelia felt even more puzzled.

"You must understand," her mother tried again. "My husband is gone ten months out of the year on his journeys. It's not as if I've…" Another pause, and then a deep sigh. "Never mind. I want you to not make the mistakes I've made." There was yet another pause before she sighed again. "I've sheltered you too much. You were my little girl from the moment I saw you. I have never wanted anything but the best for you, but I do not know what the best is."

"Because I'm Chinese." She said it because it needed to be said. "If I were not, it would be easy. I wouldn't have to go with whichever man vaguely wanted a female companion, no matter what his mother said of me."

Her mother reached out and pulled her into a fierce hug. "You mustn't say such things, little bird. There is a place for you in my heart, and so there will be a place for you in this world with me. Stop packing. You don't have to marry Mr. Flappert."

Amelia turned to look at her mother.

Her mother nodded. "We'll just have to think of someone else for you."

Someone *else*. Amelia let her mother stroke her hair, let her eyes shut, and let her mind go wandering. Her mother likely meant some other missionary.

She thought of Captain Handsome and his offer of a salary. She thought of that deep pull in her gut, the one of megalodonic proportions. His offer felt like a memory that she didn't have—as if it were something she had dreamed once and then forgotten. It seemed both strange and oh so familiar.

Make friends with your megalodon, he had said, and leaning against her mother, feeling the soft brush of those fingertips, brought back something that felt like a memory even though she knew it was not.

Amelia had been told the story so many times that she almost felt as if she *could* recall being there. Instead, the blurry images must have been invented after the fact. She had been six years old back then, and her actual memories of the time before Mrs. Acheson had taken her in were hazy and indistinct.

Nonetheless, she had a clear vision of that moment, one she had built up over countless recountings. She could see the road, dust rising in clouds. She could see the other travelers— too tired to run, too afraid to stop, faces and clothing painted in dirt and desperation. She knew the memory to be false because, in her mind, she was high—too high—above the shoulders of the adults, a dreamlike vantage point.

She knew what she had been told. Amelia and her Chinese mother had been traveling on the road. Amelia had been too big to carry for long, yet too small to walk much on her own. Amelia had been crying and feverish.

"So thin," her mother had said. "*That* woman couldn't have been feeding you much."

Mrs. Acheson had always believed charity started with kindness, so she'd offered the travelers a meal. Over the course of bread and cheese, between Mrs. Acheson's rudimentary Mandarin and Amelia's Chinese mother's tiny command of English, one important point had been communicated: Amelia needed help.

"She gave you to me," her mother had said. "She knew you'd be better off with me."

She left you, Amelia had always heard. Her Chinese mother had walked away from her into that cloud of dust and desperation.

"Which direction?" Amelia had asked as a child. "Where was she going? Didn't she want me there?"

Her mother hadn't known the answer to any of those questions. "Sweetheart," she had said gently, "we could scarcely communicate. I'm sure she might have told us, but how would we have known what she was saying?"

Amelia had dreams of that time on the road. Of her mother —her Chinese mother. Sometimes she dreamed the woman shed tears as she left. Sometimes she imagined her relief at being rid of a burden. But she always seemed to remember one last thing as her mother stooped in the dust of the road and pressed a hand against Amelia's cheek. She remembered words. One final communication.

Hold on to your heart, she remembered hearing. *I will come back for you.*

Those words were a lie. Amelia dreamed them sometimes, but they always came in English. It was a dream that she'd conjured out of time and wanting and a desperate desire to think she hadn't truly been given up like the useless burden she must have been.

Captain Hunter was wrong. Amelia's megalodon didn't want to be her friend either. Her wants had been born extinct.

And yet every road leading to every house where she had ever dwelled, she had wanted. She had looked down those roads, and especially on dry, dusty days, especially on days when the wind kicked up, she had imagined someday someone would come for her. She had imagined she had been wanted.

On every birthday (which they had assigned to the day Mrs. Acheson had taken her in), she'd been told to blow out a candle and make a wish.

She had stopped wishing for her Chinese mother to return when she was ten.

Captain Hunter had it completely wrong. She had been wanting ever since she was six years old. Sometimes if she let herself slip, she found there was nothing inside her but a deep well of unfulfilled want.

The little wants? The surface wants? Those she could look to.

Maybe there was room to look ahead of her and dream of the future instead of yearning for the past.

Her mother's hand drifted down the side of Amelia's head again, caressing her. "Did your Captain Hunter say what he wanted?"

Captain *Hunter.* She tried to fix his name in her mind.

When the devil comes courting, he offers you what you want.

That wasn't entirely apt. In all her years of desperate, unfulfilled wanting, she had never once thought, "Employment in a telegraph office, coming up with a version of Morse code for Chinese characters... That would be just the thing for me."

It was just that as soon as he had said it, she had wanted it. Desperately. He'd talked of an office in Shanghai. Amelia had been found near Shanghai, and something in her yearned to return, to find what could not be found.

He'd talked about telegraphs. She had loved her time in the telegraph office, had always schooled herself to look sober and dependable when someone came to tell her Melvin Tabor was drunk again. The captain had talked about encoding Chinese and sending telegrams to every part of China, and the megalodon part of her brain had perked up, whispering that perhaps this way she might make inquiries, might someday find the woman who had left her behind.

Another day. Another variant of that dream of her mother returning down a lonely, dusty road.

Amelia sighed. She was in Fuzhou with Mrs. Acheson, the only woman she truly remembered as a mother. She turned her cheek into the caress.

"He wants to employ me," Amelia said, editing all those wants to this bare statement.

She could feel her mother tense, every muscle in her body stiffening in reply. "Employ you as what?"

"As someone who knows the Chinese language."

Her mother made a face. "As an interpreter? Is that what he means?"

"You remember how I spent time in the Hyderabad telegraph office a few years ago?"

Mrs. Acheson smiled. "Of course. I'll never forget a thing about my children."

"I tried to come up with a version of Morse code for Chinese then," Amelia said. "He wants me to complete it."

"How very peculiar," her mother said. But she didn't say anything else. She just stroked Amelia, quiet and comforting, and Amelia let it happen.

He only wanted her for her code, but at least he *wanted* her. Mr. Alden Smith, Mr. Alden Flappert... They had both thought she would fit the bill. There was nothing about her in particular that they had appreciated except for her availability.

Captain Hunter wanted her for something that she had personally done, not just as a blank sheet of womanhood to do all the things women were supposed to do. It was a more specific wanting than anything Amelia had ever experienced, and that frightened her.

Matters would have been easy if her mother had simply said that Amelia would have to marry Mr. Flappert. There *truly* would have been no alternative then; her entire being rebelled at the thought. She'd have fled to Captain Something immediately and hoped to repair the breach later.

"You know," her mother said, "if you take employment, you'll never marry. Men won't want that in a wife."

Amelia turned to her mother and saw the grave expression on her face. As if she were speaking of the worst fate that might befall a woman.

Amelia, however, had been married once. Not being tied to another Alden seemed like an unexpected bounty.

"Really?" *Do you promise?*

"Really." Her mother nodded. "And I know that may not figure at this moment. But you've never found someone you really want before, have you? One day you might meet him and realize what you've given up."

It was an echo of the thing she'd said earlier. *You've never met a man who could obtain your full and enthusiastic participation.*

Amelia had now.

She could almost hear her wants whispering to her: Wouldn't making a telegraphic code be a lot more interesting than being a wife to a man she'd never met? If she helped build a telegraphic network, perhaps she could send advertisements throughout China, asking if anyone had lost a six-year-old child on November third seventeen years ago. But even saying that made her feel the helplessness of the endeavor. November third? They didn't even use the same calendar.

She could feel old wants tangling around her. The devil of

her wanting had come courting, and there was nothing for Amelia to do but to turn him down. Again and again. Repeatedly. Until he finally gave up and let her bury her deepest, darkest desires in the depths of her heart.

But oh. Until she did. Until she *did* tell him no...

Until then, she wanted to pretend.

CHAPTER SIX

Grayson's cousin had been making the tea run to Fuzhou since he was nine—first with his father and grandfather, and now that they'd retired, on his own as captain of the *Lenity*. When Grayson arrived back at Captain Zedekiah Hunter's ship, he found his cousin on the docks haggling with a Chinese merchant. Zed spoke Cantonese and the Fuzhou dialect fluently. He was friends with all the Chinese tea merchants—at least while they weren't talking prices.

The haggling was apparently going well since both parties were claiming the deal would send them into bankruptcy.

In the past years, Gray had become very good at pretending. If he didn't pretend, people worried. If people—especially Zed—worried, they wrote home. And if they wrote home with something like *I'm worried about Grayson; he doesn't seem like himself,* his mother would end up on a ship to China.

So instead of finding a place to hide and mull over what he'd just learned, Grayson waited for Zed to finish. And when Zed suggested a Chinese wine shop to wind down after a hard day's work, he agreed with a practiced grin.

"So," Zed said after they'd made their way down a

narrow passage, past a table where fortune-tellers were doing a brisk business at the shop's entrance, through a dark serving room, where they were waved into an empty table in the corner where they could order. "Did you get your man?"

Grayson made a face as the wine arrived in a clay jar. His cousin set out the cups and poured a generous amount into each.

"I see," Zed said. "Something of a hang-up? Nothing you can't work around, I'm sure."

Grayson took a long pull of the wine. It was rich and fruity and enough of an excuse for silence to allow him to gather his thoughts. "The Silver Fox is a woman."

The shop was crowded. Zed leaned in, cupping one hand to his ear. "Say again?"

"She's a *young* woman," Grayson admitted, a little louder.

There must have been something in Grayson's face or tone that gave him away because Zed waggled an eyebrow at him. "Aha. A *beautiful* woman?"

Grayson did his best to give his cousin a quelling look. "It's a business matter. Her looks aren't relevant."

Zed just cackled. "That's a yes."

She was pretty, he might have said objectively. *Not* a beauty, at least not until she got excited and that light shone in her eyes. Grayson rubbed his temples. "It's going to take a bit of a delicate touch."

"Already thinking about touching. Delicately. I see how things are."

He had to change the direction of the conversation. "It's not like that. She reminds me a little of Noah."

Zed's eyes lifted to his. The teasing humor slowly seeped out of him and he blew out a breath. Grayson hadn't meant to say something quite so revealing. He hadn't even realized he *thought* it until the words came out of his mouth.

He didn't talk of his deceased brothers often. Doing so reminded him of too many things he needed to forget.

"Hell, Grayson." Zed reached across the table and refilled his wine cup.

Now that Grayson had made the connection, his internal reaction to her made a lot of sense to him. "You know how Noah was." It hurt to say the words, hurt more to keep his tone steady, to pretend his heart was not scraped raw. "He would get interested in something—anything—and that's all he would talk about for months on end."

"He was bright."

"Beyond bright. With Noah, it was the railroad fascination. Then steamships and propulsion. Then eventually, gutta percha."

Noah's gutta percha obsession had changed Grayson's life. It should have changed Noah's.

Zed reached across the table. "I miss him too."

Grayson hated being so transparent. He wanted to yank his hand away from the offered comfort. "She *isn't* like Noah. Not really. Not at all. But over the course of two hours, she showed me the bamboo bustle replacement she'd been trying to make. I got six minutes of megalodon facts. And she eviscerated Viguier's telegraphic code proposal without even batting an eye. She isn't like him, but there's the same kind of single-minded enthusiasm."

Zed nodded in understanding.

His family had always encouraged Noah. When the incessant railway discussions had annoyed Grayson when he was younger, one of his uncles had taken him aside and explained. *Love is a gift,* he'd been told, *and wanting to love things is a bigger gift. Let him be.*

Grayson had breathed and let his brother be. Noah had blossomed. Latitude charts and calculations…

Zed shook his head. "So I see the need for delicacy. A lovely young white woman. Raised by sticklers in the East, I would imagine. Heavily protected and told not to do anything. How is she managing?"

"She's not white."

Zed's eyes widened.

"She's Chinese. She was, ah 'taken in'—her words—by a missionary when she was six."

Their eyes met over their wine cups. Grayson didn't elaborate; he didn't need to. Zed didn't respond. He *also* didn't need to.

"I need to be rational," Grayson said. "I need to propose employment and negotiate terms. But I keep thinking of what it would be like for Noah to be raised by someone who told him his people were savages." Grayson trailed off, shaking his head and draining his wine cup. "I can't think about the matter like that. I can't get involved."

Across the table, Zed looked into his wine cup, sloshing it slowly from side to side before looking at him. "Involved?"

"In the next year and a half, I have to lay the last two segments of the transpacific cable—four thousand miles. I have to establish telegraphy on the Chinese mainland. I need a code that will convince the Taotai of Shanghai that this is not just some Western devilry. I *have* to be rational, or I'll never get this done."

"I hear you on the difficulty of the work." Zed met his eyes. "The part I have difficulty with is that you think your plan is rational."

Grayson stared at his wine cup.

"It's not," Zed said. "There is nothing rational about this."

Gray forced a laugh. "You've seen the potential profits. What could be more rational than profit?"

"Going home to the people who love you," Zed replied, "more than once every handful of years. You're lonely, Gray."

"I'm busy." He picked up his empty wine cup, turning it

67

around. "And how could I be lonely? I can scarcely get a minute to myself. Captain Bell of the *Celerity* is an excellent man. We met in service in the war. And Ellis aboard the *Victory*—"

"I'm not insulting the credentials of the men you picked," Zed said with a wave of his hand. "Ellis and Bell are solid. But they're wildly grateful to you because Black men, even with their naval experience, would otherwise have been relegated to shoveling coal on a transatlantic steamer. They aren't going to tell you to go home for Christmas. And they certainly won't be carrying tales to your mama."

Grayson rubbed his temples. "Unlike you?"

"You see, I *like* my mama, and what's more important, because I have a sense of self-preservation, I like my mama not being mad at me." Zed shrugged. "That's why I'm always going to turn you in. I'm doing you a favor. This is a warning. My mama and yours are plotting. And I'm telling you now, you need to think about your mother."

Grayson let out a long breath. He and Zed both had been born in a tiny village in Maine in the United States that had been founded by the great-great-uncles who had started Lord Traders as an enterprise. His family home was unlike any place he'd ever been. His great-great-uncle Henry had been from good English stock, and he'd used his influence to shield the small Black community from what they'd heard of in so many other places—violence and people driven out.

Grayson's father had gone to England to lecture on trade alternatives to slavery. When his parents had eloped, and his mother had been thrown out of her wealthy British family, they'd gone back to his father's hometown.

The community was tightly knit, and his mother had wound herself into it. She'd named two of her sons after the aging great-great-uncles who had started everything. There had been a time when Grayson had unequivocally thought of his mother's house in Maine as home. Even when he was on the other side of the world, it was home.

He didn't know how to think of it now.

It was not that he never thought of his mother. It was that the thought of her—the memory of how she'd looked when he'd told her about Noah—would stay with him till his dying day.

"Look," he finally said, when it became apparent he wasn't going to get Zed away from this subject. "I know things are off with me."

Off. Like milk gone bad. Like a ship permanently tilted at sea so nothing stayed in place. He was *off;* that was the only explanation he could offer.

Zed just gave him a skeptical look. "Stop overthinking everything. I was told to tell you directly that you'd better come home or your mama will come find you. And you *don't* want that."

He didn't. He thought about what it would be like if she caught him off guard. If they ever had to have the conversation that would break them apart.

"I know I'm off," he repeated. "But I know what's gone wrong. And I have a plan to fix everything."

He could feel the disbelief rolling off his cousin.

Megalodons, Mrs. Smith had said. Beneath the surface, he also had megalodons, wants so large they would eat him alive. His weren't so friendly.

"I have a plan," he repeated. "And when I'm finished, every-thing will be…"

Put to rights? No. That could never happen. Made whole? Also impossible.

"Everything will be as well as it can be," he said.

Zed just shook his head. "Truly, Gray. You haven't told me one word about your plan, and it already sounds foolish. Just go home."

～

A melia had not woken up with the desperate need to avoid Mrs. Flappert, but shortly after she'd dressed and gone down the stairs, she'd heard the woman talking to her mother.

"Honestly," Mrs. Flappert had been saying with a little laugh, "I didn't think I would have to be considering the feelings of a little Chinese girl in all this! I'm sorry to have upset her delicate sensibilities, but gracious me, Mabel—"

The rest of the conversation had been swallowed by the clink of tea things and the rushing whirl that fury and upset and humiliation made in Amelia's ears. She'd crept out the back way.

She had errands. Definitely errands. She needed to go to the market to purchase…a vegetable, maybe? And if she left the house without money or so much as a sack to carry the hypothetical greenery she intended to purchase? Well. Sometimes she was absentminded.

Sometimes it was far better to be absent from reality than present for its harshest truths.

In the early morning, the air was crisp as she walked.

I didn't think I would have to be considering—

She pushed that voice aside. It didn't matter. She would never see Mrs. Flappert again. Especially not if she managed to make herself into Miss Out on an Errand for the remainder of Mrs. Flappert's visit.

She hadn't realized where she was heading until she arrived at the docks on the river Min. In the books that Amelia had read, European cities moved to the beat of the sun: lively during the day, a short burst of activity in the evenings, and finally falling into something like tranquility at night.

During tea season, the river Min bustled with the moon. At high tide, the only time the steamships could navigate the river to the ocean, Fuzhou positively boiled with activity. At low tide, the traders were out, bargaining as they could with the vessels that were stuck. At this time of morning, the ships were stuck in place, sitting low on the docks with the duckweed visible on the top of the water.

One of those ships belonged to...

His card was in her pocket, but she didn't need to consult it. His face came to mind before his name. The curve of his eyebrow. The smile as he'd leaned in and spoke to her of megalodons. She could imagine his skin, a lustrous brown, with the morning light shining on it. Her heart picked up a beat—surely, she thought, the exertion from the walk—but there was no point lying to herself when there was nobody to fool. She wanted to see Captain...Hunter.

There. *That* was his name. Captain Hunter because he had hunted her out—her!

She didn't know where Captain Hunter was staying, but it was easy enough to find out once she remembered how to refer to him.

"I'm looking for Captain Hunter," she tried. "Captain Hunter of..." What was the name of his ship? She had forgotten. "Captain Hunter of..." What was the name of his trading company? She pulled out his card to remind herself.

The first white sailor she stopped looked at her face and saw nothing further.

"You lookee for big captain?" he asked her very loudly in exaggerated pidgin.

Amelia suppressed a groan. "I'm looking for a Captain Hunter," she said. "From the United States."

"You lookee for American captain?" He gave her an exaggerated wink. "I givee American captain!"

It didn't make sense in English *or* pidgin. Not in any dialect anywhere at all.

"No, thank you," she said politely.

"Me givee you, um…"

Maybe she needed to be louder. "No, *thank* you!" she bellowed and fled, taking her folding fan from her pocket in case she needed to stab him in the eye.

Next she tried the Chinese trader hawking his tea. He looked up at her, his hand playing with the long braid of his queue.

"I'm looking for Captain Hunter," she managed in the Fuzhou dialect.

"Who?"

"Captain Hunter."

His eyes lit. "Ah! Zed!"

That didn't sound like the Christian name the captain had given her, but what did she know?

"There," he said, pointing west along the harbor. "That ship."

When she arrived at the ship he'd indicated, a boy was getting off. He was white with sandy brown hair.

"Excuse me," she started.

He turned to flash her a bright smile. "Yes, ma'am. Can I be of service?"

"I'm looking for Captain Hunter."

"Of course." He sounded like he knew Captain Hunter, which was a relief, but then he kept talking. "*Which* Captain Hunter?"

Which Captain Hunter? This was beginning to sound like one of the nightmares where people she knew surrounded her, demanding that she tell them their names. "I, um."

He took pity on her, bless his soul. "If you're here about tea or trade, it's Captain Zed Hunter, and he's off in a teahouse. I can take you. Almost everyone is here for Captain Zed."

"I'm here about telegraphs. My Captain Hunter—" She felt herself blushing at the way those words had come out. "Um, I mean the Captain Hunter I spoke with yesterday wanted a tele-graphic code?"

"Aha!" The boy grinned at her. "*You're* the Silver Fox. You want to speak to Captain *Grayson* Hunter. You're not what I expected. Are you coming along? This is so exciting!"

Amelia had never been exciting before. He started off, gesturing her to follow, and she did.

"I'm Benedict Worth." He glanced at her sidelong as he said the name as if he was expecting her to recognize who he was and react to it.

Ha. It was more likely that he would turn into a dove and fly away. She had already forgotten the name he'd given. The boy—he could have been no more than seventeen or eighteen —chattered merrily to her as they went along, enthusiastically recounting something about tea and how he had been put in charge of getting through the locks and something something something.

Amelia was too busy practicing what she would say. *I'm sorry, Captain Hunter, but after careful consideration—*

I do not think that I could possibly bring myself to—

As a currently unwed woman, it would be improper to—

Her attempts to conjure up words were interrupted by an insistent whine at the back of her mind of someone else's thoughts—*I did not think I would have to be considering the feelings of a little Chinese girl.*

Amelia didn't know why that of all things had stuck in her mind. She had been called far worse things than "little Chinese girl." At least this particular sneering appellation had the benefit of being mostly true by dint of race and gender and a stature that she knew was diminutive in comparison to other people. There was no reason for truthful statements to bother her. None at all.

The boy conducted her up the gangway, then up a wooden ladder, across the deck, and down another ladder. He paused to offer a hand to steady her on the ladders, a thing he did seemingly without thinking—better manners than she had been expecting from someone who was probably a sailor. Come to think of it, he didn't speak like any of the sailors she'd met.

Finally, they stopped in front of a door. The boy knocked, and Amelia's lungs seized. She clutched her fan.

"Captain," he called.

"A moment," Captain Hunter's voice called in response, and she felt her heart leap up and start to race. He was behind the door. *He* was behind the door—

The door opened. Captain Hunter stood there. Her gaze jumped to his eyes, then down, then immediately back up.

He was clothed. Barely.

He was clothed if one counted a loose pair of trousers, slung low at his hips, as clothing. He was clothed, if shrugging on a shirt and not doing up the buttons, exposing a stripe of brown chest from his navel up to his neck was clothed.

A wave of warmth washed through Amelia. She thought her fan might catch flame, clutched in the heat of her fist.

You've never met a man who could obtain your enthusiastic participation.

Amelia swallowed. "Captain Hunter."

"Mrs. Smith." He did not seem the slightest bit embarrassed about his lack of proper dress. "I did not realize there was anyone except Benedict here. My apologies."

She'd been scalded by the sight of him.

"Give me another moment. I'll be right back."

He turned around. Those loose trousers clung to his hips, his buttocks—

God.

The door shut.

Amelia was still clutching that fan in her hand, but she wasn't about to make herself look the fool by waving it in front of her face. It was morning. It wasn't hot enough yet to be this...hot.

The boy with her didn't seem to have noticed anything

amiss in her expression though, and if *he* hadn't seen anything untoward in her expression, Captain Hunter likely hadn't, either. The thought was cheering.

The door opened again, this time to a Captain Hunter with his shirt done up and a navy coat and a pair of trousers that didn't cling anywhere.

Drat.

No. What was she thinking? *Good.* That was all good. She shouldn't want to see any of that anyway.

"Thank you, Benedict," the captain said. "That will be all. Mrs. Smith, I assume that inviting you into my chambers for a discussion would not be the right choice here?"

His *chambers*. Amelia shook her head furiously, her mouth too dry to formulate an answer.

A corner of his mouth quirked up. "The deck then."

Up the ladder again, into the bright morning sun. She should have been more aware of him now; instead, she felt aware of herself. Aware of her arms at her side; aware of her skirt swishing around her ankles. Aware of the corset boning holding her straight and the prickle of her arms and the way her eyes followed him, even though she did not want them to do so.

For God's sake. She had only come here to tell him no.

"Mrs. Smith," he said in a pleasant tone of voice. "What brings you here?"

She should have concentrated more on planning her speech. Amelia found herself wincing.

"I'm very sorry," she said, "but after careful consideration of all the options, I have decided that your very kind offer, as to that, I must—"

He held up a hand. "Allow me to interrupt you, Mrs. Smith. What you mean to say is *no*."

She swallowed. "Yes." And then winced. "I mean yes, I meant to say no. Not yes."

His eyes danced at that, but he didn't quite smile.

She didn't want him anywhere near her, didn't want that well of heat to grow in her belly. She had only seen him unclothed for an instant in dim lighting; how was it that her mind retained the distinct image of the hairs on his abdomen, black against the brown of his skin, dusting the edge of his trousers?

"Well then." She nodded. "I'll be off." She didn't move.

He sighed. "You're not marrying Mr. Flappert, are you? Not that it's any of my business. But I would find that to be personally annoying."

I never thought I would have to be considering the feelings of a little Chinese girl.

Her mouth twisted. "No." She shut her eyes. "I could not have done that."

"It got worse when you went back." The captain nodded as he spoke. He didn't say what *it* was; he said *it* as if her entire morning were laid out before him. As if he had been standing on the stairs next to her that morning and had overheard that little snippet. She felt tears prick at her eyes.

She stared at the ship docked next to this one in lieu of looking at him. The vessel was painted in some nondescript gray all over save for a Swedish flag. "I don't think I have the strength to marry him," she said instead. "Not if he's like his mother in any respect. And since she is the one who came rather than him, he may very well be worse."

"You've made it all this way," he said beside her, his voice soft and gentle. "They haven't managed to break the part of you that is kind and curious and inquisitive. I don't think they could."

She swiped at the corners of her eyes because tears made no sense. It hadn't meant anything, that exchange she'd overheard. It *hadn't.* It was just one woman she would never see again; she'd forget about it in a day or two. It wouldn't mean a thing.

"Oh," she said quietly. "I think they could."

"Yet you've decided not to come with me. A pity."

She had come here to tell him no. To stand strong against his offers. Ruthless, her brother had called him, and she'd expected an onslaught of argument. She hadn't expected nothing.

She glanced over at him. The morning sun caught the planes of his face, painting it in orange and gold. King's colors, she thought wildly and looked away. "That's it? That's all you're going to say? I had expected you to…" She wasn't sure. "Black-mail me? Or something. Leland said you were ruthless."

"On the contrary. If you'll pay attention, you'll see that I am being extraordinarily ruthless indeed."

"Are you?" She frowned skeptically. "You are being very understanding."

"You want me to explain all my secrets, do you?"

Secrets. Her mind went momentarily not to extortion or threats, but to those loose, clinging trousers. She flushed hot. He smiled at her, and that smile seemed to shoot up her spine.

"I don't have to threaten you to put you under threat." His eyes met hers, deep and understanding. "During the past civil war, my youngest brother lived in England, surrounded by white people. I know what your threats look like. You are so accustomed to them that more won't move you."

That statement punched the air out of her lungs. *I didn't think I would have to be considering the feelings of a little Chinese girl.*

The rude ones—the ones who called her names and the like —she could dismiss. But Mrs. Flappert had come here intending to marry Amelia to her son. Even under those circumstances, Amelia's feelings had been irrelevant.

"From what I gather, you came up with a Chinese version of a telegraphic code because—"

"An incomplete version," she found herself compelled to

add. "Very incomplete."

He just nodded at this addition. "You started to come up with a Chinese version of a telegraphic code because it was fun. Because you enjoyed it—enjoyed the challenge, enjoyed imagining what might result if you were successful."

She nodded.

"And you think I'm not ruthless." He shook his head, smiling. "If you don't accept my offer, you're going to have to go from spending your life doing something you find wildly interesting back to that house you just came from. Please understand: you are making this decision under extreme duress. I'm just not the one applying it."

Amelia's mother had made matters entirely clear. If she took employment under him, she would never marry.

She thought of the five years of her marriage—of trying and trying to make her husband happy. She had succeeded. But after the second year of her marriage, she'd realized that *his* marital bliss did not make *hers* any more likely. She'd begun to resent his felicity, unaccompanied as it was by a similar feeling on her own part.

He had accepted what she did for him as a matter of natural consequence, as if her providing what he needed followed as surely as water flowing from high ground. He had not once considered what *she* might want. He hadn't considered her feelings. He hadn't considered them at all.

She could hear her mother's voice from last night. *If you take employment, you'll never marry. Men won't want that in a wife.*

That was what awaited her if she stayed: another man. Not Mr. Flappert, but another man. The next man might be kinder about it. His mother might be more circumspect. He might come himself instead of sending a proxy.

If you take employment, you'll never marry. Men won't want that in a wife. If Amelia had any sort of moral sensibility, the idea should repel her.

Instead, some part of her stirred in anticipation. She could provide for herself, *and* she wouldn't have to deal with another husband? It seemed like a double bonus. Captain Hunter had arrived at this very moment, offering her the very thing she hadn't realized she wanted. There had to be some kind of a catch.

Her teeth ached with wanting. Amelia turned away from him to look back at the docks. "I'm not sure."

"Aren't you?"

Her wants lurked beneath the surface. Large, she reminded herself. Vicious. Rows and rows of massive, pointy teeth.

She needed to resist. But why?

She lifted her eyes to his face—to the slant of his nose, the tilt of his mouth. Sun seemed to glitter off his skin, highlighting the brown planes of his face.

Amelia sucked in a breath, all her responses suddenly making sense. The rapid beating of her heart. The way her eyes sought him. The telltale lift of her spirits when she contemplated the offer. All of it came together into one picture, and she realized that there *was* a catch. An *enormous* catch.

She could feel his gaze like a heated caress, sweeping over her from head to toe. She felt conscious of every inch of her skin, from the hollow of her neck down the swell of her corseted breasts past her belly.

"Oh no." She took a step back. "I'm *attracted* to you."

He stood rooted in place as those unruly words actually came out of her mouth instead of staying in her brain like good thoughts. *God, Amelia,* she wanted to moan. Why had she said that out loud?

She had done embarrassing things before. She was *used* to doing them. This was, however, quite possibly the most disconcerting, distressing, discombobulating truth she had ever blurted out in a panic.

He stared at her, one eyebrow rising.

She plastered a hand over her face. "I didn't mean to say it. It just slipped out. This is ridiculous. I'm *never* attracted to people. I wasn't even attracted to my husband."

Somehow, adding that information did not make the situation feel any more comfortable. Her face was aflame. She balled the hand on her face into a fist, then thumped it against her forehead.

"Please ignore everything I'm saying. Sometimes my mouth just makes noises that vaguely resemble human speech. It's very inconvenient."

He was staring at her, a slight upward tilt to his lips.

"Don't look at me," she moaned, turning away. "It makes the embarrassment all the more acute. Look away and let's pretend I didn't say anything."

"Just to make one thing clear," Captain Hunter said, "I *may* be trying not to laugh right now. But it's *not* because you should be ashamed of what you just said."

She turned slightly to glance at him. He did look on the verge of bursting into guffaws, the corners of his eyes crinkling in amusement. What was she to do?

"Talking more is not helping." She dug her knuckles into her eyes.

"The funny part," he said, "is that you think I'll mind. I *know* I'm attractive. You've just confirmed that you have excellent taste."

That only made it worse. Amelia let out something close to a squeak.

"I know," he told her. "It's terrible manners for me to notice how handsome I am. But just between the two of us?" She could hear the cocky grin in his voice. "I'm aware."

"It's not good manners of me to *feel* it," she muttered. "Virtuous women don't."

"Well," he said, in the same matter-of-fact tone that he'd

used to tell her that he was aware of his handsomeness, "that's poppycock."

Somehow he managed to emphasize the *cock* in poppycock, and that made her face feel like fire all over again.

"There's no virtue in attraction. Some people feel it. Others don't." He shrugged. "Variation is ordinary. That's all."

She shook her head. "You're making this all sound so commonplace."

"It is." He waved this away, as if all the heat lodged in her were pedestrian. "It's normal to want things. This is one of the things that people want. Unless you're worried about what I would do about it?"

"No—of course not—I'm sure you wouldn't—"

"We'll leave Fuzhou on the *Lenity*. My cousin Zed is the captain. I'll move my things to a hammock in his room, which will leave a full chamber for you. You'll have a lock and the only key." He smiled. "It's a very small ship, and much of it will be taken up with cargo."

She exhaled slowly.

"We will go to Hong Kong, where the *Celerity* is docked. You'll get another room, another key. Bell is the captain there; he brooks no nonsense, not even from me. Once we've arrived in Shanghai, I'll be around for a few days on business, after which I will go lay submarine cable."

Something terrible was happening to Amelia's imagination. *Lay submarine cable* should not have sounded like such a euphemism, but she could not help but think of the process— long, thick cable being laid in the watery depths—

"Eep," she managed.

"I'm attractive," Captain Hunter said, "but I know my own limits. Even *I* can't attract you from the middle of the North Pacific Ocean. So rest assured." He grinned at her. "This too shall end."

"You... You..." She bit her lip once more. "But..."

"I don't mind," he told her. "It's not embarrassing. It's perfectly normal. I promise you once you understand what a shambles my encoding program is and how ridiculous a task I'm foisting upon you, whatever you're feeling now will fizzle off into annoyance. But I don't need you to want *less*, Mrs. Smith. I need you to want *more*."

She looked over at him, eyes wide. It felt as if he lived in an entirely different world. It had different rules from the one she inhabited—rules that were both kinder and far more stringent all at the same time.

"What do *you* want?" she heard herself ask.

"A worldwide telegraphic network." The answer was as swift as it was insufficient.

"Why?"

He shrugged. "Is profit an insufficient motive?"

"That's a question," Amelia pointed out. "Not an answer. You're asking me to work with you. Shouldn't I know if your aims are good? Nobody just wakes up one day and says, 'I want a telegraphic network.' So why?"

"Ah." He pulled away from her, gaze wandering over the harbor, then to the hills to the east. "That's an excellent question. Do you know how much it costs to send a transatlantic telegram?"

She shook her head.

"Four pounds. Twenty-two American dollars. Thirty grams of gold. Months of work for the average worker."

She felt shocked. "I had not realized the profit was so immense."

"Do you know what it means when the cost is so high?"

She shook her head.

"It means the only messages that can be sent are ones of business. News of a cotton shortage. Information on large trade negotiations. That sort of thing. It means that who communicates and how and to whom is limited. That shapes the world we live in."

He was still looking out over the harbor. She had thought him attractive before. Now with his gaze fixed on a faraway mountain, he seemed even more so.

"The world is going to grow in the shape of the wires we lay, and nobody is thinking about what that will look like. They don't ask what it will mean if all we talk of is business and news from the wealthy and powerful."

She swallowed.

"Think of all the things that *could* be sent. 'Clara had her baby.' 'Come quickly. Papa is dying.'" His voice sounded like steel on that one. He turned, gesturing, looking her in the eye. "Or: 'I love you.'"

Her breath seemed to come to a standstill in her chest. The moment narrowed. And perhaps he realized what he'd said because he looked up at the sky, rolling his shoulders.

"There." He said it with a shake of his head. "Now you know *my* secret."

"*Your* secret."

"My father's family has been in trade for some eighty years. I had been around the globe the first time before I was ten. I enjoy it."

She nodded.

"My youngest brother does not. It doesn't suit him. He's place-bound."

She nodded again.

A hand worked at his side. "It's really very simple. I want a worldwide telegraphic network so that I can tell him I love him from anywhere in the world."

Amelia let out one breath. Then another. Her own wants rose up in her, hard and savage. A dusty road. Her mother. Words exchanged.

Hold on to your heart. I will be back.

If Amelia did this—if she made a telegraphic code that touched every corner of China, if it were easy and available…

Every day that passed, she'd wish. And want. And hope. She'd wait for a telegram that would never come from a woman she could scarcely remember.

She couldn't possibly bear that.

"No," she heard herself say. "No, no, no. I can't. I can't possibly work for you."

He looked at her. She wondered how she must appear now. How foolish and silly and flighty, to jump from attraction to this state on the verge of tears.

But he didn't argue.

"The *Lenity* is leaving tomorrow," he said instead. "We have a launch spot at three forty in the afternoon."

Why was he telling her this? "I can't be on board."

"I heard you say no."

She wrinkled her nose.

"You said it four times. I could not possibly miss it."

"Good." She exhaled. "Then it's all settled between us. Perfect. Thank you. Goodbye then." But she didn't move. She kept looking at him, wanting, wanting.

She was going to imagine this for a long time—what it would have been like to go with him. How she might have learned what the little wrinkle in his brow meant. The way he watched her.

"You're not trying to convince me," she said in confusion.

"Yes, I am. I am convincing you with all my heart." He looked at her. "Think on it, and you'll see why."

Amelia shook her head. "You're not doing a very good job of it."

She could hear the lie in her voice. Still, she turned around and fled.

CHAPTER SEVEN

Grayson did not watch her leave. He tried not to concentrate on the swish of her skirts or the sound of her shoes traversing the deck. To do so would be a mistake; of that much he was certain.

In some other world—a place he dimly remembered from years ago—he would have flirted just a little more. He might have followed his interest in her to see where it led. But the building of a telegraphic network would not wait through idle flirtation. If he did not end up connecting the world, piece by piece, someone else would.

Grayson had only so much room in his life, and he knew what he needed Mrs. Amelia Smith for. It wasn't flirting.

If he could scarcely spare the time to see his own parents, he could hardly justify trying to woo her.

As if that were the reason, some sullen corner of his mind whispered.

He ignored it. He was *good* at ignoring it all.

"So," Benedict announced loudly from behind him. "What did it cost you to hire the renowned Silver Fox? Half a shilling and a song?"

Grayson exhaled and turned. It took a moment to orient himself. He was a captain; he was responsible for everyone in his employ. That included this delightful loudmouthed terror. He'd promised his sister-in-law years before to try to teach Benedict how to go about things, and here they were.

"On the contrary," Grayson said. "She has absolutely and unconditionally refused to be employed by me."

Benedict stared at him for a moment, then shook his head in disbelief. "Not you. Not the extraordinary Captain Grayson Hunter. You wouldn't fail."

He could. He had. Just not this time.

The boy's bafflement grew as Grayson said nothing. "I have seen you talk an entire company of Dutch telegraph officials into thinking that you're giving them the opportunity of a life-time by walking away from a deal. What is happening?"

"That's easy. The telegraph company you mentioned? They didn't respect me and I didn't respect them. Neither of us imagined we would be working together after that one event. I had no desire to correct their misapprehensions about the Japanese market, and they had no desire to inform me of what they believed to be true. It's harder when I have to engage in business with a moral qualm or two in my pocket."

"Huh." Benedict frowned. "I was so looking forward to hearing about your methodology. What you were going to use as leverage. That sort of thing."

"You can't approach hiring a person like that." Grayson shook his head. "You're working with them on a permanent basis. It makes sense to exercise a moral qualm or two."

"Hmm." Benedict nodded. "I see."

"More importantly, I'm hiring her to make a Chinese tele-graphic code in six months."

"Yes?"

"And it's going to be *hard*," Grayson explained. "She will have to want to do it, want it enough that she won't quit midway. She'll have to want it enough that she'll work through all the frustration so she can persevere to the end. When you need someone to have a will of her own, you can't just bend her to yours."

That was the difficulty.

They had quite a bit in common. They'd both lost family in a civil war—he back in the States, she in China. She'd reacted to what he'd said about family and telegrams as if he were a tuning fork that had been stricken by the same painful frequency that resonated in him.

He was older and harder; that was the main difference.

"So that's what you're doing?" Benedict asked.

"If she can't make up her mind that she wants this, she won't be able to do it. I have no set plan that she can follow. She'll be heading out in the dark."

Silence fell. Benedict tapped his lips, thinking. The boy was bright—very bright—and good at discerning how others felt. It was a useful skill, up until it wasn't. He was nice. *Far* too nice.

"Are you really just going to hire her and leave her in Shanghai? The rest of the trading office is there, but if I recall correctly, the people who were working on the code have all decamped after the last debacle. I can't imagine leaving her all alone to make code would be a good idea."

"That wasn't what I was planning."

"Of course you have a plan." Benedict shot him an easy grin.

"Of course I do." Grayson looked at Benedict and waited for him to understand.

Several years ago, they'd encountered each other when Grayson's younger brother had married one of Benedict's sisters. Benedict had latched on to Grayson with the stubborn determination of a youth who'd wanted to do anything other than the thing he was told to do. He'd told his sister, Lady Trent, that *he* wanted to be in business, just like Captain Hunter. After she'd overcome her horror—after Benedict had wheedled and whined and insisted—Lady Trent had given in and approached Grayson for his help, offering a truly ridiculous sum of money in exchange for keeping her younger brother from running off on his own. She had been very worried about that possibility, as yet another one of Benedict's siblings had done just that.

Honestly. He did not at all understand the family his little brother had married into.

Grayson liked being given truly ridiculous sums of money. He also liked children in general, and Benedict in particular, so he'd said yes.

Benedict was good at listening. He soaked up every lesson like a sponge. He looked at Grayson like he was an utter hero.

He was also too nice. Too eager to please—not just Grayson, but everyone. One day, he was either going to have to figure it out on his own, or... Well.

"What is it?" Benedict asked impatiently.

"I'm not leaving her alone." Grayson looked Benedict in the eyes. "You will be her liaison in Shanghai at least through the winter."

"What?" Benedict blinked, shaking his head. "Me? But Captain Hunter, won't you need me with you on the *Victory?*"

"I'll need you more there. She'll need someone to help her set up the office, hire people as needed, conduct tests, and prepare a presentation on Chinese telegraphic code for the Taotai of Shanghai. This cable must be laid, and it must be done this September when sea ice is at a minimum. You'll have to do it in my stead."

Benedict was the perfect choice for the position. He wouldn't order Mrs. Smith around too much, and he'd be unstintingly positive, which she would need.

Benedict frowned. "But—"

"Do you not think you're ready for it?"

"I do, but—"

"Were you not just telling me you were looking forward to spending time in Shanghai so you could look for your sister?"

Benedict blushed. He was a little too transparent. "I was, but—"

"Do you doubt yourself?"

"No." Benedict tilted his head. "Well. Maybe. But—if she says no, really and truly, I'll go with you, yes?"

Grayson looked out over the harbor where she had vanished. "I always believe in planning for the best. And if she doesn't come along..."

"Yes?"

"Then I'll leave it to you to put a team together. We *must* have some kind of a code for the taotai."

"Oh God." Benedict put his hands in his head. "That's—it sounds *impossible*—you can't really mean to put that on me, can you?"

"Glad to hear you're up for the task." Grayson slapped him on the back.

"Captain Hunter." Benedict sounded pained. "I'm not smooth. Or convincing. Or of age."

"You don't have to be perfect."

"My Mandarin is so rough. I know a bare handful of Chinese characters."

"But you're from a good family, and you'll be able to speak with those who know more."

"By *good* family you mean a family of convicted traitors?"

"They weren't actually convicted of treason." Grayson smiled. "You'll be at her side. I will be expecting reports. I know I'm pushing you, but you need to learn to operate independently. You're ready for it. I have faith in you."

Benedict looked at him and heaved a great sigh. "Yes," he finally said. "Yes, sir."

I t was past noon by the time Amelia returned home. Her mother was waiting for her near the back entrance, toe tapping, lips pressed together in a grim, impatient line. For a long moment, they looked at each other.

Amelia thought about what she had just done. She had gone to see Captain Hunter.

On business, yes, but he was a man, and quite technically, Amelia had not yet said no to Mr. Flappert.

Her mother folded her arms, one finger beating against the crook of her elbow. But when she spoke, her words were perfectly pleasant. "Did you have a good walk, dear?"

"Yes," Amelia replied. "It was very good."

It had been awful. On the way home, she'd been able to think of nothing but the skin of the captain's chest, lightly dusted with dark hairs. She had tried to distract herself, but she had kept circling back to her own words. *I'm attracted to you.*

Attracted. It seemed like such a tame word. Gravity was a form of attraction—the boring day-to-day force that kept her feet attached to the ground, except for when they were tripping over things. *Attraction* did not encompass the heated confusion that welled up in her at the thought of him.

"Good," her mother said. "That's good." She looked at Amelia expectantly.

Amelia sighed. "Where is Mrs. Flappert?"

"She went to visit another friend. She'll be back for dinner tonight."

Amelia must have made a face because her mother sighed.

"Be cordial, please?"

"When am I *not* cordial?"

This won her the hint of a real smile. Her mother stood up and came to her. "Right now, cheeky girl." She patted her cheek.

It was affectionate, yet the gesture somehow grated at

Amelia. *Was* she cheeky? Her mother would say that every so often, but Amelia never *felt* cheeky. She had always assumed that her intentions and appearance were at odds, but suddenly, everything was coming up questions.

Her life felt unsettled. She'd always held out hope for her Chinese mother to reappear. She'd held on to those falsely remembered words with a dogged tenacity. She didn't even know what they meant any longer.

Is this what I'm meant to hold on to? Is this my heart?

She should have given up long ago.

But now Captain Hunter had appeared and shaken her peace into little bits.

No. It was not just him. *She* had been trying to unsettle her own life, with her bamboo bustle and going on walks when important company was expected. She had seen the road ahead of her, and she had not wanted to walk on it.

She just hadn't wanted to admit it to herself.

She was admitting it now. She didn't want to marry Mr. Flappert. The entire idea was repellent. She'd been hoping his mother would find Amelia wanting so she wouldn't have to stir things up by rejecting him.

Her mother had been talking all this time.

"You can at least get someone who is willing to give you the bare minimum of respect, I should think. It was a sign that he sent his mother rather than come in person. I don't blame you for how you've been acting, but next time, please…"

Her mother loved her. Amelia knew that. It was just that sometimes…sometimes Amelia wondered if her mother wanted Amelia to love herself.

"Next time," Amelia heard herself say, "you'll try to find someone who will take the feelings of a little Chinese girl into consideration?"

Her mother lapsed into silence, then blew out a breath. "Oof. I'm sorry you had to hear that."

Amelia shrugged. "Don't worry. It wasn't a problem."

She could envision Captain Hunter shaking his head at her in dissatisfaction.

"I mean to say," she corrected herself, "why didn't you tell her that *of course* my feelings mattered?"

Her mother stared at her as if she had grown horns. "Sweetheart. There would be no point in doing so. She's leaving tomorrow. Why should I be so rude?"

Amelia pressed on. "Wouldn't *I* be the point?"

Her mother pulled back. "What's gotten into you? You're usually not so prideful or self-centered. Where's my sweet girl?"

"I'm twenty-three," Amelia gritted out. "I'm a *widow.* I've run my own household, and you were planning to marry me off so that I could do it again. I'm hardly a *girl.*"

"Oh aren't you?" A roll of her eyes. "You're so old and wise. Tell me that you were so clever again when you're forty-nine like me. I'm not going to tell you lies just because you want to hear them, you know. When the devil comes courting, he offers you what you want. I want the best for you even if I have to tell you hard truths."

No, Amelia realized. Her mother was not expected to lie. It was only Amelia who had to do so.

Her mother sighed. "Don't think yourself into a state. You know you do it, so don't look at me like that. It's really not that important. Be rude to Mrs. Flappert if that is what will make you happy. But realize that someone like her will talk—she likely already has. You may think that the missionary community is spread out over vast distances. You might even imagine her personal thoughts will have no effect. But your good reputation is still at stake. All I want is for you to have a chance at a normal life, Amelia. Is that so much to ask?"

A normal life. A *normal* life.

"What do you mean by *normal?*" Amelia finally asked.

"Don't be obtuse. You should get married and have children."

"I should have to hear people say for the next sixty years that they didn't realize they would have to consider my feelings and to swallow how much it hurts? To have my *own mother* not defend me when someone says *my* feelings about the rest of my *life* should be immaterial? Is *that* what you're calling a normal life?"

Her mother shut her eyes. "Amelia."

"Do you mean that I should expect so little because I am a little Chinese girl?"

"I didn't say that," her mother snapped. "But we must be honest with ourselves. You *are* Chinese. It *is* an obstacle. You *will* have to settle. *I* love you for who you are. That's why I'm telling you this—and I'd appreciate it if you'd give me credit for delivering hard truths honestly."

That was it. That was the hard truth at the center of Amelia's life. There was no point holding on to her heart because nobody but herself had ever wanted it. Nobody was coming back for her. The person who loved her most in the world believed her to be an obstacle, and she was probably right.

This was when Amelia should give in. She *knew* it. Yet some intransigent part of herself held on still. If *this* hadn't broken her, nothing would.

"No," Amelia said. "No."

"No? No to what?"

"No to all of it." She was on the verge of tears.

Her mother exhaled. "Amelia, I…"

But she didn't finish her sentence. She didn't say, *Amelia, I'm sorry.* She didn't say *I see where you are coming from.* She didn't say anything at all. She just shook her head.

Amelia stalked off, heading up to her chamber. From her small window, she could see hints of the river through shiny green eucalyptus leaves—a hint of blue, that was all, before the landscape rose into hills once more.

Captain Hunter was leaving tomorrow with the tide. If she went with him…

She scarcely knew him. She had just *met* him.

But her brother had…almost, maybe, in a way…vouched for him. Leland thought he was a man of his word, at least, and Leland didn't want her to have a *normal* life where she labored as a maid-of-all-work for no wages. Leland wanted her to be happy. Leland believed it was possible.

When the devil comes courting, he offers you what you want.

That aphorism seemed to eat up all the light inside her. *Nothing can change,* her mother had told her. *Nothing can change except you, so change. Change more. Change harder.*

Amelia was *tired* of changing to make other people happy. She was tired of feeling like she was worth so little that she should be grateful a woman wanted to hire her as a scarcely glorified housekeeper to provide her husband with all the comforts of home, sexual intercourse included.

She was vibrating with the need to elude the snare her life had made for her, vibrating so hard she feared she'd run straight into folly. *I need more.* It thrummed through her system, impossible to ignore. *I need more.* Something had to change. Something *had* to.

She wasn't going to decide; not yet. She had nearly twenty-four hours to think things through. She was going to be rational and come up with a list of rational questions.

But in the meantime…

She could keep her options open. She had started packing last night. Why not continue? She could always unpack on the morrow.

Amelia went to her wardrobe and looked inside. Dear God, what did makers of telegraphic code even *wear*?

She suspected the answer was trousers since they were

likely all men. That seemed rather risqué, even for her current mood. And she didn't have any trousers.

The green muslin gown—that would be serviceable. It didn't mean anything that she folded it up and placed it in her trunk; she was just seeing what would fit. The blue organza, in case she was invited somewhere nice. She wasn't sure how or when that would happen, but it was best to be prepared.

Shanghai, Captain Hunger had said. She would work with him in Shanghai.

Some part of her mind latched on to it, dreaming. Shanghai. Her English mother had found her outside of Shanghai. Her Chinese mother…

Maybe she lived there now. Maybe one day …

For a moment, Amelia sketched a little tableau. She had no idea what Shanghai looked like, but perhaps it would be something like the Chinese part of Fuzhou—houses of gray brick with gentle curving roofs built around courtyards, the smell of savory cooking rising from Chinese-style ranges fueled by coal. Amelia would be a very important telegraph person, doing important telegraph things. One day, Amelia would turn a corner…

She bit her lip imagining that moment. That moment when she would see…

She scarcely knew what face to imagine. Her fragmented memory and the passage of seventeen years had turned everything into murk. When she looked down at the packing she wasn't doing, she found she'd somehow tangled her corset laces with a pair of stockings into ungodly knots.

"Really, Amelia?"

She shook her head. Enough fantasizing. She should have outgrown it long before now, those moments when she imagined her mother would arrive. If she was going to be a telegraphic code person—whatever that was—she would have to be focused and serious.

Question one: how does one focus when one's thoughts always go to someone who isn't around?

A serious telegraphic code operator wouldn't daydream about a mother who had left her seventeen years before. She would... She would...

For a moment, another dream flashed in front of Amelia's eyes. She saw herself in a smart outfit at a desk. She imagined a Chinese woman coming up to her in the telegraphic office of her imagination.

"Good day," the woman would say in Mandarin. "I would like to send a telegram."

Amelia, the future serious telegraphic code operator, would nod and get out a pen and paper, a thing she would have to do to immediately write down the names before she forgot them. "And who would you like to contact?"

Her mind could have filled in anything in response—anything at all. A man about a piano, for instance.

But instead, the woman in her mind smiled at Amelia and said, "I am trying to find my daughter. Can you help me place an advertisement in a newspaper across the country?"

Amelia shut her eyes.

Chinese telegraphic code. It was one thing for Captain Hunter to offer her money and occupation and an idle chance to exercise her mind. But Amelia had never even told Leland *why* she wanted a Chinese telegraphic code.

She'd been seventeen and silly when she had the idea. The late Alden Smith had not come on the steamer he'd indicated before, and there had been nothing to do but wait to see if he appeared on another. Her mother had sighed and said how convenient it would be if they could get telegrams in Fuzhou. Mr. Smith might then have sent word.

"How simple it would make things," Mrs. Acheson had said, "if we could just *tell* people where we expect to be."

Amelia had thought: *If there had been a Chinese telegraphic code back then... If there had been Chinese telegrams...*

Maybe it wouldn't have been so inconvenient. Maybe her Chinese mother would have been able to come back for her.

Amelia let out a slow breath and looked at her half-full trunk. China was a large country absolutely full of people. She had long since stopped believing she would turn a corner and see a woman whose features she could no longer clearly remember.

But what if she could help people find each other before they were seventeen years lost and all hope was gone?

The idea gave her a lump in her throat. She looked at the bottom of her wardrobe. Her ruined gown was still crumpled at the bottom. She lifted it out, saw broken bits of bamboo bustle and fossilized megalodon teeth.

Something in her hardened into steel at the sight of them. And somehow, she packed those first.

CHAPTER EIGHT

I t was coming up on noon. The tide was coming in, the water lapping higher and higher, and Grayson had just been steeling himself to accept the inevitable and disappointing conclusion that Mrs. Smith was not coming, when she came.

The good news: She arrived. He caught sight of her standing on the dock, looking up at the *Lenity* with her lips pressed together and a disconcerted expression on her face.

The bad news: She was alone, carrying nothing but a little handbag that could not have fit more than a pair of gloves, let alone the luggage one would expect if one were to uproot one's life.

He did not move to greet her. He watched as she navigated the ladder on her own, then looked around the deck until her eyes landed on him.

"Mrs. Smith."

"Captain Hunter." She nodded at him, stiff and uncertain.

"Here to say no?"

"I have some questions." She looked at him. "If I am to do

this, I must ask questions rationally and soberly consider the answer."

"Indeed." He found himself smiling. This was promising. They hadn't even discussed salary. Talk about money and other particulars would shift the conversation from *if* to *how*.

She reached into her tiny bag and took out an even tinier sheet of paper, folded and folded over. She smoothed this out. "I wrote down my questions." She flipped the page over. "So I didn't forget any. They are all important."

"Good. Have at it."

She stared at the page, her jaw squaring.

He waited.

"I want to know," she said steadily, "how to stop thinking about someone who is absent from your life."

He felt as if he'd been punched in the gut.

If John had been here, he would have known what she meant by that. How to answer it, how to set her at ease with a few convincing words.

"What do you mean?" he heard himself asking instead, his voice surprisingly steady.

"My mother." She looked away. "My Chinese mother. I have this memory I cannot shake. I remember when she left. She told me she would return, and so I waited and waited and waited. But I cannot keep waiting."

Grayson let out a long, slow breath.

"If she were able—if she wanted to—" Her voice broke and she looked down. "She would have found me, right? The mission in Shanghai where my mo—Mrs. Acheson worked would have forwarded the information on. If she is not dead, she doesn't want…"

It wasn't the same, Grayson told himself. It wasn't anything like what had happened to him.

"But the last time I saw her was outside Shanghai. I can't go there while I'm constantly looking. Wondering. How do I stop thinking about it?"

"*That's* your question?" Grayson had heard every platitude in response to grief. *Just move on. Grieve and let go. Have a stiff upper lip.*

In his experience, none of them worked. So either he was going to repeat the lies he'd been told to her, or...

"You don't," he heard himself say hoarsely. "You never do. There's a hollow spot in your heart, and it will never be filled. You see someone out of the corner of your eye and turn your head too fast, but it's not who you think. It's never them."

His own feeling must have leaked into what he was saying because she turned wide, sympathetic eyes to him.

"Who is it for you?"

"My brothers." He swallowed. "Three of them."

"I'm sorry."

"Don't be." He folded his arms. "It doesn't help if you are."

"What does help?"

Nothing, he didn't say. "We planned the telegraph line together. I tell myself that if I do this..." There were so many things that had fallen out of balance in his life since the war. So many. "If I do this," he said through the lump in his throat, "it's as close to them as I'll get in this world. Maybe that will make up for..."

He couldn't finish the sentence. Luckily, she didn't ask him to.

She nodded, and for a moment they stood like that, stood next to one another, not speaking.

"Right." She whispered that word. She was staring over the stern of his ship. Westward into the interior of China, west toward tea.

Grayson cleared his throat. "Is there anything else on your list?"

She jumped. "Oh yes." She looked down at the page still clutched in her hands and turned crimson. "Oh. *No.*"

He waited.

"Oh. God. I can't ask you *that.*"

"Is it related to the question of your employment?"

"Yes, but—"

"Then ask."

"Ohhh." She drew the syllable out. "I…"

"Just ask."

"I wanted to know." Her lips were half-parted; the sun was hot enough overhead that a little droplet of sweat had formed on her forehead, just below the dark line of her hair, and started to trace down her cheek. Still, she didn't say anything.

"I need to know." Still she trailed off.

"Just spit it out. The question can't be half as bad as all this dillydallying."

That flush had completely overtaken her face, staining her cheeks in red and her forehead in pink. The color crept down her neck, disappearing into the collar of her gown and making him wonder if…

"I want to know what it's like to kiss someone I actually like," she blurted out, so fast that her words ran together.

He stared at her blankly. *That* was her question? She wanted him to kiss her? Not that he minded—in fact, the very thought of it had seemed to settle like a sparking firework in his stomach because it turned out he also wanted to know what it was like to kiss her, and until this moment he hadn't realized how much he wanted to know.

He cleared his throat. "This is related to your employment?"

"Yes."

God. "You know that I am going to spend my fall and winter laying submarine cable. I won't be around at all."

For some unknown reason, that simple description of his work made her blush even harder.

"What does that have to do with it?"

Very well. She knew he wasn't staying around; she wanted it. And as for him...

Saying he wanted to kiss her was a mild enough statement. She was pretty and clever, and he'd wanted to kiss her within five minutes of meeting her. The problem was what had come after those five minutes. Luring her into employment felt less and less like business and more like opening up old wounds.

"Is it so hard then?" She seemed befuddled by his hesitance.

What did it matter? she'd asked.

She was still watching him, her eyes dark and lovely and there was no reason for him to be squeamish about the affair. A pulse leaped in her neck; he could already imagine putting his fingers on it, feeling the connection, heart to heart. It was dangerous to think this way about someone who was going to be in his employ. It was even more dangerous to open this door because once it was open, once he started thinking how kissable her lips were...

He curled one finger. "Come closer."

She took a small, shifting step toward him.

"Closer still."

Another step, and still she was a foot away.

"Mrs. Smith." He sighed and looked up. "Closer."

She swallowed. Her eyes had not left his. She took another step six inches in, close enough that he could lean down and be within tasting distance. Close enough that the scent of her wafted in, something sweet that reminded him of jasmine. He reached out and set his fingertips on her cheek.

Her blush had not dissipated. It spread under his touch, her skin warming. His index finger tilted her chin up, and he leaned down, slowly, so she could stop him if she wanted, slowly, so he could sense the warmth of her breath. The soft gasp she let out brushed his lips.

"Captain Hunter!" She sounded shocked. "What are you *doing?*"

He straightened, rubbing his mouth, blinking in confusion. "Kissing you?"

"Oh." Her eyes squeezed shut. "Oh *no.* Is that what you thought I was asking for? No wonder you hesitated. How utterly appalling you must think me."

He did not think she was appalling. Not at all.

But she was looking at him most earnestly. "I wouldn't," she told him. "I wouldn't just ask you to kiss me like that. Not for employment. That sounds like one of those horrid parlor games that the men make us play when it's raining—where someone gets blindfolded and it's all an excuse for people to put their hands wherever they wish in the name of fun."

"The what the who now?" Grayson could feel his face stretching into a grimace. "No. Don't explain. I'm happier not knowing. What did you actually want then?"

"My mother said that if I took employment, nobody would ever want to marry me." She said this so earnestly that it was clear she actually believed it. "She said I mightn't mind at the time, but I would if I ever met someone I truly wanted to kiss."

The look she gave him was so guileless he wanted to stab someone.

"I want to know what it's like. Can you describe it?"

Describe it. What the *hell.* He let out a laugh—his own qualms had mixed so poorly with his barely contained desires that he'd jumped to conclusions.

Then he saw the expression on her face, the way she looked at him, as if beseeching him for a thing that she knew she wanted but didn't know how to request. He saw all her embarrassment—that red tide that rose again and again in her cheeks—and he realized this wasn't about a kiss, or about her attraction to him, or his attraction to her. It wasn't about the unrecognized want that pulsed between them.

It was about *her*. About a girl who had been abandoned by her mother to people who told her she was always lesser, that she didn't dare to hope, that she should be satisfied with whatever tiny scraps she was given. It was about that girl who'd married a man twice her age and who'd hoped and labored and lost. It was about the fact that Mrs. Smith had been overlooked time and time again until she had begun to suspect she was invisible.

It was, in a sense, amusing that she was asking. It was also heartbreaking.

"It depends," he finally said.

She frowned. "It depends. Boo. That doesn't tell me anything."

"I'm sorry, but it depends. Sometimes it's like lightning. You know how lightning works, yes? There's an electrical charge that develops, a difference between the ground and the sky. You can feel that electrical potential crackling between you before you even touch. Even if you never touch."

She nodded.

"And when you kiss… Well, as I said. It depends." He gave her a rueful shrug. "Sometimes all that heady attraction dissipates in one bolt that arcs across the sky and then is never seen again."

Her brows furrowed. "And…?"

"And sometimes," he said, "sometimes it is an entire storm. The lightning is the harbinger of rain and winds, and each strike comes closer and closer, until thunder and lightning are practically on top of each other. You can feel the wind tearing at your clothing and hear the clap-clap-clap as the shutters flap in the breeze. Rain falls in great torrents. Creeks swell to rivers, and you know that this is a storm that can remake a landscape." He shrugged. "Or, I suppose, it would be. I'm extrapolating a bit, you see."

"You've never personally been in a storm that remakes landscapes."

"I have." He looked over at her. "Real storms at sea. I've been in those. But on land and in a kiss?" He shook his head. "I'm the wrong person to ask. I'm more of a single-lightning-strike sort of person."

She nodded thoughtfully.

He'd been struck by *actual* lightning more times than this. But this hardly seemed the time to bring it up. "If you really need to know, I can fetch Zed. Or Hao, his first mate."

"No. You've answered my question."

He was even more puzzled than he had been before. "I have?"

She nodded. "You have. I don't need it."

"You don't need it." He seemed to be repeating her words.

"Yes. Weren't you paying attention? If I am employed by you, I won't marry. I won't kiss, et cetera, and so forth." She waved a hand dismissively. "Your depiction was sufficient. I don't need it."

"Mrs. Smith." He made a face. "I believe you are making a great deal of assumptions, and I'm not sure where to start untangling them. As we are talking about employment, I think it's best that we move on. Do you have more questions?"

"Yes. Might I have a dog?"

He was not yet accustomed to the back-and-forth ricochet of this conversation. "Really? *That's* your question?"

"I know, I know," she said hurriedly. "They're messy and noisy and so forth. But." She raised her eyes to his, glistening and hopeful. "The Flemings at the mercantile have a dog named Daisy, and she's whelped these puppies. They're just old enough to leave. And I know we can't take dogs on board a ship. But I'm sure Shanghai has dogs. Might I have one once we arrive?"

He stared at her. "I'm not going to be your landlord. Why would I care?"

"I might need to bring the dog into the office."

He shrugged. "So long as your dog is sufficiently trained and does not prove to be a distraction, I see no problem with that."

"Oh." She broke out in a smile. "Perfect. Then I accept your offer of employment."

He stared at her in disbelief. "Mrs. Smith. We haven't even spoken about salary yet."

"Oh, I'm sure you'll recompense me fairly."

"I—Mrs. Smith. Negotiate *before* you leave, while you still have options. It gives me too much power otherwise."

"Does it?" She shrugged. "Oh well."

"Oh well," he repeated, thunderstruck. "Oh well?"

"I need to go get my trunk. I have, what, an hour and a half to be back here?"

"Yes," he said. "So you should take fifteen minutes to discuss whether you will receive enough money to meet your needs."

She sighed and shook her head, as if it were an enormous imposition. "Very well. What are you offering?"

God. He really could offer her anything. For a moment, frugality warred with fairness. But if she were as good as he believed, it wouldn't do to undervalue her.

"Fifty Spanish dollars a year," he said.

She made a face. "That's *far* too much. But I suppose that's your lookout. I accept."

"It's a good thing I'm hiring you for code," Grayson said in bafflement, "not for your bargaining skills. At least negotiate me up by five dollars. One day you'll realize how badly I'm underpaying you, and you'll regret this."

Her mouth set mulishly. "Captain Hunter, when Mrs. Flappert found out I didn't want to marry her son, she said, and I quote, 'I didn't know I would have to be considering the feelings of a little Chinese girl.'"

Grayson winced.

She nodded at him. "Precisely so. You just spent fifteen minutes treating my feelings as if they mattered." The smile she gave him was a blast of pure sunshine. She reached out and patted his shoulder. "Keep your five dollars."

CHAPTER NINE

"So." One single word from his cousin, laden with an entire paragraph.

Grayson watched Mrs. Smith go down the ladder—God, slipping and scarcely catching herself before biting back something that looked like laughter. He should have had someone help her.

"So." Grayson gave a nod in answer.

"You got her."

"Yes."

"You got her to make a telegraphic code for Chinese characters."

"Yes." Grayson found himself smiling, which made absolutely no sense.

Zed nodded thoughtfully. "Did you mention to her that the last telegraphic expert you hired said what you wanted was not possible?"

"So-called telegraphic expert." He shrugged. "If I listened to the people who said this was all impossible, we'd never have started. And now we're halfway there. Telling me it's impossible just makes me all the more ornery. When we started talking about a cable over the Pacific, they said it couldn't be done."

"And lo." Zed grinned at him. "You haven't done it yet."

"No, but all the things they said—about the ocean being too wide and so forth—"

"Didn't do any good until Japan decided to modernize. If you didn't have a northwest base—"

Grayson just gave Zed a cocky smile. "That was all according to our plan. The transpacific cable was never impossible." He looked at Zed. "And *I'm* going to do it."

Zed clapped his shoulders. "Any more ornery and you'd turn into a mule. Which would be extremely inconvenient since this is my ship and there's no room for livestock."

"Ah." Grayson held up a finger. "Thank you for the reminder. Permission to bring livestock aboard?"

"Grayson, what are you up to?"

"Nothing much." He bit back a smile. "Very small livestock. Extremely manageable. You know Fuzhou, do you not?"

"Like the back of my hand."

"Do you know the Flemings?"

"At the mercantile? They're mostly reasonable. Why? Looking for shaving cream?" Zed reached out and rubbed the stubble on Grayson's chin. "We're going to have a woman on board. You might want to spruce yourself up a little for the company."

Grayson elbowed him away. "I wouldn't dare. If I get any more attractive, we're going to have people combust around here. It's a messy process, combustion. Very painful to clean up, what with the burn marks everywhere. I'd never burden your crew with that sort of thing. No, I'm afraid my good looks will just have to remain on the bearable side of smoldering. Now if you'll excuse me, I've livestock to fetch before the tide comes in."

Zed just shook his head. "You're the worst cousin. I don't know why I put up with you."

～

A melia had hired a cart to take her trunk to the docks. She preceded it up the hill to her home on foot. The clopping of hooves and the creaking of wheels behind her beat the time for her pace—swift, she had to be swift. If she outran the cart, maybe she'd earn enough time to explain her imminent departure.

By the time she reached home—was it even home anymore?—she was a mess. Her hair fell out of her bun, sweat trickled down her forehead, and her mind was in absolute turmoil.

She dashed through the door only to find the trunk Amelia had packed the previous night immediately inside. Her mother stood next to it, grimly tapping her foot.

"Oh." Amelia grimaced. "Mother. Good...afternoon?"

"Good afternoon, Amelia. I see you have packed all your things. Did you change your mind? Are you going with Mrs. Flappert after all?"

"To marry the man I've never met?" Amelia made a face. "No. I have accepted Captain Hunter's offer of employment."

Her mother's eye twitched. Her lips pressed together in disapproval. "And what, precisely, does Captain Hunter want with you? Has he explained your duties in detail?"

Amelia found herself flushing. "You would find it extremely boring, I assure you. He has no interest in me like *that*."

But if he *did* want her like that—no, ridiculous, *now* was hardly the time to get distracted by a daydream.

"Boring. So boring you didn't mention to me that you were contemplating leaving at any point yesterday? So boring you could not relate to me the substance of the offer?"

"I already told you everything relevant. I will be working on a Chinese telegraphic code."

Her mother looked skeptical.

"And we only just finished salary negotiations this afternoon," Amelia tacked on, thanking Captain Hunter in retrospect for giving her this very valuable piece of ammunition. *Negotiations* sounded very adult, very responsible.

"And you believed he wanted you for that? Amelia, *millions* of people speak Chinese better than you do."

It was true. They did. She felt her ears burn. "Yes, but I have been working on a similar code for the written Chinese language. He's seen the particulars."

"Your leisure activity isn't worth a salary."

Amelia's hands twitched at her side. "My leisure activity represents hundreds of hours of labor. I was stuck in India and nobody British would talk with me and nobody not British would trust me. I was all of seventeen and married and entirely alone. And you act as if I am *now* going off with some completely unknown person—"

"You *are.*"

"But Leland sent a letter of introduction, and *Leland* knows him. Leland vouched for him." In a way, he mostly had. "I know more about him than I would have known about Mr. Alden Flappert."

Her mother turned away and snorted. "Your brother is overly idealistic about human nature. That counts for little."

Amelia could hear the cart finally arrive in the clatter of wheels outside. She hefted her trunk. It was heavy, so heavy she could scarcely lift it, and yet so light to contain her entire life.

"Amelia," her mother said, coming up behind her, laying a hand on her shoulder. "Don't go. Every time I think of how I found you when you were just a tiny thing with big eyes, and so, so thin… All I want is to protect you. That is *still* all I want."

That hand squeezed her shoulder.

Amelia's heart contract.

"I love you," her mother said. "You don't need to do this. It may turn out well, but the *risks*. Just think of the risks if Leland is wrong and this man is not what he says he is. Think of how absurd his story is. He wants to hire a girl scarcely into adulthood to make tele-something what's-it-called? Think of how that sounds. Why wouldn't he hire a *man* who had experience? Why *you?* I just want what is right for you."

Amelia felt as if she were perched on a blazing divide. Of course she doubted herself. Why *was* she running off with Captain Hunter? Was it simply because she was attracted to him? Was it because she'd lost her mind?

I just want what is right for you, she could hear her mother say, and for a second, she wanted to retreat from the bargain she had just struck with Captain Hunter, retreat from the dog she was getting, retreat from everything and cry and put her face in her mother's skirts while she received reassuring pats.

She wanted to trust someone else's judgment because honestly, who was she to believe herself worthy of fifty dollars a year?

Then she remembered. "You thought I should marry Mr. Smith."

There was a moment of silence. Her mother stared at her in confusion. "I beg your pardon?"

"You thought I should marry Mr. Smith," Amelia repeated. "You've *never* protected me from people who didn't care about me. Even now, the thing you're saying in my supposed defense is that I'm not good enough and nobody could ever see my strengths. I know you want what's right for me, but you don't even think people should care about my feelings before marrying me."

There was a moment of silence. Amelia took three steps to the door, still open.

"Amelia!" Her mother called behind her. "That's not it. The

world is not kind, not to women like you, raised as you were, being who you are. I know people see only your features—foreign on the outside—and don't really understand that you're as English as they are—"

"Am I?" Amelia looked into her eyes. "*Am* I as English as they are, if I have never been allowed to be?"

"I know it's hard to accept. But just because a thing is hard doesn't mean you should avoid it."

"You believe that I have to learn to bear this." Amelia shook her head and walked out the door. Light clouds had come in, magnifying the humidity of the day. "I can't. It's not bearable."

"But what is the alternative?"

"I'm not certain, but I think I'm more likely to find it following Captain Hunter than I am staying here. What he says about my position makes me feel hopeful, and I had not realized how little hope I had." Amelia handed her trunk to the cart driver, who placed it in the back. She passed him a coin and asked him to start back down to the ship, if he pleased.

"Of course he does." Her mother came up behind her. "When the devil comes courting—"

Amelia interrupted her. "At least he's come courting at all, instead of saying that I'm a little Chinese girl whose feelings he doesn't have to consider."

Her mother shut her mouth with a snap.

"I don't have time." Amelia shook her head. "I'm sorry. I have to go. The tide won't wait, and he's leaving with it."

"Amelia." Her mother reached out and took hold of her wrist. For a moment—just one moment—Amelia thought she was going to be restrained. But then her mother loosened her grip. "Not like this. Please don't leave me like this, not in the middle of an argument. Please."

"I haven't any time. I have no choice." Her nose twitched mulishly. "And I didn't start the argument."

"One minute," her mother begged. "Please. You've made up

your mind, and you won't change it. Let me just wish you well and tell you that I love you. If things go badly, come home. You can always come home, no matter what happens, do you understand? There is nothing you could do, no choice you could make, nothing that would make me not welcome you. I knew you were mine from the moment I set eyes on you, and there is no power on this earth that would ever alter that. I love you."

Amelia felt tears spark in her own eyes. "I love you too. I *will* write. I promise."

"Go." Her mother leaned in for an embrace, squeezing her tightly. "I will send all my love and my apologies when you send me your address. And please, please, please, Amelia. Come home if you need to. Come home if you *want* to." Her voice sounded harsh with tears.

Amelia didn't want to leave, not on those words. She did not want to pull away from her mother's embrace. She almost changed her mind yet again.

But her mother was not a life, not by herself, and living with her mother meant enduring the Mrs. Flapperts of the world again and again and again. The next Mr. Flappert might be acceptable the way Mr. Smith had been acceptable—enough to send her mother into a delighted tizzy, and to make Amelia feel as if she really *ought* to accept and give up her life once again.

Amelia wanted to believe that Captain Hunter was telling her the truth. She wanted to believe that she was necessary and important and worth fifty dollars a year.

And she wanted a dog.

It was that simple. She kissed her mother's cheek, wiped the tears from her own eyes, and set off down the hill after the cart and her trunk, as fast as she could go.

⌒

I t had not taken Amelia long to accustom herself to the hum of the steam engine; here, trundling downstream at a few miles per hour, it was little more than idle noise in the background.

There were five hills in Fuzhou, each covered with trees. The corners of familiar residences poked out of those leaves. The farther they went, the more the details disappeared into an indistinct haze of greenery: first the furthest hill, built up with Chinese residences of gray brick walls topped with curving roofs melded into the hillside. The residences of the Westerners lingered in her vision the longest, white stone and waving flags lingering on the edge of visibility for miles. Finally, all she could see was trees and the occasional wisp of smoke.

Amelia felt so many things that it was impossible to feel them all, as if her hope, her tears, her sorrow, her excitement were all very far away, receding into blue haze the way her childhood home was. She felt, most of all, an inexplicable relief.

Captain Hunter came up beside her. "Is everything well?"

She nodded. The first time she had left Fuzhou, she had been newly married. She had been seventeen; she had scarcely known her husband, but she had been full of hope and imagination.

She'd been told to wait in the cabin for the departure. Mr. Smith had not stayed with her. She had become sick with the ship's jerking motion immediately.

On board the *Lenity*, she'd been asked only to stay out of the way. The crew worked around her—a mix of Black and Chinese sailors speaking a polyglot cacophony of Cantonese and English with a few words mixed in that she didn't recognize in any language.

The captain of the ship—another Hunter, which made it very easy to remember his name—stood at the bow.

Her stomach felt a little queasy, but if she concentrated on the far horizon, that feeling was manageable. An ancient pagoda of white stone stood in the middle of the river on an island. They passed it, the structure as high as the ship's chimneys, before it too began to recede.

"I first came to Fuzhou when I was seven," she said. "I don't remember much before we arrived. But my mother prevailed upon Mr. Acheson to provide a permanent home in the East once she took in me and Leland. This was the place they chose."

He didn't say anything in response to that. What was there to say?

Finally: "You call him Mr. Acheson and not father?"

She shook her head. "He's around so rarely. He's quite busy, you know; I saw him maybe two months out of the year when we were younger, and even less now."

He did not say anything, so Amelia continued. "He referred to me and Leland as his wife's strays a few times. I'm sure he wishes he had children of his own instead of us, but I gather that was an early sticking point in their marriage." She shook her head; she hadn't meant to discuss her mother's personal affairs. "But never mind. I suppose this is my childhood home; I don't recall much of anything before I came here."

Dust. A promise.

A string of ships was escaping Fuzhou on the high tide, threaded out both before and behind them. Mrs. Flappert was aboard one of them. They were all deep in the water, heavily laden.

She frowned. "Isn't it dangerous to load ships so much? We're heading out to sea. Won't we be in greater danger of sinking under waves and things like that?"

He shook his head. "Precisely the opposite. Cold water, up to a point, is more buoyant than warm. And salt water is more buoyant than fresh."

"Oh." She nodded. "Then a sea voyage over many climes must require a great deal of calculation. I had not realized."

"It's done via load line."

She turned to look at him.

"Ships have lines drawn on them to represent what they can carry and in which seas. That way, you never forget that a ship that shows no difficulty in one harbor may flounder in a different sea. All carrying capacity varies with circumstance."

"Can you see the *Lenity*'s load lines from here?"

"If you don't mind falling overboard." He grinned at her. "If you're interested, have someone show you in Hong Kong."

Amelia exhaled into the wind. The clouds hung low overhead, but the oppressive humidity from earlier had fled. The wind ruffled against her, flapping the collar of her gown. Seabirds called overhead, and she turned from where she stood at the stern to look forward.

The sea was ahead, wide and blue and so close that she hadn't realized they were upon it. A gap in the clouds lit the waters, painting them in blues and greens and white frothing wave caps.

"Oh," she said softly. "It applies to people too."

She'd expected him to make some sarcastic comment, demanding to know what nonsense she was spouting.

Instead, he just looked at her with those dark brown eyes and smiled. "Feeling buoyant, are you?"

She didn't understand why she was feeling such relief. She hadn't realized until she left that the world she'd been in had exerted such force on her. It felt strange and odd and open. Her heart lifted inside her.

"Captain Hunter." She turned to him. "I have just realized a thing."

"Have you now?" He sounded amused. "What is it?"

"I have just realized that I hated my late husband. It seems so unreasonable to have done so; he didn't *do* anything. But he took me to India and just expected me to manage everything. It never occurred to him that I had to expend *effort* to learn a new language. That I was doing that, and trying to keep his house, and *everything*. The only time he noticed me was when I failed to do something, at which point I earned his annoyance. He never thought about my load. He never thought of me at all."

Captain Hunter was watching her with a raised eyebrow.

Amelia sighed. "It's a stupid reason to hate someone. And he's dead, so it seems ungrateful in addition. And yet. I had been dreading the concept of another Mr. Smith for so long that I didn't realize how much room my dread was taking up. I feel…" She whirled around, laughing. "I feel amazing."

"I did tell you." Captain Hunter's lip quirked up. "I didn't need to threaten you. If you're enjoying yourself now, wait until the Daily Disoccupation."

"The daily what?"

"You'll see." He smiled. "It's a Lord Traders tradition. Almost a century old. We've pushed it off a bit because of the launch, but it will be time soon."

"All of this." She smiled back at him. "*And* I'm getting a dog in Shanghai. Why didn't I find someone to employ me before?"

He very gallantly did not mention how many days he had needed to employ her *here.*

Instead, he straightened, holding up a finger. "Speaking of which. Wait here."

He disappeared, leaving her at the railing. Ships stretched out behind them, dots painted in whites and blacks and grays breaking up the greenish waters of the Min. Her old home blended into a hazy backdrop of navy hills and snow-capped mountains beyond.

In front of her, the ocean made a dark blue glittering horizon in the sunlight, beckoning her forward. The wind was picking up, crisp and cool against her cheeks, and with it came the sharp scent of salt and the sound of seabirds overhead, crying out.

Her feelings were as yet unsorted, but a few leaped to the forefront now. Expectation, sharp and heady. Delight in the feel of the sun on her face, the wind going by. Adventure. She was going on an adventure, and she was getting paid fifty dollars per annum to do so.

Captain Hunter came up the ladder, carrying a small, crumpled blanket. He walked up to her and set the blanket on the deck. The fabric wriggled, moving…

"You mentioned the Flemings at the mercantile? There are of course dogs in Shanghai, but I realized after you'd left to fetch your things that you were under a misapprehension."

Her heart leaped in her throat. She leaned down, peeling the fabric back. Inside was a small yellow puppy, eyes blinking in confusion, as if it had just been jolted from a nap.

Amelia heard herself gasp. "Oh, I know you. You're Daisy's littlest girl, aren't you?"

"Mrs. Fleming did say that you'd spent particular time with this one," Captain Hunter said. "You seemed to believe dogs couldn't come aboard ship. But I obtained particular permission for this one."

Amelia could scarcely pay attention to his words.

"If you don't want her, I'll find her a home in Hong Kong. But I thought you might wish to start on her training during the voyage so that you could bring her to the office as soon as you arrived."

She had not heard anything beyond *if you don't want her*, a sentiment that seemed utterly absurd spoken aloud.

"If I don't want her," she repeated, aghast. "Do you take me for a monster?"

Amelia collapsed next to the pup, holding out one hand in hope and wonder.

The little dog lifted a nose and pushed against the palm of

her hand, then stood and flopped against her side, allowing her to stroke puppy-soft fur.

"Hello, love," she heard herself saying. "Are you a dog? Are you a dog?"

The dog gave no response except to close its eyes and lean into her hand.

She really ought to respond to her own queries. It was just good manners. "Yes, you're a dog. You're a little puppy, aren't you?"

"So," she heard Captain Hunter say as if from a great distance, "I take it you want the dog?"

"Yes, you're *my* dog," she told the puppy.

"That was a rhetorical question. I had dogs as a child; ask me if you have questions about training."

There was no point talking to Captain Hunter anymore, not when there was a dog—*her* dog!—present.

"I'm going to call you Miranda," she said. "But if you were Miranda, how would I shorten the name?" After another moment: "Merry for short, I think. That's a good name for a very good dog. Miss Merry, for Miranda Mei, I think."

"Mei?"

She finally decided to look up from her dog and acknowledge Captain Hunter's presence. "Mei. It's a Chinese name. It seemed appropriate." Amelia frowned. "I think I'll use the character that means…" She looked around. "Sunny weather, but sometimes also clarity. That's what you are, my Merry Mei. No clouds. Sunshine all the way." She leaned down and received a gentle lick on her nose. "Thank you, Captain Hunter."

"Well." Captain Hunter sounded amused. "You're very welcome, Mrs. Smith."

Amelia scarcely heard him leave. "I will have to teach you your name in telegraphic code. You're a smart pup. You'll learn swiftly."

CHAPTER TEN

Grayson had stepped away from Mrs. Smith for a while. He watched the other seamen on board fetch a few cuts of cheese from the galley and a bit of rope for Merry to tussle with. One of them sat with her and showed her how to hold the treat to get her puppy to sit, a thing Merry figured out instantly once cheese was on the line.

Grayson had needed something like a respite. He didn't have the words for how he'd felt after their prior conversation. Her questions—what was it like to kiss someone, how do you stop thinking about someone who is absent?—had brought more emotion to the surface of his life than he preferred.

It was a relief to have her attention fixed elsewhere. To be able to concentrate on straightforward matters like the list of things he must finish in order to stay abreast of the ever-present schedule in his head.

But even that could only distract him so much. Her laugh, pure and unguarded, as she watched Merry wrestle with a blanket, filtered to him over half the ship. It was a good thing he was going to leave Shanghai shortly after he deposited her there.

The waves grew rougher as they made their way out through the islands into the South China Sea. It wasn't until the men started laying out mats that Grayson realized he needed to interrupt her again.

He made his way back to her side. The puppy was sprawled on her back on a blanket, legs pointing in four directions. Amelia was watching her with a soft light in her eyes.

"You may want to put Merry in your cabin for a short space of time."

"By herself?"

"She's sleeping," Grayson said. "The cabin is small and dark, rather like a cave. It's a very cozy environment for a young pup. But the deck is about to get busy, and I wouldn't want her underfoot for what is to come."

Amelia looked up, blinking, to see the sailors on deck bringing out a chest filled with mats. They started removing them, arranging them on the deck.

"What *is* happening?"

"Put her away and you'll see when you get back."

By the time Amelia returned, the mats had been fully set up in the center of the blue ring painted on the deck. Zed had come to stand by Grayson, and Amelia, after a hesitant look around the crew, had come to stand next to them. She glanced at him, then at his cousin, then back at him.

"Captain Hunter." She nodded. "Captain Hunter."

Grayson thought about what she'd said about both her late and potential husbands being named Alden and suppressed a grin.

"What's happening?"

Zed took this one on. "Ah. It's the Daily Disoccupation."

And about time. Grayson had been in an odd, melancholic humor all afternoon. He needed something to dissipate it.

"What is that?"

"Tradition," Zed said. "It's usually at three in the afternoon.

We've a late start this evening. As many crew members as can safely do so join in, and we rotate the schedule so everyone gets a turn. It's a time to set down burdens and to bring grievances to the group as a whole. Inside the blue line during the Disoccupation, the typical rules regarding the chain of command cease to apply."

Her nose wrinkled. "That's a lot of words. None of them explain what's happening."

"It's a distraction," Gray said.

"Enh." Zed made a face. "It's rather more than that. Every ship in Lord Traders does it, but the captain picks the method. On board the *Lenity...*" Zed nudged Grayson. "It's wrestling, of course."

"Heap of miscreants that you are," Grayson intoned.

Zed just grinned. "You're going to be part of Lord Traders too, Mrs. Smith, so you should understand. We try to do things differently. For me, tea season is always difficult. We're in nonstop motion, scarcely in harbor for longer than a few days on either end. During that time, I'm always in charge. Always. As captain, I must be."

She nodded. "Of course."

"However, sometimes that means that I miss things. Someone hurts their shoulder and doesn't ask for help because they don't want to be seen as weak. The Daily Disoccupation is a way for us to drop boundaries and be honest with each other." Zed winked at Amelia. "And also to have a little fun."

"As I said," Grayson replied. "A distraction." And one he desperately needed.

While they'd been speaking, the number of people on deck had grown. The sun had sunk lower in the sky. Land was still visible, a dark line on the horizon limned by orange. But Zed's men were on deck, clapping and calling out.

"First challenger?" Zed called out.

A man stepped forward and waved a hand.

"Seaman Hao! Seaman Hao, who are you challenging?"

"Seaman Johnson," the man replied.

"Right. Have at it." The two men shucked off jackets and then faced off against each other.

"You see," Zed told Amelia, "even the question of who challenges whom tells me what's happening on board my ship. Hao and Johnson are fast friends; if they're starting with a friendly match, I learn that the crew is in good humor. That's useful to know."

Amelia's gaze fixed on the two men. Gray knew them both. Johnson had been with Lord Traders for decades now. He was one of the Black men who had made his way up north before the war and found it useful not to wait around for his freedom to be stolen. He'd taken to life at sea and had eventually made his way to work on the China end of the world. Hao was from Guangzhou; his two brothers also worked aboard the *Lenity*. He kept his forehead shaved and his hair in a long, braided queue down his back. They circled each other a few times before Hao went in, getting an arm around Johnson's waist.

Amelia gasped. "Isn't that dangerous?"

Zed shook his head happily. "Isn't everything dangerous?"

"There are rules," Grayson put in. "No punching, no tripping. Just a little good-natured grappling."

It truly was a distraction. Grayson found himself leaning in with the men, wincing at a body blow, cheering when Johnson eventually got Hao in a headlock. There was a moment of struggle before Hao tapped the mat twice in quick succession.

Grayson saw Mrs. Smith tilt her head in confusion. "It's a form of surrender," Grayson said. "I'm not sure where that one came from, but we've adopted it."

The next pair to face off was the chief engineer against Second Mate Wilder. The chief was small and wiry; the second mate was big and burly. The crew clapped and called. The chief played up his size—or rather, lack thereof—by ducking and dodging, making exaggerated faces when Wilder almost caught him and blowing raspberries when he escaped.

That was the point of the Daily Disoccupation—to let go of worries.

Finally, Wilder caught the chief around the waist. The man just shrugged dramatically and, just as dramatically, tapped out to immense applause.

Mrs. Smith was smiling at this. "I can see how this would be a form of entertainment."

"I've got a challenge," Zed called at her side. The crew turned to him. "Grayson Hunter, you stubborn mule."

Grayson looked over in surprise. Ah, damn. He should have expected something like this. Grayson sighed. "Yes, Captain Zedekiah."

Zed motioned with his head. "Get your sorry behind on those mats."

Grayson stepped forward. His smile felt fake, but nobody here had to know how he felt. "If you want to beclown yourself in front of your crew." He shrugged. "That's your lookout, I suppose."

He shucked off shoes and socks and started to take off his jacket before remembering that Mrs. Smith was on board.

For a moment—just one moment—he looked up from where he crouched to find her watching him with wide eyes. For a moment, he almost made a comment about her sensibilities, delicate or otherwise.

Then he remembered she'd watched the first two rounds without so much as a blink of an eye. What was he going to do? Posture for her benefit? That would be truly ridiculous.

Instead, he stripped off his jacket. The air was cool against his shirtsleeves. Her eyes rounded.

Next to him, Zed let his jacket slip to the floor and struck a pose, flexing his biceps. His crew cheered. "Zed! Zed! Zed!"

Oh, what the hell. Grayson absolutely was going to posture.

He moved next to Zed and flexed as well. The small crowd clapped in unison as the two men entered the ring and circled around each other.

"Now Gray," Zed said across the way. "I'm only doing this because my mother is worried." He feinted; Grayson dodged easily, whirling to face him.

"You're doing this because you're scared of your mama," Grayson taunted back.

That won him a laugh from the crowd.

Zed rushed in head down—no feint this time. Grayson let him hit center, turning so that his back foot absorbed the shock of impact.

"Fear," Zed panted as he tried to wrestle Grayson to the ground, "is a...healthy...response...to powerful things."

Grayson twisted, squeezing, and broke free. The two of them circled each other warily.

Zed looked him in the eyes. "I'm not going to tell her I didn't try my hardest. I need your promise that you're going home."

Home. For a moment, he saw home—home as it had been, his brothers so young, waiting for him when he returned from his first trip with wide eyes, demanding he tell them everything.

Then he thought of his mother's face, washed pale by funeral black, and the grim, grieving lines of his father's body next to her. He felt that old lump in his throat, lodged so far back he wasn't sure if he could breathe.

Disappointment and doubt. That was what waited for him.

All that flashed through him, cutting deep into him like the sharpest knife.

"I want your promise, Gray," Zed called.

If he said no, he'd have to explain why in front of everyone, and he could scarcely explain it to himself.

"Have it your way." Grayson kept his eye on his cousin's

feet. Zed feinted with his hands; he never could lie with his feet. "I'll go home and see everyone. You have my promise."

Another feint. One of these days, Grayson was going to tell his cousin how he telegraphed his moves in advance. Today he stepped into Zed's feinted reach, took hold of his hand, and pulled him off balance.

Zed hit the mat, and Grayson got a knee on his back.

"Choose a date!" Zed called cheerfully, nose pressing into the mats. "I'll be sure to include it in the next letter I send."

Christ. Of course he would. "You want me to have a calendar in my head while I'm drubbing you?"

"You *always* have a calendar in your head."

He wasn't wrong. They'd lay the cable to Myriad Island in September. It would take all of three months for the *Victory* to make her way back to San Francisco for the smaller load of cable. That would put him on the eastern seaboard by December.

"If you say anything other than 'I'll be home for a month starting next year...'" Zed let that threat trail off dramatically.

Grayson dug his knee. "You'll do what?"

"Then I'll lose to you every day until we get to Hong Kong," Zed said, tapping out. There was a certainty to his tone that said he would definitely do it. And if *he* was feeling the pressure, Zed's mama—Grayson's aunt—must be going even harder than Grayson had imagined.

Grayson sighed and got off his cousin. Zed turned around, coming up to a kneel.

"Have it your way." Grayson extended a hand. "I'll be back home around Christmas, precise dates to depend upon travel times."

"Perfect." Zed's smile managed to be both sunny and cutting all at once. "I shall see you there."

The air was cooling off as they returned to stand on either side of Mrs. Smith. Grayson had put his jacket back on, but he could feel sweat from the exertion running down his brow.

"You see?" Zed said with a hint of cockiness. He had a towel that he was using to wipe his forehead. "It's less about winning and losing, and more about making sure that someone hears your frustrations. The alternative is to keep all those feelings pent up. Nobody wants that."

That, Grayson was sure, was a dig at him. Something was going on. Not just Zed's remarks. Not just the insistence he spend time at home—none of *those* were new. No, this felt like an alteration in his internal weather. There was a wind picking up, something hot and dry, and winds heralded change. Ever since Fuzhou, ever since he'd admitted that Amelia reminded him of Noah, ever since that afternoon with Zed in the wine shop…

He could feel it, feel the change of pressure in his inner ears as if a real storm were coming.

He didn't have time for any of this. In reality, there was no storm. Just humidity and a few scattered clouds and Mrs. Smith pondering Zed's words, her mouth scrunched up.

Amelia glanced at Grayson, then back at Zed. "You said that the captain chooses the, um, the method of Disoccupation?"

"Of course."

"What is it on Captain Hunter's ship? We're going to his ship next, aren't we?"

"Ah." Zed stopped midswipe. "You'll be taking the *Celerity*. That's Grayson's ship in the sense that he owns it. But it's captained by Bell, and his Disoccupation is rather patchwork."

She looked over at Grayson.

"He does all sorts of things," Grayson explained. "Sometimes it's quoits. Sometimes it's other sorts of tossing games. It depends upon the sea and everyone's inclination."

"Quoits!" Her eyes grew wide. "Really? Quoits?"

"Is something wrong with quoits?"

"No. I just thought, after wrestling, wouldn't it be something more, um. More?"

"More what?" He made himself hold her gaze, made the moment stretch out as if nothing were bothering him. "Are you trying to imply something about quoits?"

"Nothing at all. I just want to know what you do on *your* ship."

Why did that make him think of a storm again? It was just words from her. Just curiosity, and she pointed that in every possible direction.

Zed snorted. "His ship used to be the *Victory,* if you can call that thing a *ship* instead of a lumbering beast. But that's now captained by Ellis, although the Disoccupation hasn't changed."

"Don't listen to Zed. The *Victory* is a beauty of a lumbering beast. You should see her cargo hold."

"What is the Disoccupation aboard the *Victory?*" Mrs. Smith turned to him, frowning. "I have suspicions. You're very competitive."

Zed laughed. "You're not wrong on that."

"Something competitive you can do aboard ship... Fencing?"

He couldn't help himself. He let out a laugh. "You think I'm a fencer!"

"It was just an idea!"

"A very wrong idea."

"Then maybe it's chess." The back-and-forth of their conversation felt like the first drops of rain.

"God no. I haven't the patience for that."

"Very well. I give up."

"Music," Grayson said.

She just looked at him. "Competitive music?"

"Just music." Grayson shrugged. "It doesn't have to be competitive."

She hadn't stopped her inquiry. "So do you play an instrument? Do you sing?"

"Oh God," Zed muttered. "Let me save you from hearing him boast. He plays the violin. He's very good."

"Nobody's truly good at violin in summer on the South China Sea," Grayson said. "The humidity is hell on the instrument. The rosin sticks to the bow like nobody's business, and that makes it stick to the strings a little too much."

"You see?" Zed gave a disgusted shake of his head. "He's bloody excellent."

Mrs. Smith was nodding along. "I was dubious until he said that bit about rosin. Anyone who is that picky is definitely good." She turned to contemplate Grayson for a moment, her eyes measuring him. "Do you play regularly?"

"As much as I can." He shrugged. "The violin is meant to be played regularly. The instrument sounds better if it is."

"Might I hear?"

"If you're aboard the *Victory*?" He gave her a grin. He didn't feel it. "Of course. Every day." It was a teasing thing to say; she was going to spend the next year in Shanghai, and the *Victory* couldn't even come close to that shallow harbor. "Of course. Otherwise, if you happen to be around when I play, I can't stop you from listening."

It was just as well he was leaving her. There was a storm on the horizon, and he didn't want to know what would happen when it broke.

CHAPTER ELEVEN

The air in Victoria Harbor was hot and heavy. Amelia felt like a bedraggled lump of fabric bound together in a heavy corset and deposited on her brother's doorstep. Nonetheless, here she was.

Leland stood in his doorway, staring at her in shock. It had been over a year since she'd seen him, and yet everything about her brother seemed familiar, oh so familiar. His beard was a bit bushier, but his eyes were just as bright and his smile as welcoming as it had ever been.

He took a step and wrapped his arms around her. "Amelia!"

Leland smelled like himself—like soap and the sea. The scent was viscerally comforting, a reminder that this was her brother and he loved her.

"You're here in Hong Kong," he muttered into her shoulder. "*Please* tell me this is not the first part of your journey out to marry that dreadful Mr. Flappert."

She laughed. "How do you know that he's dreadful? You haven't met him."

Leland pulled back from her and folded his arms, looking at her darkly. He was taller than her by two inches, which made him not very tall at all; his hair was a bright ginger, and she was so used to seeing him smiling that when he scowled, the expression made his face look odd and unnatural.

"You haven't met him either," he groused. "A man who cannot meet his wife before marriage? He's absolutely dreadful. I'm sure of it. I will tie you up and hide you from him if I must."

"Will you?" she asked, her head tilted. "Really?" It was odd to hear Leland advocate such a thing. He had always been the gentlest of creatures.

He deflated. "No, of course I would not." He shook a finger at her. "But I would do my best to construct an extremely sound argument in whatever time we have remaining."

She smiled. "Lucky for you then. I've accepted employment with Captain Hunter."

"Ah." He grinned. "Excellent. I'm glad." He looked out over the harbor. "How long are you here? Is he having you stay in Hong Kong?"

"The office for the Chinese telegraph division is in Shanghai."

"Fuzhou to Hong Kong to Shanghai? That's a roundabout journey."

"The ship he came on was en route here, and the main office here in Hong Kong had some papers for me to sign." Amelia put her nose in the air. "Be aware, Leland—I'm now an employed woman."

He did not shriek in horror, which was unsurprising since he'd been the one to put her in Captain Hunter's way. "How long are you here for?"

"I have another handful of hours before the *Celerity* departs."

It was a shame. Not that Amelia had much love for Hong Kong; she'd only been twice before. Once had been shortly after her marriage to Mr. Alden, when they'd taken a ship to

Bombay from Victoria Harbor. The second time had been on her return after his death.

She'd stayed a week with her brother then. For comfort, she'd told her mother, in her time of loss. But she hadn't felt loss or sadness. She'd just felt relieved and guilty about feeling relieved.

On both occasions, she had thought Hong Kong humid and crowded. She'd no desire to stay here except for one thing. In Hong Kong, she knew Leland, and in Shanghai, she knew absolutely nobody.

Except perhaps... Amelia was so used to her unruly imagination that she tamped down this wayward daydream—a hint of wind, a lonely road, and a woman she didn't know but instantly recognized—with scarcely a thought.

"Well then. Let's not waste time. Would you like to go for a walk?"

Technically, Amelia did *not* want to go for a walk. Walking in Hong Kong was like swimming through air so humid she felt like a goldfish in a heated pond. And she was dressed in layer after layer after layer of clothing.

"Of course," she told her brother because she was ridiculous. "Anything you like."

He took her down by the harbor. "I'm glad you took Captain Hunter up on his offer," he said after a while.

"I am too. It's odd. It had never occurred to me that employment was a thing I could do. And yet here I am. I wish the idea had struck me earlier."

"Weeeell." Leland elongated the word, shaking his head in a way that seemed a touch bitter. "That's Mama for you. She has only one definition of womanhood, and if you don't want it, she'll never comprehend."

What an uncharitable thing to say. Not that Amelia would actually disagree now that he'd put it in words so plainly. She'd just never imagined that Leland—of all people, sweet and gentle Leland—would say it.

Amelia looked over at her brother. His nose was wrinkled.

"I wasn't sure you would take Captain Hunter's offer. You've always been a bit under her thumb," Leland continued.

Amelia stared at him. *Under her thumb?* He'd never spoken like this before. Oh, he'd made a few gentle remarks about their mother previously; she knew they had disagreements. Large ones. Mother had wanted him to stay in Fuzhou. *Why not be a missionary here?* she'd asked. Leland had admitted to Amelia on more than one occasion that getting away was the entire point.

"And you, I suppose, are out from under her thumb?"

"She still wants me to marry," Leland said with a shrug. "Honestly, it's the only thing she can think of, man or woman. Is your future in doubt? Marry. Is your future *not* in doubt? Also marry. Marriage cannot be the answer to all of life's problems. Especially since *she* is married, and..." He cleared his throat. "You know."

Mr. Acheson was in Fuzhou maybe two months out of the year. They maintained very cordial relationships during that time, and not one iota of communication outside it. Amelia tried to think of a delicate way to respond. "It's not the *only* thing she thinks of. She also takes in children."

Leland let out a cackle. "Amelia! That was almost unkind. Look at you. My little sister is all grown up."

She hadn't meant it unkindly, and she didn't see what any of this had to do with growing up. But he beamed proudly at her, and she didn't want to make him frown. They lapsed into silence for a few steps more.

"Do you ever wonder?" Leland asked.

"I wonder often. Wonder about what though?"

"Why we're here." Leland gestured, encompassing the harbor around them. "What we're doing. Why we even *send* missionaries. It was all well and good when I thought I was saving souls, but what if I'm not? Sometimes I think that everyone else's soul is perfectly intact, and I'm the one without."

She looked over at her brother. Amelia *had* wondered when she was in India. She had been seventeen when she'd first married and gone to Bombay. The first few months, she hadn't thought much of anything; she'd been so wrapped up in the newness of her role. But after she'd settled in...well. She sometimes had thoughts.

It had felt to her like a horrible breach of manners to show up in someone else's country and to tell them they were doing everything wrong, and as a consequence, God intended for them all to go to hell. She had felt herself cringing every time someone spoke those words.

She'd never allowed herself to repeat those sentiments to anyone else. The questions attached felt dangerous. If *Amelia* wasn't supposed to be in India, it would follow that her mother shouldn't have been in China, and Amelia's whole life would be...what, exactly? Wrong? Bad?

She couldn't allow herself to think it. It was too much to question the entirety of her childhood. Some thoughts were too dangerous to harbor.

Amelia shook her head as if to toss those treacherous ideas out. "You've always thought yourself to bits. Maybe you're doing it now."

"Maybe other people aren't thinking enough," he countered as if he'd heard her unspoken doubts. "Either I am doing the gravest of disservices or..." He trailed off. "Or I am not well. There is no choice that leaves me in the right."

Not well? She wasn't sure what he meant by that, but it sounded like none of her own thoughts.

He sighed and shook his head. It was obviously an old argument he was having with himself, and he'd failed to rehearse large portions of it for her. She wasn't following.

"Leland, I cannot imagine you doing anyone harm."

"Can't you?" He looked over at her, his eyes sharp. "Ah well. You don't exactly know what I've done."

"I don't have the faintest inkling, but I love you. I will love you no matter what." It was easy to do so; Leland was the one person in the world who understood her.

Like her, he'd been taken in. He had been the child of a soldier whose parents had both passed away; without Mrs. Acheson, he would have been shunted off around the world to some distant and impoverished relation he had never known. He'd grown up with their mother; he understood what she was like. He had been the older brother who taught her English and letters and mathematics, showering her with praise and encouragement. He'd loved Amelia without condition or requirement. It was easy to love him in return.

"That's the thing," Leland said, turning to her. "People talk a great deal about unconditional love, but what if it's not merited?"

"That makes no sense. It's not unconditional if it has a condition."

"Yes, precisely. What if there should always be a condition?"

"If you've killed a man," she finally said, "I'm sure you had good reason."

He let out a startled laugh. "You'd forgive me murder?"

She set a hand on his elbow. "I can't imagine what else would inspire this sort of self-doubt. As it's clearly something less serious than that, I bid you not to worry."

He exhaled. "It's not fair, putting the question to you this way, with none of the facts." He looked at her sidelong, then looked away. "I'll tell you once I work it out. I'm a bit envious, to be honest. You always seem to hew to your loyalties so easily."

"Nonsense." Amelia shook her head. "I'm loyal to those who are loyal to me. There's no choice to be made there."

"Ha." But he shook his head again. "Enough with my foolish imaginings. Let's talk about something uplifting. Tell me what you're imagining for yourself in Shanghai."

Amelia found herself brightening. "Did you know I have a dog?"

"A what?"

"A dog!" And that was enough to change the conversation from self-doubt and loyalty to the benefits of hounds and the methods of training.

~

The harbor of Hong Kong was busy around Grayson, filled with little steamers like the *Lenity*—small ships intended for the coastal trade. Smaller, more agile Chinese junks darted between larger steamships heading to all four corners of the world.

The British flag flew from a high pole on the harbor; dozens of smaller flags—British, Dutch, French, and American like Grayson's own—flew from every ship.

The Chinese dock workers that Zed hired had come aboard, unloading the purchased tea with smooth efficiency.

Behind him, Zed was giving out some final instructions. "These, to the western warehouse—those to the east. That will go to San Francisco; Aaron is leaving tomorrow, so transfer it across the harbor."

"I'll be off then," Grayson said.

Zed looked up from the giving of instructions, his face a scowl. "Just like that?"

"Not quite so abruptly. Thank you for all your assistance. I'll see you in December."

Zed came to stand next to him at the rail, looking out. Victoria Peak rose across the water, lush vegetation interrupted by the cut of a road winding up and up.

"You're off to Fuzhou for more tea." That was the way these things went—during tea season, Zed made the journey as often as he could.

"If everything goes to schedule, I'll be back within a few weeks." Zed tilted his head. "Have you considered staying a bit?"

"I haven't got a few weeks to stay."

Zed sighed. "Look, this isn't just about my mother and your mother. It's about me too. There aren't as many of us Hunters as there once were. I get lonely, you know."

Lonely. He could not let himself think of loneliness.

"I can't change what needs to be done. The work doesn't become lighter for the wishing."

Zed looked skeptical.

"I have to go from the northeastern corner of Japan to Myriad Island," Grayson explained. "Then back to San Francisco for more cable, see my parents, entirely thanks to you, then return immediately for a meeting with the taotai. All of this takes time; the world is too large. And it will only get smaller if I do the work."

"You don't need to convince me what you're doing is important," Zed told him. "That's why I need you to take care of yourself. Your *whole* self."

Grayson looked away, his gaze going to the high British flag once more. "My whole self is just fine."

His whole self wasn't whole, but there was no way to mend those fractures, not with idle conversation. And what good would it do to admit the way he felt now? He wasn't even sure himself. He still had that odd feeling, the one that had started back when they were first leaving Fuzhou. The atmosphere around him felt like the build up of pressure, like a promise of wind and rain to come. He had a storm to outrun.

Beside him, Zed absorbed this obvious lie in silence. He let the quiet stretch, waiting for Grayson to break down and admit otherwise.

It would never happen.

Zed broke first. "*Mine* isn't. I was in the same war. In the same navy." *Suffered the same losses,* Zed did not say. He didn't need to. "I'm not 'just fine.'"

"Then you understand," Grayson said softly. "I'm as just fine as I am going to be. And finishing a transpacific cable won't fix everything that's wrong, but it will mend the things that are mendable. Let me do it."

"Gray."

Grayson turned to him. "We planned it together, Zed. Every mile of cable has Henry and Noah and John bound up in it. It's their monument. You can't expect me to leave it to someone else."

"Gray." Zed reached out.

Grayson shook off that hand. "I need to be off. I have too much to do."

The look his cousin gave him—piercing and not at all subtle —was too much. Too pitying. Too understanding. Grayson didn't want it.

"My whole self will wait," he said. "It will wait until the work is finished."

CHAPTER TWELVE

That unwelcome sense that change was coming lingered with Grayson as the *Celerity* left Hong Kong harbor. Thinking of his ships—thinking of what he was going to do—grounded him. And God, he needed to be grounded.

The *Celerity* was swift and small. She had a cargo hold—enough to carry precisely the right amount of coal—and a purpose as part of a mismatched pair.

Her opposite—the *Victory*—was everything the *Celerity* was not. The *Victory* was heavy, slow, and possessed the distinctly unusual characteristic of having a carrying capacity of nearly ninety-thousand cubic feet—enough to hold a cable over two thousand miles long. The *Victory,* with her heavy load, would lay the cable in deep ocean. The *Celerity* laid the line to the shore. The *Victory* crept at a slow pace, paying out cable as she went; the *Celerity* scouted ahead, alerting her larger, ungainly counterpart to coming storms or icebergs. And when the *Victory* finished her run up north, where no friendly harbors waited, the *Celerity* would be her dock, serving as coaling station in the arctic reaches.

Facts. Those were facts, and facts would keep him safe in the coming storm.

(Also a fact: The *Celerity,* in their original plans, would have been captained by his brother Harry.)

Grayson scrubbed at his face. Not *that* kind of fact. What was happening? He'd held everything together for years, all his emotions properly battened down. And *now* they were going awry again?

He did not have to guess at the reason why. She was on deck, running to one end to watch the water from the screw propeller with Merry at her heels, and then walking swiftly up one side, leaning out to look over.

He yearned for the days when he thought the Silver Fox was some kind of elderly man.

Eventually, she came to stand beside him.

"I've been thinking about our code!" Her tone was as bright and friendly as her eyes. *Our code.* It was just talk of business, this; surely talking about business would reassert the natural order of things. Grayson inclined a head to her.

"I'm sure you'll tell me if I'm off when we're in Shanghai together—"

Here was a good place to remind them both. "I won't be in Shanghai long."

"You had mentioned leaving, but surely not immediately."

"Almost immediately. I'll be there a few days."

"Well." She frowned. "In that case, I should explain what I am thinking now."

The puppy lay nearby, chewing contentedly on a bit of rope that one of the crewmen had found for her. Clouds obscured the sun for their journey up until this point, but this afternoon the winds had swept the skies clear. This was the first time he'd seen her in sunlight and wind.

He wished he hadn't. They were traveling at close to twenty

knots, and the wind caught little bits of her hair, sending it whipping behind her.

She turned to him. Her cheeks were red from the wind. She met his gaze and her cheeks turned even redder. She looked swiftly away.

She was attracted to him. He knew that. Why that should make him feel a storm on the horizon, he couldn't say. He would have recognized the signs even if she hadn't blurted it out earlier. He hadn't lied; he *was* attractive. He'd even experienced it like this. Her shy demeanor, the way she hesitated before looking at him…

Even his stirring of interest in return wasn't new. The desire to ask and know more. To flirt and grow close… He'd felt those before, and he'd ignored them often enough.

These sorts of feelings belonged to a younger man— someone who could allow sparks to build to flames.

Luckily, it also felt like the sort of new, fluttering emotion that he could starve to death in a matter of days. She would move on from him as quickly as she did from a new topic of conversation, and this storm would pass.

"You're right," he said. "We should talk code, and the sooner, the better. While we're at it, you'll need to hear what Lord Traders stands for. What I hope to accomplish." He glanced at her. "You'll fit right in."

"Absolutely."

"Let's start with our competition. The Great Northern Telegraphic Company is currently attempting to produce a code for China. The man who is leading this endeavor is named Viguier, and while I don't know his purported code, I do know the general thrust of the idea."

Mrs. Smith nodded, leaning forward. "You had mentioned it before."

"As I remember, you abused the method he came up with—

assigning numbers to each character. How do you plan to do it differently?"

She sent him a tentative glance. "I don't have a *plan* as such. I never finished a complete encoding."

He'd seen the letters she'd sent her brother. She already had a more intelligent plan than he'd seen from anyone else.

"I was looking through my journals on the way to Hong Kong," she said. "Back when I was contemplating the matter, I thought it would make little sense to treat Chinese the way Morse did English. In Morse code, letters that are more commonly used are given shorter encodings. The letter *E*, for instance, is a single dot. But written words in English are composed of letters arranged in a single dimension. Chinese characters are not quite analogous. They are composed of radicals arranged in two dimensions, and even that understates the complexity. Morse in English maps a one-dimensional arrangement—words—onto another one-dimensional arrangement—code. The difficulty with Chinese is how to deal with those multiple dimensions."

This all came out in a rush of words, a wild overflowing of enthusiasm. He understood about half of what she said, but he was still caught by the look on her face, the light in her eyes, the way her hands moved to illustrate what she was saying.

"And you doubt I hired the right person."

"I'm telling you I don't know how to complete it."

"You're telling me that you've identified the difficulty."

She made a face. "The benefit of assigning numbers to Chinese characters is that you don't have to solve any of these difficult problems."

"Of course. And the detriment?"

She blew out a breath. "It is incredibly stupid."

He let out a startled laugh.

"I'm warning you. I started learning characters a mere six years ago. I'm not a master. I'm scarcely even what you might call a journeyman. There are Chinese masters who study this sort of thing for decades. I'm liable to make mistakes."

Grayson waved a hand. "Then hire someone who has studied them for decades. You'll also have to think about training operators. You will have help with that—we've made a code in Japanese—"

She let out a little gasp. "Oh! But if you can do Japanese, then you must know how to send Chinese characters!"

"Not so fast. Wabun code is only for Japanese syllabaries. The use of Chinese characters is as yet unsolved."

Her nose wrinkled. "Drat."

"And we expect the telegraphic code in Japan to be limited to Japan itself. The global population distribution is different. The Japanese have largely kept to themselves until the era changed a few years ago. But Chinese people can be found all over the world."

"Hmm." She frowned at that.

Business. He had to talk business—things like limitations, expectations. Things that had nothing to do with the emotion she showed so freely.

"That creates an added difficulty. Your code must be able to be sent by operators who have never spoken, and will never speak, a lick of Chinese. You'll need to test this under real-life circumstances. I won't understand the details; I'm a cable expert, not a code expert. But we need a code that convinces the Taotai of Shanghai that this is a *Chinese* code, designed for the spectrum of the Chinese language, not some slapdash Western thing thrown together in an afternoon."

She made a confused face. "The taotai? Taotais are administrators, aren't they?"

"In Shanghai, the taotai holds diplomatic power. I've heard the Chinese call him the Barbarian Keeper. If we want to establish a telegraph in China, we'll have to convince him."

"I see."

"But convincing him is only the first step. If Viguier comes out with his code first, no matter how stupid, it may very well end up the standard by virtue of its mere existence. We have to get in first."

"Why, if ours is superior?"

"Because we're the Lord Traders," Grayson told her. "Someone else will make a code, ask the taotai for permission, and when it isn't forthcoming, they'll shrug, say 'we tried' and just build the telegraph in with the certainty that China won't fight a third war over a little copper wire."

"And you won't?"

"No." He let out a breath. "We won't, for the same reason we won't just throw a handful of characters next to a numbered list without caring that we're dooming a generation, at least, to a foolish code that is unworkable. If we're going to connect China, we're going to connect *China*—not just make a show of it for Western profit. I want your code for Chinese ready in rough form within the first three months. I want training methodology ready three months after that. We have a meeting with the taotai in February. And we have to be not just ready, but *good.*"

"I'll have to work quickly."

"Fast enough to beat all other comers, but slow enough to be sure it's done right," he countered. "I've hired two teams before you, thinking that maybe they might find it. They didn't; they just came up with the same sort of boring and uninspired code that you ridiculed the day we met."

"And you think I can do better than *them?*"

"Mrs. Smith." He looked down at her. "You're not a *maybe* in my mind. You've already come further than them. You can do this."

She bit her lip. "You said you wouldn't be staying in Shanghai long."

Yes, and thank God. "I'll be off laying the second section of a transpacific line."

"Oh. The *second* section?" She turned to him. "Of *course.* You're doing it in sections. I read a bit about the transatlantic cables. It took everything they had to complete those two, and they were under two thousand miles long. The Pacific Ocean is…" She gestured outward at said ocean. "So much bigger. So of course you're segmenting it. But where are you putting the middle bits? You're not just dropping the ends and dredging for them, are you?"

Her eyes were shining with interest, and for a moment, he couldn't help but smile back at her.

"We're doing a northerly route—northern Japan to Myriad Island, then from Myriad down to Moresby, on the coast of British Columbia, and from there down to Seattle. We've already laid the Moresby to Seattle segment."

"I've never heard of Myriad Island."

"It's just a name we gave to what amounts to a barren rock we discovered in the northern Pacific. We're laying the section from Japan to Myriad early this fall, and then the final segment, Myriad to Moresby, the year after that."

He could see her taking all of this in, nodding. "This fall and the next, a year later?" She frowned, chewing her lip. "In September? It must be because of the sea ice then. Is Myriad very far north?"

"Exactly. It may be possible to lay earlier than that, but the more we have to dodge icebergs, the less even the cable. And we have to keep strict records on cable location because if anything needs repair, we'll need to be able to find it again."

"What's it like, laying cable?" she asked. "It sounds exciting."

"Very dull," he replied with a smile. "The ship moves very slowly while the cable pays out. Every ten miles or so, you stop and let the cable settle. You test the circuit—"

Her eyes grew even rounder. "You have a live electrical circuit as you lay the cable?"

"We keep batteries on board to establish one. Sometimes the cable will nick a rock on the ocean floor, or the pressure of the deep ocean will expose a fault, or a megalodon will take a chomp on the way down—"

God, what was he doing? Business, he'd told himself. All business. It had taken ten minutes, and he was already teasing her, smiling at her while she looked up at him with those wide eyes.

Grayson straightened and tugged his jacket into place. "That is to say, if we didn't test as we went, we'd discover the line was bad a thousand miles into the journey with no notion of where the fault lay. So we let the cable settle and make sure we've always got current running every so often. If not, we track back, hauling the cable up as we go, until we find the fault. Then we cut it out, splice the cable, and start forward all over again. It's very boring. That's why I told you I needed someone who would have to work independently. I'll be unavailable for months." He had to emphasize that. Distance. They would be very distant.

"Well, that makes no sense. Why would you be unreachable?"

"At sea?" He gestured to the waters around them. "In the middle of thousands of miles of ocean? Nobody's trained a pigeon yet that could deliver that message."

"Nonsense. You just said you tested electrical current. That means you have a circuit between your ship and the shore as you lay the cable. If you have a circuit, you have a telegraph. Why *can't* you send and receive messages?"

He blinked. "Ah. Um."

"Come to think of it," she mused, "if every ship could just trail a cable behind it, nobody would ever be lost at sea. We could always communicate with them at any time."

"Absolutely," Grayson said. "If every ship had an enormous cargo hold large enough to carry thousands of miles of cable, a budget of a million pounds for copper cabling and enough gutta percha to insulate it from the depths of the ocean, and an itinerary so devoid of any temporal pressure as to justify a maximum speed of ten knots on a good day."

She stuck her tongue out at him. "You're making fun of me."

"Just a little," Grayson said. "But going back to what you said. You'd have to talk to Mr. Lightfoot. He's my telegraph engineer. It's my understanding that while the cable is settling, the current is unstable. You wouldn't be able to tell if the current was interrupted by a settling error or if it was part of the telegraphic signaling. And there may be some issues with battery capacity."

"Hmm." She frowned, looking out over the sea. "You know, if you could generate a slow, evenly timed signal, repeatable without variance... And you could run the current with a battery from shore, upon signal..."

He tilted his head and turned to her. "What?"

He wasn't sure if she heard him. She was nodding, looking off on the horizon. "You'd need a stable sea, so you could use the galvanometer to trace the results... With thin paper, you could overlay them, which would give you something like an average. The error would fall out with enough repetition. But how would you distinguish between error and the start of the message? You'd need an unmistakable start and end signal, or perhaps a designated time of day in which to send and receive messages? Yes, that might be easier, and yet wouldn't allow for communication in the event of emergencies."

He waved a hand in front of her face. "Mrs. Smith, where have you gone?"

She blinked once, then twice before turning to focus on him. "I have an idea. Give me a few days and I'll work it out."

Her eyes seemed to be trained in his direction, but already he could tell her mind had drifted elsewhere.

He recognized the look on her face. That faraway dreamy look, starry-eyed, fixed on some internal vista.

At least, he thought dryly, *she's not tempting you by looking at you.*

A storm was coming, and it was worse than he feared. He couldn't even pretend that what he felt was a reflection of her own feelings. She seemed to have forgotten that he existed.

And here was the truth. He liked her. He liked talking to her about the telegraph. He liked teasing her. He liked the way her eyes shone, and he even liked the way she found a problem and then completely forgot that he existed. He liked everything about her, and it was going to be a issue.

"Mrs. Smith. I didn't hire you to work out the mechanics of sending telegraphic messages at sea."

She jerked back into the present moment with a visible shake of her head. "Oh of course." She seemed embarrassed. "I was just thinking it out for the fun of it. It's all right. I do tend to get diverted." She made a face. "I'm sorry."

"No." His reply came out in a rush. "That's not it at all."

"Hmm?"

"One of my younger brothers was something of a genius," he told her. "The rule always was to let him think where he wanted. You never knew what you were going to get. If it's fun, by all means, think it through. I'll ask Lightfoot if he wants to talk to you about it. He probably will. He loves things like this."

"Oh." She seemed taken aback by this. "Really?"

A storm was coming, and Grayson couldn't stop it. Even if he wanted to, he needed her. All Grayson could do was hope to race ahead and avoid the worst of what was coming.

"I only meant you had no obligation to continue. If you want to do it, by all means. Go ahead."

~

For the next days, Mrs. Smith and Mr. Lightfoot were inseparable. Damien Lightfoot was a Black engineer Grayson had hired after the war. He was almost seven feet tall and as thin as a wire, and Grayson tried his best *not* to feel jealousy every time he saw the two of them talking together, Lightfoot bent over to match her diminutive height.

Sometimes he saw them in the mess, going over diagrams. Sometimes he saw them speaking excitedly. Grayson didn't see Mrs. Smith alone again until days later, in the middle of the afternoon at the side of the deck.

"Come on, Merry," she was saying to her puppy. "Go. You can go."

Merry was sniffing the railings eagerly but seemed in no hurry to do her business.

He shouldn't ask. He should just tip his hat to her and leave. But… "How goes the telegraph at sea?" Grayson heard himself say.

She started, lost her footing, then caught the rail, steadying herself before he'd taken two steps in her direction to assist.

Grayson put his hands in his pockets, as if he had not just launched himself toward her in a panic.

She let out a pained laugh. "It's not going. The start was promising, but, I am stuck."

This was a business matter. Talking her through the solution of problems was necessary. "Sometimes it helps to stop cudgeling your brains to give up an answer." Grayson gestured at Merry. "You can tell her to go for hours on end, but sometimes it just won't happen until the pressure is off."

She sighed. "The *pressure.* Why did I do this to myself? I told you it seemed so easy, and here I am! Discovering that it is in fact not easy."

"That's normal."

"You would know." She turned to him. "You woke up one day and said, 'I want to build a worldwide telegraphic network.' I imagine the pressure must be intense."

Not many people noticed that. Grayson let out a bark of laughter because laughing was better than grimacing and falling to the floor, clutching his head. But he didn't want to talk about himself.

"I suppose it must be," he said.

"What made you decide to do it?"

After years of answering this exact question, he had a whole little speech he could rattle off—something about power and information and profit, something that made sense and told a good story.

But he'd already told her that.

A storm was coming and fool that he was, he faced headfirst into it.

"We had the idea back when we were breaking the gutta percha monopoly," he found himself saying.

"The gutta percha monopoly? What is that?"

It was at the heart of his plans, at the heart of himself. He should make his excuses and go.

But in that moment, he could see it clear as day. He'd wanted to hire someone who would make a telegraphic code that felt right—not just done, but *right.* If that was going to be her, she had to know what he meant by that. And that meant telling her about gutta percha.

"So." He turned to her. "If you're laying copper wire on the bottom of the ocean floor, it must be insulated or current will never flow."

"Of course." The way she looked at him, the way her eyes were so wide and interested...

He looked off to the sea. "At the bottom of the ocean, it's cold and the pressure is intense. Rubber becomes brittle and ceases to insulate. So, one cannot insulate a submarine telegraph cable with rubber."

She nodded, rapt.

"Luckily for the worldwide telegraphic network, there is a latex exuded by a plant called gutta percha, which continues to insulate at the bottom of the ocean. It's produced by a tree also called gutta percha."

"And there was a monopoly on it? Did you do some clever negotiating to break it?"

He shook his head. "It wasn't a negotiation problem. Gutta percha only grows in a small portion of the earth—Borneo and British Malaya, some parts of Java. And—here's the difficulty—if you fell a sixty-foot-tall gutta percha, you'll get ten ounces of latex."

Her eyes were wide. "From the whole tree? Just ten ounces?"

"From the whole tree. And it took two hundred and fifty tons of gutta percha to build a cable to cross the Atlantic."

"But that's…"

"Three hundred thousand trees," he told her. "Unimaginable acres of forest crushed for ounces of milky fluid so that current can stutter across the ocean. How do you break such a monopoly? You might find a forest or two outside British control every now and again, but you'd run through it in no time at all. A few pounds here or there is no monopoly-breaker."

She shook her head. "I have no idea. How did you do such a thing?"

You, she said. It had not been him.

"Here's the thing," Grayson told her. "When you're starting to harvest gutta percha in the very beginning, the solution always seems so easy. The fastest, cheapest way to get ten ounces of gutta percha is to cut down one tree and extract all the latex. Keep it up though, and the forest that was growing on the coast has become a sea of stumps. Then it's not just the cost of cutting down trees. You're building railways into scarcely inhabited sections of Borneo and putting down rebellions when the locals realize you'll destroy their way of life and leave famine in your wake."

Her eyes were wide.

"This," Grayson said, "is really what I think the Lord Traders are about. We find the places where everyone chose the *first* easy solution. They stick to that doggedly, even as it becomes mired in complexity and increasing costs. That's when we try to find the second, better solution."

"Which is?"

He leaned in. "You can get ten ounces of latex from one tree, but you can get an ounce of latex from its leaves. It doesn't sound like much, until you realize that you can get that every year, without fail, from the same trees."

"Ohhhh." She turned to him. "Oh that's a truly lovely solution."

"It's slower, but instead of causing famine in the local area, you're increasing prosperity. You never have to look for another forest. You never have to build a new railway. That's how we broke a monopoly—by questioning fast and cheap and thinking about what lasts. Once we had a long-lasting source for gutta percha, we saw what people were doing with it… At some point, we realized that we could already produce the most expensive ingredient in laying submarine cable." He let out a breath. "The rest of it seemed obvious from there."

It was an oversimplification, of course; he'd left out Noah's search for a similar tree in Brazil, based on latitude and humidity charts and the runs his cousin Ben did down south on the *Reliant* that made all his cable possible. To talk of any of that, he would have to tell her about Noah.

"I could say that's where the idea of a worldwide telegraphic network came from," Grayson told her. "From having the gutta percha to build it. But it was more than that. You see, our company is eighty years old. It seems like a great deal, but in the history of trade, it's the blink of an eye. We've been trying to look for those second solutions—the ones that started off cheap and ended in expense and misery—for all that time. But the telegraph is building a new world, structured in a new way. It got us thinking. What if we were able to get in *first?* What if instead of trying to fix messes after they'd escalated into famine and rebellion, we did it right to begin with? The telegraph is new, but you can already see how it's changing the world. Do you see what an opportunity this presents? To make the world right as it's being made anew?"

"Amazing." She was watching with wide, glowing eyes.

"That's why I need you," he told her. "Why I must have you. I needed something better than a list of numbers because what we invent in code today will determine how the Chinese language is transmitted. The moment I saw your position characters, I knew—"

He cut himself off, realizing what he'd been saying. *I need you. I must have you.*

Her eyes were focused on him though. She scarcely seemed to be breathing. And he couldn't *not* tell her.

"You knew what?" Her voice was breathy.

"I knew," he said, "that I had to let you loose on the world. We can't do this without you."

She exhaled, eyes bright and luminous.

"One question. Who is we?" she asked earnestly.

It was as if a cloud passed overhead, plunging him into cold air. For the space of a few sentences, he'd forgotten. He could see Noah standing next to him, talking excitedly about balata and latex. He could hear Harry and John argue about what it would mean to be able to send messages in minutes rather than months. He could see Noah, bright and lovable Noah, shaking his head and going to hide and think where their argument wouldn't bother him.

It was ridiculous that he could still forget after all this time. But there was no *we* anymore. It was just him.

"We," he said with a hollow pit in his stomach, "is me."

She could not hear the ache in his heart. "Just you?"

"Just me," he said softly. "I lost everyone who should have been with me cleaning up the biggest damned trade shortcut humanity has ever taken."

Just him. It was just him and he *had* to finish this. Had to make what they'd planned a reality. And he could not stop until he did.

Her expression clouded.

"Merry's finished," he told her. "I'll leave you to your other thoughts."

~

He saw her a few hours later in the mess with Mr. Lightfoot at the Daily Disoccupation. Grayson had been pitted against Captain Bell, Jason Lu, and Alex Wang in a fiercely competitive, no-holds-barred game that involved shooting wooden disks into a jar.

Lightfoot was teaching her how to play. She needed all the help she could get. She could not aim her disks at all, sometimes making them limply jump a few inches, other times sending them off at wild angles.

Grayson was trying not to pay attention to her because he didn't need to give in to his every urge, and besides, he had his own game to win.

He and Wang were paired against Bell and Lu, and Bell had managed to get five out of his six disks into the jar. Grayson was going to have to get all of his in to claim the victory. He'd measured the angle, calculated the precise force to use to send the disk tilting through the air to the pot.

Three feet away from him, she was laughing. "No, really," she was saying. "This one will definitely go in!"

"Oh sure it will." Lightfoot managed to sound both sarcastic and encouraging all at the same time.

"I'm giving it a great big push."

Grayson was *not* going to let himself get distracted. He weighed his own disk in his hand and concentrated. One. Two—

On three, he pressed. On three, Mrs. Smith did as well. She did, indeed, give her disk a great big push. Her aim, unfortunately, was not as good as her vigor. The wooden disk sailed through the air to strike him in the side of his forehead. The disk slipped out of his hand, landing a few feeble inches away.

A look of horror spread over her face. Silence reigned.

Then Captain Bell started a slow clap. "Mrs. Smith," he said, "you've done it. You've felled Hunter."

Grayson picked up the disk that had gone astray and handed it back to her.

"That," he said, "must count at least five times over."

She stared at him for a little too long before she blushed and snatched the disk from his hand.

A storm was coming. God, why was he still feeling it? After so many days?

"Isn't it a bad idea to encourage people to strike the captain?"

"Maybe," Grayson said, "but Bell is the Captain of the *Celerity,* and you're unlikely to replicate the endeavor."

"Cold, Captain." Lu shook his head. "Very cold."

He saw her again the next morning in the early hours before dawn, when he'd crept out with his violin. For some reason, it took longer than his usual starting regimen of twelve-tone scales up into the harmonics to limber up his arm. That morning, he felt a bit of a Beethoven violin romance coming on. He shut his eyes and started.

He didn't exactly have the piece memorized, and so the first minutes of music slid fluidly into something of his own invention, then into the long, slow notes of an old church hymn. Usually he could lose himself in the music, finding a place empty of thought and feeling where there was nothing but the press of the violin body between his chin and shoulder, the vibration of the strings under his fingers. Today, the dyad chords of the hymn seemed off. Nothing seemed to hang together. He could feel the frequency of each note like an echo in his hands, his body, and every single one felt out of place.

He started and restarted, shifting the music to a jig, then to a march he vaguely remembered, which truly was not suited for violin adaptation.

Finally, after a few minutes, he heard someone whisper behind him. "Merry. No. Come back."

He opened his eyes to see her crossing the deck to him. He stopped, relaxing his chin against the chin rest, letting the weight of the instrument fall into his palm. She picked up her puppy, who was trying to crawl into his violin case.

The storm felt closer with every passing day.

"Sorry." She waved her hands at him. "You're very good. Sorry to interrupt."

He shook his head. He wasn't good. Not today. But he shut his eyes and tried to forget he'd seen her.

～

He managed to avoid her for most of the remaining days of the trip. He didn't even have to try much; she retreated to the mess with Lightfoot, and he didn't see her often. When he did, she was frowning over a notebook or talking with the engineer.

It was only as they drew near to Shanghai that she sought him out again.

"Here," she said, handing him a few sheets of paper. "Lightfoot says he'll give it a try. I thought you might want to go over it beforehand."

He shuffled through the pages. It was a scheme for sending telegraphs through an erratic connection. It involved special paper and some tightening of the rules for sending dots and dashes. *Repeat message five to six times,* she had written, *and overlay results. Random current interruptions can be identified upon comparison of the streams—*

"You two really came up with a way for me to send telegrams while at sea?" He shook his head.

"Well, we don't truly know if it will work, do we?" She looked over at him. "I only did it for fun."

"Just for fun. Well, you're going to have a lot of fun in Shanghai."

"Hmm." She looked over at the coast.

They were close now. That storm felt even closer. But he couldn't shy away from her completely. They had to talk about what was to come.

"You don't look excited," he mused. "You look nervous."

She exhaled. "I'm going to be in Shanghai. I told you perhaps a little of what that meant."

"Do you think there's any possibility you could meet your family there?"

She shook her head emphatically. "It will do me no good to hold out real hope. I can scarcely manage the false variety."

A breeze skittered across the deck, tugging at her skirts. She smoothed them back into place.

"I need a new thing to hope for." Her voice was very soft, scarcely audible above the ever-present sound of the screw propeller turning water.

"Have you any notion what that will be?"

"I like your idea." She looked across the sea, looking west toward the mainland of China. "Maybe one day I might be able to clean up a mess for someone else when it couldn't be done for me. I think I've accepted in my mind, if not my heart, that the reunion I've imagined so many times—one where we see each other at the end of a long and dusty road—will never happen. But if I do my work well, maybe others won't need to be separated."

Grayson turned to look at her. She was still staring out at the mainland. There was a quiet agony of surrender in her eyes, at war with the certainty of her jaw.

He'd been wrong this whole time. The storm wasn't coming. It was *here.*

Mrs. Smith wasn't an intelligent, attractive woman whom he would forget after a few months away. That was more likely to describe what she would do with him.

She was in this endeavor with him—to finish what his brothers had started, and to finish it well. His business, his feelings, *her* feelings... They were all intermingled, and he couldn't ignore any of them. He was *feeling* things, looking at her like this—feeling the sharp pain of giving up on seeing family that he loved dearly, feeling the torture of releasing connections with his loved ones, feeling the isolation of being alone in the world, unable to reach out. He hadn't wanted to feel it for himself, but it had slipped in sideways, reflected by her emotions.

He felt all those things, and that was the point where he truly felt the rain fall around him. He wasn't going to forget her. Not someone who took her misery—one she'd been bearing since she was a child—and turned it into a sincere desire to make the world a place where others didn't suffer as she had.

This moment of affinity stretched between them, connecting them. Useless thing, connection. Grayson despised it. What was he going to do with that? Tell her that he felt this way? Pointless. He was going to leave in a matter of days, and he was used to bearing his emotions alone in any event.

It wasn't just that he wanted to reach out and touch her, to cup his hand against the cheek that was reddening in the wind, to pull her close and shelter her from the weather. It wasn't just that he wished everyone else were very far away so that he could kiss her the way he wanted.

He'd told her back in Fuzhou that he didn't really know what it was like to kiss someone he truly wanted. That he was a single-lightning-strike sort of person—attraction happened swiftly and then passed on.

The thing was, Grayson had actually been struck by lightning thrice in his life. Freak accidents, every single one—and never direct strikes, but side splashes, the leap of current from one tall object to him. He had scars on his right arm as a memory from one of those strikes.

He didn't know how he'd survived *those* and yet his brothers… He took a deep breath, refusing to think of that.

He'd *told* her that he was a single-lightning-strike sort of person, and yet he'd known as he'd said it that he was the sort of person who attracted lightning.

The storm was here. He thought he'd insulated his heart, but a few inches of rubber were nothing for a bolt of energy that could cross the heavens. He didn't want to feel this. This yearning. This want. This desire to keep her safe, this connection. He didn't *want* it.

He had known something was going wrong, that there was

danger, but he'd justified all his conversation with her as business. Telling himself it couldn't hurt. He should have recognized the danger he was in. He should have protected his heart better.

How could he have? He hadn't realized he still had one.

"Captain Hunter?" She turned her wide eyes on him, and he felt himself falling. "Is something amiss?"

He nodded. "I smell a storm. It's a big one."

Her eyes grew wider. Her expression was curious and delighted. "You can smell storms? How does one smell storms?" She inhaled and let out a deep breath, inhaled and let out a deep breath, as if searching for secrets in the scent of the world.

God. He was lightning struck by her. All the way through, and he didn't have time to feel like this.

What could he do? Grayson gave in and told her.

CHAPTER THIRTEEN

They landed in Shanghai in utter confusion. Amelia had expected something like Fuzhou in tea season, except maybe larger—busy docks swirling about a busy river, with residences a little farther away. She had been found just outside Shanghai, and so she'd hoped it would prove familiar and comfortable, even if she had no memory of it.

It did not. Shanghai wasn't just Fuzhou but on a different scale—it felt as if it were on an entirely different planet. Ship after ship after ship, with so many flags painted on them, half of which she didn't recognize. A hall that had to be navigated, paperwork presented to her, everyone shouting, all the noises echoing, in layers of unknown languages.

Benedict guided her through the confusing morass of customs at Woosung, confidently telling her where to sign and what everything meant even when the noise reverberated to the point of headache.

Leaving that cacophony did little to alleviate her confusion. The foreign concession in Shanghai was nothing like Fuzhou. Everything seemed made in the English style—and bigger, taller, grander, with more squares and statues. She was, at first take, the only Chinese person in sight and that made her nervous.

Benedict seemed to recognize her discomfort—good—but dealt with it by directing a bewildering flow of information at her.

"That's the theater," he said of a spattered white stone building as they made their way through the concession. "They took up a subscription to raise it five years ago, and now they're very proud, say it's just as good as the one in London." He shrugged. "It's not. I don't know why they try."

"It looks very grand to me." It looked steep and imposing and extremely muddy. Were all the buildings she saw in woodcuts of London this muddy? Was the cleanliness all an artist's trick?

Benedict simply gestured to his right. "Over there's the horse track. It's a source of constant argument. Is it viable amusement? Is gambling a vice?" He grinned at her. "The argument itself provides half the diversion."

He kept this discussion going as they trekked along muddy paths lined by blocky Western-style buildings—banks and social clubs and residences. In Fuzhou, what she had thought of as Western buildings were made of stone and brick—long, windowed structures of one or two stories. Here, the stone was carved into curlicues and built up into ornate structures of three, four, even occasionally five stories high. Amelia had seen prints of buildings like this in books about London or Paris. It was her first time seeing something this grand in real life.

But neither Benedict nor Captain Hunter seemed to think their surroundings particularly imposing.

"This property we are going to," Benedict said, "was obtained with great finesse after the First Opium War." He frowned. "I'm told that Captain Hunter's great-great-uncle—Uncle Henry, you'll have heard of him—did the negotiations back in the forties. We don't really own it."

She glanced back at Captain Hunter.

"You'll have to get Captain Hunter to tell you about his uncle Henry," Benedict said. "Him and uncle John—they founded Lord Traders. Everyone is quite in awe of them. From what I hear, uncle John was the visionary and uncle Henry was…"

Benedict trailed off, glancing behind them at Captain Hunter who had raised an eyebrow.

"Are you planning to delve into the entire family history?" Captain Hunter asked.

"Yes," Benedict said. "As Mrs. Smith's official liaison, I am providing orientation and conversation."

Captain Hunter shook his head.

"People do it when they want to be friendly," Benedict went on. "You do it too. Why are you being so forbidding and scary all of a sudden?"

Captain Hunter sighed. "It's late. I'm tired."

Amelia could understand that. "What were you saying about the place where we are headed, Benedict?" Amelia suggested. "You don't own the building?"

Benedict flushed. "Well, *I* don't own anything at all! My understanding is that it's a lease from the original owners."

"And will I be allowed to stay here? I had thought that under the treaty, Chinese people were not allowed in the foreign concessions. And I have not seen any."

Benedict waved a hand. "Ehh. That's technically true. But that particular bit is not enforced at present."

"No?"

"After the Taiping Rebellion, there were too many refugees to keep them all out. There's some grumbling about it, but so far, no need to worry. Didn't your mother register you as a British citizen anyway?"

"I have citizenship through my prior marriage."

Captain Hunter huffed and looked away.

"We're here," Benedict said.

Amelia looked up. The stone building they had stopped before was a blocky, angular structure lacking entirely in courtyards. It was two stories tall with wide windows everywhere. She'd been traveling all day. After the bewildering cacophony of customs followed by the walk here, she was already exhausted.

But there was no time for exhaustion. Captain Hunter came forward and conducted her on a tour of the building, introducing her to the head of his staff, Geoffrey Wyatt. He showed her an office, told her it was hers, introduced the others working there—

Her head was spinning.

"Benedict will be your liaison for the first few months," Captain Hunter said.

Amelia looked at him in mute entreaty. She had known he had cable to lay. (Cable. To lay. She blushed and made herself think of regular cable.)

"I've business here for the next three days," he said, as if he'd heard her silent protest. "Settle in, start working. I'll talk to you as I can."

It had all been theoretical up until this point. Having an office and a desk made her future telegraphic work seem real. It was now Amelia's job to allow half a billion people to communicate via telegraph.

Whatever had she been thinking to imagine she could accomplish that?

"Benedict will help you find a place to live. Jump in," he told her, as if he understood her hesitation. "It won't get any easier for putting it off. It will just make you dread the work more."

She squelched all her fears into a tiny ball in the pit of her stomach. "Right. Where should I start?"

"Mrs. Smith." Captain Hunter looked her directly in the eyes. "Do you remember what I told you on board the *Celerity?*"

"Um." There had been so many things. "Which thing?"

"I have to let you loose on the world." She wasn't sure if the smile he gave her was kind or cruel. "That means you're going to have to let yourself loose as well."

But where do I start? She managed to pull in this whining complaint, managed to smile at him and nod as if that wasn't a string of gibberish that bounced in her head the way all the words in the customs hall had.

"Right." She nodded. "Perfect. Absolutely. Understood." She had no idea what she was even saying anymore.

Maybe she didn't sound as certain as she'd tried to be, because he huffed. "I'll see you again before I'm off. But for now—I've a meeting."

He nodded to her, once, and then decamped.

The room he abandoned seemed very empty. Just her, a desk, a window over a city that should have been familiar but which felt incredibly, increasingly foreign. Her and the boy who had been assigned as her liaison, and they were supposed to change the world?

"Whew." Benedict whistled beside her. "What are you going to do now?"

What else was there to do? "Find a place to sleep." She let out a long breath. "And then, I suppose, jump in."

$\sim$

Amelia saw Captain Hunter regularly over the next handful of days.

"How is it going?" he asked her the next afternoon, when she'd only had the chance to review the folders of project needs and the absolute chaos that had been the prior attempts to encode the Chinese language. "Any questions?"

"No!" She'd smiled at him brightly, hiding the fear that roiled in her gut. "It's all very clear!"

She saw him again at noon the next day.

"Everything's fine!" she reassured herself in his direction. "Just fine!"

And then again that evening: "I'm off to a smashing start!"

She thought about that "smashing start"—ha—through the wee hours of the night. Smashing, yes. It was all smashing right into her. She had steeled herself to give him another cheery and insubstantial reply when she saw him the next morning. But somehow when he walked in and saw her at her desk, with her stack of notes where she'd doodled various exclamations of doom in the margin, she realized that he would be leaving within a day.

"It's all..." *Wonderful!* she wanted to say.

Instead, she found herself squeezing her eyes shut. "Oh God."

"Mrs. Smith?"

Just say it's wonderful, she told herself. *Tell him not to worry.*

Instead, her accumulated fear and confusion came out in a torrent. "It's all a mess. I'm a mess. The project is a mess. I can't do this."

Silence. She opened her eyes enough to see him watching her. His visage seemed to be made of stone.

Panic clutched at her chest. "I'm going to disappoint you. You're going to sack me. I'll have to go back to Fuzhou—" She'd lived there for years; why did the thought of *going back* make her lungs seize in terror?

"Ah." His expression lightened. "I see." He pinched the bridge of his nose. "Mrs. Smith, I am not possessed of magical talents."

This was such an odd response that it broke through her cycling panic. She bit her lip. The mild pain felt like a grounding reassurance.

"We are going to work together." He met her eyes. "And

167

hopefully for a long while. But if this partnership is to work, you must understand one thing."

She nodded, bracing herself for his inevitable criticism.

"Don't tell me you're fine if you're not fine."

She blinked. She had been expecting him to reprimand her work ethic, her mind. Her *anything*. Instead, this admonition brought up a new, hot well of shame as she relived her own conduct over the past few days.

She hid her face. "Oh no."

"Don't tell me you're fine if you're not fine," he repeated. "I can't solve problems I don't know about."

She had been despairing before. But this was worse, much worse. He thought her untruthful. No. Worse than that, and she had to face the facts without downplaying her own conduct. She had *been* untruthful. She had never thought herself a liar before, but here it was in black and white: She had lied.

"Oh *no.* I'm so dreadfully, horribly sorry."

He shook his head. "It's hardly the end of the world, Mrs. Smith. Come. Set your work down and get your outside things. Let's have some tea."

"Outside?" She frowned. "But we have tea here—and I—"

"I don't believe I misspoke." He was still smiling, but there was an edge to his words. "Get your outside things."

"But—"

He gestured to the door. "Tea, Mrs. Smith. Come on. I have heard of a shop just outside the foreign concession. Zed has been there before. We can talk without being overheard."

Half an hour and many muddy streets later, they had found his teahouse—a diminutive building.

Inside, long doors opened onto a garden courtyard. Cozy tables of rosewood were surrounded by cushioned benches. A smoky range stood at the back, on which a large pot steamed.

The proprietress gave them an intense stare when they entered.

Amelia could sense the woman's suspicion like a palpable thing. She wasn't the first Chinese person she'd encountered in Shanghai—they'd seen quite a few on their way here—but Amelia's manner of dress, so English in origin, her hair, done up in an English bun...

She wasn't going to fit in here any more than in Fuzhou.

"So," Captain Hunter said after they settled into the teahouse. "Tell me now, and accurately this time." He met her eyes. "How has the project really been coming along?"

Amelia frowned. "Coming along?"

It *hadn't* been coming. Or going. What had been a perfectly fine code for her and her brother was completely inadequate as a general measure for communication in the wider populace.

"It's..." She let out a breath. "You were wrong about my capabilities. I would say the problem is difficult, but it's not just that. I'm not the right person for this."

He raised a skeptical eyebrow. "And what brought you to *that* conclusion?"

"Among other things? My speaking skills. I'm not native, you know. When I started to learn Mandarin... I don't know if I spoke it at all before. My tongue knew how to pronounce words, and I learned much more quickly than my brother. But I'm not like someone who knew it from the beginning."

"That is what disqualifies you?" He looked skeptical.

"I may once have known a different Chinese dialect, but if I did, I knew it the way a child did. I have done all my learning in English. There are so many things I understand but can't converse on."

"Hmm," he said. "But that's normal when learning a new language, isn't it? I would say the same thing."

The proprietress came to their table. She looked at Captain

Hunter suspiciously and at Amelia even more suspiciously. Her gaze traveled down Amelia's very English gown, and then up to where Amelia had her hair in a very English bun, so different from the way her own hair was divided into separate, intricate braids. She took note of Amelia's face, her eyes, her dark glossy hair.

Then she spoke in Mandarin—one word. "Cha?" How she made that sound so mistrustful, Amelia had no idea.

"Yes, please," Amelia responded in the same language. That earned her an even more suspicious glare.

"In any event," Amelia said after the lady had departed, "I've gotten better! I know some of both Mandarin and Cantonese and a little of the Fuzhou dialect. But every time I think I've reached the point of fluency, I start talking to someone and they pick a topic I've never discussed. And it's like I'm a child again because I don't know *any* of the words they're using."

"Hmm."

"I don't know why I thought I could do this," Amelia moaned, warming to the inherent impossibility of her situation. "In my original scheme with Leland, I had come up with my own version of Morse, a separate encoding for every Chinese radical. But your project requirements are for a *worldwide* telegraphic network. You couldn't send such a code with an operator who didn't know it. And how are we to teach operators around the world a code for a language they cannot speak?"

"I'm sure you'll find a way to manage that."

"I thought so too. But there are so many radicals and only twenty-six letters, and even if I find a way to double them up, how do I know which ones are used most frequently as one should to reduce transmission time? I don't have that level of knowledge of the language! And that's what it comes down to. I don't know enough."

He looked over at her. "That seems a bit—"

He was interrupted by the woman's return. She plonked in

front of them a teakettle, a blue-and-white ceramic pot with a lid, two teacups, and another, larger, ceramic vessel. She did not say a word; instead she started walking away.

Amelia peered into the kettle; there was nothing but heated water.

"Excuse me," Amelia said in Mandarin. "Is there tea? And, um, a…" How did she not know the word for teapot? She'd used it before. Often. It was on the tip of her tongue. Instead, what she came up with was: "A…tea…wok?"

The woman looked at her as if she had lost her mind. "Use the gaiwan."

"The, um, the lidded bowl?"

"Yes. Of course. The gaiwan."

Amelia looked over the dishes in front of her. There *was* a bowl with a lid, but it looked incredibly small for the task.

"Gaiwan?" she asked again.

The woman let out an exasperated breath. "Don't you know how to make tea?"

She managed a half-hearted smile.

"Your accent," the woman muttered. And then she said something that sounded like: "Who even raised you?"

Amelia had said this sentence to Chinese speakers so often that it was second nature to her now in any language. "I was taken in by Christian missionaries at the age of six."

That gaze sharpened on her, turning to a disdainful pity. "So, you don't know anything, do you?"

Amelia swallowed and glanced at Captain Hunter, hoping he couldn't understand what was happening here.

"Not one thing."

The woman came to stand behind her. "Take the gaiwan." She took the top off the blue ceramic pot. Inside were some tea leaves. She took hold of the kettle, poured in a little water, and waited a moment. "Wake the tea leaves." With one practiced motion, she put the lid over the top, then tilted the entire contraption so the hot water, colored a faint green-gold, streamed out into the little ceramic pitcher, leaving the leaves behind. "Pour that into the cups," she said. "Then throw it away. It's no good."

Amelia poured the hot water into the cup, feeling the ceramic heat against her fingertips. Grayson moved to take his.

"She said to throw it away," Amelia said, as he raised it to his lips.

He did.

"Now." The woman poured more hot water into the gaiwan. "This you drink. After it"—Amelia didn't catch the word she used, but she was guessing it meant *steeps*—"pour the tea into the pitcher."

Amelia nodded. "Thank you for your explanation. I appreciate it."

The woman just stared at her. "You're not pouring. Did you understand what I said?"

"You said, after it…"

"Yes, after it—" That same word, probably? Maybe it didn't mean steeps. Maybe it meant something else.

Amelia gave her a horrified smile. "But it hasn't even been a minute."

"A minute!" The woman widened her eyes. "No, no, this is *good* green tea. The first steeping finishes in ten seconds. How can you taste each steeping properly if you let the leaves sit in water for minutes on end like you're boiling soup?"

"That's how the English make it."

"Ah!" The woman threw up her hands. "The English! Fight two wars for tea and can't even make it properly! How will you marry if you can't even prepare tea for your mother-in-law? What would your mother say if she saw you? She would be so ashamed."

Amelia felt her face burn. *The English.* Of course that was how this woman saw her. How could she think otherwise?

Amelia wore English clothing and spoke the English language. She had an English mother, an English childhood. She *was* English, in every way that counted to everyone who wasn't English.

It hit her then, that sense of deep shame. It was just as well her mother hadn't come back. Just as well that the woman had never seen what her daughter had turned into—someone who couldn't even make tea.

"Thank you for your instruction," she said quietly. "You've been extraordinarily patient, madame."

"Madame." The woman scoffed. "Don't you know anything? Call me Proprietor Zhu. And throw that water out—it's no good now. Steep it right. Twenty seconds the second time." She left in a huff.

"Is everything all right?" Grayson asked after a moment.

She'd seen him use some Mandarin. Amelia didn't know if he'd followed that exchange. Even in Mandarin, Proprietor... Who? Ah, there, the character was on the wall, how convenient. Proprietor Zhu had an accent. He might not have been familiar with it, and she had been speaking quickly.

Of course, she wanted to say. But the words stuck in her throat. It wasn't right. None of it was right.

"What am I doing?" she finally asked, shutting her eyes. "Why am I doing this? I don't even know how to make tea properly for my mother-in-law. How am I expected to make a code for a language I understand so badly?"

"I didn't realize you had a mother-in-law." A bit of a pause, and then he said, more dryly. "I didn't realize you wanted one."

"Metaphorically speaking," Amelia said with a wave of her hand.

Her hand shook as she poured the hot water into the gaiwan; she could feel Proprietor Zhu's eyes on her from across the room. When she decanted the liquid a short count later, pale and lovely, the woman gave her a sharp, approving grunt.

"Captain Hunter, I don't know why I'm here. You need someone who will do this right, like with the gutta percha. That's not me."

"You're here," he said, "because you're *here*. Because you will be the third person I hired for this task, and if you finish, it will be because you stayed, and they didn't. If I didn't have you here, it will fall to some Frenchman with less understanding of the language."

Your mother would be so ashamed. It felt like hubris for Amelia to think she could do this. "I'm not going to be perfect. Someone else would be better."

"You're not wrong," Captain Hunter replied with what sounded like practiced ease. "In an ideal world, a consortium of every interested party would sit down together and develop a natural approach. We had something like that in Japan, but the Japanese emperor wishes to embrace modernization in a way the Chinese do not. So here we are. In *this* world, an American invented the telegraph, developed a code for transmission, and left the rest of us scrambling to graft something usable on top of what he made."

Amelia put her hands over her eyes, unwilling to look at him. "She said." She let out a breath. "The owner. Mrs. Zhu. She said my mother would be ashamed if she could see me. How can I do this?"

Grayson looked over at her. "I take it she wasn't talking about Mrs. Acheson."

She shook her head.

"And I take it you care."

Amelia found herself nodding. She shouldn't have. She couldn't remember her Chinese mother—just that false hope. *I will come back for you. Hold on to your heart.* She'd already lost it to the fog of memory.

"I don't know your Chinese mother." He gave her a little shrug. "Do you want me to offer false platitudes?"

She looked up, glaring. "Well now I don't! You aren't supposed to admit your platitudes are false before offering them! It completely ruins the effect."

"Then have the truth: You can't possibly know whether she would feel pride or shame if she saw you now. You can't hope to meet the standards of someone who exists only in your mind and your memory."

Her eyes stung. "I know. I'm not good enough."

He poured her more tea. "That's not what I meant. The question is not whether she would be proud of you. It's whether you would be proud of yourself. If you'll feel shame for working on this, then by all means stop."

He looked over at her. His eyes were dark and deep.

Amelia swallowed.

He continued. "But I don't think you *do* feel shame. I think you want to do this deep down in your bones. I think *that's* what scares you—that you *can* do it right, and you're afraid you won't. Am I wrong?"

That was what made it so hard. She *did* want this. She wanted to be the person who did it because if she did…

If she did, she would finally have someplace where she belonged, even if she'd had to carve it out herself at the inter-section of China and the West. She felt tears prick against her eyelids.

"Whatever you create will have traces of you in it. If Vigu-ier's version becomes standard, then Chinese transmitted via telegraph will always have his echo. It will always be a code secondary to Morse. Convoluted, tricky, difficult to send, and harder to encode."

She exhaled. "If I fail, it will prove once and for all that I don't belong."

She'd said something similar to her mother once—talking

about that fear that went deeper than loneliness, deeper than rootlessness. She usually received reassurances in return—that she would always have a place with her mother, even if she floundered. Those words had never reassured.

Captain Hunter offered her no such easy platitudes. He just shrugged. "Then don't fail."

"Oh very well." She ran a finger along the edge of her teacup. "I suppose I just won't fail then. How useful."

She wasn't trying to hide her sarcasm.

But his eyes widened. "Aha!"

"Aha?"

"Aha, as in, eureka, I have discovered something. I made a bit of a mistake there. No—don't look so despondent—I have not discovered that I think you'll fail." He shook his head. "It's just…" He looked away. "You remind me a bit of one of my younger brothers. Noah."

He wasn't watching her. He'd mentioned his brothers before. The way he wasn't looking at her, the way he was trying for a lighthearted tone…

"Noah was the one who came up with the leaf harvesting and extraction method for gutta percha," Captain Hunter explained to his teacup. "He was the one who made humidity and latitude charts and…never mind." His hands clenched around his cup. "You have his intelligence. His enthusiasm. I forgot you didn't have his experience. Noah would have known he could succeed."

Amelia felt a pit of uncertainty in her stomach. "And I don't."

"You don't know it *yet*," he said. "You'll have to learn by doing."

She made a face. "You don't learn success. You either succeed or you don't."

He finally looked up at her. "No," he said slowly. "Take it

from me. You learn. And if someone has taught you *not* to succeed, you learn that too. You'll learn."

"How?"

He looked at her across the table. "You'll learn because you'll want something more than you fear it."

She had thought him handsome before. But in that moment, that quiet assurance, the way he looked at her... Her doubts didn't fall away. Her confidence didn't soar. But it felt like the smallest parting of clouds, a single ray of sunshine bursting through and catching the two of them at this teahouse.

He nodded. "I have an idea. I'm leaving tomorrow. I'll be on the wide ocean for weeks, and you're clearly not ready to be left. There's not much to be done about that, unfortunately, but here we are. Luckily, you've already set up a potential method of communication between us."

"It might not work. It won't allow for much."

"I think it will be enough. Let's assume you're right." He gave her a small smile. "Like I said. I have an idea. I'll show you tomorrow."

CHAPTER FOURTEEN

Captain Hunter appeared the next morning just as Amelia was making her way up to her office. He had a leather satchel over one shoulder. He nodded to her in greeting and bent to pet Merry, who responded with tail-beating enthusiasm.

He said little as she went to her desk and found the notes she'd made feverishly last night after their talk. She glanced up. The morning light glinted off his skin, drawing her attention. What would it be like to trace the brown divot in his upper lip with her finger…?

He was watching her in return. She felt her whole body light up when he looked at her. *Attraction,* she reminded herself. Many women were attracted to him. It wasn't particularly meaningful.

"I'll be back as soon as I can—early February, I hope."

That was so many months away.

"It will be before the meeting with the taotai at any event. But while you're getting started, I'll be laying the Japan-to-Myriad line. We should be able to send messages: my telegraph to Japan, then via courier ship to Shanghai. The same will work in reverse."

She inhaled. "Are you saying I should write to you?"

Merry pushed around Amelia's feet, butting under her skirts, nudging her ankle with a cold nose and beating her tail against her calf. Amelia knelt beside her and rubbed her dog's head, trying to hide the loneliness that welled up inside her at the thought of him leaving. He had said he would do it; it wasn't a surprise.

He looked embarrassed. "I'm saying you must write to me."

Don't tell me you're fine if you're not fine. The idea of sending honest progress reports sent a shiver down her spine.

"And you'll respond? What sort of question can I fit in a telegram? What sort of answer could you provide?"

"Benedict has access to our commercial ciphers. He can help you get a message down to a minimum. As for me, I imagine we won't have much ability to send the lengthy return messages that might prove useful. So I'll send you a number."

"What am I supposed to do with a number?"

For a moment, Captain Hunter appeared as if he were contemplating a distasteful task. His lip curled; his nostrils flared. Finally he opened the satchel at his side and removed a stack of envelopes—thick enough that even when compressing them together, they did not fit in one of his rather large hands.

He handed them over in two hanks. On top of the first one, inscribed in dark black ink, was a number: *1.*

"When I send a number, open up the corresponding envelope. It will tell you my thoughts on the matter. Understand?"

She stared at the envelopes. "Captain Hunter. Did you write all these out last night?"

He cleared his throat and muttered something.

"I beg your pardon?"

"I said, I might have." He looked away from her. "It's just

179

another form of commercial cipher, highly compressed. Nothing else."

The thought of him sitting up at night writing out instructions, however general they might have been, made a warm, fluttery thing come to life inside her. Then she remembered that he'd asked her for honesty, which meant he would provide it as well.

Some of these envelopes must contain reprimands.

Amelia fanned the thick stack. "I suppose envelopes two through thirty just say 'no, you fool.' But thank you."

She expected him to take his leave at that. Instead, he fiddled with the strap of his satchel.

"Is there something else?"

"Unfortunately." He exhaled. "There is."

But he didn't speak. He didn't move.

"Captain Hunter?"

He shook his head and, without saying a word, crossed to the door. For a moment, she thought he was going to leave, just like that—

The door closed. She looked up to find him inside still, just looking at her. There was something fierce in his gaze, something she could not quite understand.

"One last thing." He spoke in a low voice. "I shouldn't say this. I know I shouldn't say this. Tell me to stop at any time. In fact, tell me to stop right now."

Her heart gave one thump and then another. There was something… *Something…*

"Go ahead." Her voice sounded soft, so soft in the office.

"It's a personal request. I ought not make it."

She couldn't say anything.

He sighed and came to sit on the edge of her desk, his legs dangling close to her skirts. "You mentioned the possibility of marriage."

"I did." Her whole being fluttered. "Honestly, I'm glad to have that whole thing out of the way now. It seems like a mess."

He leaned in a little closer. "Don't be so sure. You won't want for offers."

"That's a little optimistic. After all—"

He set a finger on her lips, stopping her words. The heat of his touch burned straight through to her heart and shocked her into silence.

"I mean it," he said fiercely. "You won't want for offers. You can tell yourself you won't have any. That will be a lie. If you let yourself believe that, when you get one you may end up flattered and overwhelmed."

"You've thought about me getting offers? Of marriage?"

His jaw set and he looked away. "From fools who only see that you're lovely and delightful and present in Shanghai and command a salary of fifty dollars a year. They won't realize that you're an absolute treasure."

Her eyes widened. "But—"

"No buts." His finger was still on her lip.

When she spoke, it felt as if she were kissing him. "I see." She tried to make a joke of it. "You must protect your investment. I'll do my best not to run off with the first man who asks me. Will that do?"

His voice was dark and deep. "I know someone will adore you as you deserve. Some day. And I'll accept that when it happens. But I'll hate myself forever if you waste yourself on a man because he asked and you find him tolerable."

She looked up. There was an intensity in his eyes. He leaned down, closer to her; his hand shifted so his thumb was on her chin and his fingers rested against her cheek.

Amelia had been married. She'd had sexual intercourse on a firm schedule.

She had never felt so intimately touched, not once. Her lips parted.

"Oh," she whispered.

"Don't marry someone," he said, "unless he makes you feel like this." And then he leaned down. He paused, a hair's breadth from her lips.

He paused, and he stayed there, just like that. His breath was shaky, his hand against her cheek unsteady. Those tiny movements of his fingers against her jaw seared into her. He was torturing her with want. He didn't pull back; he didn't move forward. He simply held himself in place, letting their breaths mingle.

She realized after a few exchanged breaths that he wasn't going to do it. That he was just going to let her sit in place and feel and want without so much as brushing their lips together.

What a *waste.*

Amelia pushed up an inch, pressing their lips together. It was inelegant and clumsy. Their mouths bumped together with a little too much force. He let out a surprised noise, as if he'd never thought she would do it. But before she could shrink back from him, his arm wrapped around her and his lips moved against hers. Her mind turned into stars, twinkling overhead and on a sea around them, light reflecting up and down and everywhere until she was filled with it. Her whole body seemed luminous in his touch. Their lips clung together, tasting, tasting, as if she were being tortured with a thought of what might have been if only…

If only he actually wanted this.

He pulled away first, adjusting his shirt cuffs, looking away from her, and she remembered with a sinking feeling in her gut that he hadn't been going to kiss her. That he'd only gone as far as he had, coming so close, because he expected her to marry another man.

"If I promise to wait until I feel *that* again," she heard herself saying, "I might never marry."

The first thing that crossed his face—a self-satisfied smile—

was all pride. Then he shook his head ruefully. "I'm very attractive. Many women have liked me."

It wasn't the first time he'd reminded her of that. She felt herself shrinking.

"They've all learned to do without me, every last one." His voice gentled. "You'll find someone more suited to you than I ever would be. You think that my caring about your feelings is extraordinary when it is a bare minimum. Don't sell yourself cheaply, Amelia. Not even to me."

The way he said her name felt like a caress. There was a gentleness to it. An intimacy, as if they'd crossed a boundary. There was surely something she could say in response. Something that would bring him closer. If *she* could respond in kind —if she could use the familiarity of his given name—

Amelia realized in something like profound embarrassment that she didn't actually know it. Captain Hunter. It had taken her long enough to remember even that. He was Captain Hunter to her. She had kissed him, and she didn't even know his first name.

He opened the door. "Goodbye, Amelia."

"Farewell." She held up her hand. "Farewell, Captain..." Damn it. "Hunter."

He vanished down the stairs.

CHAPTER FIFTEEN

Amelia was sitting in her office, sorting through the contents of the desk drawers: dried inkwells, old pieces of candy in wax paper, papers with monthly personal budgets sketched on them...

She was trying to get her mind on anything other than the thing that just happened. A kiss. A *kiss*. She'd *kissed* him, what the devil, a kiss. It had felt like heavens opening, angelic choir singing, all of that.

She was fairly certain this wasn't a theologically sound analogy, but that was how it had felt.

And now she was staring at someone's monthly budget. Her predecessor's, no doubt.

He'd been paid less than her.

(A kiss, her mind whispered, a *kiss*.)

Whoever had been here before her had a rather practical bent, but for the predilection for candies, if the figures were true.

A knock sounded at the door.

For a moment, her heart kicked up a notch. *Captain Hunter.* Had he come back? (A kiss. *Another* kiss?)

She looked up. It was most definitely not Captain Hunter who stood in the doorway, beaming at her with puppylike enthusiasm.

"Ah." She sighed. "Mr...." Damn. His *name?*

The boy ran a hand through sandy brown hair and gave her a smile. "Hullo," he said cheerily. "I'm your liaison here in Shanghai, here to liaise!"

Benedict, Captain Hunter had called him. She could recall that much. Would it be gauche to admit she had no idea what his family name was? She had some sense that Captain Hunter had said it before.

"What should I call you?" she asked instead.

He shrugged. "I'm not the sort to stand much on formalities. So Benedict, if you wish. But if *you* are the sort to stand much on formalities, Mr. Worth, I suppose. Are you?"

"Am I?" she echoed, looking wistfully at the dried inkwell. Would it be horrible to write his name down right in front of him? What would he think? She was just starting here; she didn't want him to have an ill opinion of her. "Am I what?"

"Are you the sort to stand on formalities?"

"I don't believe so." She grimaced and rolled her shoulders. "I have never taken employment before. *Ought* I stand on formality? Will people not respect me if I do?"

"Ooh." He looked up into the corner of one room. "That's a very good question. I had not thought of that. What do *you* think?"

She felt her suspicions rise. "Mr...." Oh. Damn. She wanted to hit her head against the desk.

"Mr. Worth," he said.

"Mr. Worth, are you *old* enough to liaise?"

His back straightened. "Yes. Of *course* I am." He looked the very picture of indignant hurt. Then his shoulders fell, and he heaved a sigh. "Although I have never done it before." Another moment of dejection before he brightened. "But Captain

Hunter gave me instruction last night on what I'm to do. It's the sort of thing that I'm great guns at."

Perfect. Neither of them had any idea what they were doing. Amelia tried not to grimace. They were not meeting each other's eyes, and awkwardness seemed to settle in. She could send him away, or…

Amelia sighed and changed the topic of conversation to one that would give him a chance to show off a little instead. "Captain Hunter said that your family name would open up doors. I'm not much conversant in…" Well, names, for one. Or the hierarchy of British families, for another. "Any of that," she concluded, "but if we are to work together, I should know who you are."

Oddly enough, this made him blush. Redness swept his face in little blotchy patches. "Well. If you must. But." His shoulders squared. "My father was the Earl of Linney."

That was all he said. No recitation of lands, no further explanation of family history. But he watched her as if waiting for her to recognize the name and respond in some fashion.

Recognize a name? Her? She looked at him. "You said *was.* Has he passed away? I'm sorry for your loss."

He winced. "Um. He was not exactly executed for treason? But that's close enough. My elder brother was transported, also for, ah, treason-related crimes. All of this happened when I was extremely young, and I have no memory of it. Not the deaths. Nor the treason."

There was an awkward pause, the kind that begged to be filled with anything. An inquiry into the weather. A dramatic shift of the conversation to breeds of sheep. A compliment on his jacket.

"What kind of treason was it?" Amelia heard herself asking instead, beset by curiosity, then wanted to hit her head against the desk again. *Anything but that, Amelia. Anything but that.*

"You know," Benedict said slowly, "I've never investigated

186

the particulars. From what I have heard, it had something to do with the war with China? Something about trying to offer them aid so as to harm Britain and alter the outcome?"

Amelia glanced out her window. On the muddy street below, she could see the white stone buildings of the American quarter, portions of Shanghai that now sat under the jurisdiction of powers from halfway around the world. "The treason wasn't very effective, was it?"

Benedict stared at her. Then he let out a laugh. "How can I know? It was two of them against all England. And *I* wasn't the one committing treason. I assure you, if—" He stopped talking. "That is to say—not that I *would*—but if *I* were to commit treason—" Another pause. "Which I definitely would not." He squared his chin and folded his arms. "If I were to commit treason, *I* would be good at it."

"Yes, yes. Great guns, just like your liaising." She waved a hand at him. "I don't really care if you betrayed Britain or whether you'd be good at it."

He looked at her warily.

She remembered Captain Hunter admonishing her to not say she was fine if she was not fine. Benedict was the captain's liaison—as close to his voice in Shanghai as it came.

"I'm not good at the whole 'polite society' thing," Amelia confessed. "And—you'll pardon me for the observation—but you seem to have a similar affliction. Can we enter a pact of nonjudgment?"

"A what?"

"A pact." She held out her hand. "I, Amelia Smith, hereby solemnly vow that I will not judge you simply because you are not perfect."

The boy stared at her hand for a while, then slowly held out his own. "I, Benedict Worth, hereby solemnly vow that I will not judge you, Amelia Smith, because you are not perfect."

They shook hands over this vow. The boy's hands were warm and rough against hers. Amelia nodded.

"First order of pact business—I don't remember your family name."

His mouth gaped. "But you've known me for weeks! And I just told you it!"

Amelia raised a finger. "That sounded suspiciously like judgment. I don't remember names. I don't know what it is about names; they just refuse to stick in my head, no matter what I do. So I may have to ask after it ninety-seven times before I actually learn it."

"I see." Benedict nodded. "As your liaison, can I suggest that we have everyone in the office put name cards at their desks?"

She blinked at him. "How?"

Benedict shrugged. "I'll just go down and say, 'Hullo everyone, Mrs. Smith is bad at remembering names, and so we'll all make her feel better if we just use name cards with profligate abandon.'"

"You can't just tell people that!"

"Why not?" He looked at her. "It's nothing to be ashamed of. Not everyone is good at names."

She was sputtering. "But—that—if we just tell them outright…"

"Then they'll know?" He seemed puzzled. "And will understand."

Don't tell me you're fine if you're not fine. It couldn't be that easy, could it?

"Captain Hunter made my duty very clear to me." He shrugged. "You've got an entire Chinese telegraphic code to work on. Why make you feel bad about not knowing names when we could just use cards to help you out? And if we're not in the office and I'm around, I can just whisper names to you when someone approaches."

"You can do that?"

His chest puffed out. "I can do that. I'm supposed to make your way easier so you can concentrate on the telegraphic work. It's really my only duty, but for—" He stopped and made a face.

"But for…," she prompted.

"It's not as bad as it sounds. You see, it's my next-eldest sister. The one who ran away."

Amelia tilted her head. It was the first non-treason-related thing she'd heard about his family. "She ran away?"

Benedict made an equivocal noise. "Technically, she took the Dowager Marchioness with her, so it was more like leaving England in the middle of the night without permission while still accompanied by a chaperone? But, yes. I've been sent to hunt them out and bring them back."

Amelia had no idea what he was talking about, but she perked up at this. "That sounds like fun. I don't know that I could help, but how is your Mandarin? If you need assistance with the Chinese language portions—"

"Stop!" He held out his hands. "No!"

She looked up at him. He colored, the pink blotches seeming so much fainter this time.

"I'm sorry for assuming. Your Mandarin must be quite good."

"It's horrid. Please and thank you. That's about it. Hopefully I'll learn more here." He shut his eyes. "I wish to do it myself. I'm the youngest of five, and everyone always thinks of me as a child. I want to do this by myself. I want it very much."

The sentiment wasn't nonsensical. It was the delivery that made her think there was something else to it.

"Mr.…" She paused. "Your name again?"

"Worth," he supplied. "Benedict Worth."

"Mr. Worth, you're not a very good liar, are you?"

He pointed at her. "You promised nonjudgment."

"I'm not judging. I'm just wondering why you're lying to me if I have already promised nonjudgment."

He mulled this over, looking away. "Did that sound very much like a lie then?"

"Yes."

"Oh." His nose wrinkled. "Drat."

"If I help you lie better, maybe you could do me a favor."

"Of course."

"What is his name?"

"Huh?" He looked around the room, as if searching for someone. "What is whose name?"

"Captain Hunter," Amelia said, feeling her forehead flush. "What is his Christian name?"

"Grayson." Mr. Worth looked—just a little bit—as if he might be judging her.

But it didn't matter. She took out a stub of pencil and wrote on a stray sheet of paper: *His name is Grayson Hunter.*

Next time she saw him—next time he touched her, next time he *kissed* her, if there ended up being a next time... Next time, she wanted to remember what to call him.

~

That afternoon, fresh out of Shanghai on the South China Sea, Grayson found himself at the Daily Disoccupation playing quoits. The *Celerity* held the materials for the game in a chest. They'd been improvised for play at sea over the years. Iron rings or horseshoes tended to slide off a tilting deck, striking people in the feet and occasionally falling into the sea. Instead, they threw loops of heavy rope.

They were on the first leg of the most important voyage of Grayson's life, and the crew was in good spirits, talking about what they would do after they'd finished that first line.

"I'm going to go home," said Abel, one of the seamen. "I'm going home and I'm eating Mama's cooking for three weeks straight. She'll have to roll me out of her kitchen."

"I've got a lady in San Francisco," said Wang.

"You've got a lady everywhere."

"Not true." Wang smiled. "I've a gentleman in London."

This was met with hoots.

On another ship, they might not have talked of such things. But Lord Traders had been founded by Grayson's great-great-great-uncles Henry and John almost a century past, and there had been no hiding what they were to one another. Crew who had problems with such things didn't get past the harbor, not on their ships.

"And what of you, Captain Hunter?" Lightfoot was less of an expert at quoits; only one of his rope loops had landed around the peg. "What are you doing?"

Bell shook his head. "He's on the *Victory.* Those poor sods. All the way back to San Francisco for the next load of cable; no time off, not for months."

"But after?"

After. Grayson stroked his chin pensively. "I'm going home for a week around Christmas, travel time depending."

This brought smiles, which told him it had been the right answer.

Lightfoot nodded. "Ah. I bet you're looking forward to that."

His answering smile was easy, reflexive, and all too false. It wasn't that he *wasn't* looking forward to it. It wasn't that he *didn't* want to go home. It was just that doing so was a stark reminder of everyone who was no longer there. He would have to go home and see the photograph his mother had had made of all her boys, crowded together and trying to hold their expressions long enough so the image would be captured properly. He already felt as if his life had been upended on *this* side of the Pacific. He didn't need upheaval on the other side.

But it was inevitable. He would have to talk to his mother. He couldn't do that anymore, not without remembering the look in her eyes when he'd told her about Noah.

That feeling of emptiness went both ways. If the absence of his brothers was palpable, at home he was always aware that he was not them.

The entire thing was a bramble of emotions, one he didn't know how to cut through. It had to be fixed; Zed had it right. He couldn't spend the rest of his life avoiding his family. He had to come home—truly come home at some point.

But before one could fix a thing, one had to have the right tools.

Once I finish the line across the Pacific, he told himself. *Once I make up for...*

He realized Lightfoot was still looking at him. That he'd asked a question, and that Grayson had smiled in answer without saying anything.

In the end, he didn't even have to lie.

"Yes," Grayson said. "I'm looking forward to it. I am very much looking forward to coming home."

He just wished it were possible.

~

Benedict Worth was a man on a mission.

Technically, at seventeen years of age, he was not yet what most people would call a "man." Also technically, given his actual intent, it wasn't what one should call a "mission." Nonetheless, when he entered the inn in the British Concession in Shanghai, he knew exactly what he was searching for. After years of pretending to look for it, he knew exactly how not to find it.

For instance, another person might have gone literally anywhere except this exclusive hotel.

Benedict, however, took a long look around the lobby. This was one of the hotels that was doing its best to be English with a capital E—so lushly, lavishly English that they hoped a British expatriate away from home would take one step inside and feel that fond nostalgia for their homeland. The furniture was adorned with ornate wooden curlicues, gilded and painted and upholstered in fabrics festooned with sheep and clouds and golden-haired shepherdesses. A large oil painting over the entrance was suggestive of Rembrandt without having his eye for color or light. Even the staff, dressed in crisp white uniforms and drowning in the humidity, did their best to evoke footmen.

"Sir," a bellman said, coming forward and taking in Benedict's English coat with his English lapels and his English trousers. "How can we be of assistance?"

He replied in his stuffiest English accent. "I say, my good fellow. I have some questions to put to you."

Having passed the language test, the man relaxed slightly. "But of course."

"I'm looking for a woman, a relative of mine." His neck felt overly warm in this heavy coat. How anyone bore it for any length of time, he would never know. "She's very young."

A tick. The bellman glanced at Benedict. He wasn't so gauche as to let emotions show on his visage, but after a pause, he spoke. "Younger than *you*? So, a *girl*, you mean."

Benedict felt a flush rise. "Maybe a year older than me," he muttered. "So, a woman, I suppose."

By now his sister Theresa *would* be a woman—old enough to marry if she wanted such a thing. If she had stayed in England, she would have been trotted out on the marriage market by his elder sister's mother-in-law. She probably would have had offers—Theresa had some money coming to her— and she would have turned them all down.

Running away had been the more straightforward option.

Instead of having to say no, no, no a thousand times, it had been one emphatic *no, and now you can't possibly stop me.* Benedict had been tasked with stopping her. To do so, he also had been compelled to leave Britain.

Well, if that's what it takes, he had said, trying to sound sincere. *Duty to my family above all else!*

Since everyone in Britain but his family hated him, it had been absolutely no hardship at all to volunteer to look for his sister. So long as he didn't *find* her, he didn't have to say no himself. No, I don't want to go to university. No, I don't want to marry one of these fine English maidens. No, I don't want to petition to take my father's title.

It was far simpler to search fruitlessly for Theresa.

Judith, his eldest sister, approved of Benedict's pointless quest and wrote him commiserating letters. All Benedict had to do in return is keep her apprised of what he was doing to not find her. So long as he never found her, they'd both be happy.

He gave the bellman a winning smile.

"She would have been accompanied by an elderly lady," he said.

The man waited for Benedict to continue. He waited a beat longer. After the silence had begun to stretch to uncomfortable lengths, the bellman spoke again. "Can you provide no other identifying characteristics?"

If anyone ever questioned Benedict about this particular tactic, he would have pointed out that identifying characteristics could be changed. He wouldn't put it past Theresa to have dyed her hair or some other ridiculous thing.

"The young woman is rather determined," he finally said because *downright dictatorial* would have been too specific. He should know; he had grown up with Theresa—or, as he had once called her—General Worth. He had been dragooned into her private army at the tender age of nine, and she had ordered him about for years. He still missed her.

194

"I see." The footman stared at him. "You're looking for a young woman and an old woman."

"Yes."

"Traveling together."

"Yes."

"With no other company?"

Benedict paused. "Probably not? But maybe so. I could not say."

"When might they have come through?"

"Sometime in the past three years?" He shrugged carelessly.

It was a miracle that the bellman did not actually hit him. "Sir." The man took a deep breath. "You could be describing dozens—no, *hundreds*—of people. Can you not narrow it down a bit more?"

Well, that was the entire point. Benedict was *trying* to describe as many people as possible.

He looked up, in apparent consideration. "Her nose looks like this?" Benedict inscribed a vaguely triangular shape in the air.

"Like a nose."

"Well, you know. Like *this* kind of nose." He repeated the triangular shape.

The bellman took a breath. He opened his mouth as if to speak, then inhaled once again. "Sir, my best advice to you is to speak to Secretary Larkin in the British Consul's office. He sees a great number of people on a regular basis; he's most likely to be of service to you in identifying these people."

"What excellent advice." Benedict cursed internally. "Thank you, my good man. There's obviously a lot that must be done here." Because he was trying to be incompetent and not a complete arse, he slipped the man a heavy coin. With a nod of his head, he left.

Outside, the sun had begun to heat the air in earnest. He could feel sweat begin to bead on his collar. This was the point where, if he were with another Englishman, they would exchange wry comments about the oppressiveness of the climate, the barbarousness of the humidity.

He was not with another Englishman. He was surrounded by them here in the British Concession, but he was—effectively—alone.

God, he loved not being in England.

It took ten minutes to return to the room he had let. It was outside the British Concession, near enough to the Lord Traders office that he'd be able to do his duties without much difficulty. A faint draft swept through the windows; he stretched out, positioned himself at a desk, found ink and paper, and began to write.

Dear Judith,

I have finally had a chance to get to Shanghai, and as you will see, there is much to do.

He smiled, thinking of the outrage the bellman had done his best to try to squelch. Benedict absolutely hated England; his search for his sister provided him with the best explanation for his continued absence.

I have asked about, and nobody seems to remember a woman of Theresa's exact description.

Because he had not given an exact description. That would be one possible reason nobody remembered her.

That being said, there are many who seem to recall someone who might possibly be her, depending on the occasion and concealment that she might have utilized.

Amazing what one could accomplish when one's description was "female, of some height, in possession of a nose."

I shall do my utmost to track those rumors to all corners of the earth.

Better to track ridiculous rumors, after all, than his actual sister. He added a few paragraphs about his personal well-being, then signed the letter with a flourish, blotting the paper and folding it up.

He hesitated a few moments before pulling out another sheet.

General Worth, he wrote. Most people would think this an odd way to address one's sister, but most people did not know Theresa Worth. If they had known her as Benedict did, they would have known she would be addressed as General Worth if she *wanted* to be addressed as General Worth. And she did.

It appears that I will be in Shanghai for at least a year or so. There may be intermittent visits to Hong Kong, so do not come to either place without informing me.

It was difficult work, *pretending* to search for his sister while *actually* being determined not to find her. In the beginning, Benedict had done too good of a job of it, and he'd actually caught up with her. Four months after he had left England, he'd encountered her in the lobby of a hotel in Bombay just as she was leaving.

"Oh for heaven's sake," Theresa had groused at him as she'd come up beside him. "This world is not large enough for the two of us!"

From someone else, those words would have been a threat. From her, it had been the simple truth.

They'd conducted a hasty, hushed meeting on the street outside the hotel and arranged a system of communication so they could most efficaciously avoid finding one another in the future. Theresa let him know she was not dead and sent him actual droll letters of her exploits months after she accomplished them.

Luckily Grayson hadn't been present to tattle on him to the rest of his family. Not that Captain Hunter would, but he wouldn't have seen it as tattling. Benedict was effectively a child on an apprenticeship. Judith asked for regular letters about her brother's performance, and even if Grayson didn't mention it to Judith, he wrote to his brother, Adrian, who was married to Camilla, one of Benedict's other sisters. Camilla and Judith talked. One could never be too careful.

Since Bombay, between Benedict's pretended incompetence in the search and his actual competence in warning his sister, they'd managed to avoid a repeat of their meeting.

He scrawled out a far more truthful, and amusing, description of how he had spent his day at the hotel before sealing up both his letters. They'd take months to arrive in the hands of his family, and by then, he'd have more non-news to deliver.

Until then... He thought of Mrs. Smith and Chinese telegraphy. He was going to be the best liaison who had ever liaised.

God, he loved not being in England.

CHAPTER SIXTEEN

The first few weeks of employment seemed to blur together. Amelia felt as if all of her time was occupied: settling into a home for her and Merry, making a list of what she needed, tentatively making decisions, panicking at the fact she had to make decisions, and then second-, third-, and fourth-guessing those decisions.

She sent her first letter to Grayson within three days—one that she'd mulled over at all hours of the night, hoping it would not make her sound too pathetic. She eventually transformed it into a twenty-word cipher with the help of Benedict.

Dear Captain Hunter, her original letter had read. *I have made a list of steps that I believe must be taken in order to fall within the timeline you have given me. In order to best accomplish this, we will have to hire two additional employees for the office. I hoped you would offer me some guidance in that regard. I had thought to provide the following criteria so you might comment as you saw fit...*

He had not yet started laying cable, according to Benedict. "It'll take a few days to send the letter to Hong Kong," he had explained, "and then a few minutes to wire to the coast of Japan. He'll answer before he leaves."

She received the telegram—one that had come from Japan to Hong Kong before being sent by courier ship to Shanghai—a week and a half later.

The telegram read in its entirety: *19.*

Dutifully, Amelia opened up the drawer where she had stored the stack of letters he'd given her. She hadn't looked at them since she'd received them; she couldn't think of them without thinking of the warmth of his hand against her cheek, the touch of his lips against hers, the scent of him, musky and slightly sweet all at the same time...

She was busy. She didn't have *time* for any nostalgic nonsense.

Yet upon looking at the unopened stack of letters, all that wistful emotion flooded back into her. She thumbed through the stack of envelopes. It took some time, as he had not given them to her in exact numerical order, a thing she found some-what offensive. She reordered the envelopes, retrieved number nineteen, commanded her heart to stop beating swiftly and her mind to stop remembering the taste of his lips on hers, and opened it.

Would there be reprimands? Would there be further information?

Mrs. Smith, his letter read, *you're doing very well. Carry on with what you believe you need. Benedict has been instructed to see to any details you need him to address.*

That was it? Her eyes narrowed. Carry on? Talk to Benedict? What if she were making a dreadful mistake? Would he even have told her?

Amelia looked up, then to the side, and threw her hands in the air. "Oh well," she told the telegram. "I suppose he shall have to bear the consequences of any of my mistakes."

∼

The rocky coast of northern Japan was still visible but swiftly receding, green and gray sliding into ocean caps. The shore line had been laid by the *Celerity;* the flow of current through the telegraph line to shore had been confirmed to cheers, and the second of three multiple-thousand-mile segments across the Pacific had been started.

It was after the Daily Disoccupation—Gray had accompanied the crew in celebratory tunes—when Lightfoot approached him.

"Captain Hunter?"

"Yes?"

"You asked me to tell you if the on-ship telegraphic system was functioning."

"Ah. Yes."

"It is." Lightfoot grinned. "Works like a charm. And I have a message for you already."

"Yes?"

Lightfoot looked at him. "It's from Mrs. Smith."

The engineer was watching him just a little too carefully. Mr. Lightfoot and Mrs. Smith had spent time together on the *Celerity.* Grayson had done his best to keep some kind of distance from them but… Perhaps they had talked? About him?

"Here," Lightfoot said, holding it out.

Talked about him. God, who cared if they had? Not he.

He grabbed the message. The first few words of the ciphered message read: *REPLEVIN ENCLOSURES…*

Grayson was going to have to consult his cipher notebook on this. Lightfoot may already have done so.

"Thank you," Grayson said. "Is that all?"

A tiny corner of Lightfoot's mouth ticked up. "I have nothing more for you."

It took him half an hour to decode Mrs. Smith's message. The Lord Traders commercial cipher was optimized for business messages, not for sending messages about Chinese telegraphy.

My problem now is how to handle enclosures within enclosures. The "end enclosure" signal is not specific—am I ending the first, larger one or the second, smaller one? The characters could go both ways. I don't expect you to answer this, but I need help—someone to talk these things over with, and Benedict scarcely understands Mandarin. Where should I go?

Grayson tried not to think of Mrs. Smith too often or too much. He definitely tried not to think of that kiss, of the feel of her lips on his, of how it had felt to give in to his wants…

It would be one thing to have sex. He'd done that before. He *liked* sex, liked being with someone and making them feel good. He liked knowing they both understood what they were to each other.

He did not understand what he was to her. If it had just been attraction, it wouldn't have mattered. But he found himself invested in her in a way that terrified him. There would be no kissing and agreeing that it meant nothing beyond a satiation of physical want.

He could scarcely even talk to his own family without guilt. There was no way to build something with a woman he had just met.

If he had encountered her in earlier times…

For a moment, he allowed himself to think about what it would have been like if they'd met one another back when he was more carefree. He might have teased her more. Complimented her. He might have found ways to stay in Shanghai so that he could answer her questions in person and watch her bloom.

He might have answered the questions he knew he shouldn't ask, like whether she blushed all over. He might have been able to have her, truly have her.

Deep down, he wanted it. He wanted her. He wanted to know her, to feel her, to—

He shook his head. It was ten years too late. She might have been a match for the person he had once been, but the man he was now? She was open. Vulnerable. Trusting.

He was very much not those things anymore. It was better that they spoke this way—separated by thousands of miles, she pouring out her questions to him, and he finding numbers that might illuminate her path forward in some tiny way. It was better for her to build a life without him.

He set down the missive he had decoded and went to his notes, looking for the right response. Not seven; not thirteen. There.

That was it. That was the number to send.

The response that Amelia received to her message from the prior week was *22*. When she opened that envelope, it read as follows.

I've given you authorization to hire who you need. Trust your instinct. Who do you want around you? What is it that your project will include? Find those people.

She stared at the page for a long while. She checked her notes on what she had sent, and then checked the number he'd transmitted and the number on the envelope.

It wasn't an answer to the question she had asked. It wasn't even close.

But it was *an* answer. Who did she want around her? What would the project include? Who did she want to be? Wistfully, she thought of turning a corner one day. Of seeing her mother down a long road...

No. She needed a new dream, a new connection. And that meant...

Maybe...that?

~

The Shanghai teahouse looked much the same as the last time Amelia had come on her prior visit. Last time she had been here, her head had been filled with the details of her coming project and the certainty of her own failure.

Today, it was midmorning. The rosewood furniture gleamed in the morning light, but the room was largely empty save for a few men in the corner.

Proprietor Zhu caught sight of her and came over, her tray full.

"You're back," Proprietor Zhu said, setting the tray in front of Amelia. "Good. You know how to make tea properly now."

It wasn't a question, but Amelia answered it as one. "Yes."

The woman nodded and left. *Where.* Where was here.

Amelia managed to use the gaiwan to get tea into a cup, her fingers only slipping a little as she held the lid in place and poured. She pulled a notebook out of her pocket and sketched. There were, she had discovered, four separate difficulties in encoding Chinese. First, her original idea wouldn't work. She'd assigned separate code values to each Chinese radical, but an English operator wouldn't know a Chinese code, making it impossible to use outside of China. So that was out. She'd have to use English characters as an encoding. It would mean sending telegrams outside China at the higher cipher rate, but that was inevitable.

Second, the—

The bench across from her seat scraped as Proprietor Zhu pulled it back, sitting across the table from her.

"Don't let the tea go cold," the woman scolded.

"Oh." Amelia gave her a bright smile. "I'm sorry. I was…" Lost in thought? She wasn't sure if the idiom would translate.

But Proprietor Zhu leaned over and pulled Amelia's notebook to her. She smiled at a doodle of Merry, frowned at the mess of characters Amelia had made.

"You're a scholar?" She sounded dubious as she looked Amelia over.

"No, I…" Amelia trailed off. She wasn't sure how much she should tell others. "Do you know what a telegraph is?" She used the English word for it.

The woman shook her head.

"It's—" Machine, machine, what was machine in Mandarin? She didn't know. "Some thingy that allows you to send a message very quickly. If I had a wire long enough, I could send a message to London that would arrive before you could blink twice."

"Every charlatan claims to have such a thing. Are you being scammed?"

"No." Amelia pinched the bridge of her nose. "This one truly works. I've seen it. I've used one to send messages from India to Hong Kong."

"Really! That far? So quickly?"

"They reach all over the globe now. The English use them all the time. You have to send the message by code, and I'm trying to work out a code for Chinese characters." Amelia's shoulders slumped. "It would be easier if I were more familiar with them."

"Ahh." Proprietor Zhu nodded. "So you *aren't* a Chinese scholar. You *need* a Chinese scholar."

"I. Um." Amelia looked at her. Captain Hunter had given her authority to hire employees and told her to do it as she saw fit. "Probably? I'm just not certain how to find one."

Proprietor Zhu stood and waved a hand. "Hey!" she called across the shop. "Scholar Wu! Yes, you. You were just complaining about not having enough to do now that you've reduced your teaching hours. And you like ridiculous things. Come take a look at this."

Amelia looked over at the woman. "Thank you, Proprietor Zhu."

The woman looked at her and shook her head. "Proprietor Zhu? You've come here twice now. Don't you know anything? You should call me Auntie Zhu. And don't thank me. This is a favor to me. He's always complaining about boredom. Now *you* can deal with him."

~

Shortly after that, Amelia got a note in the courier pile again.

32.

If you get this, we've used the system you and Lightfoot developed for a week without incident. Excellent work. You should be proud of yourself.

Proud of herself. It seemed such an odd concept, to be *proud* of herself. And yet. There it was. A flicker of happiness inside her. Amelia grinned, hugged the page to her chest, and then went back to work.

~

It had been six weeks since Amelia left Fuzhou. In that time she had sent four letters to her mother and received two in return. The one she held now would likely be an answer to the second letter she had sent.

That letter had come out of extensive soul-searching on her part. Captain Hunter's words before he took her to the tea shop had stayed with her, rankling in her soul. *Don't tell me it's fine if it isn't fine.*

She had thought herself generally truthful up until that point. But once he had said those words, she'd suddenly become aware of all the ways in which she lied. "I'm fine" was only the start. She had started a list of the lies she had told her mother, and they had been surprisingly extensive. "No, it doesn't bother me if I can't get a dog." "Of course it's no problem." "I'm willing to marry again." "I'd love to meet Mrs. Flappert."

It had shocked her sensibilities to discover that she was not only untruthful, she was a consummate, inveterate liar.

So in her second letter, she had tried being honest, turning each sentence over in her head until she was certain she was offering the truth and not the platitude her mother wished to hear. She'd written a heartfelt, honest letter. She had said that the work was hard but rewarding. For every three steps forward she took, there was one step back—sometimes two. She found herself thinking about the project at all hours, having it consume her thoughts. Benedict Worth had to remind her to take meals. She was wildly happy.

With trepidation, she opened the response and unfolded the page.

My dearest Amelia,

Between the lines of your letter, I am hearing a very different story. Sleepless nights thinking of soulless code, scarcely eating, making little progress... I can see you are putting a good face on it, but there's no need to do so with me.

She frowned at those words. She had tried so hard to be unflinchingly honest. Had she failed once again?

You and I both know that you're not suited to this sort of thing. Come home. I will never say a word of this endeavor again; I am sure we can still find someone to marry you if you like.

The letter was puzzling. Exceedingly puzzling. Had Amelia not been clear that she was happy? That for every step back, she took more forward? Did she need to be *more* clear?

She stared at her mother's words for half an hour, trying to bring to mind the letter she had sent. She'd struggled over it for long enough that she could recall large portions. There was no point in that letter in which she'd expressed unhappiness. Not one.

Where had she gone wrong? She could remember Captain Hunter telling her not to tell him it was fine if it wasn't fine. She could remember the shame that had filled her at those words. She could remember the list she'd made of the untruths she'd used to tell.

She had forgotten to ask herself one very important question.

What would have happened if she had said she *wasn't* willing to meet Mrs. Flappert?

She held her mother's letter in her hands and imagined it now. Not good. It would have been...not good.

Amelia stared at the letter a while longer before shutting her eyes. "Oh."

~

It was late at night when Lightfoot knocked on Grayson's door. Grayson had not yet gone to sleep, but he'd changed into loose trousers. Lightfoot had an entire sheet of paper in his hand.

"Captain Hunter." Lightfoot nodded in greeting.

"What is it, Lightfoot?"

"This one's quite long. Also, none of it was in cipher. It's..." Lightfoot held out the paper. "Sorry to be intruding on personal matters."

"Personal matters?" His mind jumped to the sorts of things that might be so urgent as to warrant a personal telegram across the ocean.

Some of his alarm must have shown because Lightfoot

shook his head urgently. "No, nothing like that. Just a little something from your sweetheart."

"My what?"

By way of answer, Lightfoot set the page in his hand.

Captain Hunter. I never did apologize to you for lying. I said it was fine and it wasn't. My mother told me to always tell the truth, and it pains me to realize I have fallen short. I have just realized that I was told to tell the truth, but when I did, my truth was not wanted. It has left my mind somewhat muddled. I am working to correct this flaw. Amelia Smith.

Grayson stared at this in bemusement. It was dark. He could hear the sound of waves around them. From his cabin, there was no chance of hearing the sound of cable slowly paying out, but he could imagine it, every click taking him farther from her, yet still staying this connected.

"My sweetheart?" he repeated.

"Are you questioning the first word or the second?"

Grayson thought about this. "Yes." His nose wrinkled. "Both. You spent more time with her aboard the *Celerity* than I did. Why is she *my* sweetheart?"

"Hmm." Lightfoot had a too-innocent look in his eyes. "Are you saying that she could be *my* sweetheart instead? I'll keep that in mind next time I'm in Shanghai."

His immediate response—that wash of jealous indignation —must have shown. He made himself unclench the fists he'd made at his side, relax his eyebrows, and let out a deep breath.

Lightfoot just laughed. "That's why, sir."

Gray shook his head. "I just want a worldwide telegraphic network. Is that so much to ask for?"

Lightfoot gestured to Amelia's telegram in Grayson's hand. "And look what it will be like once we get there."

Amelia had already regretted the lengthy, abject missive she'd sent to Captain Hunter. She wanted to send another: *Just forget I said anything.*

But while she was stewing over how to word that, a reply arrived.

46.

This would be the "no, you fool" envelope. Or the "hold your tongue for important matters" envelope. She was certain of it. She opened the paper with shaking hands.

Don't blame yourself for the failure of others. I am satisfied with what you are doing.

CHAPTER SEVENTEEN

In bed that night, Amelia tried to make sense of Captain Hunter's last message. She'd gone back through her record of the letter she had sent to him. She had cross-checked the reply number. But Captain Hunter's *don't blame yourself for the failure of others* had definitely been sent in response to her missive about saying she was fine. She traced the words she had sent: *I was told to tell the truth, but when I did, my truth was not wanted.*

She *had* told Captain Hunter the truth. Embarrassingly so. On multiple occasions. She could remember standing on a deck in Fuzhou harbor and blurting out that she was attracted to him.

She could remember the look he'd given her. The way he'd smiled and said that she had good taste, that yes, he *was* very attractive.

It had been arrogant. It had been conceited.

But it hadn't made her feel ashamed. He'd not poked fun at her for daring to think she might like him. As outrageous as he'd been at the time, he had actually been very kind about it.

It felt particularly kind in comparison with what Amelia

was used to. Those two things went hand-in-hand, she realized. The expectation that she would give him the truth depended on his not making her feel like a fool for doing so.

It felt like a very honest sort of connection. The sort of relationship she'd had with Leland, but without any of the fraternal companionship.

He never would, but if Captain Hunter ever blurted out an embarrassing truth about himself, Amelia would want to treat it kindly, rather than making him feel as if he had to hide away.

Thoughts of one kind of intimacy, indulged at night in her bed, led to thoughts of another. Captain Hunter's kiss…

It wasn't the first time she'd thought of it at night. It wouldn't be the last. She clung to the memory of contradictory pieces of it—the softness of his lips, but the firmness of his hold on her. The way her thoughts had all seemed to come to a standstill, compared to the way they fluttered about her now.

Someone like him, someone who valued honesty… He would be very different than her husband had been. He wouldn't want her lying in bed calculating how long he would take, hoping he would finish soon, wishing he hadn't interrupted her in the middle of a book.

Someone like him would see to her. He'd care about what she thought. He'd want to know if his touch was too rough or too gentle.

As she thought, her hand crept between her legs.

It wasn't the first time for that, either. Touching herself left Amelia confused and frustrated, as if there were something she were missing, but didn't know to look for and couldn't remember how to find. It felt like a name on the tip of her tongue, as if the introductions had been made once but she'd long forgotten what to call out.

Maybe it was wrong to imagine the rough pads of his fingertips against herself, but would he truly mind, if he knew? If he wanted her, he'd touch her there, just like that. When she said *please, a little harder*, he wouldn't ignore her. Yes. Just like that. He had more experience than her; likely, he'd have more imagination than her, touching her—there. Her other hand crept around her nipple, brushing it between thumb and forefinger, feeling a spark go through her.

There. The hand between her legs crept down. There? Her fingers slipped inside her, and when that didn't seem to do anything, crawled up, pressing—oh. There. *There.* Her circling thoughts pulled in, electrified, and she pushed the palm of her hand against that spot.

Once she had started down this road, what followed came easily. The flicker of pleasure grew to a bonfire. She swallowed the noises she wanted to let out. This, this. Was *this* what it could be like?

She had the sense of chasing something—reaching for it—

Her back arched as pleasure filled her in an electrifying circuit. Her mind went white; her hand slipped against that spot, faster, faster, until it was too much and she could do nothing but press into her own flesh and let out a cry as a sheer wave of delight passed through her.

Her breath was unsteady. Her hands were a mess. She felt alive, open, filled with light.

"Oh my God," she whispered into the night.

Her body could do *that*? Her heartbeat sounded heavy in her own ears. Her body could do *that*, and nobody had told her.

"Oh my God," she repeated. She was going to have to do some reading.

~

I t had taken more than a month, but Benedict Worth had finally exhausted all the useless leads he had generated. He'd tracked down twenty-seven separate blond ladies— ranging in age from twelve to forty-three—none of whom were his sister, half of whom weren't even British.

There was only one thing left to do, and—alas—it was the thing a competent searcher would have done from the beginning. Which was how he found himself waiting in the consular office in the heart of the British Concession in Shanghai. A salt breeze blew in from the sea; he could scent it coming in through the open window. The September weather was warm and clear. A beautiful day for a pointless conversation.

The door opened behind him; Benedict rose, nodding to the man.

Benedict had been years out of England now and had spent most of that time with Captain Hunter. His ability to judge the deference owed to someone of a different social station had once been knife sharp. That sense had now dulled to a useless blob of barely remembered facts. He was no longer sure whom he was supposed to treat as his better and who he was supposed to assume was beneath him. The result was that he made it all up as he went along and inevitably made everyone British despise him a little.

His nod, he realized from the way the man stiffened, had been a little too deep.

Benedict Worth was the son of an earl. He shouldn't even have stood.

The man in front of him crossed behind the desk, sat, steepled his fingers and stared at Benedict. His hair was jet black, and there was so much of it—running from the curled mass on the top of his head down through beard and sideburns. The depth of that color seemed out of place next to skin as pale as the underbelly of a salmon. His eyes were a startling, piercing blue, and he was looking at Benedict as if examining a bit of refuse found on the bottom of his boot.

Ah. One of *those.* A stickler for order. Well. Maybe Benedict could be incompetent. Annoying him would undoubtedly make the visit less productive. Benedict slouched back in his chair lazily.

The man's nose twitched.

All the better if he didn't like Benedict. It's not as if Benedict *wanted* assistance in his search. "Hullo there!" Benedict said cheerily, upsetting things further. "You must be Consul Secretary Larkin."

The man glanced at the brass nameplate on his desk. "A stunning conclusion to draw. Bravo."

Benedict had been told to seek out Consul Secretary Larkin nineteen separate times. Larkin knew everyone and everything that passed through the British quarter, he was told. The people he'd talked to used phrases like *keen mind* and *stands on principle* and *maybe stands a little too much on principle* to describe him.

"I was told to ask you about a personal matter."

Another twitch of Larkin's nose at this. "Sir. This is a *consular* office."

Benedict bulled ahead. "I am searching for a lady."

Larkin flattened his hands against the desk. "I don't assist in procurement, if *that's* what you're asking. The rules on such are set by the treaty between Britain and China, and the regulations promulgated by—"

"Oh no," Benedict interrupted, realizing suddenly what the man must have meant by procurement. "Not *that* sort of lady. Nor that sort of looking. I'm looking for my sister."

"Ah." Larkin's face seemed to grow darker. "She's not here."

Benedict looked around the office. "You mean she's not in China at all?" Another thought occurred to him. "You know who Lady Theresa is? Has she been here?"

She hadn't told him she was in Shanghai, but Theresa was Theresa.

A climbing vine of some sort had been trained up a lattice in the corner; little flowers bloomed on the edge. Benedict frowned. Not telling him where she was? That *would* be just like her.

"She's not at the *consulate*," Consul Secretary Larkin replied with annoying precision. "This office lacks jurisdiction over the entirety of China, and I am unable to speak beyond the purview of the consul."

"Well," Benedict said, more sarcastically than he intended. "Thank you. That's most helpful of you."

The man sniffed. "You're welcome."

This was going wonderfully. A complete shamble, of course, which was perfect for his needs. Benedict looked at the man. He knew he should leave, but...

"But you know who she is," he said slowly. "You didn't say anything about that. *Has* she been here? You must have some customs records of who has passed through the British Concession. Might I look through the records to see if she is using an assumed name I might recognize?" That would take weeks. Judith would be delighted at this assiduous point-lessness.

"No," Secretary Larkin said. "You may not."

"No?" Benedict repeated. It wasn't a problem; he didn't *care* if he got to see the paperwork at all. It was downright delightful that the man was throwing up obstacles—Judith would *also* commiserate at his hard work in the face of such obstinacy.

"No," the man said again. "You see, I not only know who your sister is, I know who *you* are."

"You should. I left my name with the consulate when I made the appointment."

"I am not referring to your name. I am referring to your

personality. Your father was a traitor. Your brother was a traitor. You are..." Larkin trailed off, his eyes not moving from Benedict, and Benedict felt cold wash down his spine. "You are apparently the sort of brother who misplaces a sister and spends a good month desultorily asking ridiculous questions of everyone who has no reason to know anything and no questions of anybody who might actually know. It does not speak well of your character. What are you playing at?"

It had been so *long* since Benedict had been in England. So long since those doubts had been cast his way. He found himself leaning forward in his seat.

"All of that is true. But the treason happened *years* ago. I was *six* when it transpired. I don't remember my father or my brother—not either of them, not in the slightest. The only thing I remember is my compatriots at Eton threatening me with nooses. So thank you *very* much for the reminder."

Larkin acted as if he hadn't spoken. "Your brother was a traitor, and now you're working with an American. Your sister is supposedly missing, and it provides you with a convenient reason to sift through consular records. My suspicions as to you are not without foundation."

"Yes, British people were just *clamoring* to work with a seventeen-year-old whose family was tainted by treason."

"You've been making ham-handed inquiries for far too long now. Odd, that you should prove so incompetent. What, precisely, is your sister doing? And what are you *pretending* to do with your insistent questions?" The man raised an eyebrow, as if to insinuate Theresa was gallivanting around the world, committing treason wherever she passed.

To be fair, Benedict wouldn't put it past her. But still. He had to stand on principle.

"Odd," Secretary Larkin continued, "that you should prove so absolutely incompetent. It makes me think your incompetence is a front."

Benedict pushed back his chair. "I don't believe I have to sit here and listen to you insult me and my family."

"You don't have to sit here at all," Larkin said. "You're free to leave up until I uncover the merest whiff of criminal conspiracy. I keep the British settlement in Shanghai clear of this sort of trouble, Mr. Worth." He articulated that title—*Mister*—with a hint of venom. "So take care. I won't help you. I don't want you here—not at the consulate, not in the British Concession, not in any part of the foreign settlement in Shanghai in general or in China at large. I think you should leave all four. Immediately."

Benedict bit his lip, stung. "And to think I was told you were fair to a fault."

The ghost of a smile slipped across the man's lips. "How lovely. I *am*."

CHAPTER EIGHTEEN

Dearest Leland,

    I'm intrigued to know how your students have got on with the geometry curriculum that you mentioned several weeks ago. I'm passing on a newspaper article for them to read, which I realize is ridiculous as Hong Kong receives the papers before Shanghai, but nonetheless, ridiculousness is happening.

    If I do my work well, I might one day be able to send you a telegram from my desk and have it arrive in your hand in less than an hour. I'll wager you never thought your little sister would be involved in something like that!

~

Dearest Mother—

    My apologies. You are right that I've communicated little in my last three letters except for information about my employment. Unfortunately, I still have nothing personal to add. I must assure you that this is not because I am angry, nor is it because someone has led me down the primrose path and I feel shame. It is because I am actually not doing anything but employment.

I shall take your admonishment for advice and shall try to do something else. The salary I am being paid is entirely adequate to hiring someone to help with meals and cleaning, and that may leave me a little more time.

Yours,

Amelia

~

To: Captain Grayson Hunter
Tasks I have completed
1 Encode radicals as English letters and numbers, reserving I, T, and E. I and T extend the remainder of the alphabet. J, JI, JT, JIT, JTI all represent separate radicals.

2 E reserved for joins. EBL equals character made by sun plus moon. E is for horizontal joins. ET for vertical. EI for contains.

3 New priority rules allow for encoding and decoding via inspection. Wins 10 to 1 in comparison to simplified numerical method

Incomplete

4 Code still underdetermines characters

5 Transmission errors radically change meaning

Your thoughts desired

~

Mr. Lightfoot had transcribed this barely comprehensible message from Amelia that afternoon aboard the *Victory*. It was a beautiful day. This far north, the light across the waves was golden and slanting, hinting at a winter that had not yet arrived.

They were maybe a week out from Myriad Island at this point, and the message had taken close to an hour to come through. It was terse—it would have taken poor Lightfoot hours to manage anything longer—and so it took Grayson fifteen minutes to understand what she was saying in general terms. They had a code. It worked. It was fast—as much as ten times faster than the alternative.

The code was not yet perfect. She was asking him if he had any thoughts on a code that she had developed entirely in his absence.

There could be only one reply.

~

The telegraph Amelia received from the courier went as follows: *4.*

Dutifully, Amelia opened up the envelope marked 4.

Mrs. Smith, I trust that you understand the intricacy of the issues far better than I ever would; rely on your own judgment.

"Thank you," she muttered to herself. "That's very helpful. *Very* specific."

"Mrs. Smith?" asked Scholar Wu.

Well. If he thought she wasn't heading for a cliff... "He approves of our direction," she said in Mandarin. "Let's go through some of the examples you have of underdetermination."

~

"Auntie Zhu," Amelia said one midafternoon in the tea shop. "We need to test our telegraphic system."

The woman paused while slipping a treat to Merry under the table, tilting her head in puzzlement. "What does that have to do with me?"

"Would you like to help?"

Her look of confusion grew. "What do *I* know about telegraphic messages?"

"Nothing," Amelia said. "That's the point. We need to see how people *want* to use the system, so we can evaluate what's happening. Think of someone far away you'd like to talk to. Imagine the sort of message you might send to them, and we'll see how our code system handles it. It's only a simulation. Without an actual telegraph line, we won't know for sure."

Auntie Zhu gave Amelia a quizzical look. "Sounds like a lot of work."

"We are paying."

"In that case." Auntie Zhu straightened, all business. "When do you need me?"

~

Dearest Leland,

I know not quite how to raise this matter, but I shall head straight into the breach. Is Mother driving you to the brink of despair? Perhaps even over it? I know it's horrid to say such a thing, but it feels as if there is nothing I can say in my letters that will reassure her of my continued well-being. Every letter I send has her writing in response that I must clearly hate her for some perceived fault of hers that I have not, in fact, perceived.

Am I truly so horrible a daughter?

~

Dearest Mother,

Thank you for your latest letter. As always, it brings me great joy to hear from you, and I will endeavor to answer the point you raised with some alacrity, as you appear to be in some distress.

To answer your query, no, I have not "gone native"—you may recall that I was born native, so to speak, and so I only ever went British, which in China is a foreign nationality. When I told you that

I was using chopsticks on a regular basis and that I had hired a Chinese woman to cook for me, I did not intend for you to see this as a rejection of your upbringing. You must know that I am still deeply grateful for everything you have done for me. I had not realized that I had left the question of my sincere affection for you in such doubt.

I know you are apprehensive for me. That it comes from a place of love. I can only send all my reassurances that you have my affection forever, whether I use a fork, chopsticks, or a machete.

∽

Dearest Leland,

Thank you for your advice on how to approach Mother. I do not know if it will relieve you to hear that it worked as well for me as it did for you, which is to say not at all.

I would fret over it substantially more, but I am far too busy.

∽

The day they connected the line at Myriad Island was a time for celebration. The telegraph worked, and Grayson knew he should feel something like excitement. But there was too much to be done to think of what it meant to be closer to his goal.

Unfortunately, Grayson had people thinking for him. The *Celerity* helped ready the *Victory* for the journey back south. They finally got on their way in the late afternoon, and Captain Ellis let the seamen choose the songs for the Daily Disoccupation.

But after the sixth song about missing love and the seventeenth slightly pointed comment, accompanied by a snigger in his direction, Grayson set down his violin and gave up.

"Is this supposed to be some sort of commentary?" he asked the crew.

One man snickered. Another nudged the other.

"Go ahead, Lightfoot," said Chief Engineer West, and Lightfoot shook his head, leaving Mr. West with no choice but to clear his own throat, take off his hat, and face Grayson with a somber expression.

"We're with you, Captain Hunter," he said solemnly. "In your time of need."

"My time of need?" Grayson made a face. "What do you imagine I'm needing?"

"All those messages with your woman," said one of the seamen, shaking his head. "Now that we've left Myriad and have no cable anymore, you won't be able to exchange sweet nothings."

Grayson let out a surprised puff of air. "Sweet nothings. Is that what you think I've been trading?"

One seaman turned to the other. "Seventeen." His delivery was gruff and forbidding. Grayson did *not* sound like that. Well. Hm. Mostly did not sound like that.

The other batted his eyelashes and simpered back. "Seventeen, Captain. Please. *Seventeen* me right here."

The last message he'd had from Mrs. Smith had indicated that she was beginning to do short tests on a twelve-foot-long telegraphic line set up in the office. *Seventeen* had been *good work, good luck, I look forward to hearing from you later.* He'd added a line indicating he was at Myriad and any further messages would take substantially longer.

Grayson sighed. "Ah, I see. It's jealousy. You want me to tell you about my woman."

They clearly hadn't been expecting anything other than gruff denial in response to their ribbing because they leaned in as one, delighted expectation on their faces.

"My woman..." Grayson looked off over the stern of the ship. Myriad Island was just behind them, but the rock was so small he could no longer see it. "My woman has eyes like fire and hair so long it could wrap around the world."

"That's it, Captain," Chu called. "Give us more of that."

"She's soft-spoken," Grayson said, "but when she has something to say, you can hear her clear across the ocean."

"Such a gentleman." This was said in a mournful tone.

"What about her thighs, Captain?" This ribald request was decidedly *not* mournful.

Grayson ignored them all. "She's a jealous lover and brooks no competition. She's demanding—she'll want me to bring her to completion as soon as I can."

That brought out the hoots and calls.

Grayson stroked his chin, pretending to remember some heated tryst. "And if I don't, she'll leave me for the British."

Silence. Out of the corner of his eye, he could see two men exchange confused glances.

Mr. West spoke first. "That doesn't sound good, Captain."

Lightfoot spoke up for the first time since they'd started. "He's talking about his telegraphic network. Hair that can wrap around the world? Hear her clear across the ocean? Needs to be completed as soon as possible?"

Groans all around. "Captain!"

"I thought we were going to get us a *good* story."

Grayson turned to face them. "A good story? I'm telling you the *best* story. It's the one you're in, fellows. And she's the only woman I have in mind. I'm making her a wedding ring of copper wire stretched across the seas. There will be no rest for me until I've satisfied her down to the toes."

Another silence stretched.

"If Captain Hunter isn't looking for a woman of the human persuasion," said one man out of the crowd, "you all know what that means, right?"

Grayson grimaced. "Don't say it like *that*. That makes it

sound as if I'm looking for—" But they were already talking over his protest. "Never mind."

"It means more for the rest of us!" called a sailor.

And with that, they started in on a ribald song involving two women and their nineteen lovers.

~

Three days into Amelia's telegraphic tests found Auntie Zhu at the table in the Lord Traders office. "Right," Amelia said. "What message would you like to send? Start with the person."

"To my husband. Mr. Zhu."

Amelia had not known there was a Mr. Zhu. She tried not to look too interested. "The, um, substance of the missive?"

"It has been five years since last I saw you," Auntie Zhu narrated mechanically, as if she were reciting from memory. "I have a tea shop now. It is profitable. I have heard the American railway is finished. I miss you."

She said this all without blinking, looking straight ahead. Amelia looked at her.

"Your husband worked on the American railway?"

Auntie Zhu shrugged. "He left to do so."

"And he hasn't returned?" Her voice was softer.

A shake of Auntie Zhu's head.

Amelia was supposed to ask for an address, but it felt impolite. "I suppose we should direct it to someone in San Francisco?"

Auntie Zhu shook her head. "Send it to Hell. That's where I think he is."

She used the English word—Hell—and Amelia did her best not to smile awkwardly at this.

"Um. Do you mean that he is in Diyu?" she asked in Mandarin.

"That's what I said. Hell."

Hell was a perpetual cross-cultural mistranslation. Christian missionaries had told the Chinese that all non-Christians went to Hell. But the Chinese had taken that to mean that the word "Hell" was the English translation for the Chinese afterlife. They'd adopted the word without any of the negative connotations.

"You know…" Amelia looked over at Auntie Zhu. "Even after our wire goes into service, I don't think Diyu will have a telegraphic station."

"But you explained it to me," Auntie Zhu said. "Isn't the telegraph like little bursts of fire going down a wire?"

"Eh…" Now was not the time to explain electrical current. "Figuratively. Yes. In a manner of speaking."

"Well then." Auntie Zhu made a little gesture with one arm. "It sounds like the message already goes to Diyu. I think Mr. Zhu is probably already in Hell. This way, I can talk to him." She turned and gave Amelia a smile. "You should try it."

"But who would I talk to?" Amelia asked.

Auntie Zhu just looked at her. And Amelia knew.

Long after the test had been completed, after Amelia had collected data on the length of time it took to encode the message and send it, after she'd looked at the decoding on the opposite end and identified that it had operated as expected, after everyone had left the office…

Long after the sun had gone down, she stayed, sitting at her desk.

What she was about to do felt wrong. When she was younger, when they'd passed shrines or temples and Amelia had wanted to go in and explore, her mother had jerked her along.

"Thou shalt have no other gods before me," her mother had reminded her. So Amelia had done her best to apply her curiosity to the Bible, where she was told it belonged.

Ever since coming to Shanghai, she'd been failing at multiple commandments. Keeping the Sabbath day holy was one of the most prominent ones. She'd been working most Sundays, a thing that became easier to do after she attended her first Anglican service and was asked by no fewer than six separate people whether she had intended to go to the missionary classes instead. No, really. Perhaps that was where she belonged.

Her curiosity about those temples, her questions about the incense she'd seen, all had been wrong. She was now going to do something that felt wrong, too. It also felt necessary.

She had imagined how she might meet her Chinese mother for years. That feeling had intensified since coming to Shanghai. She would walk down a street and find herself temporarily alone, the crowds dissipated, and the space would feel oddly disorienting. Or she'd make her way home at night and catch sight of a woman at the other end of the street, face obscured in darkness. Her heart would jump. Someone would come into Auntie Zhu's shop and speak in Shanghainese. After the first few months speaking with Auntie Zhu and the other customers, Amelia had found herself gradually understanding what they said.

She'd been born near Shanghai, hadn't she? Probably? If she were truly from here, shouldn't her understanding of the dialect have come more quickly?

In those moments, she felt on the edge of some unseen boundary. She would turn and stare, her heart beating wildly, thinking *finally* and *she's here.* Shanghai felt like a transitional space, one that stood between the child she had been and the woman she could become.

A makeshift telegraph line had been constructed inside the

office for the test. One end was situated upstairs in her office, the other downstairs in the room off the entry. All Amelia had to do to make it work was to attach the battery they used to power it. She sat in front of the apparatus and collected her thoughts.

How should Amelia address her telegram? Should she be formal, speaking to a woman she couldn't remember? Should she call her "Chinese mother," as Amelia did in her head?

What came to mind was this: *Ah Ma.* It was what she'd heard young children calling their mothers on the streets. It was a word with weight to it, a word imbued with affection and the certainty of an answer. She wasn't sure she had any right to use it.

Still, her fingers flew on the encoding. *Ah Ma.* EQEICZ EBTWI. *I have waited to know you my entire life.* That want rose up in her now, the bitter wrapping around the empty. She tapped again, letting all those feelings—the anger, the sadness, the hollowness, the wrongness—be converted into disruptions in the flow of electric current, sent out into nothingness.

You said you were going to come back. Why didn't you? Why wasn't I enough to come back to?

Her fingers fell from the transmitter and she waited in silence. Footsteps crunched outside the office. She heard the dim murmur of voices in passing. It was closing in on October, and the crickets, an ever-present chorus through the spring and early autumn, had fallen to one solemn voice in the evening. The eaves of the office building creaked around her. Merry stirred where she lay, then stood, stretching, walking to Amelia, claws clicking on the floor.

Nothing more. Just those mundane noises.

Maybe Amelia's Ah Ma was in Diyu waiting for Amelia, who would never make it to the Chinese afterlife. Maybe she was separated from this world by a dielectric gap so small that this interrupted current could leap over it. Maybe it was so large that Amelia would never pass over.

It was there, sitting in her office, that Amelia finally accepted the inevitable.

She was never going to see her Chinese mother again. There would never be a time when she rounded a corner in Shanghai and saw a woman from her past. Her only connection with where she came from was the code she'd made.

She was eternally going to stand with one foot in the British rules she'd been raised in the other in the Chinese community she didn't quite belong to. She had to accept that this was the case. She had to make it work, or she was going to be miserable her entire life.

She shut her eyes. Maybe this blow, soft as it was, urging her to make her peace with herself, was as close to communication as Ah Ma could manage from Diyu. Apparently, she was going to straddle two communities for the remainder of her life.

There was nothing to do about it but learn balance.

Amelia exhaled. "Come, Merry," she finally said, standing. "Let us go."

CHAPTER NINETEEN

The journey down to San Francisco aboard the *Victory*, and the subsequent train voyage across the American continent, was longer and more grueling than Grayson had expected. He missed Christmas at home through no fault of his own this time, sending an apologetic telegram out of Omaha two days before he arrived home. He managed to make up a day by wheedling and bribery, and that was how he arrived at his parents' home on a quiet afternoon when nobody was expecting to see him.

Their home was on the edge of town, which was a relief. If he'd had to go through the village where assorted cousins and workers and longtime family friends lived, he would have gathered a clamoring entourage. He didn't think he could handle that.

He opened the door, silently letting himself in, swapping his snow-crusted boots for a pair of slippers waiting nearby. Then he padded into the kitchen where he could hear voices.

They didn't see him as he stood in the doorway. His youngest brother, Adrian, was present alongside his wife. It had been years since he'd last seen Adrian.

Adrian had always been something of a homebody, particularly in contrast to Grayson. More like their father, less like their uncles.

Now Adrian was here, holding his first child in his arms, shushing her and bouncing her on his hip while his mother looked on, cooing from one side, and his father sat at the other, making exaggerated faces.

Grayson had heard about his niece by letter. He stood in place, exhaling slowly.

He loved children. He especially loved other people's children. Half his valise was made up of toys for little Henrietta. This tended to confuse people because there had never been a point where he'd actually wanted his own child.

Part of that was because he was inherently a wanderer. He'd had go-fever since he was able to walk. He'd listened to his uncles' stories of their travels with big eyes and an even bigger yearning. He'd begged to be allowed to come along even before he could possibly be allowed to do such a thing.

At the age of seven, he'd tried to sneak on board his great-great-uncle John's ship. He had succeeded too—or at least, he had thought he had succeeded. An hour after the ship had pulled out from harbor, his great-great-uncle had found him in his hiding place.

"Well," Uncle John had said, looking up at Grayson's startled, pleading eyes, "do you want to see your bunk?"

He had discovered that his mother had packed his things for the short journey and written him a letter saying that if he was going to sneak off, he might as well do it properly.

He had, apparently, not been as sneaky as he'd thought he was. Ever since that time, it had been a constant struggle between them, inasmuch as his mother ever struggled. She asked him to stay, allowed him to leave, and sighed when he grew restless. If she'd had her way, all her boys would have stayed home forever and surrounded her with grandbabies. Now she had only Adrian for that.

They looked happy here. For a moment, he could watch them laughing and cooing over the baby, his heart a tangle, feeling outside the circle of their love.

Then his mother looked up.

She hadn't had a chance to prepare for the sight of him, and he remembered an instant too late that this was going to be a problem. She turned to look at him. Her eyes widened. And in that first instant—before the smile, before the greetings—he saw a flash of something pass through her eyes.

His mother was English. It had been a hell of a shock for her, moving to America, moving to be with his father's side of the family. His cousins and uncles and aunts tended to be direct and plainspoken—exactly the opposite of how his mother had been raised. She'd grown used to it, somewhat, but she was never going to be the sort of voluble person who told him exactly what she thought at all times.

Grayson had grown up with her. He'd learned to infer her emotions. Unfortunately, he was far too good at it.

"Grayson," she said. "You're here early."

His father was *not* English. He jumped up from his seat, barreling across the room, folding Grayson into a hug. Adrian got up gingerly, his child in his arms, and came to stand beside him.

"Merry late Christmas," Adrian said, touching shoulders to avoid squishing little Henrietta between them.

"I'm sorry I couldn't quite make it in time. I ended up delayed by travel. I had to cross the country, second class by rail—"

"Not first?" His mother interjected.

Grayson let out a long sigh. "I *bought* first. I was put in second."

Adrian made a face. His father sighed. But his mother… Her eyes flashed in something like resentment.

How well Grayson knew what resentment looked like on her.

"Intolerable," she said. "And this isn't the first time we've heard of this." A slash of her hand indicated who her *we* encompassed—the world of people she was connected with who were like-minded. "Your father and I have been donating to a subscription for legal challenges to such practices. If you'd like, we could—"

Grayson cut this off with a wave of his hand. "Mama, I'm too busy making my own network to be bothered with the problems from someone else's."

John might have done it, if he were still here. He was the sort to appreciate such intricate machinations. But Grayson hardly trusted the courts that had given the country *Dred Scott* to treat transportation fairly, no matter what the law supposedly said. Better to make something for himself.

His mother sighed. "Go wash up. Let me get us some tea before we are inundated with cousins."

By the time Grayson had returned from the washroom, tea was served, and Adrian was back, sans baby. Camilla, his wife, was putting her down, he said; they had a little time. Just for themselves—him, Grayson, their parents.

"We're looking for a property," Adrian said. "We may move back here now that everything is settling down."

God. His mother must love that. Grayson was happy that she had someone to love. Truly he was.

His mother leaned over and set a hand on Grayson's knee. "I'm so glad you've taken a week from your busy schedule to see your family."

Here was the thing about having a mother who had been raised to express herself in the politest terms possible. When she was angry, *this* was how she sounded. One had to be attuned to her every nuance to recognize that statement for what it was: a thorough denunciation of the way Grayson spent his time.

"Mama." Grayson thought about apologizing, but he'd been raised to believe apologies were meaningless without changed behavior, and he didn't know how to change. "We're behind schedule as it is."

"Schedule?" She glanced at the clock ticking against the wall. "You're in charge. I thought *you* set the schedule. Why would you set a schedule so that you would be so behind it that you couldn't even see your family?"

Here in this room, with one other brother and room for so many more, with his mother and the resentment he occasionally caught behind her eyes...

Here, he could have said it. *Harry set the schedule; I can't abandon Harry's schedule.*

But he hadn't talked to his family about his brothers, not since the day he'd come home alone and had his mother ask why Noah wasn't with him. He hadn't been able to do it.

Instead, Grayson leaned over and kissed his mother's forehead. "Mama, I know how hard it is for you to have..." He couldn't even say *that*—how hard it was to have only two sons now. He changed his words. "It's been hard on you, having a son who wanders the world."

Her eyes shivered shut. "Gray." Her hand found his. "Don't worry about how hard it is on *me*."

Of all his parents' sons to survive the war, it had to have been Grayson who did it. He wasn't loving and ebullient like Harry. John enjoyed a bit of travel, but he'd been more interested in politics—at home or abroad, he'd taken after his father in that regard.

His mother had never said it—she would never have mentioned it—but Noah had been her favorite, so bright and full of life and enthusiasm for the entire world that everyone couldn't help but love him with all their heart.

Grayson was the one who didn't want children of his own. Who never wanted to rest in any one place. He knew his mother loved him. He also knew—although she would never say it—he was her least favorite son.

When he had come back from the war—when he realized the letter he'd sent informing his family of his brother's passing had never arrived, when he'd had to tell her in person that Noah had died of a fever in his arms—he had seen that now-familiar flash of resentment. It had been her first response, before tears, before sorrow.

He might as well have heard her words: Why *you?* Because if she'd had to pick one son to survive, Grayson knew it would never have been him. Not that he blamed her for it; if he'd had a choice in the matter, he'd have done anything in his power to have his brothers come home instead.

Matters had only grown worse when they held a service for his brothers. Grayson had been supposed to speak. He'd had hours of stories he could have told—things that only he knew, stories of what his brothers had done, what they'd planned together—and yet standing there in a crowd humming with expectation, he'd somehow not been able to utter a word. Not one.

He'd turned and left, and that had only made the gulf grow.

There was a reason he didn't make it home as often as he should. The emptiness. The quiet. But most of all, the knowledge that no matter how much his mother loved him—and she did love him—he always reminded her that with any justice in the world, it would have been someone else who survived. And his mama loved justice.

"I don't worry," Grayson told her. "I haven't the time."

She let out a huff at this. "So. How long are you here for?"

"Not long enough, I'm afraid."

She fixed him with a look. "A month, at least."

"Five days," he admitted. "And not an iota longer."

"Really." Adrian stared at him. "Really? You've come how many thousands of miles, and *five days* is what you have to offer?"

"It will take fourteen days to cross the country," he said, ticking time off on his fingers. "The *Celerity* headed back to Hong Kong after we laid the cable to Myriad, so I'm on commercial transport back to Asia. Twenty days from San Francisco to Yokohama, if I'm lucky, then eight days from there to Shanghai. I have a meeting with the Taotai of Shanghai on February the sixteenth that I cannot miss. I must be there by the twelfth to prepare."

His parents exchanged glances.

"It will be better," he said, "once we've finished the Pacific line. We'll start making a profit on what we've put in. I'll be able to have some time off."

That was what he *said.* Truth was he had a plan. He couldn't do anything about the fact his brothers were gone, but after he'd left the service, after he'd found himself struck to silence, he'd wandered alone on roads he'd once trodden with his brothers. He'd thought about the journals in which he'd chronicled their plans for a telegraphic network.

He hadn't been able to speak them aloud. But what if he did it one better? What if he made it?

A telegraphic network wasn't enough, but it would be something, *something* he could give to his parents, something that would serve as a monument to what his family had lost.

So he'd formed a plan. He'd finish the transpacific line. He would show them his journals. He'd talk about what Noah added, what Harry had said, what John had conceived. And his mother wouldn't stop resenting him, he didn't think, but maybe, if he did enough, she would understand that he was trying to make up for it all.

"So." She frowned. "What I'm hearing is that next *year* you can spare yourself. I don't suppose you could manage any sooner for the sake of your dear mother?"

The fact that she was pressing it meant that she wanted it—really and truly wanted it.

Grayson didn't want to deny her.

He sighed. "Maybe I can manage a week in April. I'll be in San Francisco to inspect the cable aboard the *Victory* for the last segment then. If I don't go back with the *Victory*... She's slow."

She made a face. "Only another week?"

Until he finished the transpacific line, until he had something to offer her... This was the best he could do. More time with her wouldn't make the gap between them any narrower.

She said *only* a week, but a week of this emptiness was a week of remembering. It was a week spent feeling the grief he tried to hold in. It was a week knowing that he wasn't enough, that he could never fill the gaping hole in their lives, but that he had to try harder to do it.

It shouldn't have been Grayson who'd survived—but it had been.

He looked in his mother's eyes, then his father's. "I'm sorry," Grayson said. "I'm sorry. I'll make it up to you one day. I promise."

∾

It was not February the twelfth when Grayson arrived in Shanghai. It was the fifteenth, the evening before the planned meeting with the taotai. Grayson arrived with the skies spitting water that froze to slippery danger on the Shanghai pavements and into daggers of ice dripping from bare tree branches.

He was chilled through and through, rubbing his hands

against the cotton towel he'd been given at the entry as he ascended the stairs to Mrs. Smith's office. He came to stand in the doorway, and that was how he saw Amelia Smith for the first time in so many months. Lightning struck. That was how he felt all over again.

She had changed. She was wearing loose Chinese trousers and a Western blouse covered by a smart jacket. Her hair was pinned up messily with rosewood hair sticks. She stood at her desk, arms folded, shaking her head.

"Stop whining," she was saying to Benedict. "If Captain Hunter really doesn't show, you *will* have to do it all. I'm not going to let you muff the formalities. Try that bow again."

"Yes, ma'am," Benedict said, giving her a salute.

She didn't seem embarrassed to be receiving it.

God. She was beautiful. Grayson had been aware before he'd left that he had a problem where she was concerned. He'd kissed her, after all. He'd thought about her. He'd wondered how she was getting along, not just for the code, but for herself. He'd pored over the occasional stripped-down telegrams he'd received aboard the *Victory*. Even the packet of letters that had awaited him in Yokohama explaining the code in detail, with a sample presentation for him to give to the taotai, had brought her to his mind. He could sense her exuberant enthusiasm even in those few pages. He'd felt it in the completeness of the packet, her evident pride in work well done.

He'd been lightning struck before. He'd known he had a problem, a deep one, a yearning one that pulled her to him.

He'd known nothing. Watching her now, watching her be comfortable where she had once been hesitant, confident where she had used to be unsure... It was worse. How had it gotten so much worse?

She glanced in his direction. Their eyes met. And he felt his world tilt off its axis.

"Oh." Her face lit in a smile. "You're finally here! I had feared we were doomed."

"Doomed." He found himself echoing her smile and her words. "Doomed." It sounded prophetic. He *felt* doomed in that moment—drawn into her, his hands frozen by rain when her entire person seemed to radiate warmth. "Why would we be doomed?"

She just smiled at him. "We need *someone* to make the introduction to the taotai. We're glad it's you."

Grayson folded the towel he'd been using to swipe water off him. His hands still felt clammy, but she was here with him. It felt as if his frozen limbs were awakening to pins and needles, slapped to life by her presence.

"You made my code," he said. "Well done."

Her nose twitched. "I made *my* code."

Their eyes met once again. It was so, so different from their first meeting. He'd thought her delightful at the time, but seeing her like this—eight months into a project he had set for her, eight months away from the place where he'd found her— meant he could see all the ways that uncertainty had pushed her off-center in her former life.

She'd found something like balance, and it made Grayson think of his own instability—how impossible it was to stop running once you set off down a hill at breakneck speed.

He swallowed his careening thoughts and gave her a broad smile.

"Behold." He mustered all his confidence. "You're not doomed. I've arrived just in time."

CHAPTER TWENTY

The meeting with Taotai Tu went about as Grayson had expected. They were ushered into the taotai's yamen. The official residence took them through a garden of frozen ponds and dry rustling leaves. Even in the depths of icy winter, there was a sense of beauty, as if the icicles had been planned. Their party passed through a gate flanked by lions and decorated with triangular flags, and into a courtyard bounded by four long buildings. The ridgelines of the roof tilted up in graceful curves at each end. But there was no time to dawdle and appreciate the space.

The servants opened a set of doors facing the courtyard. In summer, Grayson imagined they'd remain open. For now Grayson and his party passed into a receiving room where a small handful of men, with long beards and longer braided queues awaited. This was the taotai and a handful of accompanying ministers. They exchanged greetings and gifts in Mandarin, and after the pleasantries were over, Grayson started his presentation.

He could feel Mrs. Smith's eyes on him as he sketched out his proposal. He could feel when her attention shifted to

Scholar Wu, who was giving the in-depth discussion of their telegraphic code.

He had to take care to make the case for what was coming. It was not just about navigating the complicated, stubborn morass of Chinese–Occidental politics.

When he'd first met Mrs. Smith, she'd shone with a brightness that could not entirely be suppressed, no matter how her circumstances had conspired to do so.

Her circumstances had now stopped suppressing her, and it showed in a dozen small ways. There was a confidence in her smile, an assurance to the way she quietly directed those who'd worked with her on developing the code. Her eyes were the brightest part of her.

Mrs. Smith had attracted him before. Now he found his eyes drifting toward her even from across the room, found his ears straining to hear a sound from her over the talk that Scholar Wu was giving to the Mandarin officials about the code.

"One fundamental characteristic," Scholar Wu was saying, "that sets the Chinese language above the Western alphabet, is this. One must *read* Western languages to know what they say. With our Chinese characters, you can see an entire page at a glance."

Gray looked up to see the taotai nodding.

"I am proud to say that an experienced operator, such as myself, can see our code as well. Let me show you how that works."

Grayson had examined her presentation in detail on the final leg from Yokohama. Every radical had an encoding in the English alphabet. But the highlight of her invention was what she called "join characters." *E*—the simplest character—was used to join radicals vertically. Other combinations represented horizontal joins and enclosures.

"It seems still possible to confuse two characters," said a minister.

"Ah," Scholar Wu said. "We've done testing on that. Here are five instances that we've come across." Mrs. Smith was already in motion, smiling as she handed papers out to the officials. "As you can see, one can tell quite easily from context which character is meant. And in the unlikely event that is not the case, we've come up with guidelines for distinguishing between them."

She'd mentioned that difficulty in an earlier telegram. She'd solved it. She'd left the bulk of the presentation to others, and yet to his eye, she was undoubtedly in charge. After Wu finished and stepped back, an official lifted a finger.

"Mrs. Smith," he asked. "Where do you come from?"

She blinked, as if surprised to be included in the conversation beyond handing out materials. "I was taken in by missionaries when I was six years old."

"Missionaries!" said the man, recoiling. "Don't they take the hearts and eyes of our children to make unholy medicine?"

Mrs. Smith looked singularly unperturbed by this charge. "No," she said with a smile. "Although I have had much to learn to make up for the shortcomings in my upbringing."

"Hmm." The man frowned at her, squinting as if trying to make her out. But his perusal didn't last long. The taotai gathered up his ministers, and they decamped to a corner of the room, consulting one another in quiet murmurs.

Mrs. Smith met his eyes with a tense smile; he returned a solemn nod. But they were not kept waiting. After a long pause, the men returned.

The taotai spoke. "Your presentation was very edifying. But the treaty allows only for the construction of buildings and streets. Telegraph wires are not included, and we therefore respectfully decline your request, as telegraph lines are unsightly."

Grayson had been expecting this answer. The Great Northern Telegraph Company had received the same answer when they'd approached the taotai earlier. One of the men involved had complained about Chinese backwardness in preferring natural harmony without modern innovation.

The man he spoke to hadn't even considered the possibility that this was an excuse.

"Taotai." Grayson nodded respectfully. "I understand your decision. Undoubtedly something could be done with the lines themselves to beautify them. We would be happy to work with your engineers on such a project. But—if I may speak plainly?"

"Of course."

Grayson was good at many things. Persuasion yes, when he didn't particularly care what someone thought of him after the fact. But this wasn't mere persuasion. It was a partnership, one that would hopefully become a leveler after a series of Unequal Treaties, a partnership that built trust where it had been absent before.

If John were here... The thought rocked him on his heels. Instead, he smiled and did his best.

"I suspect you have other worries. As to those, I must ask. Do I look like a man who wants to outfit China for copper shackles?"

The taotai tilted his head, his expression not giving anything away. "Continue."

Natural harmony? No doubt the taotai cared about that. But it wasn't the only reason the taotai had said no.

"I am a Black man from America," Grayson said. "My people have endured the shackles of the West for far too long. I have no wish to chain anyone else in turn. I have no love for a trade enterprise that treats my people—and yours—as perishable goods."

The taotai met Grayson's eyes. "Speak on."

"I understand the burden you are carrying on a physical

level. I have fought to end the West's shackles. I have lost brothers in that fight who would be standing beside me right now in that fight, as you, too, have lost people." He held on to the cutting grief that rose temporarily, holding it close in his heart. "I propose that China will own its telegraphic lines and control them entirely. China will collect revenues on those lines exclusively. We have come up with a code that encapsulates the clarity and beauty of the written Chinese language. We offer a partnership that grows out of respect, with nobody in a subservient position."

"Do you now?" The taotai did not sound convinced.

"I ask only the right to establish telegraphic offices in treaty cities. This would give Chinese people worldwide the ability to communicate with anyone in China."

Another shake of the taotai's head. "That would allow those in treaty cities the right to communicate with anyone in China as well. Why even have treaty cities if foreigners will be able to make their presence known in every village anywhere in the country?"

"Taotai, you and I both know the West. What they do not get from politely asking, they will take by force. I've heard half a dozen Englishmen say they should just run a telegraph line to Shanghai in secret."

The taotai did not react. He had undoubtedly heard the same.

"That," Grayson said, "is your question. Not *will* there be a telegraph line to China, but *when* will you have it? Will you control it? And most of all, will you be a partner in the enterprise or will China be shut out of its future altogether? That's what I'm offering. A partnership. A chance to own your own wires and set your own rules. It's a chance to wrest the reins of your future from the West. It's a shot at a more equal future for both of us. It's up to you."

"Thank you." For a moment, the taotai tilted his head, as if he were about to say something else. Then he turned to the officials who had accompanied him. "We will discuss."

It was not an outright no. It was also not a yes. It was as good an answer as Grayson had expected for now, and yet...

He held his disappointment in and instead executed a low bow. "Thank you. I look forward to hearing from you."

❦

On the way back to their offices, Grayson felt as if he were a frozen block. This was expected, he told himself. This was natural. But his dissatisfaction did not vanish simply because he knew it was irrational.

Mrs. Smith's expression echoed his feelings. She worried her bottom lip between her teeth, her brow furrowed. A blustery wind blew about them; long-dead ginkgo nuts crunched underfoot, letting out an unpleasant odor. They passed a gray stone bank, a brick trading house, and a genteel club before finding the street down which the Lord Traders Telegraphic Company offices stood.

He thanked everyone, repeated his thanks for their hard work, and gave assurances about their future success that he had to work to make himself believe.

Finally, he was alone with Mrs. Smith in her office. It was natural to speak with her at a time like this. Quite natural for him to close the door to discuss where they would next proceed. Yet the moment he had done so, he became aware of her. Of the bright expressiveness of her eyes infected by worry, of the purse of her lips.

She was watching him, her forehead wrinkling with worry.

"That..." She exhaled slowly. "I thought, during the presentation, that we were missing something. I wish I'd seen it earlier."

He shook his head. "Don't worry." He'd known it would

happen, after all, and it was his problem to solve, not hers. "It went as well as it could have."

"But in the middle of it I realized that the proposal was all about encoding and money, with not one word of the things that matter. If I'd made it *better*—"

He waved this all away with a sweeping gesture. "You made it to my precise specifications. If there is fault, it is mine for not advising you on the political situation here. We've come further than any telegraphic company thus far."

"But…" She looked up at him. Her eyes were glossy with almost-shed tears.

"None of that," Grayson said gruffly, coming to stand directly in front of her. "The only immediate answer the taotai could give was no. And I honestly suspect we'll still hear that as well. It's fine."

For some reason, those words made her bite her lower lip and tilt her head down so he couldn't catch her expression. She contemplated her hands as if they were endlessly fascinating.

"It's fine," Grayson repeated. He felt as if he were convincing himself as much as her. "I have always expected that we would be refused at first. But we will be first to introduce our code in Hong Kong, and as it catches on—"

She raised her head abruptly. There was something like fire in her gaze, something hot and indignant. "Captain Hunter." His name felt like an admonition, and he stopped speaking.

"What is it?"

"It's not fine." She sounded so indignant that at first he didn't understand the source of her ire. "*You* don't think it's fine, no matter what you're saying. Don't tell me it's fine if it isn't fine."

He was stunned speechless.

"It's not fine!" She took a step forward, jabbing a finger into his chest, glaring up at him. "I know what you sound like when you believe what you say, and it's not that."

He exhaled and wrapped his hand around her finger, arresting it midjab. She was close, so close that he could have leaned down and tasted her. "I believe what I said." He felt weary. "I believe very much that your code is brilliant. That there was no fault in it, or in how you presented it." He realized he was still holding on to her hand, warm in his, and dropped it hastily. "I believe in you. None of that is a lie."

But, he didn't say. *But...*

She heard it anyway. "But?"

He could not leave her in doubt of her accomplishments. That was it—the only reason he spoke.

"But," he said softly, "my brother John would have done a better job of convincing the taotai, and I am very much aware of my own limitations."

Said out loud, the words had weight to them, a cold crackling sharpness that cut through the emptiness in his heart, threatening to cleave straight through his studied equanimity into the well of grief he couldn't let himself acknowledge. Grayson swallowed and looked away.

"We'd planned this together," he told her. "What I said to the taotai was all a memory of what John had once told me. He said it better six years ago, with no time to study it. If he had been here, he would have done it right."

His grief had edges, but it also had pressure. He could feel it on his soul—not just the pain of loss, but the unspeakable burden of carrying what must be done.

"Now you know why I didn't tell you." He made the words mocking. "It's to my advantage if you don't realize that the most grandiose portions of my plan aren't even mine. Let's pretend I never mentioned it."

"Grayson." There was a subtle reprimand in her tone. In the use of his Christian name. "I have been thinking much lately about why I... Never mind me." She met his eyes. "I understand that sometimes it is necessary to lie and claim everything is well. I told myself I wasn't doing it, but I was. But if you never tell *anyone* you're not fine, who will take care of you?"

God. The sheer density of the load on him felt unbearable. Take care of him? The concept felt impossible.

Take care of him? Not Noah, his sweet younger brother. Not Harry, his longtime confidante. Not John. He thought of the flash of resentment in his mother's eyes, of the five days he'd spent with his family, of her saying, *I'm so glad you've taken a week from your busy schedule to see your family.*

At least this way, with his visits eked out to them five days at a time, she could forget. Forget that he wasn't the bright one, wasn't the one who would bring her babies. She was always going to resent him just a little for being the one who survived, and he couldn't blame her. He couldn't blame any of them.

How could he ask anyone to take care of him, when he hadn't been able to care for his younger brothers?

Who would take care of him? The answer, desolate and lonely, was obvious. Nobody. Not even himself. And he couldn't think that—he couldn't let himself wallow in any of the feelings that arose with that admission. Feelings were the enemy.

Perhaps that was why he reached out and took hold of the hand he had relinquished a half minute before. Perhaps that was why he pulled her in, leaning down until he could smell the warm scent of her hair, until he could see the way her eyes divided into black and brown and little gold flecks. Perhaps that was why he kissed her.

He hadn't meant to do it. He acted before his mind caught up with him. She let out a surprised gasp. The noise was enough to bring his rationality back in line. But then she took his face in her hands and pulled him in, kissing him back with a fierceness that drove all rational thought away.

Grayson let himself fall into the kiss, into the softness of her lips against his, the taste of her mouth, sweet like jasmine. The play of her fingers against the side of his face. Kissing her was like forgetting. The whisper of their kiss. The slide of fabric as her skirts rearranged as she tipped forward, leaning closer to him.

Kissing was dangerous. But it was safer than speaking, safer than the painful jolt of emotions that he needed to keep buried. Kissing was action, and action distracted from thought. Lust singed through him, driving out melancholy.

Grayson had once been told sharks needed to move to force water through their lungs, that moving was breathing. That knowledge had settled into him. He had no time to stagnate in feelings. No time to allow his old worries to catch up with him.

He opened his mouth, catching the sound of surprise she made. Their tongues met, and he pushed in closer.

He could feel the heat of her body, the press of them against each other, the curve of her chest. He pushed in between her legs, her skirts pushing back against him. A short step forward, and he ground his pelvis into hers, feeling desire spark. Again, and—

And reality intruded in the feel of fabric. What was he doing?

He pulled his mouth from hers and stepped back an inch, a sense of shame dawning in him.

"Grayson?" Her voice shook.

He couldn't do this. For him, it had been an escape. For her?

He let out a long sigh. "God. I'm so dreadfully sorry."

Her eyes narrowed as she contemplated him. Then she shook her head. "Put your apology in a fire pit and burn it to ash."

"Amelia," he said quietly. "I cannot—I must not—do this. I *am* sorry."

He made himself look into her eyes as he enunciated each syllable, waiting for the hurt to take over her features.

It did not. She tilted her head to look at him. Her brow

furrowed. Then it smoothed and she gave him a tight-lipped smile.

"For what, precisely, are you apologizing?"

He gathered his wistful desires and clenched them into a tight knot around his heart. The things he might feel if he let himself go down that route... They were unthinkable.

"I'm sorry." He took his hand from hers. "I shouldn't... The way I feel about you, I shouldn't have..."

Her nose scrunched. She didn't look hurt or disappointed. She looked, at first, puzzled. Then a thought crossed her mind —he could see it in the widening of her eyes—and she pressed a fist to her mouth to hide a laugh.

A *laugh*. He didn't understand at all.

"Ahem." She brushed an imaginary piece of something off the shoulder of her gown, straightened her spine, and tilted her head back, peering at him as if she were looking down on him, even though she was so much smaller.

"You're attracted to me," she said with a lift of her chin.

"Isn't that obvious?" He shook his head in confusion. "I said I was *sorry.*"

She giggled. There was no other word for it. She actually giggled. "You have no idea. I've wanted to do this for such a long time."

"Why are you laughing?"

"The amusing part," she said in a voice pitched a few notes too deep, "is that you think I will *mind*. You have excellent taste."

His mouth dropped open.

"It's bad manners of me to admit it, but I *am* attractive." She gave him an arrogant look. "Many men like me. And who can blame them?"

"I..." He could remember the exact moment he'd said something like this to her. They'd been on a ship. In the harbor in

Fuzhou. She must have gaped at him exactly as he was looking at her right now. "I did not say it like *that*."

"Very much like it." She reached up and patted his shoulder. "Don't think I have not noticed. There was an apology and there were kisses, but you haven't answered my question. Who is taking care of you?"

His breath punched out. He didn't have the strength to resist any longer. "Nobody," he confessed.

It had been months since he'd teased her about her megalodons. Now she was doing it back to him. He felt like a pane of glass, liable to shatter at any moment. His throat seemed full of sand.

"Nobody," he repeated through the gravel that seemed to clog his speech. "Everybody who did was killed." He could hear the yearning in his words. "I'm the only one left, and dammit, what do I need with something so paltry as care when I was so selfish as to survive?"

She didn't say anything, but her eyes—wide with compassion—said it all.

She'd seen his megalodons—giant sharp-toothed beasts lurking under the surface, waiting to shred him if he ventured forth. His ambitions only seemed so large because they substituted for a want so cavernous and impossible that it would always go hungry.

"Mrs. Smith." He was choking on his want now. He had to— he didn't know—shove it back. Push it away. Bury it beneath the ocean waves before it ate him whole. He had to get away. "With your leave." He nodded at her and turned to go.

"Absolutely not!"

"Then without your leave," he told the door to her office. And he was gone before she could answer.

CHAPTER TWENTY-ONE

I t was still dangerously slick when Amelia returned to her office the next morning, cold enough that the paving stones were slippery and icicles formed spears down tree branches. She'd woken up throughout the night, hearing the wind howl.

Normally, when she heard wind, she thought of her mother —of that long-ago dusty, windy day when she'd been left behind.

Last night she'd thought of Captain Hunter instead. How easily he wore his arrogance. What a mask it had turned out to be. She'd thought about the burn of his kiss and the touch of his hands. But most of all, she'd thought about his telegrams. About the confidence he'd given her.

That morning, she'd come into her office, gone to her desk, and removed the stack of letters he'd given her. Over the last eight months, she'd received a slew of numerical telegrams from him. Every time she'd received a number in the correspondence sent up from the Hong Kong telegraph office, she'd felt a queasy trepidation. This was it. This was the time he would be disappointed with her.

Now, though, she definitely had suspicions.

She found a letter opener, seated herself on the floor, and took out the envelope labeled *1.*

She had opened sixteen envelopes from him. Thus far, they'd all said some variant of the same thing: *Trust yourself. You can figure out the answer.*

Now with the inkling of a suspicion, she slit open the first letter and pulled the paper out.

I'm not sure why you asked me a question, since you clearly know the answer already. Simply do as you think best.

Ha. She set this back in its wrapper and went on to the next one. *2. There's no need to sound uncertain. Your first impulse was correct. Go with that one.*

Just as she'd thought. Next was *3. You've got the right idea. Keep going.*

On and on she continued, through *13. You've made excellent progress; at this point, you understand the matter better than I do, and so I must defer to your superior expertise.* Through *27. You don't need me to tell you what to do.* On and on, past *31. I trust your judgment.* Her fingers grew colder and colder as she opened them. Half an hour passed while the stack of letters grew around her. She'd not had much of a plan when she started; she had less of one now.

"This is it," she told envelope number 59 balefully. "If you are going to disprove my hypothesis, it must be you."

The letter lay innocently in her hand.

"Well?" said a voice behind her. "What is it you expect it to prove?"

Amelia shrieked and turned. She had still been holding on to the letter opener as she did so, and it slipped from her hand and hurtled across the room. She screamed again as it flew through the air, turning, and clattered at Captain Hunter's feet. She tried to rise, but her leg had somehow fallen asleep in her lengthy letter-opening session. It didn't quite function any longer; she tripped over it and spilled ignominiously back down on the floor.

Carpet met her nose. She scrunched her eyes shut. Maybe if she never opened them, she would not have to acknowledge what had just happened.

A long silence passed.

Then: "Did you just trip?" he asked. "While sitting down?"

"Impossible," she muttered into the carpet.

"I had thought so too. Truly I am amazed at all you have accomplished here."

With immense effort, Amelia managed not to bang her head against the floor in frustration. Slowly, she peeled herself up into a sitting position. "Can we pretend this didn't happen?"

He picked up the letter opener at his feet and crossed over to set it on her desk.

"What were you doing?"

"I figured it out last night." She looked at him. "My entire goal these last months was to do so well that you would never have to send me the number for the 'no, you fool' envelope."

"Ah." He settled himself cross-legged a few feet away from her.

She glared at him. "There *is* no 'no, you fool' envelope."

He shrugged. "No."

"How were you supposed to tell me I was a fool?"

"I wasn't supposed to do it," he said, "for the reason that you are not a fool and lying is bad."

She tried to take this concept in, but there wasn't any place in her head for a thought that seemed so warm. Soft. Comforting.

Her nose wrinkled. "Did you not just see me with the tripping? And the letter opener?"

"Amelia." He said her name so calmly. After everything that had passed between them last night, it felt *too* calm. "I asked you to do something that had never been done before. I hired you because I had no idea how to do it. There was nothing I could do to help you but convince you that you were capable of doing it." His eyes met hers over the vanquished detritus of his letters. "And I was not wrong. You never needed someone to say you were a fool; you do that to yourself far too often. You needed someone to tell you the truth about yourself. And you needed someone to make you believe it."

She stared at him in confusion. The months of his absence had gone by in what felt like the blink of an eye—so swiftly that she'd scarce had a chance to look at herself or to think about what she had done.

She had gone from *I can't do this* to *I can,* and every time she'd questioned or faltered, his letters had been there to catch her.

Amelia gathered her courage. She inhaled.

"Sorry—" he started to say just as she spoke.

"Thank you," she said.

They stared at each other.

"Thank you," she repeated. "This has been good for me. I always thought that I was just, um. Clumsy and odd with a mind that darted around to ridiculous ideas and pushed all sense out of my head."

"And you've discovered that your ideas are not so ridiculous."

Amelia let out a little laugh. "I note you say nothing about being clumsy and odd."

"Nobody is perfect." He smiled at her. There was something weary in his expression. He sighed and looked away. "Speaking of imperfections. Last night, I shouldn't have kissed you. Or mentioned my feelings. There are often expectations that arise—"

She couldn't hear this out. "I have none."

"Listen to me, Amelia. You *deserve* to expect things from a man who kisses you. I said it last night, but I scarcely allow myself to feel anything anymore. I'll spend the rest of my life traveling. I can't spend five days with my mother without knowing how much she resents me for who I'm not." He looked over at her. "I couldn't bear it if you grew to resent me too."

How completely absurd. She shook her head.

"You might say now that you won't, but—"

"It has been good." The words spilled out of her. "I don't *want* a husband. I had one. I don't want someone who is constantly expecting. I have *had* someone who is always there, always demanding, never caring if I'm fine or not. It has been good for me to just…"

She wasn't sure she would be able to complete her sentence, but the sting of him saying she would *resent him…*

"I needed to just believe." She picked up one of his letters at random and waved it in his direction. "This. About myself."

His eyes shut. "Amelia."

"I've never much wanted children, even though other people told me I would one day. I found marriage stultifying. I can't tell you what it has done for me, being away from all that. Knowing that I can be *this* person, and not the woman everyone expected."

"Amelia." He hitched forward a few inches, close enough to lean his forehead against her shoulder. He had to curl his head down to reach. She reached out tentatively, touching his head. He arched up into her fingers.

"Grayson Hunter," she said. "I don't know about anyone else in our life. But I could never resent you. Not ever."

His hands clutched her skirts, scrabbling at her knees, but he didn't lift his head. Time seemed to shift. The tick of the clock on the wall slowed to match the feel of the back of his neck, shaved close but still prickly, against her fingers. She didn't know what she was doing, what she was asking for.

"I realized," she told him after a few minutes of silence, "that

I could not tell my mother when I wasn't fine because she preferred to believe I was. Her happiness depends on her belief that she has rescued me. Any sign that she has not feels like a threat. To her, personally."

He let out a long exhale.

"I don't want to care about you like that," Amelia whispered. "If I care, I want to know."

She reached out and took hold of his hand. There was a little scar, a pale brown line, across the knuckle of his thumb. She turned his hand over to examine his palm. He flipped his hand back, clasping their fingers together.

Slowly, he lifted his head. "Amelia."

"Grayson."

Their hands twined together.

He let out a breath. "You should know. This is not what I had planned. I was going to separate myself from you, but this is much more intimate than a kiss."

"I was married for years." She looked into the dark brown of his eyes. "I know."

He looked down at their hands where they touched, tilting his so that their palms pressed against each other, fingertip to fingertip. His hand was larger than hers by an inch, and warmer by degrees.

"In some other world," he said carefully, "I would wish you were mine. It turns out that I very much like odd, clumsy women whose heads are full of delightful ideas. But I'm asking you to be nothing."

"No." Amelia looked around the room at the piles of letters still stacked around them.

She could hear his voice now, whispering those remembered words. *You've got the right idea. You've made excellent progress. Trust your instincts.*

"You're asking me to be myself," she said.

He exhaled. His hand swallowed hers, pressing convulsively. She needed to memorize the feel of his touch on her skin for when he wasn't here.

"Every time I see you." He swallowed. "Every time I see you come into yourself more and more. Every time I do…" He reached out with his free hand, tapping the letters. "I mean these more and more."

She bowed her head to brush her lips against the back of his hand. They stayed like that—fingers tangled together, her lips against his knuckles, while the clock behind them ticked and ticked.

They stayed that way until a knock sounded at the door.

"Mrs. Smith? Captain Hunter?" It was Benedict.

Amelia pulled herself away, slowly peeling their fingers apart before clambering to her feet and brushing her gown into place. "Yes?"

"The taotai has sent his answer."

Captain Hunter stood as well, arranging his jacket. He did not look at Amelia. He did not hesitate. "I'm coming."

CHAPTER TWENTY-TWO

The reply from the taotai was succinct.

"Many thanks for your honored presentation," Grayson read aloud to the office floor, "but Shanghai will not be in need of a telegraph service."

Grayson could see Amelia—no, Mrs. Smith; he *must* think of her as Mrs. Smith, no matter what had just transpired—exhale, shoulders slumping. He reached out to her, his hand moving a half inch in her direction before he caught himself and pulled back.

Instead, Benedict touched her arm. "Don't fret, Mrs. Smith. Captain Hunter has a plan. He always does."

He did have a plan. He always did. His entire life seemed made up of contingencies layered upon contingencies, and all he needed to do was hold himself and everything together long enough to bring it all to fruition.

"I had hoped," Amelia said, "that we might spare Captain Hunter the planning."

Benedict seemed faintly puzzled by that. Grayson himself was bemused. But Mrs. Smith wasn't the only one wondering what would happen next.

"I do have a plan," Grayson said. "Chinese laborers and merchants travel the entire world."

Her eyes met his, but he couldn't stare at her. Not in front of the entire office. He made himself look away, making eye contact with everyone here.

"They live in Hong Kong and Macau and Singapore and Brazil—so many that the places are too numerous to mention. Your work will mean those people can communicate."

Scholar Wu frowned. "But China itself..."

Grayson made sure his easy smile encompassed the room. "I promise you when the alternative becomes sending Chinese messages to Japan rather than shipping them over via courier, the taotai will come around. The better our system, the easier it will be for the Chinese abroad to adopt it, and the faster China will follow. We knew the taotai would oppose change at first. We've planted seeds. We must expect that they will take some time to bloom."

The mood in the room warmed a little. People nodded.

"Your next step," Grayson said, "is clear. Start readying codebooks and a method for training operators. We will launch in Hong Kong shortly." He looked over them all, one by one, doing his best not to single out Amelia in particular.

"I'm leaving imminently for San Francisco to inspect the cable that will connect Myriad Island to Moresby. Once that's finished, we will have a transpacific cable in place. And that will open our options considerably. I trust you will all continue with your excellent work."

He could feel Amelia's eyes on him as he spoke. He touched his forehead in something like a farewell salute and went to get his coat.

Amelia followed him. "Captain Hunter. If I could have a few words on logistics? May I walk with you as you leave?"

"Of course." He donned his coat and hat, waiting for her to

find her outdoor things before ushering her out the door ahead of him.

He wasn't sure what she would say. They hadn't spoken nearly enough. Comfort and reassurance were well and good, but he couldn't promise her anything.

She followed him outside, pulling on her gloves in the crisp air. Her breath made white clouds. Then she smiled up at him, and all his inchoate worries seemed to shift in place.

"This was according to plan?" Her lips twitched. "Let me guess. Every setback is always according to your plan."

"Of course." He gave her a sardonic grin. "Bow before my prescience."

They hadn't spoken much at all, he was beginning to realize. True, they'd both said a great many things, but they didn't have an understanding. They weren't *supposed* to have an understanding.

"Amelia," he said, "I'm leaving."

"I know. You have said."

"I won't stay for you," he replied bluntly. "And you say you won't resent it now but—"

She made a face. "Grayson, I like you for who you are."

He stared at her dumbly.

She gave him a cheeky smile, one that pierced right through him. "Your leaving at this exact moment is entirely according to my plan."

"*Your* plan," he echoed. "*Your* plan. What is your plan?"

"I suspect it's about as firm as your plan. Just to confirm, while you're away, I'm expected to operate independently."

"Yes, of course. But I'm suspicious now. I'm very suspicious. What is your plan?"

"Oh dear." She looked away. "You're leaving imminently. I suppose you'll just have to find it out, won't you?"

~

After Grayson had left, Amelia retreated to the office where her staff waited.

"We'll start work on compiling codebooks immediately," she told them. "I have some thoughts. And we still have the problem of error correction to manage. But Benedict, I have an additional duty for you."

The boy perked up, smiling. "Yes. What is it?"

"I want you to get us a second meeting with the taotai. Not immediately; I think we will need a few months to prepare. April or May will do."

Benedict stared at her. "But I've never done anything like—that is to say, Grayson made the first meeting—is *that* what he asked you to do just now?"

Amelia just beamed at him. "Didn't you hear him? It's all according to his plan."

CHAPTER TWENTY-THREE

Three days after Benedict began to inquire about making an appointment with the taotai, he received a message via courier. It was not from the taotai.

He read it, crumpled it, threw it against the wall, then retrieved it and read it once more.

Benedict had his own little cubby on the ground floor of the Lord Traders' office, which meant that nobody had seen this childish display. It also meant that nobody would ask him what the message said.

The worst had happened. His competence had intersected with his incompetence.

He stared at the words, sighed, and went to craft a response.

The appointment Benedict received in response to his missive was seven days later. "First available opportunity," he'd expressly said, yet it had been almost March when Benedict made his way to Consul Secretary Larkin's office.

He was made to wait half an hour once he arrived, even though he'd been ten minutes early. Finally he was escorted back to meet the man.

Benedict didn't think he had much of a temper. He liked pleasing people. He enjoyed listening to others. He was always willing to help. And it was hardly any secret to himself as to why. He'd grown up with two sisters who scraped along like flint and steel. Benedict had done his best to keep Judith and Theresa from sparking too often.

Now he felt the start of sparks of his own.

By the time he was escorted to the secretary's office, those sparks had begun to smolder. It didn't help that Secretary Larkin looked at him once—dismissively—then rolled his eyes, looking away.

"Why are you still in Shanghai?" The man sounded bored. "You *do* recognize the risks, do you not? If treason is committed in Shanghai, *you'll* be the one blamed for it."

Was the man *expecting* treason? Honestly. Benedict kept a firm hold on his temper. "I'm simply arranging a meeting with the taotai. Is that treason?"

"It rather depends on what the meeting is for, doesn't it? I prefer not to risk it. You may not meet with the taotai."

Benedict sighed. "It's not my meeting. It's on behalf of the Lord Traders Telegraphic Company. It's my *job* to arrange meetings."

Consul Secretary Larkin made a precise notation on the paper in front of him. "Find a new occupation. Or go home."

Benedict exhaled slowly. He needed to be patient. He could be patient. He was good at being patient. He…

"No," he said surprising himself.

The man looked up. "No?"

"My father committed treason," Benedict told him. "My brother committed treason. But I'm not like them."

"You're loyal to England then?"

"It's not that."

Benedict saw the man's eyes widen at this admission, so he bulled on before he could be interrupted.

"They were cowards who couldn't speak up for their principles. My father was an earl. He had all of Parliament at his fingertips. He could have forced them to listen by taking advantage of the privileges he had by dint of birth. And with all of that, he decided the proper way forward was underhanded *ridiculousness*. If you believe in a principle, you should be willing to own it in broad daylight."

"I see. You're not like them," Larkin said mockingly. "*You're* honest and forthright."

The truth took Benedict by surprise.

He *was* like that. He was absolutely an underhanded coward. He hadn't told Judith what he truly wanted because he'd wished to avoid the ruckus. He'd used excuse after excuse to hide the truth from her to justify what he wanted to do.

He'd been fourteen when he'd started to lie to Judith—young enough that the thought of telling his much older sister that he didn't want to do what she'd wanted had seemed impossible. In the intervening years, he'd done a lot of ridiculous things simply because he could not make himself stand and give a simple no.

He had to learn to be the person he wanted to be. And he had to do it now.

So Benedict Worth took in the mocking blue of Consul Secretary Larkin's eyes, the lanky pitch color of his hair. He felt as if he were looking at every last person who'd ever mocked him during his horrific time at Eton.

It was time for Benedict to stand. He glared at Larkin. "I have had enough from you. I am Captain Hunter's liaison in Shanghai. He has taught me more about bravery than all of England. It is *my job* as liaison to make an appointment with the taotai."

"And it is my job as consular secretary to—"

"No it's not," Benedict said. "It's your job to help British citizens interact with Chinese officials, not to make up stories about them so you can hinder their work. You are not the taotai's secretary. You're the consul's. Furthermore, you're not my mother. You're not my sister nor my caretaker. You are the secretary to the consul, and you have absolutely no business insinuating yourself in this matter."

Consul Secretary Larkin looked at Benedict, his eyes wide in surprise. Finally he shook his head. "I don't like you. I don't trust you. Put one foot wrong, and I will have you thrown out of my territory."

"The feeling is abundantly mutual. I'm here as liaison. Now get out of my way and let me liaise."

Larkin just sighed. "If you want the rope to hang yourself with, by all means." He ran a hand through his thick, dark hair. "Have at it."

"I've spent enough time aboard ship." Benedict shrugged. "I'm good with rope. By your leave?"

Larkin just shook his head.

~

It was dark by the time Benedict sat down at his table and started another letter.

Dear Judith,

I have not been telling you the truth. I haven't really been trying to find Theresa beyond a few half-hearted, ham-handed attempts. I do not want to go back to England. I am employed as a liaison for a telegraphic company in Shanghai, and I love doing this. I want to stay here.

You've made your home where you are, but when I think of England, I think of boys who bullied me because of my family name. I don't want to come back. I never will.

~

Grayson had tried not to think of Amelia during the first nine months he knew her. In the months that followed after, he surrendered to the inevitable.

Commercial transport took him to San Francisco, and with no cable trailing behind him, he had no way to contact her. No short messages informing him of what she was doing. Nothing. He sent off a packet of short inquiries when he landed in San Francisco; he would receive updates as time went on. But for the next months until the *Victory* returned to Asia, they were truly apart.

That left him time—too much time—to puzzle out their last hours together. He thought of the way her fingers had felt against his as they'd sat on the floor together. He thought of the light in her smile just before he'd left. He thought of her telling him it was all according to her plan. He thought of her asking him who cared for him.

He thought of what it might be like if he'd not had a telegraphic empire to establish—if someone else other than him could be put in charge—but that thought brought to mind Harry, and he could not go down that road.

So every time he spent a few idle moments thinking about her, he packed up his wistful longing and focused on what needed to be done. Get the cable loaded in San Francisco. Take a few weeks to go visit his family in Maine. Steel himself so he could ignore the unspoken truths that lay between them.

One day after inspecting cable in San Francisco, a packet of letters arrived.

It contained copies of manifests and budgets and reports of negotiations gone well. A note from the Yokohama office told him he would have to stop in Tokyo to discuss the scheduling of internal telegraph lines. Revenue from the Singapore line was up. Good, except that also meant a renegotiation of the agreement with the connecting telegraphic lines. There was too much to do, and he'd promised his mother he'd return in April.

He should have been looking forward to it.

He rubbed his temples. A letter from Amelia was a nice interlude, even if it was entirely about something mathematical —error correction and something, something modulus? Grayson skimmed the math enough to get the idea behind it, but lingered on her final words.

Take care, Amelia.

He traced the *t* and the *c* in "take care," once and then again, something unknown welling up inside him as if it were the antidote to the burden on his shoulders. Then he packed it all away and picked up Benedict's report.

The codebooks were going to plan; Benedict would be going to Hong Kong to deliver them and start the training, but he would return before the second meeting with the taotai…

Grayson stared at those words.

"The what?" he said aloud.

Benedict was not here to answer.

The *second* meeting with the taotai? What second meeting?

In a rush, he remembered how Amelia had looked in the final instants in which he'd seen her. She'd been bundled up in the cold outside the office, stamping from foot to foot. She'd looked up at him with a grin and said, "Your leaving at this exact moment is entirely according to my plan." And then she'd innocently added something about operating independently.

"Son of a bitch." Grayson exhaled slowly.

His first reaction should have been anger that she'd moved without his approval.

The problem was, he trusted her. Also, he'd specifically told her to move without his approval. That had been the entire point of all the letters he'd written to her.

His second reaction should have been fear. She might mishandle delicate negotiations.

But Amelia wasn't stupid.

And so the thing that he actually felt when his thoughts cleared from the shock was relief. Relief that this was one thing someone else was managing for a change, relief that everything did not have to be done by him.

I should be there, he thought, and then, *no, I shouldn't. I promised my mother I would come back.* But that opened up another unfortunate realization. He'd been dreading the visit.

He'd already been subtly regretting the time he would have to spend crossing the country, making his way to Maine, visiting with his parents pretending that nothing was wrong.

He practically *had* to go to the meeting with the taotai, didn't he? And if he didn't go home now, if he postponed the visit until after he was finished with the transpacific line, well. Then he'd have something to show for himself. Things would be less awkward in the first place. It would be a better visit.

Grayson got up. Paced around.

Don't tell me you're fine if you're not fine.

Amelia had the right of it. If you couldn't tell someone you weren't fine, you couldn't tell them when you needed care. But there was a time to descend into polite fictions, and his mama, British to her core, understood that in her bones.

He and his mama, they'd been lying to each other. *Neither* of them was fine, and they couldn't talk about it because you couldn't go back from some things.

I wish you had died instead of your brothers was not a thing a mother could say to a child.

On the one hand, if Grayson skipped out on this meeting *now,* there would be hell to pay. His aunts, far more direct, would be sure to let him know precisely how he'd stepped wrong. Zed would convey every ounce of their wrath.

And the next time he saw his mother, she'd be less able to hide that resentment from him.

But on the other hand, if he postponed their meeting? Maybe later he could actually speak of what lay between them. *I know I'm not enough. I know I will never make up for it. But I'm trying, I'm trying, to do what they would have done.*

If he left for Asia now, he'd save a full month of travel. More, because he could return via commercial ship faster than the *Victory.* He could handle the matters in Tokyo, the renegotiation of the Singapore contract. He could see Amelia and manage the taotai and push aside the uneasy truths that would break apart his family for long enough to maybe finally address them.

In the end, it wasn't even hard.

Dear Mama, Grayson wrote. *I must unfortunately cancel my upcoming visit...*

CHAPTER TWENTY-FOUR

G rayson only managed to land in Shanghai the morning before the meeting. He counted time in his head as he crawled his way through the paperwork associated with arriving in the foreign concession.

He'd spent a week in Tokyo untangling details of interior telegraphs, and yet he'd not announced his return to Amelia. He wanted to catch her by surprise.

But when he made his way to the office, the front room was empty. Instead, he could hear them upstairs.

"Order, order." That was Amelia speaking in Mandarin. "We're practicing, not making fun of me."

He couldn't hear the reply, but he found himself smiling just at the thought of seeing her. He crept up the stairs. The door to Amelia's room was open a good three inches, and when he peered inside, he saw it had been filled with chairs. His eyes landed on Amelia where she stood up front with a group of Chinese women. More than a dozen, he thought at a glance.

The presentation they were practicing was entirely in Mandarin. Grayson's Mandarin was decent, and the topic of conversation—telegraphy and travel—was one where his vocabulary was regularly exercised. It was easy enough to follow.

"For me," one of the women gathered at the front was saying, "if I could send a telegram, I might find out if my son was alive. He went to Brazil as a laborer three years ago. We haven't received any letters, so we wait without knowing."

She bowed deeply and stepped back.

The next woman introduced herself as Zhu Yiwei. "My husband went to work on the American railway," she said. She sounded tired. "It was finished several years ago. If I could send a telegram, I might find out what happened to him. If he's alive or..." She trailed off. "I don't even know if I should make offerings."

There was a quiet despair to that.

Grayson stood back against the wall, not wanting to disrupt them, slowly sinking to the floor in the hall outside. He took in stories about grandparents, brothers, children. *This is what a telegraph would mean to me,* they said. *This is why I need it.*

It painted a very different picture from his first attempt. He'd talked about code and characters, about pricing and partnerships.

She'd hit on what was missing: a picture of how the telegraph could help China not to be more like the West but more like *China.*

"There," Amelia said with satisfaction. "That's everyone. I have notes, if you would not mind—"

"All of us?" said one of the women. "Of course it isn't. What about you?"

"Me? But..." Grayson couldn't see Amelia, but he could hear her hesitation. "I'm an outsider. A Westerner." Her voice sounded so brisk. "This presentation is about you, about what the telegraph would mean for China. Auntie Zhu, I am legally a citizen of Britain."

"Stupid," said the woman who had spoken before.

"Very stupid," said someone else, a woman with a higher voice.

"Of course you're an outsider if you always stay outside," said the first woman—Auntie Zhu? Grayson realized with a start that this was the woman from the tea shop. "I had to practically hit you over the head before you realized we were friends."

"Didn't you say that a minister asked about you at the last meeting?" This was another voice.

"Yes, but—"

"Nobody wants your excuses. Go, say something. Say something."

Grayson could imagine the face she was making.

"Well?"

"I'm thinking," she retorted. "Give me a moment to think of what a telegraphic system would mean to me."

There was a tremble to her voice. Grayson let out a breath. A long time ago, Amelia had told him exactly what it would mean. She'd told him about her mother, about hopes that had died. He could imagine that look in her eyes now, the harrowing look of memory that had left her behind, but not quite.

And then she spoke.

"The last time I was here," Amelia said, "your minister asked if the English missionaries removed the eyes and hearts of the children they took in order to make unholy medicine."

Grayson could remember that.

"I recall."

"When I was growing up in Fuzhou with the English woman I called Mother, she would sometimes take me out to show other Chinese people that I was living. That I had not been made into medicine. But I don't think they ever asked the right questions. My eyes and my heart remained in my body, but they always yearned for something they could not remember seeing."

Grayson was frozen where he was seated outside her office. The wood floor was hard; the office wall he leaned against cold. He could not have moved to interrupt her, not in a million years.

"The mother who gave me up during the Taiping Rebellion… I have wondered what happened to her almost every day. Who was she? Where did she come from? Did she live or die? Who was my father? What was my family name? Do I have sisters?"

Amelia's voice was smooth and low. How had Grayson come to know her well enough to understand she was wrestling with tears?

"I accept that I will not ever know. I accept that I have other family now. But when I was writing this code, I thought every day about what it would mean if I could complete it. What it would mean for families who were separated, for children who did not know their mothers, if there were a swift means of reuniting people after a calamity."

Grayson had known how personal the telegraphic system was for her, and yet hearing those words spoken aloud, hearing her say it to someone other than himself, touched something deep inside him.

"I have a brother I grew up with. A woman who has served as my mother. But there are grandparents I will never know. A name that once belonged to me is lost. My eyes and my heart are mine, but they've been changed, and I cannot recall the things that no longer belong to me. And if I can save one other person from that loss…"

He understood her more deeply than he ever had before in that moment. Wanting to build back with copper wire what time and war had destroyed. Knowing, deep down, the futility of what she was doing for herself, but throwing her all into the project for others.

That was when Grayson realized he was in love. The feeling was sharp to the point of pain.

He couldn't build back what he'd lost with his family. He couldn't even imagine it. But he listened to Amelia baring her soul for the sake of his—of *their*—telegraphic network. He thought of her brother who had told Grayson almost a year ago that his sister was *criminally* undervalued.

He thought about what he'd just done—walking away from his mother because he couldn't face her yet, and he thought about Amelia losing more of the connections she cared about. How long had it been since she'd seen her brother in Hong Kong?

Close to a year, he imagined. She'd been here in Shanghai, plotting how to get the taotai to accept his partnership so she could help lift the load he shouldered.

Who cares for you? she'd asked. He hadn't needed to come here to talk with the taotai. But, he realized, he had needed to know what she was doing.

Who cared for him? It didn't matter. Who cared for *her?* It couldn't be her mother, not with what she'd said. It couldn't be him. He couldn't let it be him.

But listening to the woman he loved talk about the pain she would always bear, Grayson knew there was an answer. It wasn't him. It was the one person in the world who had valued her as she was before Grayson found her.

Amelia finished her speech.

"Good," Auntie Zhu was saying. "You see? You were stupid to think you shouldn't say anything."

Amelia hadn't seen him. She didn't know he was here. Grayson inhaled and stood. He'd come to Shanghai, but he would have headed to Hong Kong after the meeting to negotiate the contract with Singapore. If he was going there anyway, there was someone he would have to see.

Before they finished, before they left and discovered him here, he slipped down the stairs and out.

CHAPTER TWENTY-FIVE

It was a Saturday—the first Saturday in which Amelia had not gone in to work in a very long while.

"In my defense," she had told Auntie Zhu when the woman had berated her and asked her how she would ever marry, "if I didn't go into the office, I'd *still* spend all my time thinking about my work. And I don't want to marry."

"Sister, do you hear that?" Auntie Zhu had turned to one of the Chinese telegraph operators they were training. Miss Ho wasn't her sister—she was actually some kind of cousin by marriage—but they'd both rounded on her.

"You can't think of anything besides work?"

"That's not the defense you think it is. It's a sign that you never get away."

"Do you even remember what men are like?"

"She might like women," said Miss Ho. "Nothing wrong with that. We know *lots* of women who—"

Amelia had tried to protest. "Stop!"

"Pah."

"I can't believe this ridiculousness," Auntie Zhu had said.

"The taotai just approved the start of negotiations on the tele-graph line. And how are you celebrating? With more work?"

To be honest, she was still nervous about that. Grayson wasn't due back in Asia for another month at least. It had taken a week after her meeting with the taotai before she'd received the official indication that negotiations should move forward, and her letter to Grayson had just gone out to Hong Kong.

"Well," Amelia had tried to explain, "I thought I would cele-brate by testing the error correction on—"

Miss Ho had dumped Amelia's coat on her desk, covering all her papers. Auntie Zhu had stolen her pencils.

"Get out," they'd said together. "It's spring! Enjoy the sunshine tomorrow."

Amelia had given in.

So now she was still at home, lingering over the soy milk soup and youtiao she'd obtained from the cart down the street. Merry sat at her feet and Amelia read a newspaper from Hong Kong (only a week old), breaking off bits of the fried dough and soaking them in soy milk until they were the perfect mixture of soggy and crisp. Spring sunshine spilled through her window.

"This isn't for dogs," she informed Merry, popping a bite into her mouth.

Merry knew better. She waited, her eyes a melting puddle of need.

"Oh very well." Amelia gave in, as Merry had known she would. "Just a little piece."

She held out a corner—and Merry jumped up without taking the treat, running to the door, and letting out a deep baying bark. A second later, a rap sounded at Amelia's door.

Amelia frowned.

Then the pitch of Merry's bark changed, higher and more excited—changing from "Intruder! How dare you!" to "Hello! It's you! You pet me!"

Auntie Zhu had probably come to check on her. Amelia

rolled her eyes fondly, took a firm hold of Merry's collar, and opened the door.

There, standing in the sunshine, with a little sardonic smile on his face, was Captain Hunter.

Thought one: Oh *no*. He was early.

Thought two: Oh *yes*. He was beautiful. The sunlight caught his ears, tingeing the brown of his skin in golden light. His eyes met hers, dark and deep, and she could scarcely breathe.

Thought three: Help. Did he know about the taotai? Was he angry at her interference?

She realized she'd let go of her dog when Merry bounded forward eagerly, prancing at Grayson's feet.

His eyes dropped from Amelia to her dog. "Ah." He leaned down, petting her. "You remember me, girl."

"Of course she does," Amelia said, feeling as if she were speaking through a long tube. "Her memory is excellent."

He glanced up at her. "And you?"

"Um." She felt her mouth do something very complicated.

What language was she speaking? The office was now mostly Chinese—she'd spoken nothing but Mandarin for three days straight—English. She was speaking English.

She gave him a little wave. "I also. Remember. You."

He let out a laugh. "Why are you looking at me like that?"

"I…um. You may have heard about the taotai?"

"I may have." He said that with a little smile, one that made her heart skip.

"I didn't consult you," she confessed.

"I specifically remember telling you to use your initiative and to not wait upon my every response. I am delighted that you have done so."

Merry nudged his hand with her head. He bent to pet the dog, and as he did, he glanced up at Amelia.

The last time she'd seen him, they'd held hands on the floor of her office. The months that had elapsed since then should have attenuated that feeling of intimacy. Instead, their connection felt all the more immediate—the way a warm stove was particularly welcoming when one came in from a snowstorm.

"Oh," she said. Her faculties did not seem to be functioning. "Hello then."

"Hello to you as well."

Amelia swallowed. She had yet to look away from his eyes —dark, deep brown, pools of warmth twinkling in a way that made her think of a smile even though his expression seemed solemn.

"Surprised?" There was his smile again. Warm and inviting and just a little soft.

"I am surprised." She frowned. "If you're not here to berate me, then... You told me that one day I would realize that I deserved a raise. I believe that day has come."

"Of course," he said easily. "As my new vice president of telegraphic encoding, you must command a higher salary."

She started forward. "Vice president of telegraphic encoding!" She felt as if she were glowing. "That's a lovely surprise! But are you *certain?*"

He laughed. "That wasn't even the surprise. That's just ordinary advancement in exchange for good work."

"It wasn't?" She looked at him. That warm, fluttery feeling rose in her belly again. Maybe, perhaps...

Oh. God. Where were her manners? She hadn't even asked him in yet.

She was about to do so when he turned around. "You can come out now."

A familiar face peered around the corner of the building.

Amelia forgot everything she was thinking in the sheer joy of seeing him. She ran forward, wrapping her arms around her brother. "Leland!"

"Amelia. You've been revolutionizing telegraphic code, I hear."

She grimaced. "Ugh. What nonsense have you been hearing? It's less revolutionizing, more beating it into submission with blood and sweat and tears."

"Mmm. I'm not sure I believe that, given what I just overheard. My sister is the vice president of telegraphic encoding. I'll have to fight Captain Hunter to make sure he's compensating you properly."

She grinned at him, holding tight to his hands, afraid to let go. "Have you eaten yet this morning?"

"Not a thing. We've just made our way through Woosung."

"Then come," she said, taking hold of Leland's sleeve and pulling. "I know just the cart."

Captain Hunter stood to the side, smiling wryly. "Well then. I'll be off."

He touched his hat in farewell and turned to go. Amelia realized that he thought he could show up on her doorstep, deposit her brother, and then depart without a further word.

"Grayson Hunter." She folded her arms. "Don't you dare."

He turned back to her.

She frowned at him. "How can Leland fight you over my salary if you slink away? You absolutely *must* come or I'll demand an even better title."

She knew it was a foolish argument. She knew he wasn't likely to agree. He looked at her for a long moment. She could feel the phantom brush of his thumb across her hand. The late spring air was warm against her face, and the sun was brilliant overhead. Little green plants in the box at her window were starting to bud. Birds were singing. He was here.

"At least come have breakfast," she said.

He shook his head. "Very well. Breakfast. I'll allow breakfast."

Grayson felt incredibly foolish dangling after Merry, Amelia, and her brother.

He'd intended to show up, deliver her a new title, hand over her brother, and take his leave while they were talking. He had business of his own in Shanghai. There were precise terms to discuss with the taotai, after all, and plans to lay the telegraph line in now that it had been allowed. There were enough business matters to occupy his time. As for Amelia, the pleasure of her brother's company would keep her busy.

He had not planned to trail behind the two of them.

At some point, he was going to have to stop and consider how to go on. But for now, he allowed himself to enjoy a rare respite. Walking behind them, he could watch her obvious joy in interrogating her brother. It lit her from within, made her smile and throw back her head.

After a bit of a walk, Amelia led them to a cart where she ordered youtiao for all three of them.

"These are really the best within a two-mile walk," Amelia said gravely as she watched the cook press long strips of dough together with a chopstick and then throw them in a wok to fry in oil. "When I have a chance, I always make my way over here. It takes a little time, but Merry enjoys the walk and I enjoy the food."

She laughed.

God, he was really a fool for her laughter.

The cook turned the dough in the oil using chopsticks, rolling them in swift sure movements. Finally, when the dough was golden brown, he lifted them out. Amelia held out her own chopstick; he skewered the sticks on, one by one, so they could dangle.

A shop a few doors down sold soy milk. Amelia purchased some, and then the three of them traipsed back to Amelia's home, where they settled around a table. Amelia found table-cloths and spoons and chopsticks for all, and Merry situated herself at Amelia's knee.

His youtiao really was delicious, crunchy on the outside and steamy on the inside, with the sweet, beany taste of the soy milk proving a perfect contrast.

"So," Amelia said to Mr. Acheson. "Any thoughts on how you will tell her?"

This appeared to be part of a conversation the two of them had been having for a while.

"Well." Mr. Acheson grimaced. "She will be extremely annoyed with me, that's for sure. But the issue is less 'how do I tell her I've quit being a missionary' and more 'what will I say if she asks why.'"

Ah. Grayson hadn't known Leland had quit his work as a missionary. He turned to the man. "And the truth won't work, I suppose."

Mr. Acheson exchanged a glance with Amelia.

"Mother is not always good with the truth." Amelia said this diplomatically.

Her brother snorted. "The truth would go like this: 'Mother, it turns out that I think you and your fellow missionaries are doing a great deal of damage. Now that I've experienced it firsthand, I can no longer take part.'"

"She will be extremely annoyed," Amelia said, turning to Grayson, "in the way that only Mother can be. She will send letters. Annoying letters."

"Lots of them." Mr. Acheson scrubbed a hand through his hair.

"She'll come to an understanding eventually."

Leland sighed. "No, she really won't. And you wouldn't know because in the end, you always do side with her. I can never quite understand it."

Grayson glanced across the table.

Amelia was frowning. "Side with her? Mother and I disagree. That's why I'm here in Shanghai rather than married to another missionary."

"Yes," Leland said with a patient sigh. "But you *chose* her, you know."

"What do you mean? I'm *here*. Not with her."

"I don't mean that." Leland shook his head and dunked a piece of fried dough in soy milk. "Tell me to hold my tongue if you wish, but I've never been able to understand. If *my* actual mother had been coming around asking to speak with me for years on end, I would at least have met her."

Mr. Acheson said that so casually, popping the dough in his mouth, that Grayson at first thought he must have misheard. But no. Cold crept up Grayson's spine.

There was utter silence at the table. Amelia looked rooted in place, her chopsticks poised over her soy milk while her own bread grew soggy.

Perhaps, after a few seconds, Mr. Acheson realized something was amiss.

"What?" he asked. "You *did* freeze her out."

Amelia's left hand curled into a fist around her napkin, knuckles white. "What do you mean?"

Leland shook his head. "I know you don't like talking about this. It's your decision. I have tried to respect that over the years, but—"

"No, no, go back to the first part. What do you *mean?*" Amelia dropped her chopsticks. "Tell me what you mean, *my actual mother.*" Her voice was quavering now. "Coming around? My decision? *What* decision?"

For a moment, the two looked at each other, eyes wide. Then Leland put a hand to his mouth. His skin went deathly pale, then shaded into green.

Without saying a word, he crossed to the door and opened it.

"Leland?" Amelia jumped to her feet. "Leland? Where are you going? You can't say something like that and just leave."

He didn't answer—at least not in words. But as Grayson stood, Amelia's brother lurched forward onto his knees, facing the shrubbery just outside Amelia's door. His shoulders heaved. And then he vomited into the bushes.

CHAPTER TWENTY-SIX

Amelia's heart was rabbiting in her chest. She felt disconnected from the world around her, as if the ground had suddenly tilted beneath her feet. As if gravity had suspended its operations.

It took all her strength to see to the necessary physical details of the disaster that was unfolding around her. A towel for Leland. Tea. A pitcher of water. Her brother kept apologizing over and over.

By the time the mess had been cleaned up, a little color had returned to Leland's face. Not much. He still looked wan and sickly.

His voice was shaking. "I owe you an explanation. And an apology."

Amelia shook her head. "Just the explanation will do."

He exhaled, rubbing his temples. "I met your Chinese mother when I was twelve. You were almost seven."

Her head spun. *Seventeen years ago* he had met Amelia's mother. *Seventeen years.* A year after she'd been left behind. Back when she still believed her mother would return. Seventeen years was so long ago.

"Go on." Her voice didn't seem to belong to her. Her lips felt numb. The words might have come from nowhere.

Leland just shook his head. "Mother said you wanted nothing to do with her. That's why she insisted on moving from Shanghai to Fuzhou—so you wouldn't have to know about it."

Amelia felt very, very cold. And confused. So confused. What he was saying did not seem possible. It did not seem likely. She had imagined her Chinese Ah Ma coming back for her so many times. She had convinced herself the memory or her promising to do so was a lie.

But if her memory of her mother saying she would come back *wasn't* a lie, then... Amelia shook her head. Logically, she knew what the answer must be. But her brain skipped every time she contemplated it. Skipped like a stone that refused to acknowledge the lake.

Leland went on, unaware that Amelia's entire world was combusting inside her head. "She said that she had asked you, but that you were angry that you had been abandoned. She said you didn't want to speak of the woman, that doing so was painful for you. I asked you about it a few times, but you always said you were never going to see her..." He trailed off.

"It *was* painful," Amelia replied slowly. It had been the source of deep, searing pain. Because she remembered her mother saying she would come back, and however confused and muddled that memory was, she'd been told over and over that she had *imagined* it. That it *hadn't* happened. That she needed to *move forward.*

The stone stopped skipping, dropping into deep, still waters. There was only one explanation.

She'd been lied to. Repeatedly. She'd been told that nobody wanted her but the woman she called mother. And she'd believed it.

"Mother said," Leland said, perhaps not seeing how close

Amelia was to losing hold on her emotions, "that you were terrified of being made to leave our family. That we shouldn't mention it so you knew you were safe and wouldn't be sent away."

Safe. Amelia couldn't help it. She found herself unable to hold back tears any longer. They stung her eyes, dripping down her nose. She hated those tears even as they started down her cheeks. She squeezed her eyes shut.

"I'm sorry." She could hear Leland let out a slow breath. "I am so desperately sorry. I should have said something."

She didn't even want to imagine what he could have done. What her world would look like if the truth had been an option.

A warm hand made contact with hers. The comforting weight of a linen handkerchief slid into her palm. She pressed the cloth into her eyes, trying to push back years of pent-up anguish that could only be felt, not comprehended. It was embarrassing. Embarrassing that Captain Hunter had to watch this happen—that he heard how foolish she had been for so long, that he saw how it affected her, that he saw that she couldn't get herself under control.

She wasn't sure who set their hands on top of hers. Those thumbs made light circles against her inner wrists, a warm, comforting touch. That convinced her it wasn't Leland. There was an intimacy to that touch. She knew those thumbs.

It should have been a relief that Grayson was seeing her like this and not scoffing at her, but somehow, his kindness made it worse. The acknowledgment that this *wasn't* fine threatened to flood her with emotion.

She wasn't sure how long she cried, how long Grayson rubbed her wrists. She didn't even know when Leland came behind her, setting his hands on her shoulders. She wasn't sure when Merry pushed a warm snout between Amelia's legs, pressing against her in comfort.

We're here. We care for you.

Amelia wasn't sure where one emotion inside her ended and the rest began. She felt anger, fear, confusion, sadness.

Her brother was saying comforting things in a low tone. She heard, "There, there," and "I'm so sorry, Amelia. God, I can't ever forgive myself. I should have said." She shuddered, blowing her nose into the handkerchief before lifting her head.

Captain Hunter had moved closer to her. The breakfast things were still strewn across the table. The youtiao must have gone cold, she found herself thinking with dismay, and then she wondered why she was thinking about the temperature of bread at a time like this.

"I don't know what to think." She exhaled. "I really don't know what to think. Withholding that information from me seems…"

Heartless, she wanted to say, but her mind rejected that possibility, unable to fit the warmth and love she had known from her mother with what felt like the calculating cruelty of making her believe her Ah Ma didn't want her. Maybe Amelia would have thought it of someone else, but it didn't fit *now.* She couldn't *make* it fit into the life she'd had.

"It seems violent." Captain Hunter completed the sentence she hadn't been able to finish.

Violent. Such an ugly word. Violence made her imagine being struck hard across the face. Her mother had never, ever been violent.

Yet this had that same feeling—of a great, bruising blow, hard enough to send her reeling.

Amelia stood, pulling away from the warmth that they had provided her. Her brother's arm fell to his side. Merry came to her heel, and Amelia began to walk slowly around her room. Walking made more sense than sitting; walking, at least allowed her to attempt to outpace her feelings.

They were all out of order. Jumbled together. She didn't

know what to do about her mother—that was entirely too much of a mess to manage. She didn't know what to do about the word *mother.*

But one thing seemed to rise out of her confusion. One simple, clear thing.

"I need to find her."

But it had been so many years. One woman, whose name she didn't know?

She shook her head. "I don't know how. Did she leave a name? An address?"

Leland shook his head slowly. "If she did, I heard nothing of it."

"Damn." Amelia turned back to pacing. "What can I do?"

"What about your liaison?" Leland asked. "Benedict Worth? I talked to him when he was in Hong Kong a while back. He's searching for his sister. Doesn't he have some skill in the matter of searching for people who are missing?"

Amelia tilted her head and looked at Leland through her disbelief. "Benedict is delightful, and I'm sure he would love to assist in any way. If my mother were British, by all means I'd consult him. But he has never been to the interior of China. And I don't have a name for him to ask about. Besides, what spoken Mandarin he knows, I've taught him, and he's not literate in written Chinese."

"Ah." Leland looked taken aback. "I had not really thought that one through."

Amelia shut her eyes. "It's impossible. But it must be done. But—but I haven't time." Her voice was straining. "I have employment. I cannot simply stop. I have error correction to finish. And the codebooks to go over. And—"

"Amelia." Grayson interrupted her with a hand on her arm. "Amelia. Listen."

She stopped and looked at him. Under her perusal, he looked away.

"I saw some of your presentation to the taotai," he told her. "Benedict sent me a letter that brought me back from San Francisco... Never mind. I came in at the end of your practice. I heard what you said."

This made as much sense as what Leland had said. As the ringing, bruised sensation when she thought about her mother —Mrs. Acheson—God, she didn't even know what words to use for anything.

"You were there? But you didn't stay."

He shook his head. "I heard what you said. I wanted you to have the thing you'd lost—family. That's why I brought your brother with me."

She shook her head. "But my employment..."

He turned back to her, a determined set in his jaw. "You may recall what I told you a year ago. There was nobody qualified to encode Chinese characters then because it had not yet been done."

"Yes?"

"It has now been done. By you. That makes you the only qualified vice president of telegraphic encoding in the entire world. Your employment will wait if you need time to attend to a personal matter. Your employment has no choice."

"You." She stared at him blankly. "*You* are saying that the work will wait."

"I brought your brother here to see you because I know what it's like to ache for family and never have them present. I have a mother who I can't—" He cut himself off with a shake of his head. "You have the chance to make that connection. There is absolutely no world in which I would deny you that."

"But I don't know what to do."

"Forty-three," he shot back, looking straight into her eyes.

Since that time he'd left her with a stack of opened envelopes filled with universally positive things, she'd gone back and read them. More than once. Enough that she'd maybe memorized them a little.

Envelope *43* had said this: *I know the task may seem impossible, but everything is doable if you break it into small enough pieces. You can do it.* She felt her eyes sting again.

"Grayson." She looked down at her hands, blurry through her tears. "It's been eighteen years. I don't know her *name.* She came back, but she thinks I don't want her. She's probably angry or something. I don't know if she still wants to know me."

"Forty-three," he repeated. "You said it had to be done. You know how to do things."

"Very well." She glanced at Leland. He still looked like wax. "It's been eighteen years. I don't know her name. What I do know is…" Amelia shut her eyes. "Eighteen years ago, she found Ah Ma outside of Shanghai. They spoke. Mother hasn't said what she knows, but she must remember something. She knows more than she told me."

He nodded at her. "You see. You do know where to start."

"I don't want to talk to her yet." She knew that much. Her head hurt. She felt bruised.

"I know, sweetheart," Grayson said.

That simple acknowledgment was crueler than pressing the point would have been. Amelia sighed. "I have to, don't I? I have to go back. I'll have to get Benedict to watch Merry."

"Sweetheart?" Leland said to their side. "Captain Hunter, should I inquire after your relationship with my sister?"

Amelia felt her breath freeze in her lungs. She didn't want to hear Grayson deny any connection. She knew he would, but right now—right in this moment—she didn't want to hear how unimportant she was to another person she cared about.

Their eyes met. She inhaled. She wasn't going to cry. She wasn't, damn it. She wasn't going to make him have to comfort her or push her away. She wasn't fragile. She wasn't in need of care.

"I'll be damned if I know what our relationship is," Grayson said. "But I know this much. If she needs to go back to Fuzhou, I'm taking her. If she'll allow it."

Amelia let out a shocked breath. "Don't you have things to do? And surely Leland might accompany me."

She had been sure of it up until the words came out of her mouth. But instead of agreeing, her brother turned even paler.

"Amelia." He let out a shaky breath. "I can't. I can't—I simply can't look at her and…" He trailed off. "I can't. I'm sorry. Please don't ask it of me."

That refusal stung. But her brother seemed genuinely distressed by her request. He'd actually vomited when he found out the truth. Amelia let out a breath.

"Captain, I can't ask you to…"

"You didn't ask. I offered."

She should say no. She should remind him of his duties. But she didn't think for one second that his memory had lapsed.

"Then yes." She exhaled. "Yes, I would like that very much."

CHAPTER TWENTY-SEVEN

Fuzhou had not changed, Amelia thought, as she made her way up the hill where she had once lived. Not in any real detail.

It was she who had changed. After months of working on telegraphic code with Scholar Wu, after spending time with Auntie Zhu and Miss Luo, Amelia had found her footing. The world looked different when you weren't afraid of falling.

Amelia had never felt as if she fit in. Now she was all the more aware that this hill where the Westerners resided, with the flags of other nations flying, was painfully out of place.

The *Celerity* was docked in the harbor below. This time of year, the harbor was only half empty. Most of the tea would still be growing on the bush. Despite the gold pollen that dusted the waters, filling the river with tiny specks of yellow, Fuzhou's harbor seemed relatively bare.

The voyage here had been short enough. Amelia and Grayson spoken over meals, and she'd done her best to think through her bruising pain—to break down her problem into little pieces. Grayson had offered to come along with her to the meeting as well, but she could not imagine her mother offering the truth in front of a virtual stranger.

So she was here, climbing the hill alone.

The last time she had been here, she'd still been holding on to her mother's strictures. *Don't use slang, Amelia; people will think you have no culture. Don't slouch, Amelia; how will they think you were raised?* And there were those other rules, deeper rules, rules that she could scarcely remember being taught. Rules about how to pronounce words, drummed into her over and over.

Be English, Amelia, or people will think you Chinese.

She had thought those rules were a part of her, but after more than a year of absence, they'd begun to peel away. She'd left with her mother's warning ringing in her ears, the inevitability of failure and ruination ahead of her.

She was coming back as the vice president of telegraphic encoding for the first company to strike a telegraphic deal with China, and it had happened because of *her*.

With that certainty to steel her spine, she knocked on the door. She nodded at the maid, who'd jumped at the sight of her. She'd asked her to fetch her mother and tell her she had a visitor. A surprise, she said.

The drawing room was as it had always been. Imported glass windows looked out over the Min. It was the picture of British opulence—British-style furniture, Persian-style rugs, Japanese vases—the best of everything from everywhere in the world. Amelia waited in this parlor decorated with the breadth of British trading.

She heard the door open behind her, the shock of breath.

"Amelia!" Her mother shrieked her name in joy. "You've come back to me!"

It had been more than a week since Leland's revelation. Long enough that Amelia's emotions, confused and angry and sad, felt as if they'd crystallized into something sharp and unbending.

Amelia turned to greet her.

Her mother looked as she always did. Beautiful. English.

"Have you come back for good?" Her eyes glistened with tears. She hastened forward, wrapping Amelia in an embrace that was so like old times that Amelia could not help but return it. "Are you mine again?"

The last question coiled like a knot in Amelia's stomach. She let her arms drop and pulled away.

"I came back because I had some questions to put to you."

Her mother must not have sensed the undercurrent of agony in Amelia's voice. Amelia could scarcely feel it herself; it felt as if she were being carried out to sea on a strong riptide. As if she would never see this place again.

"Of course!" Her mother gave her a brilliant smile. "Let me get some tea."

She called out, and a few moments later—the maid must have prepared in anticipation—the tea arrived.

Porcelain teapot. Little cups. One little teaspoon of tea for the entire gigantic pot. Milk and sugar to mask the taste.

Fought two wars for tea and don't even know how to drink it properly, some part of her whispered as she observed this ritual.

Amelia wasn't here to fight over tea.

She let herself be shepherded into a chair, let her mother ply her with sandwiches and a biscuit and milky tea that tasted sickly and sweet. Had she really drunk it like this? She took a bite of the biscuit. It tasted like sand.

"Come," her mother said. "Talk to me. You seem troubled. Is there some problem with your employment? Have you been let go? You know I'm here for you. Anything you wish. How *are* you?"

That was all she could imagine—that Amelia had returned

to her a failure. Yet Amelia had been sending her letter after letter, week after week, detailing every stage of her success.

How are you?

Those words were like a handshake. *How are you? I am well. Nobody wants to know anything more.*

Amelia looked her mother in the eyes. "I am not well."

Her mother's eyes widened. "Oh dear. Are you ill? Have you been let go?"

"None of that." How *was* she? If she shut her eyes, she could see an entire maelstrom of emotions, blue and red and orange. She finally settled on this: "I am angry."

"Who has wronged you? Are you in need of assistance?"

Amelia didn't answer the first question. "No. It's not that kind of…" She shook her head. "I just need to understand. Can we talk about my Chinese mother? Tell me everything."

Her mother looked at her. A wrinkle in her brow deepened; her lips pressed together. "Dear. Are you still letting that bother you? I thought you were past it. If the circumstances of your abandonment are still giving you pause, it won't do any good to stir it up."

Amelia shouldn't have phrased it as a question, one that could be avoided. Amelia bit her lip, the slight pain centering her. "I *need* you to tell me everything about her."

Mrs. Acheson looked over at Amelia. Maybe she finally saw something of what was happening because she exhaled, long and slow. "Very well. I don't think it's wise, but…" A shrug, as if to say that it was all on Amelia. "What would you like to know?"

"Everything." Amelia was not calm; she was frozen solid.

Her mother tapped a finger against her teacup. "You know there isn't much to tell."

She still looked sincere—so sincere that for a moment, Amelia wanted to doubt Leland's story. What if he had been wrong?

"I'm not sure what specifically you're asking for," her mother said, shaking her head. "But I've told you how it went already. More times than I can count. We were offering water and a meal to refugees when your mother came in with you."

She had told Amelia this story more times than Amelia could count. Amelia had a mental image of that moment in her mind, just as she had an image of all the stories she'd been told.

"You were small for your age and yet wide-eyed and inquisitive, looking about everywhere. I held you for a moment to give your mother a chance to rest. And I think she saw how happy we were together. She told me that she wanted me to have you."

"What was her name?" Amelia had asked this before.

Not so much as a blink. "I don't know." Same answer as before. "We only had a few words in common; we could hardly communicate well enough to exchange names or directions."

It was so odd. *So* odd. Amelia had been told this story so many times and from such a young age that she had accepted it as absolute truth. Not once had she stopped to question what was now so plainly obvious after eleven months of working out how to transmit information in the Chinese language, working alongside Chinese men and women who spoke slightly different dialects, trying to make sure they all understood one another.

"If you couldn't communicate with her well enough to obtain her name," Amelia asked, "how could you communicate well enough to know she wanted you to take her child?"

There was a long pause. Her mother stared at her, and there it came—the first hint of uncertainty. Blink. Blink. That wrinkle on her forehead popped out again.

It lasted only a moment.

"There are ways to communicate such things," her mother said, three seconds too late. "Gestures. I could see it in her eyes."

Gestures. Amelia had spent nearly a year of her life hammering out efficient and effective modes of communication. She'd read books about it. She could have written one now; if one counted the telegraphic manual, she *had.*

"Oh," Amelia said. "How extraordinary that you both knew semaphore."

Her mother looked at her.

"Or was it some other form of gesture-based language that you had in common? A sign language? Those differ from region to region."

"If you're going to be sarcastic," her mother said snippily, "this conversation is over."

"I wasn't trying to be sarcastic. I was listing gesture-based forms of communication. Which one was it?"

"None of those. Just gestures. *Human* gestures."

Amelia didn't even know what to say about that, so she went on. "Was there anything else that happened? You've never heard from her after?"

"Of course not," her mother said.

Amelia shut her eyes. "Mother." She said the next item as matter-of-factly as she could manage. "I know you've heard from her since. Did she use human gestures the next time you met as well?"

There was a long pause. Even now her mother did not look upset. She simply sighed before rubbing her temples.

"Oh dear." She said this the way she might respond if a servant knocked over a teacup. "You must have talked to the mission in Shanghai."

Amelia blinked. The mission in Shanghai?

"And they told you. How upsetting for you that must have been. I told them not to. They don't know you the way I do. And now look where we are. They've upset you."

"*They* have upset me?"

"I didn't tell you about any of that when you were younger

because I knew how hurt you already were when your mother abandoned you the first time. Was I going to subject you to upheaval a second time? No. Of course I was not, and I will not apologize for it. She *left* you. You were *mine.*"

Intellectually speaking, it would be fascinating how swiftly her mother transitioned from *of course I've told you everything* to *I lied to you about everything, but it was for your own good.*

"I was yours?" Amelia felt her anger rise. "On the basis of what? Human gestures? I wouldn't take a dog without clear, unequivocal communication that it was allowed, and I'm not a dog. I'm not *yours.* You don't *get* to own me."

"There you are. Talking nonsense about dogs again." Her mother shook her head. "I didn't mean it that way. I *love* you."

"I know." The truth was beginning to break through the confusion in Amelia's heart. "But love doesn't give you the right to take a child."

"Listen to yourself. Take? I didn't *take.* I *gave.* I gave you a life, an opportunity. It was for your own good."

"Was it?"

"It's always been for your own good."

"When the devil comes courting…," Amelia said slowly.

Her mother looked up sharply. "He tells you what you want to hear," she finished.

"You were always so quick to tell me not to want things. You came up with an explanation even now why I shouldn't hear the truth as a grown woman. You told yourself it was right to take me in. It was right to lie to me. It was right for you to send my mother away without even letting her see me."

"*I* am your mother."

Amelia ignored that. "And you say it's for my own good. Until I left here, I felt like nobody would ever love me unless I got everything right. That a year of employment would spoil me like a fruit. How was *that* for my own good?"

"Amelia, you must understand. I know how the world

operates. It wasn't *I* who believed it. I know it must sting for you to contemplate it as well. But I did it all for your own good."

"No." Amelia finally realized through her confusion what she was feeling. Her heart was breaking open like an ocean wave against the immovable black rock of her certainty.

Her mother opened her mouth again, and a torrent of words poured forth. Amelia could not concentrate on them. She could scarcely hold the seams of her own emotions together, let alone listen to what someone else had to say. Not when that person (*your mother*, her mind whispered, and *not your mother*, another part whispered back) had lied to her throughout her entire life, had been offered the chance to tell the truth and had lied brazenly again.

She would have accepted an apology. An explanation. She had hoped for one.

"I cannot believe you are accusing me like this," her mother was saying through tears. "Have you no gratitude? Do you not realize that, in actuality, it is you who—"

Amelia held up a hand. She did not think she could stand to be told she was apparently at fault for removing herself from her Chinese mother, for not knowing her Ah Ma had come for her, and for being upset the knowledge had been concealed from her.

"You taught me to question myself when I wanted something too much," she said. "You taught me to be careful about my own desires. But you never questioned yourself the way you questioned me. When the devil came courting *you*, he told you that you could take a child. Why did you never ask yourself if that was right?"

Her mother sniffled, then wiped at her eyes. "Why are you doing this? Can't you see how you're upsetting me?"

A part of Amelia still wanted to step forward. To apologize as she was expected to do. Making someone else cry... It had to be her who was wrong. And yet were her own tears of lesser value?

It was, maybe, the first time in Amelia's life that she saw clearly. Those tears were a weapon. They openly proclaimed her mother's hurt, demanded attention to heal that harm, and in so doing, declared the harm that she had done to Amelia unimportant. In fact, Amelia was rude and invasive for mentioning it.

"You didn't answer my question," Amelia said. "Why did you think you could take me?"

Their eyes met. Her mother shook her head.

"What does the mission in Shanghai know?" Amelia asked.

"Nothing." Her mother muttered sullenly.

"Not her name? Not her direction? Nothing? If I went to them and asked, what would they say?"

Her mother looked up, a hint of fear in her eyes.

"Did they write to you?" Amelia asked. "Did they tell you she was still coming to inquire? Did they give her your direction?"

Her mother's eyes widened, and a memory caught at Amelia's mind.

"Is that why you wanted me married off so quickly? Has she come here as well?"

Her mother just stared at her, unblinking, and Amelia wanted to cry all over again. But her well of tears felt dry and empty.

Finally, "Yes," her mother whispered.

Yes. She hadn't just come *one* year. She'd come more than once looking for Amelia. Often enough that her mother feared its recurrence.

Amelia shut her eyes. "Is that why you thought I should marry at seventeen?" To get her out of the way?

"I have always wanted what was best for you," her mother replied in quavering tones.

Amelia stood. "I think I've heard enough."

Her mother also stood. "Where are you going? What are you going to do? You can't just leave me like this!"

For a moment, Amelia thought her mother might physically bar her way.

Amelia's heart was bruised, and that made her feel a little wild. She'd had enough of being handed around like a dog that nobody really wanted. She stared back into her mother's eyes.

"I'm leaving," she said. "But before I do, you're going to tell me every last scrap you've heard about my Chinese mother. You're going to do it because if you don't, I *will* never talk to you again. I want letters. I want names. Places. Everything you've heard from the mission. Everything you remember. You're going to tell me all of it."

"And if I do? What then?"

Amelia hadn't the capacity to make threats. She wasn't even sure what threats to make. For all her anger and her confusion, this woman had raised her and she still couldn't bring herself to examine what that meant.

Amelia shook her head. "If you do, you'll get to believe that maybe one day, if you figure out how to apologize for this, I might forgive you."

CHAPTER TWENTY-EIGHT

Amelia felt odd when she returned to Grayson's ship.

Odd did not quite cover the way she felt. A freezing numbness had set in, and her veins felt full of creeping crystals of ice. She made her way to the cabin that had been assigned to her and sat.

She now had letters in her possession. Plural. She spread these out in front of her and started reading from the beginning.

None of these letters were from her Ah Ma.

Instead, the letters had been sent by the mission in Shanghai where Mrs. Acheson had once volunteered. The first letter, from a Mrs. Wilson, said That Woman (that was how she was referred to) had come again. They had promised her that they would pass on the information she provided. Further letters came at irregular intervals—sometimes once a year, sometimes twice, sometimes more.

They always said some variant of the same thing.

We have promised That Woman that we would pass on this information, and we are doing so now.

"That woman" had a name. Eventually, a Mr. Tallent used it.

He called her "Long" in one letter, and "Liung" in the next. Mrs. Wilson named her as "Ling."

Amelia strained her memory, trying to hear the echo of that family name in her mind. Surely her own name would have to feel familiar.

But her memory for names didn't improve no matter how much she wanted it to do so. She could remember nothing but silence.

No personal name was ever given in those letters. The writers reported dutifully that she lived up the Yangtze River from Shanghai. Four days, one said, although no mode of transportation was given to qualify what that meant.

One letter finally provided more. Lee Yong City, that letter said. Near Chang Chow. That was how those words were written: Chang Chow. Lee Yong. The transliteration was no doubt a mess. But it was something to go on.

Amelia's Ah Ma had been making the voyage from the place four days up the river down to Shanghai at least once a year for the past seventeen years to ask where her daughter was. When that hadn't turned up anything, she'd apparently made her way to Fuzhou a handful of times.

The letters from the mission in Shanghai concluded in much the same way: apologies for the annoyance, promises not to give the woman any information, best wishes for Mrs. Acheson's health.

Amelia finished reading through this correspondence and shut her eyes. She had tried to imagine her Ah Ma all her life. She had wisps of memory, barely enough to construct a face, and even that she wasn't sure about.

But this gave her a little more. She imagined the determination of a woman who kept coming and coming. Who refused to give up. Who kept caring after all hope and reason should have fled. What kind of person must she be?

Oh, she thought. *She sounds like...me.* Emotion simmered in her heart.

A rap sounded at the door.

"One moment."

She stood, swiped away her tears, dabbed a handkerchief in cold water and pressed it underneath her eyes. When she thought that the puffiness had been dispelled, she found a smile —it was easy to make her lips pretend—and opened the door.

Grayson stood there. He was watching her, his gaze dark on her. "Well?" he asked. "What have you found?"

Amelia bit her lip. "She is in some place that sounds like Lee Yong, four days up the Yangtze River."

His eyes met hers. "You see? Forty-three."

"Forty-three." She felt her eyes sting. "You were right."

"I can speak with the consulate's office back in Shanghai. It will require a bit of paperwork, but we should be able to get interior passes."

He said this as if it were a small thing to offer to convey her to the woman she barely remembered.

"We?" she echoed. "You don't need to come with me. I'm perfectly capable of going on my own. You've done more than enough..."

He shrugged. "I haven't done much of anything except help arrange transport."

"Grayson." Amelia shut her eyes. "You've done a lot more than that. You're here."

He exhaled, pressing a hand over his face.

"You're always so busy. Haven't you things to do?" She found the thread of a smile on her lips once more and let herself pretend all her other emotions no longer existed. "Are there no employees to bother or other languages to commit to telegraph?"

"Amelia."

He looked down at her. He seemed close, very close. Probably because he *was* close. She wasn't sure when he'd drawn near.

"It's not just about you."

She looked up at him.

"My mother." He shrugged. "I'm her least favorite child— and don't look at me like that. I can't fault her for it. If you'd known my brothers, you would have loved me least too."

"Grayson." Her heart was breaking for him, and yet he said this all so nonchalantly.

"She can't help how she feels. She'll never admit it, but I know she resents that out of the four of us who went to war, I'm the one who survived. And I didn't make it easy on her surviving, either, with how I've been after."

"Grayson."

"I can understand it all from her perspective. The resentment. The guilt about the resentment. I don't *want* that from her. I can hardly bear to be around my parents because of it."

"Grayson."

"But I'm fixing it." His eyes blazed and he looked at her. "If I can build the transpacific telegraph—well, never mind how it will work. That's not the point. I'm fixing it, and damn it, if I can do it for you, maybe I can do it for me too."

"Grayson." She felt horrified by how quickly he moved on from what he'd just said.

"Just to make things clear between us, when I first met you, before I knew I needed to employ you, I thought about seducing you."

"Oh." She felt faintly disappointed. "You stopped?"

He let out a huff of air. "Amelia."

"What a pity."

"It has only become worse. I want it more than ever." He set his hand on her chin, fingers stroking along her jaw. She felt heat ripple through her at his touch. She wasn't sure if she tilted her head back or if he did.

"Grayson." She looked up at him.

His hand slid around her to cup her head.

"Gray—"

She could manage no more. He leaned in and kissed her. There was nothing sweet to this kiss, which was just as well because anything sweet in her had burned to bitterness in the past hour. It was searing—his tongue against hers, his mouth open on hers, need pouring out all at once, demanding every fiber of her attention.

He was kissing her. He was *kissing* her, and she was kissing him back, refusing to be taken by surprise in this. Her own hands came to his shoulders, pulling him close. Then they were kissing deeper, deeper, as if she could inhale the warm solidity of him into her lungs, as if she could take in the happiness he made her feel and drive out all her sorrow.

His arm came around her waist, holding her in place. She could hear the lapping of the waves against the ship, the call of gulls, the buzz of the docks.

He kissed her on and on until time disappeared and the sadness in her chest lightened.

He finally pulled away, his breathing heavy.

She looked up into his eyes. "Thank you."

"Don't. That was pure selfishness." He smiled at her. "I've wanted to do that again for months."

His thumb trailed down her cheek. He smiled sadly. Then he leaned in and kissed her again, this time gently on the lips.

"There," he said. "I should let you go before we do something neither of us is equipped to handle."

～

The days that followed felt like a dream to Grayson. Time passed, but it seemed to run at ninety-degree angles to reality.

The journey back to Shanghai should have been fraught with tension. His own want felt too large to be contained. But the time wasn't right. He could sense her discomfort in the way she looked out over the gray waters of the ocean with a troubled expression. Yet there was an ease to their time together that defied all explanation.

She'd learned to play Go while in Shanghai, and while he had no experience, she taught him. After a few games that were outright slaughter on her part, he managed to put up a decent fight, getting better and better as the voyage went on.

Then there was the lust. It should have made matters awkward between them, those glances drenched with yearning, the times their hands met not entirely on accident.

It should have been a morass, those moments when she caught him looking off over the horizon to the west, when she took his hand between hers in silent comfort. It all should have been delicate and painful and uncomfortable to be in love with her, to want her, and to know he could do nothing other than offer scant relief, to bid her good night and then imagine her with him when his door was closed.

Instead, it was perplexingly easy to want her. The want fit into his life.

Arriving back in Shanghai didn't shake the dream either. It just made it feel more like a fantasy. It took a little time to arrange passes to the interior from the consul and to inquire after the places listed in the letters. "Chang Chow" they determined to be Changzhou; that made "Lee Yong" to be "Liyang." An interpreter fluent in the Wu dialect was added to their retinue.

Going up the Yangtze was its own form of an unreal dream.

For all the time that Grayson had spent in Asia, he'd only ever visited the ports in China that were opened to foreigners by treaty. The waters of the Yangtze delta passed through low, rolling hills covered by bamboo forest—endless miles of spiky green leaves that rattled with the wind. The riverbanks had swollen, overflowing in the spring. They passed by paddy after paddy being planted with rice by laborers in wide-brimmed hats.

Canals and streams fed into the Yangtze. The banks were dotted with the artillery-darkened ruins of bridges, remnants of decades of wars that had been waged up the river.

Amelia watched all this go by with a sense of wonder in her eyes, and Grayson watched her.

"Is any of this familiar?" he asked her late afternoon on the second day as she watched the sunset in orange and pinks and golds over the smooth river waters.

"It's not *unfamiliar*," she said. "But I don't know it. It's unsettling how much it doesn't unsettle me."

That was how he felt about her. This thing between them felt at home in his heart; it was just that his heart didn't know the feeling of home.

After several days traveling upstream, they arrived in Liyang. The entire journey had been comfortable. *Too* comfortable.

Grayson and Amelia presented their passes to the local district registrar who shook his head. He spoke Mandarin, but swiftly enough that Grayson couldn't completely follow. The interpreter started to speak, but couldn't keep up with the rapid-fire questions. Something about passes, business…

Amelia managed to smooth everything over. She offered humble apologies for not knowing the proper protocols and begged for the official's instruction in the matter. The man looked at her, then at Grayson. Finally he nodded and took their letter.

"He says your passes look to be in order," the interpreter finally told them. "You may stay here, but you must report where you are staying on a daily basis."

"Xie xie," Grayson said.

The man cast him a searching, curious look, then turned to the interpreter, asking something else. Amelia colored and tensed.

"He wants to know what kind of barbarian you are. I can set him straight," Amelia started to say.

Grayson shook his head. "The Chinese think all non-Chinese are barbarians."

It was not as if Grayson could fault that belief, not when China's contact with the West included two wars fought over the West's supposedly God-given right to opiate the Chinese people. *They're barbarians to me too,* he wanted to say. But there was no real way for him to explain centuries of chattel slavery and a family that had grown up on the edges of that travesty, fighting it. And he was not without ties to Britain.

How could he explain this to someone who saw the entirety of the world outside China as an undifferentiated mass of barbarianism?

"Funny you should ask," Grayson said instead. "Let's have dinner and discuss the matter. I'll buy the wine."

When this was translated, the man nodded, pleased.

"We're looking for Mrs. Smith's family," Grayson told the man. He waited a moment for the interpreter to translate that, and another for the man to turn his head to Amelia.

"Se-mi-su?" He shook his head.

"That's my English name," Amelia explained. "I was separated from my family years ago."

"Ah." The man looked disturbed. "What is your Chinese family name?"

"It's Liang," Amelia said. "Or Leong or Lang or something like that?"

The official stared at her a moment before shaking his head rapidly.

"Useless," the interpreter conveyed to Grayson. "He wants to know what character they use."

"I don't know. An Occidental told me."

A long sigh. "He says that could be practically anyone, the way Westerners speak."

The official said something else. Amelia blushed, and the interpreter cleared his throat and didn't translate.

"I suppose we'll have to inquire." Amelia sighed. "This might take a while." That last was directed at Grayson in English. But the interpreter translated it, and the district registrar just tilted his head, considering.

"There are thirty thousand people in Liyang," came the apologetic reply. "Luckily, everyone will want to see you."

~

The district registrar had it right. The two of them were curiosities and everyone turned out to catch a glimpse. Grayson, who was used to the British and Americans doing their damnedest not to see him at all, found the whole endeavor of being noticed a little nerve-racking.

Word quickly got out about the Black barbarian and the English Chinese. Within a few hours, the courtyard at the inn they took rooms in was crowded with those who wanted to meet them in person.

Grayson had always been good with language and dialect. But he could see Amelia leaning forward, little flickers of confusion on her face crossing with wide-eyed moments of understanding. At one point, she answered a question before the interpreter had a chance to translate.

"I don't know," she said, after Grayson inquired. "I've spent months with Auntie Zhu and Miss Chu speaking Shanghainese, and this is closely related. But it's more than that. It feels like…" She wrinkled her nose. "It's not that it's in my brain somewhere. But it feels like…it fits in my brain. Like there's space for it."

Grayson had imagined there would be difficulty getting people to speak to them. He'd imagined bribes and snubs. Instead, it was the opposite. They were bombarded with questions and when they responded in a friendly way, inundated with offers of help that it would take them years to take advantage of.

Someone at the inn started bringing food out as the sun flirted with the horizon. Mutton strips with hearts of cabbage, some rice porridge cooked with a dark, rich black substance that the translator told Grayson was thousand-year egg.

It was impossible for the interpreter to keep up with the crowds; Grayson sat back and left the majority of the talking to Amelia. At some point, she explained the concept of a telegraph —the interpreter tried to translate that, and it turned out that neither dialect nor enthusiasm was up to the task. Still, she sketched Western codes and Chinese characters, using claps to convey the concept of dots and dashes. She gestured to Grayson as she did so, and apparently, the news that the Taotai of Shanghai had made an agreement with him brought a widening of eyes, some deeper bows, and a dish of chicken feet that had been simmered in sweet soy sauce until the meat melted off the bone.

As Amelia was finishing her rice, someone said something that had her laughing, blushing, shaking her head, and then glancing at Grayson.

"He said she's obviously from here," the interpreter informed Grayson. "The way she said 'xia xia' just now—very Liyang."

"It's not necessarily that." Amelia was still blushing. "I've always mirrored the speech of people around me."

The translator went on. "He said she should marry the district magistrate's son."

That set Grayson back. He'd once told Amelia that she would have no trouble marrying—that she might make herself unsuitable for boring men, but that all the interesting ones would be all the more drawn to her. He'd known it was true, and yet time was ticking on. He couldn't hold on to her, and someday, he would lose her.

He just didn't want it to be today. But she blushed again, shaking her head, and he had no right to selfish jealousy.

Sometime after someone pressed orange slices preserved in a sweet syrup on them, he saw Amelia turn to a man in front who shouted something at her. Grayson *thought* the man was speaking Mandarin, but it was late enough—and the accent rough enough—that he wasn't sure.

She gestured him closer; he spoke again. As he did, her eyes widened.

She set her chopsticks down with unsteady fingers. He could see her hands shaking, her eyes lighting up with hope.

Slowly, she stood.

"She asked him to repeat himself," the translator murmured to Grayson, "and for everyone else to be quiet so she can hear his words."

After the friendly babble of the past few hours, the silence seemed strident. The man spoke. Next to Grayson, the interpreter whispered. But he hadn't needed a translator to know what was being said. He could tell from Amelia's face already.

"He said that someone told him the story about Mrs. Smith, and he needed to come by. He thinks that this sounds like Madame Lang. She goes to Fuzhou every year looking for her daughter. Do you think that's her?"

～

When Amelia had imagined finding her mother, she'd always envisioned them alone—Amelia at one end of a long and dusty road and a dimly remembered shape at the other.

But when she asked for directions to Madame Lang's so that she might make the journey in the morning, the entire crowd laughed at her.

She couldn't understand most of what they said. They spoke to her in swift, accented Mandarin and Northern Wu. But she did understand the woman who shook her head with a smile.

"Silly," said one woman. "We'll take you now."

"There's no need—" she started to say.

An elderly man clucked at this. "There's *every* need," he'd told her in careful, slow Mandarin. "Between the rebellion and the wars, do you know how many of our children have not come home? And here you are. This is for all of us."

In the end, they ventured out in the night in a large group, armed with lanterns and laughter. As they passed through the streets, people asked what was going on. Once they heard, they followed along.

"Didn't you hear?" someone shouted to someone else. "Madame Lang's daughter has come home. We're going to—" She couldn't understand the rest.

"There," someone said after they'd been walking for fifteen minutes and their numbers had swollen threefold. "That's it. That's the Lang household."

In the dark of the evening, the blue-gray compound they stopped in front of looked like any of the other buildings they'd passed. A wood gate was opened to the street. Little flowers grew outside the blue-gray walls.

"Come out, Madame Lang!" someone next to her shouted. "We have your daughter!"

The light from the paper lanterns flickered through the shadowed courtyard. Amelia caught the silhouette of some tied animal—a mule perhaps—shaking its head. She could count the beats of her heart as the crowd cheered around them. Then a door opened and a figure stepped forward.

"Madame Lang!" someone called.

"She's here!" cheered someone else. "Madame Lang, come out!"

"What are all you fools shouting about at this hour of the night?" the woman called out.

"Ei, don't sound so—!" She couldn't catch that either, nor the rest of the exchange.

Then she felt hands on her shoulders. She was being escorted forward—not quite pushed, but moved faster than her feet seemed capable of taking her. The press of the crowd behind her brought her to the forefront of the throng with firm hands. Amelia felt dizzy with want, dizzy and uncomprehending.

It wasn't a dusty road. She wasn't alone. The woman's silhouette was dark in the night, and Amelia was blinded by the lanterns shining into her eyes.

"Madame Lang," someone called out by her side. "Come out, come out! We've brought your daughter home."

CHAPTER TWENTY-NINE

Amelia took a deep breath. Or, rather, she tried to. Her lungs seemed to be constricting. She glanced over at Grayson. He'd said nothing the entire walk—not that she would have heard him through all the ruckus—but he gave her a warm, reassuring nod.

For a moment, nothing happened. Then the woman in the courtyard crept forward cautiously, poking her head outside the gate and peering around.

The lantern light fell on her face.

Amelia had planned a speech for this moment. She'd been planning it for over a decade. She'd recited it three times last night on the boat until it was perfect down to the very word.

She couldn't remember a single syllable of it.

The woman looked at Amelia. Amelia couldn't hear anything—not the clamor of voices around her nor the sound of her own feet on hard-packed dirt as she took one step forward, then the next.

What Amelia remembered was a woman who was tired and weary. She remembered smudges of dirt and dark hair, disheveled and unkempt from an arduous journey. She remembered more the impression of a woman than an actual woman.

And yet as this woman came toward her, eyes widening, she felt...something. Some deep sense of recognition, as if time were drawing a line between those useless recollections and this moment. As if that whispered, remembered promise—*I will come back*—had always been heading here.

In the end, Amelia could manage only one word, squeaked out. "Ah Ma?"

The woman rushed forward, taking hold of Amelia's arms, looking into her face.

She looked a lot less weary than Amelia's memory and a lot cleaner. Tracks of wrinkles were visible around her eyes, but they seemed the sort of wrinkles that laughter would make.

"Mengmeng?" she asked. Her voice shook. "Is it you?"

Had that once been her name? Perhaps. But Amelia was apparently no better at remembering her own name than anyone else's. She felt not a flicker of recognition.

"Madame Lang," someone called in the crowd. "Is this your daughter? Is this Limeng?"

Amelia couldn't answer the question. Her mouth felt dry; her hands were chilled.

"I'm sorry." Amelia bit her lip. "I don't know that name. I don't remember what I was called. I am now called..." The words of the name that she used seemed foreign here, as if they would set her apart. "Amelia Smith." The diphthongs felt odd and strange, as if they had no use in the Chinese sentence.

"Amelia Smith," her mother repeated with a frown, and then, to Amelia's great shock, she spoke in halting English. "Do you like that? What is the meaning?"

"You speak English?"

"I learned. A little." Her mother's jaw squared. "I thought one day I might meet my daughter again. The missionaries told me she had gone away to be an English lady. I needed to know how to say…" She trailed off before smiling and switching back. "Everything. I needed to know how to say everything. But my Limeng was taken by a Madame Acheson ten miles outside of Shanghai, not a Smith."

"Oh." Amelia's whole body felt fluttery. The whole tableau seemed very distant. She'd dreamed of this so long that now she wasn't sure this could be real. "That's my… That is to say, I was taken by Madame Acheson. I suppose that's me?"

"You hear?" someone called. "It's her!"

Cheers rang out. She could make out some of them— "Madame Lang's daughter has come home!"—was simple enough and composed of words she'd repeatedly heard throughout the evening. But someone said something that sounded maybe like cow? Her whole brain ached trying to understand. Amid the din and confusion, Amelia took a step forward, close enough to hear what her mother was saying.

"I'm glad you came." Her mother gave her a tentative smile. "I know you didn't want to—"

Amelia shook her head violently. "Madame Acheson." Her voice shook. She waited until she felt steady and tried to speak loud enough to be heard. "She told me that a…" Refugee, what was *refugee* in Mandarin? Cantonese? She could remember it in French of all things. What was the use of that? Amelia gave up. "A person running from the Taiping Rebellion gave me up. Asked her to give me a home and to raise me as her own daughter."

Her mother took hold of her hands, her eyes wide. "No. That's not right." She shut her eyes. "You had a fever. She had medicine and food. I thought she would make you healthy again."

"I remembered you saying that you would come back. I believed it for years, but my…" She didn't know what relationship to use to describe Mrs. Acheson. *Mother* felt odd and out of place, especially talking to the woman who had given birth to her. "Madame Acheson told me it was a false memory. Just a hope. She never told me that you came looking."

"I was always looking." Her mother met her eyes. "I told you I would come back."

Amelia nodded. "I was always waiting." A long pause. "I remember you telling me to hold on to my heart. Did you say that?"

"Yes."

Amelia felt tears prick her eyes. "I tried." She whispered the words. "I think I lost it for a while. But I found it again."

Their arms came around each other, and Amelia felt something inside her burst—the emotions she'd been holding close, that strange, detached feeling that had taken over her limbs ever since she'd spoken with Leland. It seemed wrong that she should be crying. She could not have put a name to her feelings, but there was joy threaded with deep, nameless sorrow. She rather thought her mother was crying too. She could feel her petting her hair, soothing her with a language older than the halting speech they had in common.

"Limeng," Amelia managed, after long minutes. "Is that what you named me?"

"Lovely dream." Her mother said the words in English with a shake of her head. "Your father always had his head in the clouds. I told him to give you a practical name."

"I didn't remember my own name."

"Ei ya." Her mother shook her head mournfully. "You never could remember names as a child! But I never imagined you would forget your own."

Amelia started laughing through her tears until she was choking on something between mirth and sadness.

"Come," her mother said. "We'll send those louts away."

"No, you won't," someone shouted.

"Come inside," her mother said, waving a dismissive hand at

the crowd. "Tell me about yourself. Are you married? What are you doing with yourself?"

"Oh." Amelia straightened and realized that in the shock of the moment, she'd rudely forgotten Grayson's existence. "This is—"

She turned, looking for him. But he was gone. She searched the crowd, but he would have stood out—both his height and color would have made it impossible for him to blend in. That was so like him. Slipping away at inopportune moments.

She turned back to her mother, a smile on her lips. "I'm sure I'll be able to introduce you to him eventually. I came with Captain Grayson Hunter. He's my, um." Oh. Drat. She'd lost the word again. "Employer," she said in English.

Her mother gave her a confused look.

"We've been working on a telegraph system. It's a way of sending messages over very long distances."

"Ei." Her mother shook her head and smiled. "Just like your father. Always wanting to fiddle with something new. You used to help him when you were younger, you know."

"My father?" She reached out and clutched her mother's hands. "Tell me about my father. I have no memory of him."

"Of course." The woman reached out and patted Amelia's hand. "But you should meet him too, you know. He's off in Changzhou, but he should be back in a day or so. And you need to meet your little sister—she's just married—and your younger brothers. You've come home. It's time to celebrate."

CHAPTER THIRTY

I t was long past midnight when Grayson heard Amelia return to the inn. She was still accompanied by a retinue of people squawking away at her good-naturedly. He heard her shoo them away, laughing. Heard the door next to his own room click shut and the tinkle of mule's bells and laughing exchanges as people left for the evening.

He checked his watch. Almost one.

He shut his eyes, not wanting to imagine her readying herself for sleep. His room seemed very dark and still around him in comparison with the rest of the world. A shout of laughter from the street drifted his way. The clop of some animal's hooves. Then, from her room, through the thin walls, he heard the faint splash of water.

He didn't want to imagine Amelia washing, but the image came to mind anyway. He could imagine her dampening a cloth, tracing it down her neck, beads of water forming momentarily on her lips before her tongue darted out, licking them away.

What passed for a bed in his room was a bench of brick. In the winter, he supposed the little grate could hold a small fire, making it a cozy place to sleep. The nights were warm enough now that the brick was cold. He shifted on the thick mats covering the bench.

The bench doubled as a place to set his trunk. Grayson, being rather taller than the typical Chinese man, found the space mildly cramping. He shifted, turning first, then tossing.

He thinks she should marry the district magistrate's son.

It was foolish, foolish, foolish to feel jealousy over a man she had not yet met. Beyond foolish when he would do nothing himself. But Grayson knew what it was like to talk with her, hold her, kiss her. The magistrate's son would never understand what it was to yearn the way she did. To need. To burn. He would never understand Amelia the way Grayson did.

But maybe he would give her what she had longed for. He might give her a place to belong, a connection to the family and the people she had lost.

It wasn't as if Grayson got a vote in who she was to marry. Still, he could not help himself. He hated the magistrate's son.

That emotion, ridiculous as it was, felt more welcome than the shock that had gone through him when Amelia had locked eyes with her mother. He'd told Amelia a little about his family, about the difficulty he was having. He was accustomed to it at this point; it was a problem, and he was going to solve it. He knew, after all, what it was like to have a wound in his family made by war and ambition.

Watching them meet, watching barriers of time and lies and distance and language fall away, watching the light in Amelia's eyes be answered by her mother's had awoken something in him, some deep, sparking yearning.

He wanted that. He remembered what it was like to feel loved without reservation or condition, to be able to come home and to feel like he had a place there.

God. He *wanted* that.

When the transpacific line was finished. When he could sit

with his parents and show them what he'd done. Grayson inhaled. He'd have it too. He would.

He turned over once more, but as he did, he stretched a little too much. He kicked the trunk he'd placed at the end of the brick bench. It fell to the ground with an immense clatter, and he swore as pain shot up his foot.

He exhaled slowly, gritting his teeth. He could still hear Amelia moving in her own room. The street was quiet now. How long had it been since she'd arrived? Wasn't she going to sleep?

Then he heard the creak of wood scraping against wood. A moment later, a light tap sounded on his door.

"Grayson?"

Grayson took a deep breath. Of course. Of course she would come over once she heard him.

"Grayson, I know you're awake. I just heard you say 'damn.'"

"Damn," he muttered, this time more quietly. Then he spoke loudly enough for her to hear: "One moment."

He picked through the fallen remains of his luggage, feeling in the dark until he found candles and matches. He lit one and opened the door to her.

In the guttering candlelight, she was the most beautiful woman he had ever seen. He swallowed.

"I don't know a lick about Chinese propriety," he told her, "but how do you think the district magistrate's son will feel about your visiting a man in the middle of the night?"

A strange expression crossed her face—confusion first, then surprise, then...amusement?

Surely not.

"Oh," she said. "Of all the things that happened tonight, *that's* what you remember?" She seemed barely able to contain her mirth.

He folded his arms.

She swept into the room and closed the door behind her. "If

the magistrate's son objects to my talking to you, then he'll likely have a conniption about the fact that I'm the vice president of telegraphic encoding for your company. Alas. The two of us are doomed before ever we started." She dusted off her hands. "And isn't that convenient? It will save me all the trouble of rejecting him."

Some absolutely petty thing inside Grayson made him want to laugh. "Ah. Is that so?"

"Grayson." She shook her head at him. "I adore my work. I'm not giving it—or you—up."

"But you found where you were from—"

She took a step toward him and set a finger against his lips. "I'm not an urn that's been returned to its rightful owner. I've been away for eighteen years. I will not pretend that those years never happened."

"Oh?" He wanted to reach out and bring her to him. "What do you envision?"

"I have so many thoughts." She gave him a tired smile. "And my brain is so completely finished with words. It has been doing words all afternoon in so many languages."

He couldn't help but smile at that. "So you came over to my room in the dead of night in order to do more of them?"

"Yes." She looked at him gravely. "I did. And if you were sitting here in the dark thinking about the magistrate's son, I clearly needed to do so."

He sighed and made the mistake of looking down from her eyes. She had exchanged her brown traveling gown for a robe, one that seemed more suitable for the moments before bed than a visit to the room of... What precisely were they? Friends? Acquaintances? Lovers?

He should have said something in response. He could not make himself do so. She seemed so...bright was the wrong word. She seemed happy. God, he wanted that for her. He wanted it for himself.

"I had to come here," she said. "I had to say thank you."

"It's nothing."

She made a little derisive noise. "You took weeks from your schedule for me."

"If it hadn't been for you, I would have been aboard the *Victory*, heading to Myriad. Boring stuff."

She took hold of his hands. "Grayson. You *told* me why you were doing it. That you wouldn't let my relationship with my mother languish if you had the power to change it."

He exhaled.

"You told me your mother resented your survival. And you gave me *this*, Grayson."

"There's no point poking at the bruise," he said softly. "What good will it do?"

"Gray."

"It's all under my control. I can't blame my family for how they feel, but I have a plan. My brothers and I came up with the idea of the line across the Pacific. I have..." He exhaled. He'd never told anyone this before. "Journals." He shrugged. "Logs. All these things with their thoughts in them. I've been making a journal of the transpacific line. They're a part of it. Once the line across the Pacific is finished, I'll be able to..."

He trailed off. Said aloud, his plan seemed flimsier and less solid than it had felt in the privacy of his own mind.

"Grayson."

"Once it's done," he said, "once I've built what we planned as an inescapable part of the world, I'll be able to show everyone that..."

There was a reason Grayson didn't talk of these things aloud. In his heart, the emotions lined up, one right after the other. He'd complete this impossible quest. It had stretched across the world. Something that hard, so tied to his brothers— surely it had to be enough. It had to be. It was all he had.

Out loud, his words made no sense. He could sense the

arguments, the questions, the ways his plan could be picked to pieces with whys and hows. But the alternative to this was surrendering hope entirely. He had come so far. He had to hold on, no matter how nonsensical it felt.

"Talking won't help," he told her instead.

She swallowed. "Are you at least happy?"

Happy. He could remember what happiness felt like. He had to because he performed it so well. His body knew what it was to smile, to laugh. Sometimes he could even fool himself into forgetting the weight he bore. He'd been holding on to it for so long that the anchor crushing his heart felt familiar.

"No," he said softly. "I do not think I am."

Those words slipped into the night, burning a hole in the silence. She took his hands. Her fingers were cold in his.

He could feel the corner of his lip quirk up in something that felt too cynical to be a smile. "I'm accustomed to it by now. Don't let it eclipse your joy. Not when you are my solace."

She wrapped her arms around him. He could feel her shoulders shuddering, could feel the gasp of her breath against his chest. Her heart beat against his, out of synchrony with his.

"Ah Meng," he said softly, running a hand through her hair. "Don't feel sorry for me. Look what I'm about to accomplish."

She pulled away. The shadows cast by candlelight deepened her scowl into something stormy.

"You," she said, "are such a buffoon." And before he could make sense of that, she kissed him.

The first touch of her lips felt as fierce as her frown— mouth on his, unrelenting, fingertips clenched against his forearms. She opened her mouth to him and their tongues met with a searing intensity born out of months of wanting. He tasted a hint of soda and salt, then just her. Just Amelia.

The intensity between them shifted, like a windstorm turning into driving rain. He wanted to be washed away. Their bodies pressed together. The thin fabric of her robe meant that he could feel her thighs against his leg, feel how little it would take to join more than just their mouths.

"God," he whispered, "I need to be close to you."

Her hands seemed tiny when he clasped them between his palms, tinier still when he spread their intertwined fingers against his chest. It was not easier undoing his buttons with four hands instead of two; it was just more pleasurable. The feeling of her fingertips against his chest, the way she looked at him, her eyes latched on the growing area revealed by each undone button. She made him feel strong. She made him feel wanted. And hidden in the tempest between them, she made him feel safe.

Her hands fumbled against his chest, and he looked down.

"Amelia." He shook his head. "That's not a buttonhole, love."

"I am bad at buttons," she informed him. "I can never do them properly. Why are buttons?"

"Bad at names." He took her hand in his and kissed it. "Bad at buttons. Best at being Amelia."

She caught his hand in hers, turning it. "Best at being Grayson," she whispered back. "My dearest Grayson."

There were other words she did not say. He found himself not saying them back. Words like *I love you.* However true it felt in his heart, those words smacked of promise, and he could make none.

It felt like arrogance to believe that he could hear them in her actions anyway. He could hear them in the feel of her body against his. He could feel the emotion in the way she squeezed him tight and angled her head up for another kiss. And he could feel his same response, those same unspoken words reverberating between them, communicated in his arms coming around her, holding her like something precious.

He let out a shaky breath. "Amelia. I have wanted you from the moment you showed me that damned bamboo cage just outside your mother's household."

"I figured that out about you." She smiled. "Eventually."

Somehow, she'd finally managed to undo his buttons. He shrugged out of his shirt. She leaned in, touching her lips to his bare shoulder. The heat of her mouth, the tenderness of the gesture… He felt those deep inside, a warmth blossoming in winter. She tilted her head, leaning into him, her lips brushing his bare neck with searing kisses.

She put a hand over his mouth. "Before I met you, I felt like a lamp dimmed to the point of extinguishment. I could not let myself feel anything—not joy, not anger, not sorrow. Meeting you was one of the greatest joys of my life. You have brought a kaleidoscope of color into my world."

He let out a breath and found his lips pressed against her forehead. "No. You did that for yourself."

His hands came to clasp her arms, and he inhaled. He could smell the scent of her, something sweet and lovely and indeterminate. Her arm went around him, stroking his hair. Her fingertips were soft and sweet.

"I walked this path," she said. "But you told me it was here."

His hands slid down the edge of her robe, skirting that boundary between fabric and skin. He could feel the softness of her. He wanted her so much it was painful, so much he felt an urge to make some jest to hide it all.

But she would see through him. And if she didn't, he didn't want his humor to hurt her. Not now. Not like this, when they were both already so bruised, when she was his comfort and he wanted to be hers. Instead, he drew her to sit next to him on the brick bench that served as bed, then set his head against her chest. His fingers played with the sash of her robe. And he told her the truth.

"I'm afraid," he confessed into the fabric covering her breastbone.

Her touch on the back of his neck was soothing. "Of what?"

"I disappoint everyone in my family." Those words felt

more naked than his bare skin. "When I see them, I'm so aware that I can't make up for the emptiness that remains. They expect me to be more than who I am. I find myself playacting the person I used to be and leaving as soon as I can."

"Grayson." She nuzzled him.

"They ask me to come visit, so I do. Occasionally. But more often than not, if an excuse comes up, I'll take it. If I'm there, I disappoint them. If I'm not, I disappoint them."

"Grayson."

His fingertips dug into the meat of her thigh. "I'm going to leave after this," he said desperately. "I'm going to disappoint you too. Because that's what I do. And if I were a good person, I would care what that means for you. But I'm not. I'm just tired of disappointing the people I care about."

"Grayson." She tightened her grasp around him. "Grayson. There's nothing disappointing about you."

He let out a long breath. Easy for her to say that now.

"There is nothing disappointing about you," she repeated. "You could leave me right now and for the rest of my days I would remember you the same way." Her voice shook. "With affection." A kiss on his nose. "Admiration." Another kiss. "A certain amount of annoyance because I want you so much, and if you walk away now, I'll have to take care of this myself."

He let out a surprised laugh against her neck.

"But disappointment?" She shook her head. "Never. Never, ever. If you believe nothing else, believe that. Every bit of you is precious to me."

"Every bit?"

She nodded. "Even the annoying bits."

"Well." He cupped her cheek. "Then. If I'm going to leave you, let me not leave you annoyed."

He kissed her. It felt different, this kiss. It wasn't just heat and want. It came from somewhere deep inside him, filled with all the yearning for her he'd refused to let himself acknowledge until now.

God, he knew he couldn't stay, that he would *never* stay. But he *wanted* her to be his.

Her hands came to his face, and she kissed him back with a fervor that felt connected to his very center, as if she had the same dream. It felt right, that kiss. As if this moment transcended the tomorrow that would never be and made something infinite in his soul.

He untied the sash of her robe. The fabric had been cinched around her waist; as he freed it, it slithered loose, showing him what she was wearing underneath.

Nothing. She was wearing nothing. He saw smooth skin, light brown in the guttering light of the candle. So much skin. She had a little mole above the swell of her left breast. Her nipples were a warm brown in the dim illumination. Her waist was a gentle curve leading to the arc of her hips. A dark tangle of curls between her legs made his breath stop. He could practically feel the blood rushing south.

"Amelia."

She pressed herself to him and kissed him. Instead of wrapping her arms around him as she had before, her hands worked inside the waistband of his loose trousers. He could feel her fingers as she undid his buttons. It took her half a minute fumbling at his groin to manage that, and he wasn't about to offer his assistance. Not when he could swallow her laughter with his kiss, not when she was touching him there, fingers trying to find the buttonhole in dim light, groping along his hardening length. Finally, she succeeded. She slipped the fabric down his hips, underclothing and all, and his erection snapped free, heavy and hard, pressing against her.

"Grayson." She eyed his member. "Oh. That's interesting. May I touch?"

He nodded, and she reached out. He let out a shuddering

breath at the spark of pleasure that raced down his spine at that first contact. The warmth of her hand, the gentleness of her touch. She patted the head softly.

He pulled away from her. "There's something I need from my trunk."

She frowned but let him pull away to rummage through the fallen things until he found a lambskin condom in a wallet. It took a little more time to find the water and pour it over the item.

"Come here." He gestured her forward.

"What is that?"

"It prevents pregnancy." He bit his lip. "And the spread of disease. If we're going to do this, that's a necessity."

"Oh." She looked intrigued. "I suppose it goes over the, um. Thing."

"The thing." He found himself smiling.

"I suppose you're putting it in water to make it more pliable, yes?"

How very like Amelia to focus on such a thing. "Of course."

"Hmm." She frowned. "I wonder if there might be another material that could be used, one that would work just as well, yet without such an unfortunate lag in time. Maybe India rubber, if vulcanized…"

"Those already exist. They're very thick though, and the rubber dulls sensation." He made a face. "Significantly."

"We can't be having that." She trailed off, staring. "I wonder about gutta percha."

He waved a hand in front of her, smiling. "Amelia," he whispered, "come back to me. You can't have my gutta percha. I need it for my telegraphic lines. Invent a better condom at a later time."

She started, looking up at him and shaking her head in bemusement. "Might I put it on then? For the purpose of inquiry so I can answer questions of fit and the like?"

"For the purpose of inquiry only," he agreed with a grin.

She took the condom out of the water, holding it in front of her, turning it around before reaching out for him. While they'd been waiting, he'd softened just a little. She frowned at this.

"For the purposes of experimentation, I suppose you had better be completely hard."

"I had better be." His throat seemed just a little scratchy.

She shrugged. "For science," she said with a flush that left her cheeks red. And she stroked lightly along the line of his cock.

"Harder." He reached down and closed her grasp around him. "Like that. God, yes. Like *that*." He could feel pleasure spark to life again, coalescing to center around her touch.

"May I try something?"

"Of course," he started to say, but she leaned down, his erection still in her hands, and took the tip of his member in her mouth.

The wet heat of her tongue sent a shock of pleasure through him. It felt good, so good, as she licked the head of his cock, taking more and more of him into her mouth, sliding slowly. She was so hot around him. His hips yearned to thrust, needed to move, needed to *go*. Still he held back, letting her explore. Her hands went to his hips. She slid another inch of him into her mouth.

His responding thrust was involuntary. But she just smiled up at him.

"Amelia," he gritted out, "if you keep that up, there will be no need for the condom and you'll lose all chance for experimentation."

She pulled away.

"I've been reading," she said earnestly. "I was married for years and I didn't know a thing except lying down and waiting for him to be done. When I figured out there was more, I was so annoyed." She gave him a brilliant smile. "Can you *believe* they didn't tell me about it?"

"Yes," Grayson said after a pause that felt just a little too long. "Yes, I can...actually believe that. They're like that."

She took the lambskin, turned it around, finding the opening before rolling it slowly down his length. He hissed at the cool, wet touch, but her hand followed, smoothing and warming, and the sensation sent him tilting his hips up into her hands.

"Interesting," she said.

He shook his head. "Unbelievable. Now it's my turn."

"Your turn?"

"You've made me ready," he said. "I ought to return the favor."

"Ready?"

"Did your reading not cover that?"

"Um."

He let his hand slide between her thighs. "You should be wet," he said, "and it's been a while for you since the last time you had intercourse, isn't it?"

She swallowed. "Years."

"You might find the stretch a bit much if we're not careful."

He slid his thumb inside her, pressing deep into her channel, finding the wetness and coaxing it out. She laid back, opening to give him passage. A finger followed, slowly stretching her out. She let out a gasp.

"Your husband never did this for you?"

She shook her head.

"Not even the first time?"

Another shake of her head. "It was never actually too horrid. I heard it was supposed to be. Mostly, it just seemed boring." Despite the factual nature of those words, her voice trembled. He could see the flush on her face spreading down her neck.

"Bastard," was his only comment.

She was slick, delightfully so. She took his finger well, letting out a surprised noise when he crooked it inside her, another one when he rubbed his thumb over the bud just above her entrance.

"Gray." This was a moan. "I need… I need…"

"Good," he said. "Keep needing. Beautiful. Perfect. Lovely. You're all of those things, did you know that?"

"Please." She pushed up onto her elbows. His hands fell away, and she climbed atop him. "Please. I need more."

"Then come take it."

Her reading had apparently covered that much because she straddled him, her entrance lining up with the tip of his erection. He could feel the slick heat of her, couldn't keep himself from nudging his cock up to nestle against her entrance. She let out a little noise and sank down.

"Oh God." She wasn't even a quarter of the way there, and she was trembling. "God, Grayson."

Even just this much felt amazing. She was so tight around him, fitting to his body.

He held his hips in check, wanting to thrust, wanting to lodge himself all the way inside her. Her back arched over him like a cat, her forehead leaning down to his.

"Breathe into it," he advised her. "It's all right."

"Grayson." She sank another inch, then another, bit by bit. "Grayson. You feel so good."

"Yes," he agreed. His voice felt like gravel. "I *do* feel amazing."

He slid his hands up her sides. His palms cupped her breasts. He could feel the involuntary clench of her body around him, could feel the air leaving her on a gasp. His thumbs found her nipples, rubbing gentle circles. She let out a moan and slid the rest of the way down, engulfing his length, her entrance fitting against his groin.

God, she felt good. *So* good. It wasn't just the heat that clutched him nor the physical feeling of her. It felt as if she was giving all the best parts of herself into his care.

"Gray." Her nose nuzzled against his forehead. "Gray."

"I'm here," he told her. He arched into her, pressing his pelvis up. His hands came to her hips, holding her in place before gently urging her to make the tiniest of motions. She pulled herself up a fraction off his length, then slid down again. He let out a groan as desire spiked through him.

God. He'd wanted her for so long. *So* long.

It took her a moment to find a rhythm. His thrusts, her hips —for a few seconds they felt off. But then they found synchrony.

He was lost. Lost in the feel of her. Lost in the heat of her body around him, the slide where they came together, the press of flesh against flesh. Lost in the pleasure that enveloped him, stroke after stroke, as she opened up to him.

He caressed her, took her up, up, higher and higher as he groaned, gasping into the feel of her. God, the warmth of her walls around him…

"Amelia."

He had to hold on and so he did, feeling his pleasure rise. He slid his hand between them so he could press between her legs.

"Oh." She let out a noise and he pressed against her, finding that perfect angle of his hips that made her gasp and contract around him. It couldn't possibly get better.

But it did. The heat of her body around him grew. He was aware of everything. Of the little noises she made, desperate and pleading. The brush of her breasts as she leaned over him. He was aware of *her* as she came apart around him, trembling around his cock and he finally let go of everything—all his tension, all his worries—and released into her.

It was bliss, pure and untouched by any other concerns. He

couldn't breathe, couldn't talk, could only feel the rightness of the instant stretching around them until nothing else existed.

He opened his eyes. He was hot and sticky; she was slumped against him. She leaned down and kissed him, a delighted smile on her face.

"Gray," she said. Her arms came around him, holding him close. He held her in return, not wanting to let go.

"Amelia." He nuzzled into her. There was so much he wanted to say. So much he wanted to ask for. But what he said was, "I need to leave tomorrow. In truth, this has taken me too long as it is. I must make plans to lay the line to Shanghai. I have so much to do."

She exhaled. "I know." But she wrapped her arms around him as if afraid to let go.

"Once I've ordered the cable and established a schedule, it will be time to connect the line from Myriad to Moresby Island." Gray swallowed. "I likely won't have any chance of seeing you until all that's finished."

"I know," she said again. "I told you. I wouldn't want you to be anyone else."

He nodded into the palm of her hand.

"Let me stay with you tonight," she said.

And so he did.

CHAPTER THIRTY-ONE

Amelia woke to the feeling of lips. First, they touched her forehead. Then her nose. Then they brushed lightly against her mouth. As she struggled into wakefulness, she felt the warmth of Grayson's arm around her and heard the low murmur of his voice.

"Amelia," he was saying. "Amelia."

She opened her eyes to slits. It wasn't even close to morning.

"Why." She squeezed her eyes back shut. "Dark."

An amused huff followed, which was ridiculous. Nothing was amusing about being awakened at this hour.

"Amelia," Grayson said. "You should go back to your room."

She snuggled into his shoulder joint and contemplated this. "Cold."

"And I must go back to Shanghai."

That woke her, jolting through her petulant sleepiness. She sat up, staring at his silhouette in the gloom. "Already?"

"Spend time with your mother," he said. "And your family. You've worked hard on your code. You deserve a rest. And there's no place for me in this reunion."

She wanted to argue. But in the dark, she couldn't make out his features, and this newly awake, she wasn't sure she'd manage to convince him. He leaned in, brushing her hair back.

"Grayson." She shut her eyes. "We..." She trailed off, unable to formulate a sentence.

"I don't know what we are either." His hand brushed her cheek. "I only know what *you* are. You are the closest, most valuable person to my heart."

His lips found hers, warm and reassuring in the deep black of the early morning hours.

"I want you to take your time here," he whispered. "Don't rush on my account." For a moment, he seemed to choke up. "You should know your family. Understand?"

She nodded into his embrace.

"By the time you've returned, I'll be out of Shanghai. I've work in Japan, then Hong Kong. Finally, in September, I must sail to Myriad Island and bridge the gap across the Pacific. I don't see how I can visit you until next year at least. Amelia, I—"

She kissed his apology away before it could come out. "Stop. You'll be able to get signal via the cable, yes?"

"Of course. Like last time."

She pressed her forehead to his.

"Then send me a number occasionally."

He let out a long exhale. "I don't think the envelopes I gave you encompass what I want to say anymore."

"Then we need to make new numbers." She reached out and pulled him into a kiss. He exhaled against her mouth, then melted against her. Into her. Into the kiss. They only had a few precious minutes left before months would separate them. She couldn't let it go to waste.

"What do you think," she said, after they'd kissed until he was breathless. "Three hundred seventy-two?"

"Yes." His hands met her hips, and he slid down her body.

"This will be four hundred twelve." He spread her legs and slid between them. Amelia's mind went blank. His tongue lapped out at her, tasting her, running along the folds of her entrance. He dipped his tongue into her a bit, then slid out, kissing up, finding that nub that sent pleasure sparking up her.

"Four hundred and twelve," she agreed, breathless. "Then four hundred and fifteen must be this. Please, Grayson. Please. There. That's it."

She'd never experienced pleasure so intense, so concentrated. She could hear the liquid sound of his tongue, of her staccato gasps. "Please. That's—just like that. Grayson. Grayson." He had no mercy at all, none, and she had no desire to make him show her any. She canted her hips up into his face. Her climax came on her quickly, burning through her with a savageness that took her by surprise.

"Five hundred seven," he growled. "That means I want you. Most desperately. And this, then, I suppose is five hundred nineteen."

It took him a moment to find another condom, to prepare it, and to roll it on. But her body was still sparking with pleasure when he pushed her back to the mats covering the bench. He slid inside her, the slickness drenching her easing his entry.

"God," he whispered against her ear. "I'm going to miss you. I'm going to miss this." The rough slide of their bodies—the heat between them—Amelia felt herself tense. "Please," she said. "Again. Again."

He reached underneath her, tilting her hips so that his thrusts angled right into—oh, right there, brushing pleasure so intense into her that she could feel her whole body flush. Right *there*. It was so perfect. She found his lips and kissed him, kissed up his nose, kissed the sweat beading on his forehead, kissed him as he took her again and again, until she felt her muscles tensing, until he groaned on top of her. Until he came, and when he'd finished, pressed his hand against her and brought her the rest of the way.

The heat of his breath whispered against her forehead. She felt a prickle in her eyes that might well have been tears.

His hands came to cup her cheeks, brushing down her face. "Six hundred and two," he whispered. "I am thinking of you."

"Six hundred and seven," she shot back. "You are in my heart, even if you are not here."

"Eight hundred." He exhaled. "I ache for you."

"I will need to write these down," she said. "I'll forget them otherwise."

"Oh, I'll just add them to our commercial cipher books for distribution," he said airily, and when she gaped at the thought of new versions of this particular code being given out to everyone—with *this* added—he let out a long, low laugh. She could feel the rumble in his chest above her.

She buried her face in her hands. "I actually believed you were going to do that."

"I know." He laughed again. "That's why it was such a good joke. You're adorable."

Their mouths met again. God, she was going to miss him. She tried to memorize everything about this kiss—the feel of his fingers on her hips, the strength in his body as he pushed her against the mats once again, the feel of his chest against hers.

Then he pulled away. The morning air was cold, so cold in the empty space left behind.

"I need to finish packing my things," he said. "You need to write down the code. And I think you should go before we throw all sense to the wind."

She almost reached for him. What was the point of having sense? But she remembered. She *wanted* to stay here. She'd wanted to know her Ah Ma all her life. She wanted this. She did.

Over the weeks that followed, Amelia learned much about her Ma. She heard the story her mother recalled of their parting—similar to her own memories, and yet so different from what she had been told. She told her mother what she remembered (little) and found comfort in the truth.

"Of course you remember it as if you were high up," her mother had said puzzled. "I was carrying you on my shoulders."

She was introduced to a younger sister and two brothers. They met each other, talking excitedly, embracing. Her father was quieter, but he listened to Amelia speak about the telegraph, making interested noises and asking questions that demonstrated real effort in understanding. She met an endless stream of cousins, ranging from five years older than her to ones who were still toddling about.

It took her an eternity to learn their names, and so she made them all badges of paper to pin on their clothing.

It was an embarrassment of riches—so much family she didn't know what to do with them all. Her heart had never felt so big. She had never cried so much from happiness.

"What does Amelia mean?" one of her littlest cousins asked. "Why did they give you that name?"

"I think my…" She still didn't know what to call the woman who had raised her. *Mother* was the word that reflexively came to the tip of her tongue. But Amelia didn't know what that meant anymore. There were mothers enough in the world who had made mistakes with their children. It was just that *this* mistake was less of an accident, and more of an intentional choice.

It was so much. *So* much. What were you supposed to do with someone who raised you, lavished affection on you, and who had also taken you from your rightful family? What were you supposed to do when you were angry, upset, outraged, and yet still wildly conflicted?

Amelia sighed. There would be time enough to ponder that difficult question, and talking to a four-year-old cousin wasn't that time.

"I believe Mrs. Acheson chose the name because she thought it sounded pretty," Amelia said instead.

"But what does it *mean?*"

"Hmm." Amelia frowned. She had asked long ago, and Mrs. Acheson had given her an odd look followed by a bright laugh. Eventually, Amelia had looked it up herself. "I think it means... industriousness? It's rather amusing. I'm the least industrious person I know. I always have my head in the clouds, thinking of things and managing to mess up basic items like..." Amelia smiled. "Buttons. Or walking in a straight line."

Ah Ma gave Amelia's shoulder a playful shove. "You? *Not* industrious? What does that mean? Did you not invent a way to send Chinese characters across great distances with wire?"

"No, I didn't!" Amelia protested. "Samuel *Morse* invented the telegraph. I just came up with a way to use it for Chinese characters. It wasn't hard. It just took a long time and was very hard."

She trailed off, looking at the group around her.

"I thought," she said quietly, "that there would have to be more people like me. People who had been separated from families by war." She thought of Auntie Zhu. "Or for other reasons. I thought if I worked hard enough, maybe one day they would be able to find each other. I never expected that *I* would find *my* people."

Her mother set a hand on Amelia's arm. "You're going back to work on this wire code, aren't you?"

Amelia hadn't spoken to her about it yet, but she nodded.

"I don't think," she said in a low voice, "that I belong here. I don't think I belong with Mrs. Acheson either. I've never really belonged anywhere." She shook her head, brushing away that melancholy, and tried for a joke. "I suppose I shall remain something of a nomad then!"

"Nonsense." Her mother laid a hand over hers. "Belonging in two places makes you a bridge. Not many people can do that. Look at what you've done to bring people together."

~

Since returning from their trip to Liyang, Grayson had told himself a hundred times not to think of Amelia. Yet he couldn't help doing so. Was she well?

(Of course she was; he had received a letter yesterday informing him that she'd returned to Shanghai.)

Was she happy? (She'd sounded like it.)

Had she forgotten him? (Unlikely, given the aforementioned letter.)

But he was good at putting off his feelings, so he worked through his lingering sentimentality instead. He wrote a letter to the cable company in San Francisco to start work on an eight-hundred-mile cable to lay to Shanghai. He discussed the precise specifications of that cable with his engineer, and then again with his navigator. He went over depth charts in the Sea of China to plot the best route. He drowned himself in preparations.

And every so often, he sent Amelia a letter. With no telegraph to Shanghai, the distance between them seemed impossibly far. With the possibility of his letters being read by others, he restricted himself to numbers.

Sometimes he sent *507: I want you most desperately.* Sometimes it was *372: a desperate kiss.* Sometimes it was *412,* and he thought of her thighs around his head and the taste of her. But most often, it was *602: I'm thinking of you.*

He sent those off when he drafted a plan for instructing

Chinese engineers on building lines to Beijing, to Fuzhou. A schedule emerged.

He was good at using work as a substitute for emotion, and yet this emotion lingered. *607: You're in my heart.*

He'd see her again in eight months. Maybe they'd exchange heated, hurried kisses. Or maybe she would have given up in disgust at his absence and moved on to someone else, someone who would appreciate her *and* be present.

602, he sent. *I'm thinking of you.*

~

Amelia's plan unfolded on accident before it happened on purpose.

She had returned by junk, watching the bamboo-covered hills give way to wide waters and then villages, and finally, the splendor of Shanghai. She'd arrived to chaos—a million things needing to be done all at once. There was a training course to develop for Chinese telegraph operators in advance of the line into Shanghai. There was still the question of error correction hanging over her head.

But all that chaos was welcome. She'd found a deeper confidence in herself and who she was. Every day she grew into her own certainty.

And so her plan started with the little things. Walking to the office one morning, Merry sniffing at little blue flowers, with the sun high overhead and the weather not too oppressively humid, Amelia found herself smiling.

You are the closest, most valuable person to my heart, he had said, and she had a handful of numbered telegrams to prove it.

He'd kissed her. They'd shared a night together. But he'd given her more than just those physical moments. She could feel that sense of sunlight he'd imparted to her. The confidence she'd learned, that she could stand on her own two feet and find her happiness. He had given her something important, and she wanted to return the favor.

And so yes, her plan started on accident with a blue flower. Merry sniffed about them; Amelia thought they were rather pretty. She reached down and spontaneously plucked one, humming to herself. When she reached the office, she slid it between two sheets of paper and slipped it in the middle of a heavy book. She thought nothing more of it.

Two days later, she found herself taking a midday meal while Merry sat at her feet, eyes luminous and begging as if she'd had nothing at all to eat in years.

"Goose," Amelia said, ruffling her fur. "I know the truth." Still, she'd taken a pencil and paper out and sketched those wanting dog eyes, the yearning face.

When she looked at her little drawing, she thought of Grayson. She'd been uncertain in the beginning, and he'd handed her a sheaf of letters. That memory coalesced idea into action.

Amelia folded the picture of Merry before she could talk herself out of the plan and dropped it into an envelope.

She wrote on the front *1*.

The flower, pressed now into desiccated flatness, became envelope *2*. *3* was a sketch of an egg tart that she purchased from a street vendor and a description of the smooth custard, the sweetness that lingered on her tongue, the flakiness of the crust. *4* was a clipping from a newspaper about a cage containing hundreds of chickens intended for market. The cart that carried them had jostled on a stone, and the gate had come loose. The chickens had taken over an entire thoroughfare, squawking and fouling up the way. *5* was a tiny sample of tea in a twist of paper—a variety that was dark and oxidized, leaves loose and fragrant with an astringent scent that held hints of caramel. *6* was another newspaper clipping, this time describing the bones of some ancient creature that had been uncovered in Kansas in the United States—something with wings. Amelia stared at the clipping for moments, tapping pencil against paper before drawing her best impression of a winged lizard chasing down a stick figure of herself and Merry. And so on and so on.

She wasn't supposed to see him again, not for many months. But as the stack of letters grew, so did Amelia's plan. When she wavered on the possibility, wondering if it would go badly, she pulled out one of the old letters he'd written to reassure her a year earlier.

Trust your instincts, she'd read in his assured handwriting. And she would.

602. 607. 412.

Every time she smiled, she thought of him, and she tried to capture some small thing that had brought her joy in a tiny way. Maybe this way, she could give him some small portion of what he'd given her.

The envelopes in her drawer grew day by day. By the end of the month, there were ninety-seven of them.

CHAPTER THIRTY-TWO

Benedict received the telegram from Theresa in Shanghai at the office of the Lord Traders Telegraphic Company on a Wednesday.

The line to Shanghai was at least a year out, so the five-day-old telegram had arrived by courier ship. "Lord," he muttered to himself. "What now?"

B, read the telegram.

HAVE FOUND HER IN HONG KONG OF ALL PLACES STOP

BOARDING PASSENGER SHIP STOP

ARRIVAL MID-AUGUST STOP

DO NOT COME TO HONG KONG UNDER ANY CIRCUM-STANCES STOP

Benedict let out a snort. There was Theresa for you. No please, no thank you. She'd been telling him what to do since the day he was born.

And as soon as he'd been capable of complying, he'd always done it.

"I'm in Shanghai," Benedict informed the inert telegram. "I'm liaising. I have work to do. It's lucky for you that Captain

349

Hunter doesn't need me at the Hong Kong office." And so he put the note in his pocket with a shake of his head.

He scarcely thought of Theresa's desperate missive until the first week of August, when Mrs. Smith popped her head into his office.

"Benedict?"

He jumped up. "Yes, ma'am?"

She tapped her lips. "I'm in need of liaising. I've been thinking about the telegraphy instruction in Hong Kong. We're making instructions here, but it might make sense for me to go in person to talk to the people there."

"Of course." He looked at her. "That does make sense."

"Out of idle curiosity," she said, "how much longer will Captain Hunter be in Hong Kong? You know his schedule, don't you?"

"He's there now," Benedict said slowly, "but in another week or so, he'll leave on the *Celerity* for Myriad Island, where he'll rendezvous with the *Victory* to lay cable. There's time to get a letter to him if you hurry."

"Excellent," she said, trying for innocence, as if he might somehow not have noticed the immense quantity of correspondence the two of them were now exchanging. "If there's a way to have a letter arrive, we can go in person. Could you arrange passage for us immediately?"

That was when Benedict thought of Theresa's telegram. *DO NOT COME TO HONG KONG UNDER ANY CIRCUM-STANCES STOP*

He bit his lip.

"I, um." He grinned uncertainly. "Um."

DO NOT COME TO HONG KONG UNDER ANY CIRCUM-STANCES STOP

It was instinct, pure and simple, to let Theresa define all the terms. But whyever should he do that? Was he to avoid Hong

Kong the entirety of the time Theresa was there? What was the purpose of that?

They'd hashed out their agreement in a hotel in Bombay. If they avoided seeing each other, Captain Hunter would never know that Theresa was not, in fact, missing, and he wouldn't tell his brother who wouldn't tell Judith…

But Benedict had already *told* Judith. She might even have received the letter by now. Her return missive was likely making its way to him.

It was that simple. Benedict didn't have to listen to Theresa. He could go wherever he wanted—or in this case, wherever Amelia wanted.

"Benedict?" Mrs. Smith asked. "Is there a problem?"

"Not at all. There's very much not a problem. You would not believe how little of a problem there is."

"Well, then," she said in confusion. "That's good, I suppose."

"It's excellent." Come to think of it, Theresa was looking for the half-sister Benedict had never met. She claimed to have found her in Hong Kong. And she thought Benedict shouldn't get to meet her?

"I'll go find passage." He grinned at her. "We'll have to leave *immediately.*"

CHAPTER THIRTY-THREE

Grayson was used to Hong Kong in August by now. He was used to the sticky humidity that made even the finest linen shirts cling to his person. He was used to sweat-covered skin, used to fanning himself desperately in the heat of the day hoping for relief that never came. There had been a breeze earlier that morning; it had died down, and now the air was stultifying.

This afternoon though, he'd be leaving, heading north to drier and cooler climes. One last stack of papers on his desk beckoned. Once that was finished, he'd have to go make sure the *Celerity* had everything it needed.

He was used to thinking of Amelia from time to time, and so when he looked up from the papers strewn in front of him to see her standing in front of his door, his first thought was that this was a rather unusual daydream.

He turned back to his papers. It was only when she let out an outraged squeak that he realized it was she. Here. In the flesh.

She'd closed his door behind her, which was probably why there was no longer any breeze.

He blinked at her. "Amelia?"

"Grayson."

He stood and stalked to her.

"I'm here for many reasons," she explained. "The, um, training? I want to see to it in person. Also, I need to consult with an expert here about mathematics. The error-correction problem —I believe it can be solved with, um."

He stopped an inch before her so that they were nose to nose.

"I believe," she said, "I was also motivated by a desire to see you."

He gathered her up in his arms, pushed her against the door, and kissed her. God, he'd missed every bit of her. She didn't hesitate, winding her arms around him and kissing him back.

If he had known she was coming, he would have shaved that morning. He could feel his stubble brushing against her with every swipe of their lips.

"Goddamn," he said pulling away. "It is warm in here."

"Is it?" Little strands of her hair were plastered to her forehead. "Do you think it would be cooler if we took off some of our clothing?"

They'd been sending each other codes back and forth for weeks now. He'd been thinking about her, about being inside her, about feeling her around him in the Hong Kong heat.

"No," he informed her. "It won't help at all. But let me show you, lest you find that unbelievable."

He took a handful of her skirts, hefting them up, and then grabbing more, and more, until he could see her drawers. He reached out and pulled them down.

"Grayson." The word sounded like a plea.

"Yes?"

"There are *people* here."

"Oh." He met her eyes. "Can you not be quiet?"

She turned the most interesting color of rouge before licking her lips. "I can try."

"Good," he said and pressed his hand between her legs before kissing her. She was already wet. Perfectly slick for him. He kissed her a little longer. "Five hundred and seven," he whispered into her ear. *I want you most desperately.*

"Then why are you waiting?"

He undid the buttons of his trousers and let himself free. He pushed her against the door. Her eyes grew wide when he lifted her, even wider still when he spread her legs around him and let her weight fall onto him.

She was obviously trying to not make noise. Not as he breached her, sinking into her tightness. Not as she wrapped her arms around him. She bit her lip, and that was no good—he wanted to do that. He pushed in hungrily, devouring her as their bodies joined.

He could feel the warmth of her channel swallowing his length, could feel the keening noise she bit back vibrating in her throat. He could feel the two of them, joining roughly, pent-up want stoked by the numbers they'd been exchanging. His imagination, run wild over the last weeks, burned with the reality of their bodies.

"There," she whispered as he tilted his hips. "There, there, *there.*" She was not perfectly silent, but the sound of her biting back her cry as she pulsed around him pushed him over the edge. He pulled out and spilled heavily into his hand.

She looked at him. "Well. That definitely is *not* a method to cool off."

He was sweating and hot, so hot. But he smiled at her as he went and found handkerchiefs. One was not enough; he needed one for himself, another to clean her up, and then, after that, still more to wipe the sweat from their faces. When they were finished making themselves presentable, he took her in his arms, pulling her to him despite the heat and inhaling the scent of her.

"I missed you," he said.

"I missed you too."

He exhaled. "Amelia. If you are ever dissatisfied with anything about our affair, you must tell me."

"Right." Her eyes shivered shut. "You have reminded me. There is one thing I should like to change."

His chest squeezed. He had known it. He'd been waiting for it, waiting to hear that he'd disappointed her. Of course this couldn't last. The demands of his schedule had always been going to break them apart.

"Go ahead," he told her in as sure a voice as he could manage.

"There *is* something I want." There was an intensity to her. "No. That I *need.* I have come to realize it in the past weeks. There is something I desperately desire, deep down in the bottom of my soul."

He waited to hear his doom.

Her eyes met his. "Grayson," she whispered, "I want you to be happy."

It was not what he had expected at all. He stared at her in confusion. She wanted *him* to be happy. Out of all the things she could want. That was what she came up with?

"Amelia." Grayson shut his eyes. "It's not that I'm unhappy." He shook his head. "It has nothing to do with you."

She pressed her lips together. She looked on the verge of tears for some reason, and he couldn't understand that. "On the contrary. Your happiness has a great deal to do with me. I feel it." She tapped her chest. "I feel it here."

"You shouldn't." He looked away. "I don't feel it at all."

"Don't you?"

He did. Somewhere, he did. He knew it because if he

opened the floodgates to his feelings, he would drown in them. "I don't," he said softly, "because I can't."

She exhaled. "I brought you something for this purpose."

"For which purpose?"

She stood and went to the door, where she'd left her satchel. She rummaged through it. "I have something for you. Yes. Here you are."

To his great surprise, she withdrew a neat stack of envelopes tied with a red ribbon.

He stared at them. The top one was adorned with nothing more than the number one; he didn't know how many there were.

"Here," she repeated briskly, holding them out. "You know the system. This is in case you ever need to consult me about anything while you are away."

He didn't take them, even though his hands itched to hold them all. "And I suppose you'll send a number occasionally? I won't be able to get them until we are connected to the cable at Myriad Island, you know." He frowned. "And if you're in Shanghai, there will be quite a bit of delay."

"I'll send my usual notes." She smiled at him. "And I'll be in Hong Kong for these next weeks anyway. But don't wait for me. Count something when you need it. Breezes. Seagulls. Whatever you wish. There are numbers enough in the world. Whichever number you choose, that's the one I want you to have."

He reached and took the stack against his better judgment. He fanned the corners of the envelopes, felt a gentle breeze arise as he did. The last one was numbered ninety-seven. That was so many.

I want you to be happy. It was the hardest thing she could have asked for, and he didn't know what to do with her wish. *I feel it. Here.*

A rap sounded at the door. He shut his eyes. "That will be Lao. The *Celerity* is supposed to leave this afternoon."

"I know."

"I must go make sure she is ready."

"I know," Amelia said again softly.

Grayson had neither the words nor the time to tell her what he was thinking. He wasn't even sure he knew it himself. Instead, he took her face in his hands and kissed her. He kissed her gently, tongue running against the seam of her lips, then deeper as she opened to him. He kissed her, searching, not knowing what he was looking for. He kissed her over and over until the rap sounded at his door again.

"Captain Hunter?" Lao called.

He nodded, pulling away from her. "Coming."

CHAPTER THIRTY-FOUR

The indistinct green silhouette of Victoria Peak stood in counterpoint to the rolling gray-blue waters of Victoria Harbor. Benedict stood at the pier watching passengers disembark in ones and threes and sixes. He only set forward when his eyes lit on a two: two women, one young, the other graying, talking to a Chinese porter about the disposition of their luggage.

He came to stand behind the two women, hands clasped behind his back, waiting for them to notice him.

"I'm so nervous," the younger woman was saying. "It's been more than a decade. She won't recognize me. She might not even remember me."

She shook her head, and as she did, she turned enough to see Benedict watching her and obviously listening to their conversation.

Their hair was not the exact same shade of blond. Hers was sun-bleached at the ends to something paler than his sandy curls. But their eyes were the same shade of blue. They had the same nose. The same mouth, even if hers scrunched in annoyance while his broadened into a grin.

Benedict raised one hand in greeting. "Hullo, there."

It had been years since they'd seen each other, and yet his sister rolled her eyes. "We don't want whatever you're selling," she called, turning away from him. "We have neither time nor interest."

He had one moment of shock, followed by a swell of unholy amusement.

"Are you sure?" Benedict asked. "I'm selling—" He stuck a hand in his pocket, fishing about. "This fine linen handkerchief. A mere five hundred pounds. It's only slightly used."

She stared at him in utter disbelief and he burst into laughter. "She really *won't* recognize you," he managed to get out between guffaws. "It's been three years since you saw me, and you *already* don't know me."

A pause. Benedict saw Theresa's shoulders draw together. She raised one hand, finger already pointing, ready to jab.

He caught her hand before she could manage so much as a single poke.

"You!" She snatched her hand away from him entirely. "Did you not get my telegram? Did you not see my words? I said under *no* circumstances were you to be present."

"Oh," Benedict said cheerily, "I got it."

"Explain yourself! These are *definite* circumstances. How can you be here? Have you any defense?"

"The best defense." Benedict motioned her to lean in closer. She did so.

He whispered, "I decided you were being ridiculous."

The older woman—the Dowager Marchioness of Trent—simply sighed. "Good afternoon, Benedict."

"Oh." He straightened and turned to her. "My lady. Um. It's been a while. I hope you are well?"

"As you can see." She shrugged. "Theresa, talk to your brother. I'll go find transportation."

Theresa nodded before rounding on Benedict. "What's this

about me being ridiculous? I'll tell you what's ridiculous. It's ridiculous how tall you've become. And your voice. What *is* that thing?" She dropped hers an octave. "You sound like a brute."

"I've grown a bit."

"You seem to have outgrown basic facts alongside everything else. Must I remind you? I have indulged in fugitation! And you have been allowed outside of England only to bring me home. If we meet and are discovered, the jig is up. We are finished." She made a slash with her hand across his chest.

Benedict shrugged. "Why?"

"Why? Why, he asks. We agreed! Has your head become a turnip?"

"It's a serious question," Benedict said. "Explain to me how we are finished. Suppose I sent Judith a letter six months ago saying that I have no intention of going back to England and doing my duty. Then what happens?"

"Why are you asking?" Theresa stomped her foot. "Judith would be upset and angry and then..." She trailed off. "Um."

Benedict couldn't help himself. He laughed. "Ah, see. I always thought you were so clever."

"I *am* clever."

"But you were hung up on this longer than I was! It makes sense that you ran away from home. If you hadn't, Judith would have sat on you."

"Exactly." Theresa nodded.

"And it makes sense that I used *you* as an excuse to get her permission to leave. I was fourteen and had no money at the time. It makes sense that we had to do ridiculous things to get out."

She nodded slowly. "Yes."

"But she can't actually make us go back. And I *did* send her a letter months ago. You can do the same. You're only fugitating for the fun of it."

Theresa took this in, biting her lip. Finally, she looked up at him. "My God." She shook her head. "You *have* grown. Ridiculous."

He *had* grown. He could feel it in him, a sureness of purpose he had once lacked. He wasn't sure he could communicate all the ways he had changed yet. He wasn't sure he understood them himself.

"You're about to go introduce yourself to a sister I've never met," Benedict said. "It's absurd that you think I can't come with you."

Theresa met his gaze. Then she gave him a sharp nod. "Very well. Let's go. I suppose it's lucky we met. Without you, I would have had to hire someone to show me the way."

~

Myriad Island in mid-September was a chilly—but not yet freezing—spit of rock and ice. From Grayson's vantage point on board the *Victory*, half a mile away, the island where they had built the telegraphic junction was scarcely more than a dark blob the size of his fist.

The *Celerity* had laid the shore end of the cable out to the deeper waters where the *Victory* waited. Now the entire crew was on deck, waiting and watching the start of this final leg. The shore cable would be spliced to the two thousand miles of cable in the *Victory's* hold, and then…

Grayson held his breath as the cable was passed up. Lightfoot spliced the cables, then checked the connection.

"We have current," Lightfoot announced.

The cheer that arose was sheer excitement. Grayson found himself smiling alongside his crew. The sea was calm and Captain Ellis was in charge. Grayson left them and slipped down to the cargo hold. Lightfoot joined him a few minutes later.

"Mr. Lightfoot."

"Captain Hunter."

"Is the current steady enough to send a message?

The telegraphic engineer checked a few things, letting the galvanometer trail a message on thin paper before nodding. "Aye, sir. I believe so."

"Then send this one. T1S43G."

They'd set up the codes in advance with the Hong Kong office.

"Aye sir." Mr. Lightfoot set up the telegraph and a chronometer. Watching him brought Amelia to mind. The way she'd frowned and puzzled on the question of how best to send telegrams at sea. The way she'd worked with Lightfoot back then.

They presently had a circuit to a station thousands of miles away.

The code aboard ship was even more terse than most commercial ciphers in general usage. Those six characters would convey all of this: *To: Hong Kong office. Shore cable has been laid. Splice is successful. We are on our way. Captain Hunter.*

He waited as Mr. Lightfoot sent the message once, then again, then a final time.

Finally the answer came—the single letter *D.*

"Received, sir. Anything else?"

He could not help but think of her at a time like this. Grayson nodded. "T74S602G."

Mr. Lightfoot tilted his head. "That's someone in the Shanghai office. Anyone I know?"

Grayson met his gaze with a raised eyebrow.

"Oh very well," Lightfoot said. "I know it's to Mrs. Smith. And, of course, this is a fine business telegram you're sending, not anything personal. Because she's definitely not your girl. Is she?"

There was a question there—and also, there wasn't, not with the knowing smirk on Lightfoot's face.

I want you to be happy, she'd said.

Happy. The emotion seemed so prosaic. So ordinary. So impossibly out of reach.

Maybe. Maybe, once the line across the Pacific was laid. Maybe if he could settle things with his parents. Maybe then…

He wasn't sure if he *could* be happy even then, not with the grief that never went away in the center of his soul. But maybe he could have *something.*

He looked down at Lightfoot. The man was giving him a look, and well he should. He knew Grayson had run off with Amelia for weeks in the middle of one of the busiest times in his life. He had probably even heard that she had shown up in Hong Kong.

"She's not," he said quietly. "She's not my *anything.* Not really."

"Is she not?"

"No," Grayson said. "She's just my everything."

~

Grayson thought of Amelia a week out from Myriad Island.

He was on a gray sea with gray clouds overhead, with China to the southwest and the country he'd been born in to the southeast. On that day, he counted seventeen rays of sunlight through clouds.

Later that day, he slipped into his cabin and opened the seventeenth envelope. It contained a little pencil drawing of a tablet of paper. There was a wooden mechanical arm over it, bearing a pen nib. He had absolutely no idea what he was looking at, but the sketch showed signs of having been erased and drawn over multiple times.

Underneath, there was a simple notation: *I can already tell this won't work!* Next to it was a little sticklike drawing of someone in a skirt shaking stick fists in frustration.

He found himself smiling.

Before he went to sleep, he found Mr. Lightfoot. "How's the connection?"

"Not ideal," the man replied. "But workable."

Grayson nodded. "When you can, send this." He set down the paper.

"T74S602G." Lightfoot looked up at him. "You've sent this message already."

"Yes, but I haven't sent it today."

Two days later, Grayson sat at the stern of his ship, listening to the steady click, click of cable spooling into water. The noise was barely audible above the sound of the steam engine and the swoosh of the screw propulsion. He counted thirty-two clicks before his attention wavered.

Envelope 32 was a sketch of an angry cat. A large-eared mouse hid between two bookshelves, contentedly munching on a piece of cheese, while the cat pawed futilely at the gap.

Lightfoot took one look at Grayson's face when he came down. "T74S602G again, Captain Hunter?"

"Precisely."

A week after that, he was jolted to wakefulness by the quiet sounds of the ship. The now-still waters of the Pacific Ocean lapped around his boat. He counted the sound of those waves, rhythmic and comforting, and when he lost count at seventy-two, he picked that envelope. This one was a short letter, in which Amelia started by admitting she was a letter-writing enthusiast.

"That comes as no shock to me," Grayson told the letter out loud.

She talked about writing to her brother Leland. About sending letters up the Yangtze to her mother and father. About how she was awaiting a reply from the sister she had only recently discovered. She mentioned that further correspondence with Mrs. Acheson was proving difficult.

As for my British mother, I am not sure what to say to her yet. But I am thinking about what it means to be a bridge. What must I do in that capacity? Every possibility makes my heart feel sick.

None of Grayson's thoughts on the matter would fit into their telegraphic code, and the commercial cipher they'd developed contained no cursing. That night, when he went down to the telegraphic station in the hold, Lightfoot just shook his head. "Is it going to be T74S602G once again?"

"Absolutely."

"Then shouldn't it go without saying?"

"It can." Grayson thought about their last conversation. About her telling him she wanted him to be happy. He wanted her to know he was considering it, that he didn't know how to go forward but he hadn't forgotten her wish. "But perhaps, I need to say it. To remind myself."

He returned to his cabin. He lay in bed and thought of the half-opened pile of envelopes she had given him.

I wish for you to be happy, she'd said. It *hurt* her that he wasn't. He had to do it. It was that simple. He'd been happy before. How hard could it be?

The problem, Grayson knew, was less that he felt *un*happy and more that he didn't allow himself to feel much of anything at all. If he did, it wouldn't be happiness that came.

He shook his head.

Three days later, after he'd spent seventy-seven hours fighting through a squall that demanded his constant attention to make sure the cable would not snap as it was paying out, he stumbled into his room in the middle of the day. But he was so tired he could scarcely sleep. He tossed and turned. He counted his breaths, heavy in the stillness after the storm, and then opened envelope 94.

Daylight drifted in under the door, enough to read her words.

I think about you sometimes at night, she confessed. *And in the day. I think about coming to your bed in an unsteady sea. I think about kissing your lips while the rocking of the ship tries to tear us apart, about finding a rhythm with you when the world is rough around us. I think about how you would have the superior pace from years of being at sea—how you would establish a rhythm that would allow us to ride the waves as I rode you.*

He felt his entire body flush. My God. She hadn't told him she'd included letters that were downright pornographic. He was tired to his bones, but he felt himself grow hard at the thought of her here. Of her riding him.

Of their bodies coming together. He shut his eyes and thought of the storm he had just been through, of mastering not the paying out of cable but the intricacies of her voice, her body.

His release was sweet comfort. He cleaned himself up and finally fell asleep.

Many hours later, after a much-needed rest, Lightfoot nodded at him. "Is it to be T74S602G again tonight, sir?"

"Not tonight." Grayson clasped his hands behind his back. "Tonight, it's T74S412G."

"You seem to be in fine fettle."

Grayson bit back a smile. "Just send the message."

Shore grew closer, and he started to encounter sea-birds. Early one morning, with the final connection on the islands dotting the coasts of British Columbia a day or so distant, he counted seven gray and white terns playing above him.

Seven was a clipping from an older English newspaper that must have made its way across the ocean through the usual winding paths. The article was about a display in New York—a complete skeleton of some prehistoric creature.

Amelia had supplied her own sketched version of what the

THE DEVIL COMES COURTING

beast must have looked like back when it was enfleshed: a large creature walking on two legs, cropping at plants. She had sketched a little stick figure next to it, one wearing a captain's jacket and a hat that looked suspiciously like his own.

Don't worry, she'd scrawled. *It has the teeth of an herbivore! Likely it would only stampede you flat if you disturbed its young. Even more luckily, the species is entirely extinct, so you should have no difficulty avoiding even that unlikely fate.*

Grayson smiled and set the envelope back in his drawer. It had been a month since he'd seen her; it would be many more months before he would see her again.

But Moresby Island was close at hand. Once the shore line was laid, he'd be able to send a real message. A longer one.

He was no closer to fulfilling her wish than he had been before. He would have to think of what to say.

~

Amelia had put off one of the tasks she had set herself for far too long.

When she'd first arrived in Hong Kong, she'd sent her brother a letter letting him know that she was here. She'd given him a direction, even, and told him she understood he might not want to see her at present, but here she was. Close. So close.

She'd received no response to any of her inquiries.

Never before in her years of knowing Leland had she received no response. They'd been separated before, but they'd traded letters back and forth for years—week after week, without cessation, and while the mail would sometimes fail her, Leland never had.

It had been months since she'd last heard from him, months since he'd told her the story of her mother with a waxen face after being sick outside her home. It had been so long since he'd taken his leave in Shanghai, and Amelia didn't know why he wasn't writing to her.

She'd avoided finding out for the weeks she was there. She was busy. He would come to her, she was sure. Whatever it was that was keeping him away... He would come.

He had not come.

Finally, with her departure imminent, she made her way to his door. She knocked and waited, heart thumping in her throat so wildly that she could taste her own nerves.

The door opened, revealing her brother. His eyes met hers, widened, and then he paled. He looked like he might be sick again.

He looked as if he'd never stopped being sick.

"Amelia." He took a step back. "Or should I say, Mrs. Smith?"

It hurt to have him speak to her with that tense air of formality. "Amelia," she told him, appalled. "Why would you not call me Amelia?"

He swallowed and looked away, guilt painting his features. And he did not answer.

She bulled on ahead. "Leland." She didn't understand this. Not one bit of it. People were often strange and horrible, but... not Leland. Never Leland.

Yet here they were.

She gritted her teeth and dove in. "I know you don't want to talk to me right now. I can imagine reasons why that might be."

Her imagination had been eating away at her.

"But I have need of counsel, and you are the only one who will understand the particulars. Leland. Please. I need you." She tilted her head, biting back tears. The truth of the statement had not hit her until she'd said it. She *needed* her big brother.

He let out a long, slow exhale. "Amelia." He stepped aside. "Of course. If you need me. Of course. Anything you need. Come in."

His abode was small and sparse. She sat in the spare straight-backed chair he indicated and looked at him.

It felt awkward, and things had never been awkward between them. He lit a range, bit back something that might have been a curse, and boiled water. She waited until the tea was before them, trying to figure out where to start... But it was no use because he started first.

"Amelia," he said in a low voice. "I'm so dreadfully sorry."

"For not writing?"

He grimaced. "I keep looking back over everything in our childhood. I was older than you. I should have known better. I should have understood what was happening. I keep thinking of my own culpability, of every excuse I made to myself. I just wanted to make things easy on myself. Think of my own comfort. I should have questioned what I was doing."

She couldn't make any sense of this. She stared at him. "Leland. Precisely what are you apologizing for?"

"Everything," he said in a rush. "I cannot think of what happened when you were a child with fondness anymore. I participated in it. Amelia, I *participated*."

"I don't understand."

"She told you, you weren't allowed to speak anything but English," Leland said, his voice breaking, "and I *helped* her do it. She called you by another name, and I didn't ask for your real one. She gave me a story and even if I thought you didn't want to know, *I* knew. *I* knew your Chinese mother was there. I knew she wanted you. And I didn't say anything."

"Leland. You were..." She calculated rapidly. "You were twelve when this started. I couldn't blame you."

"Old enough to understand when things weren't right. Old enough to know right from wrong. But I didn't want to know. There were too many things I didn't want to know, so I didn't ask. I have spent too long not asking because it's comfortable. Because it's easy. I don't know if I ever *would* have asked, were it not—" He cut himself off. "I can't ask you to forgive me. What I did—it's unforgivable. But Amelia, please understand. I'm sorry." He looked over at her. Misery was etched in every line of his face. "I'm so dreadfully sorry."

She couldn't help herself. Not when he was so utterly distraught. She stood and moved to him, wrapping her arms around him.

"Leland," she said. "You are my brother. My big brother. You have been my everything. When I took a ridiculous interest in telegraphs, you encouraged me. You sent me a book about encoding all the way from Hong Kong so I could learn more." Her voice shook. "When we were younger, you listened to me. I could always count on you. When I felt I had no choice but to marry a second time, you found me a solution and you broke the shell of my world wide open. Don't you dare apologize to me for something you didn't do, do you understand?"

His eyes were glossy. "But, Amelia."

"You and I," she said, "we were always in it together. We will be in it together as long as you allow it. I thought..." She choked on her fears. "I thought you'd decided that I wasn't really your sister, not anymore now that you'd realized that I had another mother. A living one who wanted me."

"No." He brought up his hands, tentatively, touching her elbows. "No. I just knew that what I had done. It was not forgivable. I couldn't ask for that. I can't let myself want it."

Amelia nodded. "When my Chinese mother left, she told me she would be back."

He nodded.

"And she told me to hold on to my heart."

He exhaled.

"I could not have done it alone," she told him. "I could not have done it without you there with me every step of the way. If what happened to me didn't crush me, it was because you were there holding me up."

"Amelia." He shook his head.

"And you are the only person in the world who can help me with my conundrum. I have a stack of letters from our mother. One every day or so. They keep coming and coming. I've read a handful—I can show you them. She acts as if nothing has happened, and I don't know what to say. I don't know what to do. I don't know how to forgive her."

Leland let out a pained noise. "Forgive *her*? Has she even acknowledged she did anything wrong?"

"Should it matter? Should it matter what she's acknowledged? Should I hold my resentment against her, when she raised me? When she expended effort and care and...and everything that she did?"

"Amelia." Leland pushed her away, but only so he could search her expression. He shook his head. "After I left, after I realized what I had done, I got drunk for three days and vomited out the contents of my soul. Have you any sense that she's harbored a tenth that much remorse?"

"No, but..." This was why she needed to talk to Leland. He would understand what she owed and help her measure out her feelings. "Leland. She took me in."

"Amelia." His voice was softer, gentler. "Amelia. What she did to you was not 'taking you in.' That is not what you do with a child who is wanted by her parents. The word for what she did is *abduction*. The word for what she did when she kept you from your language is *theft*. The word for what she is doing by pretending that nothing is wrong—by making you feel that you are at fault for not forgiving her without explanation—is *shite*."

Amelia exhaled. "When I was talking to my Chinese mother, we talked about my feeling as if I didn't belong. As if I didn't fit."

He nodded.

"She told me that I was a bridge. That I fit perfectly in the space where I was. And if I'm a bridge, don't I owe it to someone?" She felt desperate. "To something, to try to bridge?"

Leland sighed. "You can't be a bridge to someone who tries to steal the ground from beneath your feet. You will break your heart trying to find steady footing, and it will never come."

Amelia's heart twisted. It was painful, so painful, the realization that came to her with those words. It hurt every part of her to understand what her brother was saying. But she could not make one person into a different one. She could not alter the course of another person's mind. Accepting that she could not solve this was hard.

"I thought the same thing for a while," Leland told her. "That I could bridge. The reason I quit being a missionary?"

"Yes?"

"I haven't told you all of it." He looked away. "I'm *afraid* to tell you all of it, but…"

"Leland. You must know I'll love you anyway."

He let out another breath. "I don't want to marry a woman. Ever."

"How could I blame you for that? I've been married before. It wasn't exactly good." Although she'd started to think…but no. Never mind Grayson.

"I'm not sure you understand," her brother said, blowing out a breath. "I'm in love with a man."

She turned to look at him.

"He tells me it's normal—mostly normal anyway. Understood in some places, if not all. And there I was, a missionary, working for an organization that was telling people that it's wrong." He looked at her. "It wasn't just the hypocrisy of the thing. When I finally realized I was allowed to believe myself normal, I couldn't stay any longer. I tried for a little while, tried to talk to people about bridging the gap between local beliefs and ours, but you can't build a bridge on ground that wants to shake you loose. Trust me, Amelia. I've tried."

She didn't know what to say to that, to the emotion in his voice or the way his eyes avoided hers. Instead, she reached out and took his hand. "I won't shake you loose. If you say it's normal for you, then it's normal. I promise."

For a long while, they sat there, hand in hand, not speaking as the light changed. Amelia's thoughts turned round and round.

"Will I ever meet the man you're in love with?" she asked.

"You'd want to?"

She nodded. The silence stretched a while longer. Leland wasn't her brother, not by blood, not by appearance. He was her brother by history. By love. By choice. And that thought that she had a choice meant...

Amelia let out a long exhalation. "I believe I mentioned I have a stack of letters from her." She didn't say who she meant beyond the single pronoun.

He knew anyway. "Do you want me to read them through with you?"

She'd read some of them already, enough to know that the apology and the understanding she needed to see was never going to come. She could choose to let the ground shake beneath her feet, or...

Instead, Amelia shook her head. "Would you help me burn them?"

He squeezed her hands. "Of course," he said. "Of course I will."

CHAPTER THIRTY-FIVE

The morning that Grayson connected the Asian and American continents via electric current dawned clear. Clear enough that as the sun rose over the waters of the Pacific, he could finally make out snow-capped, blue-gray mountains made insignificant by distance, dancing on the horizon.

He turned to Lao. "Signal the *Celerity*. It's time."

A few crew members gathered on deck, celebrating the sight of their destination.

"Have the *Celerity* lay the shore cable and meet us at the rendezvous," Grayson said.

Cheers rose. This was it: the day Grayson had been waiting for. Today he would solve everything. The temperature was pleasant. The sun was warming. His entire crew buzzed with energy.

And Grayson didn't feel a thing.

Maybe it was because he had too much to do. It took another three hours of carefully laying cable to come up on Moresby Island. Somewhere in those hours, Lightfoot reported the current had cut off. They then had to retrace their wake, hauling up cable and testing as they went until they found the flaw. Cut, splice, check the insulation, check the signal. The crew cheered when the current was restored and off they went again.

Moresby Island started as a line on the horizon, gradually expanding into dark green forests and grassy meadows.

It was midday when they caught up to the *Celerity*. She was anchored with Moresby close enough to taunt them with the end of the journey. From here, Grayson could see another ship —the *Reliant*—visible in the harbor. She'd come up with a support crew for the aftermath of this. The shore line had already been laid; everyone was waiting so Grayson could complete the task that had taken so much of his life. Just one splice—connect the shore line to the line aboard the *Victory*. One splice and it would all be done.

Grayson had stood here once before, on board a different ship roughly nine years ago, plotting this enterprise. Even back then, he and Harry had planned to complete the line here.

And he'd done it. Just as planned—he'd done it. He should have felt a sense of accomplishment. Pride, at least. If there were ever a moment for happiness, this was one.

Except, he had never planned to be alone when it happened. Harry was supposed to be on the *Celerity*. Noah should have been at his side. John would have been waiting on Myriad with a feast ready to celebrate the occasion. Instead, it was just Grayson.

Seamen gathered as Mr. Lightfoot performed the final splice and a final check. The mood was exuberant. There were jokes and laughter amid ebullient, expectant waiting.

Grayson found himself mimicking the proper emotions alongside everyone else. He laughed. He clapped, holding his breath alongside everyone else as the two cables were spliced into one.

"That's it?" someone asked, when that was complete. "We're finished?"

If they'd done everything right, the line they'd just laid would complete the work they'd set out to do—Japan to Myriad Island, Myriad to Moresby, Moresby down to Seattle. The circuit should be complete. They could now send telegraphs halfway round the world.

Lightfoot looked over at Grayson, gesturing with the now-joined cable. "Sir? Would you like to toss her overboard?"

The line was heavy, copper coated in gutta percha. Letting go of the cable would signal that he'd finished, that he could move on. Grayson shook his head. "You do the honors."

Lightfoot looked honored. Delighted. Not conflicted, the way Grayson felt. "Me?"

"Who else?" Grayson smiled at him. "It's thanks to you that we've kept the line in working condition this whole time."

Lightfoot walked the spliced cable to the railing. He held it gently. He bit his lip, then kissed the cable for good luck. Finally, he heaved it over the side. A half second later, a light splash sounded.

For a few moments, Grayson could see the line disappear, a dark black snake vanishing into the murk of the Pacific.

"Well?" someone asked. "Is that it? We just wait for it to settle?"

Grayson counted. He knew the precise depths at this spot, knew exactly how long it would take for the line to fall to the ocean floor.

"Now what?" someone asked.

"Now someone on Moresby sends the signal that the line is live." Much of the crew on the *Celerity* had likely rowed in to shore for that purpose—that and the celebration that would follow. Grayson shut his eyes. "Then Sapporo signals Seattle, and Seattle signals Sapporo in return. Whoever is listening on shore tells us if we did it properly, and if not, we haul it up, find the fault, and toss it back in."

"That's him then?" One of the seamen gestured behind them. "The signaler?"

There was a man out on the deck. At this distance, the man appeared as little more than a stick with flags.

The *Victory* was a mile offshore. Yet something like silence fell—the silence of the sea. They could hear the waves slapping against the hull, the call of gulls circling overhead.

"I can hear it," someone whispered. "I can hear the vibrations of the telegraph passing, a hum."

"Dunce," someone responded with a slap to the head. "You can't hear a telegram."

"Then tell me, what did I just hear?"

Grayson exhaled. Nine years ago, he and Harry had stood on this ocean together. They'd bickered good-naturedly about what the first message should be.

Grayson had wanted something grandiose, a quotation like, *be of good cheer; I have overcome the world.*

Harry had rolled his eyes and told him, "Just say, 'We did it.' Or better yet, 'Harry was here.'"

They'd bickered about it good-naturedly.

Harry wasn't here though, so it was the first message—*we did it*—that was being sent. If that was received, Sapporo would reply, "Apparently so."

At the cable junction built on Moresby, the waiting crew would be able to listen in on the transmission. If they'd been successful, the man on the dock would signal via semaphore.

The seconds that passed felt like hours. They waited. Two of the *Victory*'s seamen clutched hands, dark and light brown fingers twining nervously together.

Then the man on the dock turned to face the *Victory*. He picked up his flags and signaled—one flag at his knees, the other pointing to the sun.

C.

The ship didn't need the rest of the word to know what would follow: *clear*. They'd done it. They'd connected two continents over the widest ocean. The cheer that went up could have wakened the whales in the deeps.

It wouldn't wake the dead.

Grayson had accomplished everything. He'd made his transpacific line, and he felt—

Gutted. Empty. He felt as if he were playacting all the proper emotions—clap everyone in his crew on the back, accept congratulations from everyone, and thank them for their hard work.

He didn't feel satisfied. He didn't feel pride in his accomplishments.

He felt *alone*. So alone. He never should have been the only one of his brothers here. It wasn't supposed to be like this. It was *never* supposed to be like this.

That sense of loss rolled over him, strong enough it threatened to wash away the barriers he had built. It took all his will to hold back the tide of his emotions. To command his smile to stay on his face. He couldn't let anyone know.

"Now what?" Lightfoot asked him after the cheers had died down.

"Now we go ashore," Grayson said with that false smile. "We go ashore, and we celebrate."

CHAPTER THIRTY-SIX

The junction on Moresby Island was housed in a small building next to a cabin. The *Celerity* had taken all but the bare minimum of the crew over for the celebrations. Grayson had planned for the party in detail. There would be provisions present: real food, not just sea-faring grub in larger quantities. Wine. Beer. He'd even had a small staff brought up to make everyone as comfortable as they could be in such a desolate setting.

But as he walked up the path, he smelled something frying. *That* hadn't been in his plans. He was trying to make sense of this as they rounded the turn through the woods into the meadow where the junction was built. That was when he saw a tent. No, not just one. Four of them, one almost large enough to be a pavilion, and three that could sleep a small army.

He stared at them in confusion. "What is going on?"

There was no time for anyone to answer because people started pouring out into the sunshine. The first man out was his youngest brother, Adrian. Grayson let out a shocked noise. Then his cousin Aaron, his father, Adrian's wife, Camilla, more cousins, uncles, aunts, nieces. So many people from his father's side of the family had all come out. At the end came his mother. Their eyes met over the crowd.

Ever since he'd seen that first flash of resentment in her eyes, Grayson had been contemplating his plan. He was going to make it up to her. He was going to set things right by building this impossible transpacific memorial and…and…

And…

And he'd just done it. He'd held on to hope for years because he refused to surrender. Now he felt his hope crack in pieces on the unyielding certainty of reality. What the hell had he been thinking? How was this supposed to work? What was he supposed to do? Say, "By the way, Mama, I know your other boys are gone, but I made you this telegraph line?"

What kind of compensation was *that?* What was she supposed to do with an insulated mess of submarine copper?

She made her way to him. She was smiling, holding out her hands to him. "Congratulations!"

"Mama." He swallowed a lump in his throat. "What are you doing here?"

"Well." Her warm tone grew just a bit frostier. "My son seemed to be avoiding me. I figured I would have to come directly to you instead of waiting for the reverse."

"Mama."

"You're lucky your father and I didn't take a ship to Hong Kong after what you pulled in April. I wanted to, but we weren't even sure where you would be. Asia is a large continent."

He let out a careful breath. "Mama." What was there to say? "I'm sorry."

She shook her head. "Say you're sorry by visiting more often. But for now, stop giving me that hang dog look." She warmed up, lecture finished. "Look what you've done. I'm so proud of you, Gray."

~

I t took hours for Grayson to be able to slink off alone. The little building holding the junction was cold. He could hear the click of the galvanometer, already moving, as the flood of international telegrams had already started.

He waited until the line was free before signaling that he had something to say.

T74S...

But what was he to transmit to Amelia after all? *Why aren't you here? I need you desperately. This didn't fix anything.*

None of the codes they'd come up with would do.

He eventually went with *602G*. The old standby. He sat in the cold and the dark, with the sounds of celebration behind him.

To his surprise, she answered immediately, meaning she was still in Hong Kong.

T1S How did everything turn out? A

Perhaps she'd gone to Hong Kong to await the news in person. To celebrate at the same time as him, whatever time it was there. He shut his eyes. How *had* everything turned out?

T74S Megalodons far off still. G

There was no more opportunity to speak; commercial transactions took priority, and the Seattle operator took the line back immediately. The galvanometer clicked away with a merry chatter. Just as well. What would he say to her? Somehow, he was supposed to figure out how to be happy? It seemed further away than ever.

The door creaked behind him and he turned. "Grayson?"

"Mama." Grayson shut his eyes. Of all the people. He didn't know how to talk to his mother.

"Grayson?" she queried again. She looked tiny in the moonlight, the darkness blurring the lines on her face. She looked young this way, too young to have had five sons and lost three.

"What are you doing all the way out here?"

"What it looks like. I'm sending a message." He didn't say anything more. Neither did his mother. They stayed there like that, she stood and watched him as he sat at the transmitter. He couldn't give up. He *had* to fix this.

"Are you waiting for a reply?" she asked.

"She's already replied."

"She?" His mother came to sit next to him, looking at him with expectation.

God. There was so much he wanted to tell her. He didn't even know where to start. She felt as distant standing next to him as when he'd been on the other side of the world.

"My vice president of telegraphic encoding." He swallowed. "She's responsible for the Chinese telegraphic code."

His mother shook her head. "You're always thinking about your work."

There was nothing he knew how to say to that. Nothing except the truth. "I'm sorry, Mama. I'm so, so sorry."

"For not coming back in April?" She exhaled. "Grayson... Well. Apology accepted. Just don't do it again."

"I'm sorry for so much more than that." His grief felt so raw. So present. He was drowning in it. "I'm sorry it was only me who completed the line. I'm sorry I'm the one who's here." He felt his spine curl as if he were a hedgehog seeking shelter. "I'm sorry it wasn't Noah or Harry or John. I'm sorry it's me. I tried to fix it, but there's nothing I can do."

His bent head pushed into his knuckles. His hands had clenched into fists. He held on, trying not to let his emotions run wild.

"Grayson, what are you talking about?"

He took her hand. "I know." He squeezed her palm between his. "I don't mind, Mama. I can't blame you."

"What are you talking about?" This echo was just a hint more strident.

"When I told you about Noah." He let out a breath. "I saw it. Your first reaction. You resented the fact that it was me who came back."

Her breath was shaky.

"I don't blame you," he told her. "I don't, I really don't—"

"Gray. No. Oh God, no."

He lifted his head and looked her in the eyes. "I know what resentment looks like on you, Mama."

Her lips trembled. Her hands were shaking in his. But she looked in his eyes. "Of *course* I resented that my sons were taken away from me!" She spat out those words. "Of course I resented it! I hate it! I hate everything about it! I will never forgive the greed and cruelty that foisted a war on us for it. *Never.*"

"I know, Mama, I know."

Her eyes glistened in the night. "But I never resented your surviving. Never. What did I do to make you think such a thing?"

He stared at her. He didn't understand. How could she *not* resent him? God, he resented *himself.*

That was when reality broke. Of course. *He* resented himself. It was him, all him, his own acrimony and bitterness coiling together into venom in his heart. Compared with his brothers, his own survival felt like a colossal mistake. And *this* —this crushing grief and inadequacy—*this* was why he didn't want to sort through his feelings.

"Ah." He felt frozen. "That's why. It's because *I* wish it had been me. *I* shouldn't be here."

"Shh," his mother said, stroking his face. That was how Grayson realized that he was crying. That he was actually making an embarrassing noise while doing it.

"Shhh. Don't talk such nonsense. It was senseless. There was no reason to who came back and who didn't."

"Mama."

She folded her arms around him. "I'm glad it was you," she told him. "I'm so glad you're still in this world. I'm so glad."

His face was wet with tears—utterly shameful—and his nose was running when the door opened again. Gray tried to choke back his emotions. But it was Adrian who entered—Adrian and his father.

"Ah," said his father jovially. "You've found the man of the hour... Oh." He cut himself off.

"Grayson," Adrian said slowly. "Is everything all right?"

I'm fine, he almost said. But he could hear those not-yet-uttered words overlapping with Amelia's. *Don't tell me you're fine if you're not fine.* And: *Who cares for you?* He'd been holding the truth back because he was afraid to ask for the care he wanted, the care he *needed.* He'd wanted to fix everything else before he could believe that he deserved to be fixed himself.

He finally saw his error. He could not fix this. He had known it all these years. He'd known it and refused to admit it. He couldn't fix this because one man could not fill a gaping hole, no matter how far he stretched. Grayson had to know; he'd stretched himself six thousand miles now, and it hadn't been enough.

Everything seemed lost in despair. His family's wounds? Irreparable. Amelia? She wanted him to be happy, and here he was, brought to his knees by what should have been his greatest victory.

Grayson shut his eyes and touched his fingers to his temples. He thought of Amelia's drawing of a mouse hiding in a corner, munching cheese. He thought of hiding away.

And yet in the cold, dark night, with the telegraph chattering noisily away, his mother squeezed his hands. Adrian came to sit on his other side, arm coming to his shoulder. His father pressed in front of him. The three of them squeezed him in a hug so warm, so tight, that even Grayson could not help but feel embraced by it.

"What's wrong?" Adrian whispered.

Don't tell me you're fine if you're not fine, he could hear himself say, and yes, that was right for *other* people, but surely, for himself? For himself, it was a weakness.

Grayson lifted his head long enough to lean his forehead against his brother's chest.

"Oh Gray."

"I wasn't supposed to do this alone," Grayson said. "Harry and John and Noah and I were all supposed to do it together. I thought if I finished the transpacific line that we'd worked on together, it would..."

He didn't even know how to complete the sentence. Serve as a monument? Preserve their memory? Bring him peace? He'd thought all those things.

"I thought if I finished the last thing we planned together," he said, "that it would mean there's something of them still in this world. But they're still not here. It's just me."

"There still is." His father cupped the back of his head. "There is in our hearts. And in your telegraph."

"But it's not enough. This isn't enough." He'd spent so long flinching from this truth. There was nothing he could do. Nothing. Nothing would ever be enough. "*I'm* not enough."

Tears came again like the opening of floodgates, a violent unstoppable torrent of water sweeping through the barren landscape of his heart. He could scarcely think beyond the grief that swept through him.

"I miss them too," Adrian said. "I'm still sad too."

Grayson could feel his brother's arms around him, surrounding him with love and affection and a grief that was so close to his own.

"I miss them every day," his father whispered. "Sometimes I forget for a day, and then one thing reminds me..."

"We were talking about Noah on the way up," his mother said. "Remember his steam engine phase?"

Grayson let out a laugh. "Who could forget?"

But that was what he had tried to do, pushing his grief away, denying it a place in his heart. He listened to his mother tell a story about how his younger brother had disappeared on a train for three hours while his parents had searched for him, more and more frantically, only to discover he'd found his way to the engine where the Black crew of engineers was answering his questions and feeding him lunch.

Then there was the time Harry had gotten into a scrape overseas. The time John had gone to Brazil. Painful memories. Precious memories. He couldn't fix them, not without jettisoning them in their entirety. He couldn't fix anything, broken as it was.

"My ship's logs." He put those words out there. "My journals. I have so much of them saved in there. Maybe when I come home next, we could...?"

"I would like that," his mother said quietly, her lips pressing against his forehead. "I would like to go through them together. I hate thinking of you out in the world all alone."

Grayson exhaled and thought of Amelia telling him she wanted him to be happy.

"On the subject of being alone." He looked away. "I have a confession to make."

"Hmm?"

"I need to tell you about my vice president of telegraphic encoding. She is..."

He searched for a word, but the truth must have come through in his struggling silence.

"Tell us about her?" his mother said. "From the sounds of it, I believe you need to bring her home. Or am I wrong?"

He exhaled. "You're not. You're not wrong."

CHAPTER THIRTY-SEVEN

Grayson's family had come up aboard the *Reliant* with his cousin Ben as captain.

"Well, of course you should sail back to San Francisco with everyone," Ben said, when Grayson asked the next morning. "I thought I was going to have to hit you over the head and toss you in a sack to make you come along, and here you are asking, pretty as you please."

It felt odd to be idle aboard ship, odd not to have to worry about the paying out of cable or the coming storms, odd to be so disconnected on the waters when he'd spent weeks with a copper connection that could fill in all the details of what was happening ashore. It felt odd to bid the *Celerity* and the *Victory* farewell until they reconvened in San Francisco a little later. It felt odd to sit at a table with his cousins and tell tales of their exploits. It felt odd to fit in.

He brought up his brothers one afternoon during the Daily Disoccupation. Ben and Zed had been teasing him because the Disoccupation aboard the *Reliant* was kites—flying, crafting, making, and of course, since he and his cousins were involved, being competitive about the entire thing.

Grayson was not good at kites. He always managed to tangle his kite with someone else's, or snap the string, or misread an eddy and end up watching his kite plunge into the ocean while everyone else's soared high.

"You really are spectacularly bad," said Louis, his sixteen-year-old something-removed nephew.

Grayson turned to him. "Well, if my brother Noah were here…" He trailed off. That spike of grief was still there, sharp and ever present. But it felt like a cold wind on a sunrise, the sorrow tempered with warmth.

The kid just gave him a perplexed look. "Who's Noah?"

Intolerable that a generation would grow up not knowing. "Let me tell you about Noah," Grayson said. "You know that telegraph line we just completed? Well, Noah was the one who figured out how to make the line."

"Didn't people already know?"

"In a sense." Grayson met his eyes. "But as Noah's not here to do it, let me explain to you about insulators and where they come from."

~

There was work to do as soon as they landed in San Francisco. The *Victory* needed to be laden with the cable to connect Hong Kong to Shanghai and Grayson had an entire packet of letters detailing what had happened in his absence. He would need to return to Hong Kong on board the *Celerity;* the *Victory* would follow. Zed was going to Maine for the winter, and Ben was heading south to Brazil.

Grayson had taken a few hours off at the beginning of the week to visit a specialty shop, and then, just before this final dinner, he'd gone back to pick up his completed order.

There was a bittersweet feeling when everyone gathered for

one last time. Grayson's aunt Meg told him that he needed to come *home*, really come home, as soon as he had the chance... perhaps now? His mother countered that he had a woman to bring with him.

At the end of the evening, Grayson found himself at a table drinking scotch. His brother Adrian was on his right; Lightfoot was to his left. Across the table from him sat Zed and Ben, while Captains Ellis and Bell were interspersed among them all.

Harry should be here, he thought, not for the first time. He could pick out the empty places in the conversation where John would have made a joke. He could try to imagine what it would have been like for Noah to drink.

Those places would always be empty. And yet the time that had passed had not been empty. He thought of Lightfoot teaching Amelia to play tiddlywinks. Of Zed challenging him to a wrestling match. Of Ben, whom he'd scarcely seen, doing gutta balata runs that had helped Grayson build his cable. He thought of the great-great-great uncles who had come up with a Daily Disoccupation in the first place—a ritual that had meant that even when he'd been at his lowest points, he'd been surrounded with human companionship.

Grayson could see the net that had been holding him up now. It had only been invisible to him because he was so intent on the holes that had been made in it.

"Ah." Grayson set down his drink. "The scotch is making me sentimental."

"Blaming the scotch, are you?"

"I've thought often that I should have been laying the transpacific line with my brothers. There were times when I felt isolated. Because of their absence." He looked around the table. "It's taken me a while to realize this, and so I hope you'll forgive the tardiness of this statement. I could never have done this without any of you."

"Ah, Grayson," said Zed. "You utter sap."

"I wanted to lay the transpacific line with my brothers." He reached out and tapped Mr. Lightfoot's shoulder. "And I suppose I did. Thank you all for being the family I needed. Even if you weren't my brothers by blood."

"Excuse me." Adrian cleared his throat. "What am I?"

"Well," Zed shot back, "that's obvious. We're his fake brothers. You're not—that makes you a fake-fake brother."

"Fake-fake, am I?"

"Look," said Lightfoot. "I believe we are missing one very important and valuable member at this table. Captain Grayson Hunter, don't you think you should be telling *someone else* this whole thing about being family?"

"You've met her, Zed," Adrian said. "Tell me about this vice president of telegraphic encoding. Has our Grayson got a chance?"

Zed looked at Grayson. He looked around the table. "That's going to depend."

"Depend on what?" Ben demanded.

Grayson leaned forward. "I would also like to know."

Zed shrugged. "On whether he can remove his head from his ass long enough to ask her," he said with a cackle. And so the topic moved on.

❧

On the journey back to China, Grayson found his strategy changing. Instead of counting birds or breezes to unlock Amelia's envelopes, he found himself counting things in his memory.

He remembered lying under a tree with John in autumn, bright red maple leaves falling on their faces—*one, two, three, four, five.* One time he and Harry had stolen their great-uncle's good brandy. How many sips had they managed each? *One,* before their coughing had given them away.

From there it was a matter of counting other things. There was an ache in Grayson's heart that had never gone away. Instead of steeling himself to ignore those moments of pain, he stopped fleeing his grief and finally let it wash through him. How many breaths did he have to take until the pain lessened? *Eighty-four* was the answer.

One morning, Grayson came onto the deck of the ship, violin in hand. The sun was tilting over the horizon, all gold and pink and orange, dyeing the wake of the ship with splashes of color. The air was crisp and cool against his skin. He inhaled and started his scales. To the side of the ship, a large silver-backed fish breached the water in a sleek arc, then another, then another. He matched the pace of his scales up and down in time to their leaps. Four. Five.

Somewhere around seven, Grayson came to a realization.

This. This feeling out on the waters, with the sun rising around him. With the ache in his heart still present, but now an acknowledged acquaintance rather than an enemy to be fought at first sight—

This was happiness.

Happiness was not the antonym of sorrow. The two existed, side by side, holding hands, and he could not deny one without barring his way to the other. This feeling now, out on the waves, was bound to the moment under the trees with Harry, leaves falling in his face. It was tied to the burn of Uncle Henry's brandy.

This instant was connected to every other instant, to the memories of his family. *This* was what he had tried to avoid— this web of connection.

Grayson inhaled. He imagined himself cradling the precious feeling to his chest. And then he breathed out, letting it pass on into the music he was playing.

⁓

Grayson had last been in Shanghai five months ago. His absence seemed much longer. It felt as if a gray fog had lifted. Back then, he'd scarcely known how to want, let alone *what* to want.

Now he stood in the doorway to Amelia's office, watching her frown over a contraption on her desk.

Her hair must have once been in a bun that morning, he thought. It had fallen from that into something that now looked like a loose twist across her neck. Little tendrils of dark hair drifted across her face; she brushed those back and concentrated on the metal cylinder in front of her.

Grayson found himself smiling. It wasn't just an expression on his face. He felt a wave of affection and warmth down to his toes. God. He hadn't known how much he adored her.

Amelia sighed, pushed back her chair—and froze as she caught sight of him.

Her entire face lit as if she were mirroring his warmth. "Grayson." She stood. "I thought you wouldn't be back for months!"

He didn't know if she hurled herself across the room or if he raced to meet her. He just knew that in one second, they were apart; in the next blink of an eye, she was in his arms. He pulled her in, breathing in the scent of her hair—sunshine and sweetness with notes of India ink and turpentine. He would find out what she was doing soon enough, he suspected.

"Grayson." She whispered in his ear. "You're back."

He pulled away an arm's length. "I am. Amelia, I've been working on the thing you asked of me."

She looked at him, her eyes wide.

"Happiness doesn't last," he told her. "It comes and goes, but that just makes the moments when it arrives more valuable.

Before I could find it, I had to go through all the other things I hadn't let myself feel."

"Grayson." She took his hands.

"And once I let myself feel..." He inhaled and looked at her. "Once I let myself feel everything, I came to a realization."

He had thought of this moment often on his return journey. What he would say. How she would respond. He took a deep breath.

"Amelia, you should know. I will never take up residence in one place. I will spend the next decades of my life expanding the telegraphic network. I don't want children of my own. The concept of 'settling down'—it's not in my blood. I'm not much of a catch, but—"

She tilted her head, frowning. "Oh. Speaking of which, I've been working on a mechanical method to transcribe telegraphic messages. It doesn't work yet—"

He let out a noise of exasperation.

Her nose wrinkled. "What?"

"'Speaking of which,'" he echoed back at her. "How is that related to what I was saying?"

"Um." She looked up, tapping her lips with a finger. "They were both in my head at the same time."

"Amelia, I love you, but I am trying to ask you to marry me."

She looked even more perplexed at this. "Really? And that's how you start? What happened to 'I am so attractive; all the women want me?'"

"It seemed gauche to mention other women at the time."

"'Not much of a catch.'" She shook her head. "Boo. It should be more along the lines of 'Look, Amelia, what other man will make you feel like this?'"

"Well. There is that."

"You should lead with your strengths. 'Amelia, what other man will give you a telegraphic network?'"

"That is true. I do have a telegraphic network."

"You could have said, 'Amelia, you may have noticed that neither of us particularly want children. Do you not find that convenient?'"

"I *do* find it convenient."

She glared up at him. "The Taotai of Shanghai got 'I'm Grayson Hunter, and I'm going to irrevocably alter the shape of Chinese communication' for a proposal, and you just wanted him for a telegraph. Where is *my* aggressive proposal? Deliver it, if you please."

"Here." He pulled the ring he'd had commissioned in San Francisco out of his pocket. The metal was gold and shiny, but the stone...well. Its luster came from polishing, as much as one could polish a fossil.

She blinked. Reached out. Touched the dull gray triangle that had been carved and smoothed underneath to fit her finger.

"Is that...is that made with a megalodon tooth?" Her voice was shaking.

"Of course it is." Grayson shook his head. "Was I supposed to ask you to marry me with anything else? It was hard enough finding a megalodon tooth small enough to fit the bill. A megalodon vertebrae would have been approximately the size of your head. How were you supposed to carry that around?"

She looked up at him.

"You could have not involved megalodons at all."

Grayson gave her a look. "This ring means that I love *you*. I couldn't have used anything else."

"Well then." She held out her hand. "It's a good thing I love you, too. Put it on."

EPILOGUE

Being introduced to Grayson's parents ended up being less nerve-racking than Amelia had thought. She managed to curtsy properly, and once they'd settled in, she gave his parents a sampling of teas that she'd picked out in Shanghai. When she handed over the blue-and-white china tea set that Auntie Zhu had helped her pick out, she didn't trip or break anything.

They'd promised everyone to attend a lengthier celebration in the evening—"Don't worry," Grayson had told Amelia, "they won't expect you to remember anyone's name, and you'll know Zed already"—but for that afternoon, they were ensconced in a room with Grayson's mother and father and his brother, Adrian, and Adrian's wife, Camilla.

"You know," Camilla had said, "Grayson has never told us how you met."

"Oh." Amelia glanced at Grayson, then smiled. "The first time I met him, he was very direct. He told me he was looking for a man, and then ten minutes later, he said something like, 'It's you. I'm looking for you.' I would have left with him on the spot."

"I think you did not," Grayson reminded her. "I had to do a great deal of convincing. It took me two entire days."

"He's very convincing, our Grayson." Adrian gave Grayson a look. "Well done."

"The second time we met," Amelia said, "I proceeded to embarrass myself by talking about megalodons."

"That's hardly embarrassing. Who *doesn't* want to talk about megalodons?" Asked Grayson's father.

"There are some people." Amelia glanced upward. "Some hundred million or so. Grayson was very encouraging." She smiled at him.

Grayson just shrugged. "She was very encourageable."

"And now we're here." She was aware that she had skipped quite a bit in that retelling. "I'm a little nervous."

"My dear." Grayson's mother set a hand over Amelia's. "I haven't seen Grayson smile like this in half a dozen years. It's normal to be nervous in new situations; I won't tell you that you must stop. But I promise you, you have nothing to worry about. We already love you." She reached out with her other hand, reaching for Grayson across from her. "We love you both. With our whole hearts."

The camphor trees along the docks in Liyang were still green in December. The weather had turned to mild briskness, and the last few dark-black camphor berries were littered underfoot as Grayson stepped off the junk, leaving a faint medicinal smell all around them.

Grayson should not have been nervous. During his last visit here, people had been friendly enough. But it was one thing to arrive as a stranger with an Englishified Chinese woman as a mere associate. It was quite another to go back to the place that had decided Amelia should marry the district magistrate's son.

Amelia was the daughter who had returned to the village; now he was taking her away again.

But on his return, the registrar greeted them both. "Ah, Jin Haowei! And Lang Limeng. Everyone will be so happy to see you."

Before Grayson had a chance to ask what was meant by that, people began to gather. He heard Amelia's Chinese name over and over; she waved to everyone happily.

He also heard the other name—Jin Haowei—being shouted over and over. Once again, they were conducted to the Lang compound. This time though, they were expected. Madame Lang—whom he'd seen briefly before—and her husband were waiting for them.

Apparently Amelia had made the journey again before now. She introduced her father to Grayson. "He is, um. I'm not sure how to say this? He's now a prefectural archivist. He was a sergeant second class during the rebellion and the second war."

"Jin Haowei," said the man in greeting. "How have you been?"

The exchange of gifts, guiding him through the requisite ceremonies, took the remainder of the time. It wasn't until later that night when Madame Lang was pressing a tea on Grayson while extolling its virtues for marital purposes that he was able to ask.

"Why is everyone calling me Jin Haowei?" The question was asked both out of desperation and curiosity. It seemed better than having a long conversation with his mother-in-law about his sexual relations. And he genuinely wanted to know.

She looked at him. "You have to have a business name if you are going to operate in China. When Amelia told me about you, I thought, hmm. He will need a Chinese name. So I asked her to tell us about you so that we could pick a fitting one."

Grayson had not known how he would be accepted. He had

expected that it would be a bit of a struggle. But this was so touching a gesture that he found himself smiling.

"What does it mean?"

"I thought maybe of translating your name directly." She made a face. "But Hunter... The translation feels too violent. And 'Gray' uses the same character as ash. That's bad luck. So that won't work either."

Grayson exhaled. "A narrow escape indeed. I must, by all means, avoid being ashy."

"So, I thought for a family name, I would use Jin."

"Jin?" Amelia had come to stand in the doorway as they were talking. "I knew quite a few Jins in Shanghai." She took out a pencil and her notebook. "This character?"

Her mother nodded. "Jin, meaning gold or metal. It's what the wire you lay is made of." She gave him a sly look. "And what you make as a result."

Amelia looked pleased. "What do you think, Grayson?"

"Jin," he repeated. "Jin. I like it."

"Then there is Haowei."

"Haowei." He looked at Madame Lang. "What are the characters?"

She took out a sheet of paper. "Hao." It was one of the more complicated characters—it would have needed seven English letters to encode. "This means grand."

"Well." He looked over at Amelia. "I do think I am rather grand in all respects."

She smothered a smile.

"Flirt later," Madame Lang said with a smile she could not quite hide. "Learn now. Wei is like this." A great many strokes, but this would have been a four- or five-letter encoding. "It means to tie together or to link."

"Grand linkage," he started to say, intent on making another flirtatious remark to his wife. Then the full meaning of the name hit him. Jin Haowei. Grand linking with metal.

He'd been happy to be accepted. For people to speak to him politely. But this? This was someone spending time thinking about who he was. What he did. What he wanted to accomplish. This was a gift. A gift of understanding. A gift of acceptance. A gift of linking—not only him with Amelia, but their families.

He met his wife's eyes and smiled at her. "Where do you think we should link next?"

THANK YOU

Thank you for reading *The Devil Comes Courting*. I hope you enjoyed it.

Would you like to know when my next book is available?

You can sign up for my new release email list at www. courtneymilan.com, follow me on twitter at @courtneymilan, or like my Facebook page at http:// facebook.com/courtneymilanauthor.

Reviews help other readers find books. I appreciate all reviews, whether positive or negative.

If you're wondering about great-great-uncles John and Henry, mentioned in here, their story is told in *The Pursuit Of...* The novella can be read in the collection *Hamilton's Battalion* or purchased as a *standalone story.*

If you want to know more about Benedict's older sisters Judith and Camilla, and Grayson's little brother, Adrian

Hunter, their stories are available in *Once Upon a Marquess* (Judith and Christian) and *After the Wedding* (Camilla and Adrian).

What's next?

The next book in the Worth Saga will be the story of the Worth half-sister that Theresa has tracked down in Hong Kong at the end of this book. You'll meet her and see a lot more of Theresa in *The Return of the Scoundrel.* I do not have a release date for this book. I used to give estimated release dates, but it turns out my estimates were off by about two and a half years on this book and I don't want to do that to any of us again.

The next book I release will be the next book in The Wedgeford Trials series. If you haven't started that series, *The Duke Who Didn't* is a delightful book about a half-Chinese duke who hasn't mentioned he's a duke, and the full-Chinese woman in the small town of Wedgeford, England, who has absolutely no time for him because she has sauce to make. *The Duke Who Didn't* has won a handful of awards, so maybe you will like it?

AUTHOR'S NOTE

I did not intend to take years to write this book. In my defense, those years—which included a whole pandemic, an attempted coup, and before that, a whole mess of wild things in the Before Pandemic Times—were *pretty* stressful.

But I also did not realize what a task I had set for myself.

I got the idea for this book in 2008, and I remember exactly where it came from. I was talking to my then-editor, on the last day in which she was my editor, about a book (*Trial by Desire*, to be specific). I had written one version. My editor didn't like it. At all. (And there were good reasons for that). But we spoke, and the thing she suggested was that Ned, the hero, who spent a few years in China investigating the circumstances surrounding the Opium War, should return from China with a Chinese baby as a method of sparking conflict with his wife.

I think I heard her say that at a far remove. One of the causes of the second Opium War was this: Missionaries in China kept taking Chinese kids, and the Chinese didn't actually like having their kids taken from them. There was a rumor that Christian missionaries were actually taking the children and killing them in order to remove their eyes and heart, which they were making into medicine. (I did not make that one up when it shows up in the book.)

End result of these rumors: Chinese people would also sometimes kill missionaries, and it turns out, this puts a strain on diplomatic relationships.

So I heard this and I think I stammered out something like "uhhh well actually that might help precipitate a war? I don't want my hero doing that?" And we moved on.

It stayed with me over the years, the thought of those children. What was it like? What did they do? How were they raised, what did they think of themselves, did they remember where they were from? Where *were* they from?

These were not idle questions for me, a (depending on how you count) third- or fourth-generation child of Chinese immigrants.

Amelia's story has been in the works for a long time. (I structured the Worth Saga to lead to it, for reasons that I now think were probably misguided, but hey, you learn from experience.)

About all the telegraph stuff

So! Obviously I rewrote a lot of telegraphic history in this book! Let me acknowledge what I changed, and what is real.

The actual transpacific telegraph line wasn't built until 1902. There are a lot of reasons for that, but none of them were technological. The transatlantic line was made many decades earlier—before the time-period of this book—and the transpacific line was just three transatlantic lines long. In our reality, the transpacific line went from Midway to Hawaii to San Francisco, and if you're wondering why it took until 1902 to establish this, it's likely because Hawaii was not annexed by the United States until 1898.

I personally did not feel like advancing the timeline on the annexation of Hawaii by thirty years was a good idea, and so I had to find another route. I ended up coming up with a northerly route (northern Japan to a made-up North Pacific island and then down the coast of British Columbia in what is now Canada and what was then a British conquest) in large part because the timing was just right to slip into the early Meiji era, in which the Japanese emperor wanted to modernize.

Japan did in fact adopt the telegraph very early on, and Wabun code was used extensively in Japan. (More on Japanese code in a few paragraphs.) But their telegraphy was actually built in collaboration with a Dutch company, and so I also had to rewrite history there so that Grayson would handle the telegraphy in exchange for being allowed to start his transpacific cable there.

So now we get to the question of Chinese telegraphic code. The first Chinese telegraphic code in reality was in fact made by a Frenchman, and to put it mildly, it sucked. It was 1000 characters long and you looked up a character and then sent that number, and when I first contemplated writing this book, I said, "ha ha this sucks so much, surely I will be able to come up with something better with the benefit of one hundred and fifty years of history on my side!"

I was, in fact, right, but it was not actually easy. My first version of Chinese telegraphic code in this book was simply a different 1000 character encoding that was arranged so that it was easier to code and decode. Was it better than the first version? Yes.

But then, while I was reading about Wabun code, I found copies of old Japanese commercial codebooks. Commercial codes for telegraphy were common. You paid for telegraphs by the word, and so if you had a very common phrase, such as "let's go jump in a lake together" you could pay for seven words to send that phrase, or you could agree that the word "puppy" meant "let's go jump in a lake together." Companies made entire codebooks that took common commercial phrases and boiled them down to one word.

In any event, Japan also did this, but their commercial codes were in fact structured differently than English codes. The Japanese ciphers were composed of pairs of kana (the elements of the Japanese syllabary), so that companies could assign a Chinese character (or perhaps four, and you'd have to determine from context which was meant) to two (some used more than two) transmitted characters. (My Japanese is very bad, and Japanese written 150 years ago is much harder to parse than modern Japanese, and 98% of my Japanese was acquired trying to read figure skating interviews...anyway, long story short, I had lots of fun figuring out Japanese commercial ciphers.)

This was the first not-terrible method of transmitting Chinese characters that I had found—in fact, in at least some cases, the kana pairs were associated with the Japanese pronunciation of the Chinese character, and so it made sense both for coding and encoding as a solution. It wouldn't entirely work for Chinese as a native encoding, but it got me thinking about how to transmit Chinese characters using pairs as a sort of cipher.

At this point, I fell back on something completely unrelated that I did a while back. Back in 2016, I noticed that there were no dinosaur emoji. There were other extremely serious problems in 2016, but I asked myself the very important question: Why are there no dinosaur emoji?

The answer I got was this: Because nobody had proposed them yet.

And that was a silly reason. *I* was a person, and *I* had a computer. So I wrote a proposal to the Unicode Technical Committee, which you can read, and behold, dinosaur emoji. In the process of doing this, I learned a lot more about emoji than I had ever known before, including learning about a character called a "zero width joiner."

As an example, if you want an emoji that is going to be a thumbs up, but the thumbs up is colored a dark brown, that emoji is actually three emojis: the yellow thumbs-up emoji, the zero width joiner, which signals to the computer that you're joining two emojis, and an emoji that corresponds to the dark-brown skin color.

I put these all together and realized that if you wanted Chinese telegraphy that actually represented Chinese characters with radicals instead of just encoding it, you could do it with zero-width joiners. You'd have to have multiple zero width joiners—three in total, to specify horizontal joins, vertical joins, and containment. But hypothetically, those would provide you all the tools you needed to represent Chinese characters.

In theory, this would have a lot of advantages. In practice, I don't actually have a team that would be able to do any wide scale testing of it, and it really is just fiction, so anyway... yeah.

Back to telegraphy: yes, the first transatlantic telegraphs were in fact that expensive—on the order of four or five pounds, which is an enormous amount of money.

Yes, the whole shebang about gutta percha is real. They really did chop down an entire tree for ten ounces of gutta percha. They really did chop down forests of gutta percha for the transatlantic telegraph alone.

I read these articles from the time that went something like this: "ha ha people say we will eventually run out of gutta percha, but it hasn't happened yet, so who is to say it will ever happen? Let's ignore all the conservation issues with this."

Yes, when they hit the point that people were like, "oh no we are about to make the gutta percha tree extinct?" people did eventually have the bright idea of harvesting just the leaves and it turns out that this works just fine, and yes, there is a tree called the balata that produces a latex that is indistinguishable from gutta percha.

Today we use a version of plastic called Bakelite to insulate our cables. Anyway absolutely amazing to me that we have come so far and yet not far at all.

Also, if you are wondering if Grayson's comments about how the British would just build a telegraph line into Shanghai without permission was just me casting unnecessary aspersions on the British, sorry. These are necessary aspersions. This is actually how the Shanghai telegraph line was built in our reality. The British asked, the Chinese said no, they asked again, the Chinese said no, and so they just built it under the cover of darkness and then said, "oh well, what are you going to do about it? Wanna fight?"

The Chinese did not, at the time, want to fight, and so the telegraph stayed.

Fun times.

Finally, about the being able to send telegrams at sea while laying cable: I have not been able to find any references to people being able to send telegrams. However, accounts of laying the long telegraphic lines all mentioned checking current every so often to make sure the lines were functioning. If you have current, you can send telegrams because a telegraphic signal is nothing more than current that gets interrupted in a systematic fashion.

There may be some battery-based limitations (if the battery is on the ship, they may not have enough capacity to continually run a current), but there is no reason the battery could not be powered from the shore for some periods of time in order to enable the sending of messages.

Hence: Grayson has very slow internet access on his boat.

Some other random non-telegraph related stuff

Grayson's reference to travel in first versus second class across the United States may not make sense for those who are used to thinking of travel in the US before the 1960s as inherently segregated. But there was actually a period when it wasn't clear that segregated travel was legal. Before *Plessy* v. *Ferguson* (and in fact the reason we got *Plessy* v. *Ferguson*), there were active attempts to bring court cases against segregated travel. Some of these were successful. Others, not so much. It wasn't until 1896 that the Supreme Court (erroneously) ruled that state-mandated separate but equal travel arrangements were Constitutional that this became temporarily settled, until overruled by *Brown* v. *Board of Education.*

I put the factory that produced cable in San Francisco. There was not such a factory in San Francisco at the time, but since I'm already rewriting the history of gutta percha, I think I can invent a cable factory that would process and use that gutta percha.

I actually tried to make other options like Boston and London work, but the travel time would have been utterly enormous and I didn't want to have multiyear gaps between when Grayson and Amelia met.

I want to say a little about what trips to the interior of China would have looked like, and that is this: I don't actually know, and with almost everything I read about China, I had to do a lot of extrapolation. The main reason for this is the incredible, intense racism. The racism impacts how things are depicted. But more than that, if you're asking the question of "how will Chinese people in the interior of China react to Westerners?" you have to ask if Westerners who look down on Chinese people will receive harsher treatment.

If you read Western accounts of trips to the interior of China in the late 1800s, you hear about petty, vexatious Chinese officials over and over again—so much so that I had initially taken it as a fact that Chinese officials would be vexatious. The thing that changed my mind on this point was Henry Lansdell's *Chinese Central Asia: A Ride to Little Tibet.* Lansdell seeks advice from a great many people about how to deal with vexatious Chinese officials. The advice he gets goes like this:

- "Threaten complaints to the great men I knew in Europe."
- "Ask nothing, but demand everything. With small officials, send for them to call upon you, and not vice versa. Do everything by force and never allow a Chinaman to take the least liberty with you."
- "The Chinese respect nothing but force."

This all sounds very grim. But finally, he asks his friend who he describes as a "heathen" (probably not a white person, is my guess). His heathen friend says this: "There is one rule that is useful all the world over... In short, be humble; and apologize to the officials for not knowing their ceremonies as you should, asking that your shortcomings may be attributed to ignorance, not to lack of good intention."

That kind of broke something open in me. Are you going to get people being polite to you if you barge into their territory, threaten them with important people half the world over, demand they come to you instead of going to them, and do everything by force? I mean, if *I* were a Chinese official and Westerners I'd never heard of kept telling me I had to go to them to do my job, I would probably be annoying to them, too.

I had to do an enormous amount of extrapolation to figure out what things would be like. Every story I read I had to feed through a filter to try to remove judgment, to try to understand what was happening on the other side.

I struggled a lot with how to depict Amelia's mother. Would she have bound feet? What would she be like? What would she allow? The book didn't give me a lot of space to include information, but 1870 is late enough that reformers in China had already pushed back against feet-binding. One of the things I had decided was that since she had known that her daughter was raised by the English already, she'd come to peace with the inevitability of cultural differences that would arise between them, and while they would arise, they'd approach them like adults with the expectation that they'd need to talk things through, rather than with the weight of knee-jerk reflexive demands behind them.

One of the things that I had to calibrate for this book was the question of how much racism to include. This is not a book where racism is a thing that happens in the background. Amelia's story may feel particularly salient today, when children have been separated from families on the US border and in some cases, given to other families without their birth parents' consent. But when I came up with the idea for this book in 2008, this was not on the national radar. I struggled with the parallels between the past and the present. I hadn't intended to write a book that was a response to those current events, but I knew it would be impossible to read it outside of that context.

I found my peace in this by recognizing that taking children from their families is something that has been happening for centuries. I based this story on the fact that Christian missionaries literally took Chinese children from their parents in the nineteenth century. This behavior is not new, and it's not limited to one racial group. This *is* a part of that history. It's not the same as our current situation, but it comes from the same place.

The amount of racism in this book is upsetting. The truth is, I have toned it down considerably. The comments made by Mrs. Flappert in the beginning (and to a lesser extent, Mrs. Acheson) were very much inline with the tone I read from works from that era, and honestly, very, very mild in the historical scheme of things.

ACKNOWLEDGMENTS

First and foremost, thank you to everyone who helped me make this book a reality, including everyone (and there are so many of you) who took time to make this book what it is, in some cases on very tight deadlines. Rose Lerner, Rawles Lumumba, May Peterson, Linda Kay, Rashi Rohatgi, Michelle Li, Lillie Applegarth, Savannah Frierson all provided immeasurable assistance. Thank you. A special note of thanks to Melissa Blue who kicked my ass in the right direction once and helped me break this book open, and then kicked my ass again when I was on the verge of despair.

I also could not have written this book without the encouragement of everyone in the 'Rona Writing Group. Special thanks to Bree, Beks, and Alyssa, for that point near the end when I dropped a text in a group chat in which I admitted that I didn't know how I was going to get this book finished and got the love, encouragement, and the kick in the pants that I needed to take a deep breath and make it happen.

Thank you to Pele, as always, for being the very best dog.

And thank you to everyone who has been waiting for this book for a very long time. I hope you enjoyed the megalodons.

OTHER BOOKS BY COURTNEY

Talk Sweetly to Me

The Turner Series

Unveiled

Unlocked

Unclaimed

Unraveled

Not in any series

A Right Honorable Gentleman

What Happened at Midnight

The Lady Always Wins

The Carhart Series

This Wicked Gift

Proof by Seduction

Trial by Desire